Margaret Thornton was born in Blackpool and has lived there all her life. She is a qualified teacher but has retired in order to concentrate on her writing. She has two children and four grandchildren.

Her first novel, *It's A Lovely Day Tomorrow* ('a gentle novel whose lack of noise is a strength' *The Times*), was runner up for the Netta Muskett Award, and is also available from Headline.

Also by Margaret Thornton

It's A Lovely Day Tomorrow

A Pair of Sparkling Eyes

Margaret Thornton

KNIGHT

First published in 1993
by HEADLINE BOOK PUBLISHING

First published in paperback 1994
by HEADLINE BOOK PUBLISHING

This edition published 2002 by
Knight an imprint of The Caxton Publishing Group

10 9 8 7 6 5 4 3 2 1

ISBN 1 84067 514 4

Typeset by
Letterpart Limited, Reigate, Surrey

Printed and bound in Great Britain by
Mackays of Chatham plc, Chatham, Kent

Caxton Publishing Group
20 Bloomsbury Street
London WC1B 3JH

For my daughter Elaine, and son David, with love.

And for my husband John, with my love and thanks for all his encouragement and understanding.

AUTHOR'S NOTE

Donnelly's Department Store and Tilda's Tavern are fictitious places, and the characters in this story have no connection with Blackpool families who might have the same names.

I hope, however, that this is a true representation of my home town, Blackpool, as it was at the turn of the century.

Chapter 1

'There it is! Can you see it? Over yonder.'

Grace Turnbull's eyes followed the direction of the young lad's finger which was jabbing excitedly at the grubby window of the railway carriage. Yes, there it was, just coming into view on the distant horizon, Blackpool Tower, looking like a pepper pot from this distance but, as she knew from the reports in the newspapers, a staggering 518 feet, a huge iron finger thrusting upwards into the sky.

'Oh aye. Look, our Sally. Just look at that.'

'I'd never have believed it were possible . . .'

'It's a miracle. It is that.'

The eyes of all the folk in the crowded carriage were now fixed on the fascinating structure, and the children – there must have been half a dozen of them – were clambering on the seats, jostling and pushing one another for a closer view, their noses flattened against the glass, their fingers leaving smears on the grimy pane.

Grace looked across at her sister Hetty, and they smiled conspiratorially at one another. It was exciting to be going to Blackpool, and not only for a day trip this time but for the whole of the Whit

1

weekend. Josiah Baldwin wasn't a bad boss as bosses went and he had said that those that wanted to could finish work earlier on the Saturday, which would enable them to get away for the weekend. Their pay would be docked accordingly, of course – old Josiah wasn't one to give you 'owt for nowt', for all his leniency – but the two girls, with their mother's approval, had deemed it worthwhile. Indeed, it had been Martha Turnbull's idea in the first place that they should have a weekend away.

Grace was longing for the sight of the sea and the smell of the salt-laden air. She knew that just a few lungfuls of the bracing Blackpool breezes would be enough to make her feel better right away, to bring the roses back to her pallid cheeks and the sparkle into her eyes. Hetty, she knew, was looking forward to her weekend away for entirely different reasons. Hetty loved the crowds, the excitement, the fun . . .

Martha fondly watched her two daughters as they stared through the window at the flat, featureless landscape of the Fylde, field upon field, bordered by hawthorn hedges now in bloom, with here and there a lone farmhouse and a few cattle grazing. No hills; you had to go further inland towards Blackburn or their native Burnley for the sight of the hills. Martha knew that she would miss the hills if the plan she had in mind came to fruition, for she was looking forward to her visit to Blackpool for yet another reason.

She looked keenly at Grace. She had been concerned about her elder daughter for some time now. Grace had always been pale, but her present pallor seemed unnatural. Her brown eyes were as loving and as bright as ever – a reflection of the girl's warmness and generosity of spirit – but now they were sunken in her face, ringed by ominous black shadows. Her cough, too, had been more persistent lately. The cough was an occupational hazard amongst the workers in the weaving sheds, caused by the irritant dust from the sizes containing zinc chloride that were used for the warps, and by the inhaling of fluff from the cotton. Martha was worried about Grace's cough. Fred's final illness had started in just the same way and he had been gone these last eight years, leaving Martha a widow with two daughters to care for.

It hadn't been easy, but she had done her best. Up to the time of her husband's death, and afterwards, Martha had worked long hours in the mill to make ends meet, leaving the two growing girls, when school finished for the day, in the care of a good neighbour. It had eased the situation a little when Grace had started work the following year, at twelve years of age, and a year later Hetty had done the same. Now Martha stayed at home and took in washing and, once a week, she had a stall at Burnley market where she was famous for her home-made cakes and pastries.

Things were not too bad, financially that was. Martha knew that they could be a lot worse off. Many of their neighbours, with hordes of children in their families, had scarcely two ha'pennies to rub together. But Martha was determined that her girls were not going to spend all their young lives in the cotton mill, as she had done. The hazards were numerous; apart from the distinctive cough that many of the mill workers were prone to, there was the danger from the flying shuttle, a deadly object with pointed metal ends which, if it accidentally left the loom, could inflict terrible injuries on anyone it hit. To say nothing of the belts whirring dangerously all around and the threat of deafness from the clatter and din. No, Martha wanted something better for her lasses.

She had been richly blessed with her two girls, and she never ceased to thank the good Lord for the joy they had brought her. Hetty could be a handful at times, to be sure – she always had been, ever since she was a little bairn, high-spirited and inclined to be wilful. She took after her father, not only in looks – her ginger hair was a legacy from her father – but in temperament too. Fred had been a right one for the lasses before he had settled down and married Martha. Grace was a different kettle of fish altogether, quieter and more serious, more like her mother. Martha knew that they often said that opposites attracted, but with her, that was not the case. She knew that if she could be said to have a favourite – something she would hardly admit, not even to herself, for everyone knew that mothers were not supposed to have favourites – then it was her elder daughter. But she loved them both, there was no denying that, and Martha felt that there was nothing she wouldn't do for either of them. Not that she ever told them so; like many North-erners, Martha was not one to wear her heart on her sleeve and she kept her feelings for her daughters well hidden, often disguised by a brusque manner.

4

'We're here, Mam.' Hetty's words broke into Martha's thoughts. She rose and tugged the battered suitcase from the rack above their heads, also a square tin box, tied round with string, which contained food for the weekend. The lodging-house keeper – when they found a lodging house – would cook it for them.

But if they had thought that the sight of the new Tower was a sign that their journey was nearing its end they were mistaken. The train staggered to a halt outside the station, waiting for a platform to become vacant. They waited half an hour; the Fylde railways in this summer season of 1895 were proving inadequate to deal with the vast numbers of people converging on Blackpool.

The scene outside the railway station had to be seen to be believed. Grace closed her eyes for a moment, feeling faint amongst all the noise and commotion. Hansom cabs, landaus, a horse-drawn omnibus piled high with the luggage of incoming visitors, and people everywhere, jostling, shouting, swearing, trying to push their way through the thronging crowds. It was every man for himself. The acrid scent of the horses' steaming flanks and the stale sweat from human bodies assailed Grace's nostrils as she stood, almost swooning, in the midst of it all. She was beginning to wonder if it had been such a good idea to come to Blackpool after all.

'Come on, lass. Let's get away from here.' Martha noticed her daughter's discomfiture and put a protective arm around her. 'You'll feel better once you get a whiff of them sea breezes . . . No, our Hetty, we'll walk,' she said decidedly. Hetty was

5

already fighting her way towards the omnibus, her elbows shoving relentlessly into people's backs, her pointed little chin tilted aggressively. 'Anyroad, we don't know where we're going yet. We'll have to find some lodgings.'

All around them they could hear the shouts of the 'touters', landladies from the lodging houses near the station, vying with one another with their offers of accommodation.

'Come along wi' me, missus. You'll not get better lodgings anyweer in Blackpool . . .'

'Half-price lodgings . . . Half-price lodgings . . .'

'Half-price me Aunt Fanny! Tek no notice of her, luv. At th' end o' t'week she'll charge yer extra for t'cruet . . .'

Martha stared at them unflinchingly. She wasn't going to be taken in by any of their blarney. A pack of lies, most of it, she reckoned.

'You'd be all right at our house, missus . . .'

Martha glanced round in surprise at the sound of a softer spoken voice, a male voice. The speaker was a young man in his early twenties, she guessed – a couple of years older than Grace – shifting from one foot to the other and looking at her appealingly. His coarse tweed jacket was a size too small and his flat cap, perched atop his straight fair hair, a size too big. She warmed to him immediately. 'You say you've got a room to let at your house, lad?' Martha put down her heavy suitcase and looked at him enquiringly.

'Aye. At me mam's. It's just round t'corner. Right handy for North Station it is.'

'And do you reckon you can carry this suitcase for a weary old woman?'

6

The lad grinned at her. 'You bet I can, missus.' He picked it up easily, then he turned to Hetty. 'And yours an' all, if you'll give it 'ere.' There was no mistaking the admiration in his eyes as Hetty handed over the smaller case.

Martha smiled to herself. Her younger daughter was working her provocative charm already. But he seemed a decent lad. She grinned back at him. 'Right, lad. You're on. Lead the way . . .'

Grace and Hetty stepped out briskly behind their mother and their young guide. Grace was feeling better already, now she was away from the congestion at the station. She stared around her, as she walked, at the unfamiliar surroundings. There were crowds of people mostly heading in the same direction as the Turnbull family, bound no doubt, as they themselves were, for a lodging house. The day was warm, but they all wore an abundance of clothing. Many of the women were wearing their dark winter coats; Grace knew that it was doubtful if they had a more suitable one for the warmer weather. Some of them, however, sported straw hats, as Grace herself did, and several of the younger women had their long hair flowing round their shoulders, a concession to the holiday mood which would be frowned upon in their workaday life. But the bowler-hatted and cloth-capped men who walked with them, in their uncomfortable-looking tweed suits and high collars, appeared to have allowed themselves no such indulgence.

The children looked happy, though, and Grace found herself smiling at the families going in the opposite direction who must have already unpacked their belongings and were now bound for the beach. Many of the little boys, and some of the girls, too, wore suits and dresses of a sailor design which had been made popular by the Royal Family and taken up by the upper classes; now costumes such as these were common even amongst children of the working classes. Many of them carried tin buckets and little wooden spades and obviously could hardly wait for their first glimpse of the golden sand and sparkling sea. Grace knew just how they felt.

The lodging houses along the street were all identical – tall, narrow buildings of shiny Accrington brick – except for the colour of the paintwork and the curtains at the windows and the signs outside the front doors bearing the name, if any, of the establishment and of the owner. A horse-bus passed by, packed with people and piled high with luggage, then a brewer's dray loaded with wooden barrels of draught beer, for Blackpool was well known for its profusion of ale-houses. Grace admired the huge black shire horses that pulled the dray, magnificent creatures with their tails and manes plaited and decorated, and their leather and brass harnesses gleaming in the sunlight. Grace felt that she loved everything and everybody today. Oh, she was glad that she had come!

She turned to look at Hetty. Like her mother, she had noticed the looks exchanged by her sister and the lad from the lodging house. Trust our Hetty, she thought. She said she was going to enjoy herself, and it looked as though she intended to waste no time. As for Grace, all she wanted was a change, a couple of days away from the smoking chimneys and grime-filled air of Burnley. It was grand to exchange her woollen shawl and heavy clogs for her high-buttoned boots and straw hat, and her crisp white blouse with the leg-of-mutton sleeves. It was last year's – none of them, neither she nor Hetty nor their mam, had money to throw away on new clothes – but she had livened it up with a brown satin bow at the neck and added matching brown ribbons to her hat. A deep, rich brown which highlighted the colour of her eyes and her hair. There was no other word to describe the colour of Grace's hair but brown. Not chestnut or auburn nor golden; just brown, a warm colour that echoed the warmth of her personality.

Hetty was walking more quickly now to catch up with the lad, and Grace found herself recalling Walter's words when she had told him that she was going to Blackpool for the weekend.

'Now, think on. You behave yourself. You're my girl, Grace Turnbull, and don't you forget it.'

His pale eyes had held a trace of suspicion and Grace's heart had filled with despair.

But she had answered calmly enough. 'Don't take on so, Walter. There's no call to be jealous. Me mam just wants us to have a day or two by the sea. She thinks it'll do us all good. And of course I'm your girl. You know I am.'

His lips had closed possessively over hers as he had said goodbye to her last night outside the front door. Grace had felt contented and secure in her love for him, all her misgivings swept away by the ardour of his embrace. As her mam said, she would go a long way before she met a finer young man than Walter Clayton. He had a steady job as an overlooker – commonly referred to as a 'tackler' – at the mill, he was God-fearing and went regularly to the Bible class at the chapel. That was where they had met and where they had been that evening.

'I'll not come in tonight, love,' he said. 'You'll have a bit of packing to do with you being off on your jaunts tomorrow. Have a good time . . . but not too good, mind.' And the suspicious glance had been there again. Grace loved him – or thought she did – but she wished he wasn't so jealous.

The lad from the lodging house had introduced himself. 'I'm Albert Gregson and me mam's Alice. I reckon you'll get on a treat, the pair of you. You're much of an age.'

Aye, no doubt I seem as old as Methuselah to you, lad, thought Martha, smiling grimly to herself. She was only in her early forties, but she felt as though her youth was far behind her. It had vanished when Fred had gone but, all being well, there might be something just round the corner, a new beginning for them all . . .

'And do you work for your mother then, Albert?' asked Martha.

'Just now and again,' the lad replied. 'When it's extra busy, like now, when it's a Bank Holiday. I really work for me Uncle Sam. Samuel Pickering – he's a joiner and builder, in the centre of town. He's done right well for himself, has Uncle Sam. Me father works for him an' all. Anyroad, he lets me off now and again to help me mam.'

10

'Touting for custom at the station, eh, Albert?' said Martha with an amused glance at her young companion. 'I reckon it's not much in your line. Am I right?'

Albert nodded and grinned. 'Aye, I'm not much cop, I know. I'm a bit backward in coming forward, as me mam would say. But she's even worse than me where this 'ere touting's concerned. She thinks it's common and she won't do it herself. But all the neighbours do it, so I can't leave 'em to take all the trade away from us, can I?'

Martha laughed. 'You're a good lad, Albert. I'm sure your mother's proud of you. Tell me, it can't be true, surely, what that woman was saying? Half-price lodgings?'

'Oh, a few of 'em try that old trick. It might be a bit cheaper, I daresay, but then they stick it all on t'bill at the end of the week. Extra for sauce and sugar and suchlike. They call it charging for t'cruet. Me mam doesn't approve of shabby tricks like that. You'll find she's fair. You'll get good value for your money.'

Alice Gregson's lodging house certainly looked inviting from the outside. The paintwork was clean, the stone step well scrubbed and edged in white with a donkey stone, and freshly laundered lace curtains hung at the windows. By the door was a glass-framed notice which read, 'Sunnyside, Alice Gregson, Blackburn'.

'That's where me mam comes from,' Albert explained. 'The family moved here when she were a lass, then when me gran died she took over the business. We get a lot of folks from Blackburn and round about.'

Martha smiled at him. 'We're from the same neck of the woods, or as near as makes no difference. We come from Burnley.'

But it was the house across the street that was claiming Martha's attention. Not so spick and span as the Gregsons', the paintwork was chipped and fading and no curtains hung at the windows. The house had a forlorn look, but in the tiny paved area which was all it could boast of as a garden there was a sign, 'Property to let'. Martha's eyes narrowed speculatively as she looked at it.

Alice Gregson was every bit as welcoming as her son had said.

'Trust our Albert to choose a nice little family,' she said. 'He never goes far wrong. Come on in. I'll show you to your room, then I'll make a nice pot of tea. I daresay you could do with one.'

The room was sparsely but adequately furnished with a double and a single bed, a heavy mahogany wardrobe and dressing table and a marble washstand on which stood a rose-patterned jug and basin. A matching chamber pot stood on the shelf below. There was scarcely room for the three of them to move around and the view from the window was unprepossessing; a concrete yard with a couple of dustbins and a door leading to the outside lavatory. But they were here. They were in Blackpool. The sun was shining and it was going to be a marvellous weekend.

Martha smiled at Alice Gregson sitting opposite her on the other side of the fireplace. 'It's real kind of you to invite me to sit with you, Mrs Gregson.

To tell you the truth, I didn't feel like doing any gadding-about tonight. I thought I'd let the lasses have a bit of time on their own, especially as your Albert agreed to go along with 'em. They're good girls and I know they won't go far wrong.'

'No, they won't come to any harm with our Albert,' Alice Gregson replied. 'He's a grand lad, though I say it meself. A bit shy, mind. It'll do him a world of good to have a couple of lasses to show around. He'll be like a dog wi' two tails. And you're right welcome . . . to sit with me, I mean. Mind you, I wouldn't do it for anybody. There's not many visitors as get invited into me parlour, but I knew as soon as I set eyes on you that we were two of a kind. And you can call me Alice. That's me name and that's what most folks call me.'

Martha nodded contentedly. 'And I'm Martha.' She glanced approvingly round the parlour, small and overcrowded, but very comfortable. A plethora of pictures and framed photographs – some obviously family groups and some of royalty; Queen Victoria and the late Prince Albert and their family – almost covered the brown patterned wallpaper. A pair of pug-faced Staffordshire dogs sat one each side of the cast-iron fireplace – where a fire burned in spite of the warmth of the May evening – together with a pair of gleaming brass candlesticks and, in the centre of the mantelpiece, another family photograph. Martha noticed a younger Alice and Albert, with a small moustached man – obviously Henry, who, his wife said, had gone for his usual evening pint – and another older boy and two girls. 'Your family?' asked

Martha, gesturing towards the photograph. 'Do they all live here?'

'Bless me, no! They're all married now, the two girls and Joe, our eldest lad. There's only young Albert left now. And what about you, Martha? Just the two girls, have you?'

'Aye, that's right.' Martha sighed. 'I've been a widow these last eight years, and two bairns in the churchyard an' all. Both of 'em lads, but we couldn't rear 'em. Ne'er mind, I'm not complaining. All told, God's been good. I've always had to work hard, mind you, but haven't we all? I'm surprised you find time to sit of an evening, Alice, with all you have to do.'

'Oh, I make sure I don't kill meself.' Alice nodded meaningfully. 'I won't take too many in. There's sixteen here this weekend and that's quite enough, I can tell you, in this little house. Six bedrooms we've got, apart from the family ones of course, but I won't pack 'em in like sardines. Not like some folks round here, greedy beggars they are. D'you know, Martha, they have 'em sleeping three and four to a bed, and I've even seen 'em queueing up outside till their breakfast's ready. Mind you, the visitors don't seem to mind, I must say. They're nearly always jolly types as we get in Blackpool.'

'Isn't it hard, though, cooking all them different kinds of food? It's a wonder you can remember which lot it belongs to.'

Alice laughed. 'Oh, they're quick enough to tell you if you get it wrong. "That's not mine," they'll say. "I'd never buy meat with all that fat on it . . ." To tell you the truth, I'm thinking of

14

changing over to "all found". You know – break-fast and dinner and tea, and providing all the food meself. But there's for and against like there is with most things. It'ud mean a lot of shopping, but I reckon it might be worth it. Like you say, Martha, it would save messing about with all them different kinds of food.'

Martha had been listening intently, taking it all in. Like Alice said, they seemed to be two of a kind. They might almost be taken for sisters, Martha thought. Alice could give her five or six years, she guessed, but it was strange how alike they were; dark hair drawn back into a bun, a round face and a figure that inclined towards plumpness. Alice was an inch or two taller, though. Martha, at barely five foot, found that both her daughters now topped her by several inches.

What Alice was saying was of great interest to Martha. She leaned forward and spoke eagerly to her new friend. 'I've been thinking, Alice . . . That house across the road, the one that's to let . . .' She paused for just a second, then went on, speaking more quickly. 'To be honest with you, I've been thinking of moving here, me and the lasses, and when I saw that house over the road, well, it more or less put the tin hat on it, you might say. That is, if it's still vacant . . .'

'You mean you want to take a lodging house?' Alice stared at her new friend with undisguised pleasure. 'Well, I think that's grand. Aye, it's still vacant, as far as I know. The landlord's not a bad old stick. Lives a couple of streets away. I can take you round and introduce you, if you like. He

15

owned this house an' all, but we bought it off him a few years back.'

'And you wouldn't mind me opening up across the road. Seems as though I'm setting up in opposition . . .'

'Nowt o' t'sort!' said Alice vehemently. 'There's plenty trade for all of us, you mark my words. No, I think it'ud be grand. What about your lasses? What do they think about it?'

'They don't know anything about it yet . . .' Martha spoke slowly. 'I haven't told them. It isn't that I'm trying to keep it from them, but I wasn't that sure meself. In fact I'm still not sure. There's a lot to weigh up. But I'm determined to get our Grace away from that mill. I fear it might be the death of her if I don't. She's not very strong, and come winter her cough gets worse. She's still got it now, even though it's warmer . . .'

'And how about the girls? Would they work in the house with you? You might find that you didn't make enough to keep all three of you in work. It's only a small house, compared with those big places on the prom.'

Martha shook her head. 'I haven't thought that far ahead. The main thing is to get here if we can. I daresay our Grace'ud do well enough working there, but I'm not so sure about Hetty. Anyroad, it'll be up to her. I've never believed in telling 'em what to do. They're both sensible enough to make up their own minds. I'm just a bit worried about how our Grace'll feel about leaving Walter.'

'Her young man?'

'Aye, I think so. Not that they're engaged or owt

16

like that, but they see a fair bit of one another and he's a nice steady lad.'

'And what about Hetty? Has she got a young man at home?'

'Not her!' Martha laughed. 'She's a flibbertigib-bet. There's a few of 'em at work and at chapel as make eyes at her, but nobody special like. I don't think Hetty's one for settling down, not yet awhile anyroad. I noticed your Albert making sheep's eyes at her when we walked up from the station, and she didn't seem to be discouraging him nei-ther. She's a monkey, is our Hetty.'

Alice laughed. 'That'll be the day! Our Albert's a bit shy where lasses are concerned. I sometimes wish he would push himself a bit more, but I reckon I shouldn't grumble. He's a good lad.' She nodded, then went on, 'Well, like you say, Martha, the first thing is to get yourself here. I'll take you round to meet Mr Butterworth tomorrow. And I think you're making a wise move. Blackpool's coming on by leaps and bounds. There's more and more folks coming every year. It won't be able to hold 'em all before long, the way things are going. Of course, the Tower's been the big attraction since it opened last year. It's been a power of good for the town.'

'Have you been to t'top, Alice?' A note of incred-ulity crept into Martha's voice. 'I don't think I'd like to go right up theer.'

'No, nor me neither.' Alice laughed. 'Our Albert's been, but I like to have both me feet on t'ground. It's not just the Tower itself, though. There's all sorts in the buildings underneath – a ballroom an' a menagerie an' aquarium, even a

17

circus. Aye, it's a real money-spinner, there's no doubt about that. Specially on wet days. The folk fairly flock there then. And we've three piers now, you know, and electric lighting on t'prom and electric tramcars. I tell you, there's no holding the place, now it's got going.'

As she listened to Alice, Martha could feel the excitement bubbling up inside her, something she hadn't felt for many a long day. Life to her had become humdrum and colourless in the Lancashire mill town where she had been born and where, till now, she had spent all her days. It was time for a change.

'Now, you two ladies, where shall we go?' Albert beamed at the two girls as they stood on the pavement outside the Sunnyside lodging house. 'Where d'you fancy?'

'I think you'd better choose, Albert,' said Grace, smiling at him. She turned to her sister. 'Don't you think so, Hetty? He knows the place so much better than we do.'

'Anywhere,' said Hetty, swinging her arms and almost jumping up and down with excitement. 'Anywhere . . . I don't mind. It's just so exciting to be here.'

'Righto then.' Albert nodded decidedly. 'We'll go to Uncle Tom's Cabin, up on the cliffs. That do for yer? Come on then, let's be havin' you.' He held out his elbows and Grace linked an arm at one side and Hetty at the other.

Albert felt as pleased as Punch. Not only one girl tonight, but two. Just wait till the lads at work found out about this. They were forever

18

teasing him about his shyness, for the way he always preferred to be one of a crowd instead of being alone with a young woman. Albert couldn't help being shy. He had tried to overcome it, but girls, on the whole, made him feel tongue-tied and embarrassed. Forever giggling, they were, and making pointed remarks, leastways the girls he had come across were like that. Maybe he hadn't met the right sort? These two lasses seemed different, what his mother would call 'well brought up'. Albert was ashamed to admit – in fact he wouldn't have dared to admit – to his pals at work that he had never yet kissed a girl. Perhaps, before the weekend was over, that might be remedied.

He had glanced at Hetty once or twice and she had glanced back at him from under those long eyelashes, and smiled, not coquettishly, just . . . friendly like, her green eyes dancing with merriment. He was sure that Hetty would never make fun of him. Nor Grace . . . Now *she* seemed a nice lass, gentle and serene, exuding a quiet happiness. But it was Hetty that Albert found himself thinking about as they walked along the clifftop. It was Hetty that tickled his fancy.

They walked through Claremont Park and then took the cliff path that led to Uncle Tom's Cabin. They could have boarded one of the new electric tramcars, but both the girls agreed with Albert that it was a lovely evening and they would prefer to walk. It wasn't very far, not much more than a mile.

'It's one of my favourite places in Blackpool,' Albert told them. 'You can see for miles, right

19

across the sea, as far as the Isle of Man on a clear day. And the sunsets . . . I've never seen owt like 'em. They're just . . . well, they're reet grand.' Albert paused momentarily, embarrassed by his own eloquence. He wasn't much of a one for poetic oratory and he had run out of words to describe the beauty of the sun setting over the Irish Sea. The lasses would just have to see it for themselves. 'Aye, Uncle Tom's Cabin's a grand little place,' he went on. 'You can dance and have a drink and have yer picture took, and there's a telescope there an' all. You can see the hills in Wales as clear as anything.'

'How did it get its name?' asked Hetty. 'Who's Uncle Tom when he's at home?'

'It'll be named after that book,' replied Grace. 'You know, that one about the slaves.' She had heard of Harriet Beecher Stowe's book, although she hadn't read it.

Hetty shook her head. She hadn't even heard of it.

'Aye, they reckon it's named after that,' said Albert, although he hadn't read the book either. 'Some folk say that it's called after the first owner, though. He were called Tom Parkinson, but that's ages ago. The place has been there as long as I can remember. It's not so popular as it were, though, since the Winter Gardens opened. A lot of folks prefer to stay in town rather than come all the way up here. But I like it.' Albert nodded emphatically. 'Anyroad, you'll see for yourself in a minute.'

'There y'are,' he said a few minutes later when the buildings came into view. 'There's old Uncle

Tom.' He pointed towards the roof of a wooden building and there the girls could see, perched high on the roof, three roughly carved figures which represented the characters of Uncle Tom, Little Eva and Topsy.

It was a memorable evening for all of them. Albert danced with each of the girls in turn on the open-air dancing platform, to the music of a piano, violins and cornets. The wooden boards reverberated with the pounding of scores of heavy-booted feet.

'I'm called little Buttercup, dear little Buttercup, Though I could never tell why . . .' Grace sang softly to herself as she watched Albert twirling her sister round, somewhat inelegantly, to the strains of a fast waltz rhythm. She sipped her ginger beer, which tasted so much better out of doors, and watched the sun gradually disappearing on the far horizon. The scene was every bit as beautiful as Albert, in his halting way, had tried to describe. The sky glowed with flaming colours, orange, scarlet and vermilion, and the darkening sea danced with millions of shining, shimmering golden coins. As Albert had said, it was 'reet grand'.

Later, as they strolled back along the cliff path in the deepening dusk, Grace noticed that Albert had shyly put his arm round Hetty's waist. Grace looked away out to sea, in a pretence of watching a distant fishing boat, and smiled to herself as Albert clumsily placed a kiss on her sister's cheek.

Grace wasn't jealous, nor did she feel that she was intruding. She had her own young man, back home in Burnley. If only he were here too, it

21

would all be perfect. Then Grace realised, to her amazement, that it was the first time she had thought of Walter all evening.

Chapter 2

'What d'you suppose our mam's up to?' asked Hetty as the two girls strolled arm in arm along the promenade. 'Going off on her own again today. What d'you think she's doing?'

'I don't suppose she's up to anything,' Grace replied. 'You know how she loves looking at the shops, even if it's only window-shopping, and she likes a bit of time on her own now and again, just like we do.'

Martha had accompanied the girls on the Sunday when they had walked along North Pier and then taken a ride along the promenade in one of the new electric tramcars. That was after they had been to chapel. Martha had insisted that they should pay their usual morning visit to a place of worship, and so they had gone to the Methodist chapel at the end of the street. Albert had been with them, singing lustily, Martha had noticed to her satisfaction, in his pleasing baritone voice. He was a good lad, was Albert, and she was pleased that he and Hetty seemed to like one another. They didn't know yet, of course, that very soon they might be able to see a good deal more of one another.

Alice Gregson had stayed at home to see to the visitors' dinners. There wasn't time for chapel on a Sunday morning, she said. There was far too much to do. Martha had secretly thought that where there's a will there's a way but, tactfully, she hadn't voiced her opinion. She knew that she might very well find, when the time came, that Sunday worship had to take second place.

'Aye, she's a good sort, is our mam,' said Hetty. 'She lets us off the leash a good deal more than some of the mothers I can think of. Young Aggie as works next to me at the loom, she has to be in at nine o'clock every night. Just imagine that! And she's not allowed to so much as speak to a lad. Her mam watches her like a hawk. 'Course, she's only sixteen, you know.' Hetty nodded with all the superiority of her eighteen years, her ginger curls bobbing beneath her flat straw hat. 'But her mam makes her that scared she can hardly say boo to a goose. Frightened of her own shadow, she is.'

Grace squeezed her sister's arm. 'Yes, we're lucky, aren't we, love? Mam thinks the world of us, you know, even though she doesn't say so. And aren't we having a grand time, Hetty?' Grace's brown eyes glowed fervently. 'I am glad we came, aren't you?'

'I am that!' Hetty turned and grinned at her sister. 'And you know what, Gracie? I haven't heard you cough once since we came to Blackpool. And your cheeks are all rosy – you look real well.'

'Yes, I'm feeling much better.' Grace nodded. 'And I know you're having a good time.' She looked slyly at her sister. 'What about Albert, eh? I reckon he's fair smitten with you. D'you like him?'

'Oh, he's all right, I suppose.' Hetty shrugged, but Grace could tell by the pink tinge that flushed her sister's face all of a sudden that she was rather taken with the lad. 'He's a bit shy. Not much go about him, but – yes – I must admit I do like him. I don't know just what it is that I like about him. He's very ordinary, but I feel as how I can trust him. Some of them fellows at work, I wouldn't trust 'em as far as I could throw 'em. And some of 'em at chapel an' all, for all they crack on they're so pious like . . . I'm sorry Walter's not here though, Gracie. You'd have enjoyed it a lot more, wouldn't you, if he could have come along with us?'

'Yes . . .' replied Grace slowly. 'I daresay I would . . .' But she was not sure. Not sure at all. Until Hetty mentioned him, Walter hadn't even been in the forefront of her mind.

'We'd best make the most of the time we've got left,' said Hetty. 'We'll be catching the train back sometime this afternoon, I suppose, after we've had our dinner. Now, what would you like to do? Shall we go to the top of the Tower?'

The two girls stopped and stared at the gigantic structure opposite them on the other side of the tram track. It really was a wonderful sight and a magnificent piece of engineering work. 'Ooh, no. I don't think I'd like to go to the top,' said Grace. 'It makes me legs feel all wobbly just to think of it. It's grand though, isn't it? Fancy, workmen having to climb all the way up there.'

'Yes. Albert was telling me that one of 'em fell off and was killed,' said Hetty. 'Not that we'd fall off,' she went on hastily, after a look at her sister's panic-stricken face. 'We wouldn't have to climb up. We'd be in one of them lifts. Can you see it, going up behind all that ironwork? And another 'un coming down? We won't go though, Grace, not if you don't want to. Perhaps another time, eh?' Although neither of them knew when the next time would be. Visits to Blackpool were few and far between.

'I'm surprised there was only one fell off,' said Grace with a shudder, staring up at the Tower again. 'No,' she added decidedly. 'I don't want to go up. Just look, Hetty. It seems to be swaying when you look at it.'

'Go on with yer bother! It can't be.' Hetty gave her sister a playful shove. Then she looked up and gave a gasp of surprise. 'Oh aye . . . you're right. It does look as though it's moving. Can't be though, can it?'

'No, of course not.' Grace laughed. 'It'll be what they call an optical illusion. How's that for high-falutin' words on a Monday morning? Let's go on to the sands, Hetty.'

Blackpool beach, south of the Tower, was crammed full of bustle and activity of every sort imaginable. At the edge of the promenade was a row of wooden pit props, intended to break the force of the waves at high tide, and from there a granite slope led down to the sands. Two wooden breakwaters, some 150 feet in length, reached out into the sea and the stretch in between was the most popular and the most crowded part of the

26

whole of the seven miles of sand which bordered the Fylde coast.

At the edge of the sea was a row of bathing huts for the more daring of the visitors, but the rest just strolled along or sat beneath huge black umbrellas which kept off the glare of the sun, whilst sailor-suited boys and girls paddled in the shallow rock pools or dug furiously with their wooden spades, building sand pies and castles. A crowd of them sat around the red-and-white-striped kiosk of the Punch and Judy show, laughing uproariously at the antics of the funny hook-nosed character whirling his wooden baton. 'That's the way to do it.' His nasal voice drifted across on the summer breeze, while his dog Toby, with a frill round his neck, sat patiently watching it all.

A group of donkeys, their bells gently jingling as they shook their long ears, stood waiting for customers. Goodness knows how they would find room to trot through all that seething mob, thought Grace as she smilingly watched them. She wasn't much of a one for crowds, but she couldn't help but feel stirred by the excitement of it all.

The two sisters wandered along happily, savouring the rumbustious delights of the scene that surrounded them. They resisted the appeal of the oyster vendor plying his wares, a bottle of vinegar in his hand, a round basket hooked over one arm and, over the other, a grubby towel to wipe his customers' hands. But they succumbed to the enticement of the Peeney Brothers' ice-cream cart, and laughingly bought huge cornets which

27

dripped and ran in sticky streams down their fingers as they poked their tongues into the delicious, creamy yellow confection.

'Hair-restorer. Sixpence a bottle . . .' yelled a salesman, a pseudo-professor with a head of thick frizzy curls. 'Roll up, gentlemen. Only sixpence and you can have a head of hair like mine . . .' Bald-headed gents parted hopefully with their little silver coins while their wives, further along the sands, stared in fascinated horror at the chiropodist publicly extracting corns from the horny feet of his clients.

There were amateur phrenologists – bump-readers as they were commonly called – acrobats, ventriloquists, men playing concertinas, fortune-tellers . . .

'Come along, ladies. Come and have yer fortunes told.'

Grace and Hetty paused at the booth of a dark-eyed, dark-haired young woman. The golden circlets dangling from her ear lobes and her garishly patterned red skirt and shawl pronounced her to be a gipsy. Grace, in spite of an immediate apprehension, felt mesmerised by the girl's haughty stare. She shook her head and hastily turned away. She felt as though this young woman could see right into her inner soul. Yet how could she? They hadn't even met until this moment. Anyway, reading palms and telling fortunes in tea leaves and suchlike was all nonsense. It was more than nonsense, it was wicked. Mr Arkwright, the minister at the chapel, had often told them so. 'Come on, Hetty. Let's go.' Grace tugged nervously at her sister's arm. She couldn't imagine why they had lingered in the first place, but the young woman's eyes were so compelling.

But Hetty could not be persuaded to budge so easily. She returned the girl's imperious look with an equally disdainful glance. 'No, ta,' she answered pertly. 'We don't need you to tell us our fortunes, do we, Grace? We can take care of our own future, we can.'

'You may think you can,' replied the gipsy girl, 'but I wouldn't be too sure if I were you. I've met many a one as thought she knew best, but you'd do well to take heed. Both of you . . .' She stared first at Hetty, then at Grace. Hetty stared boldly back, but Grace, seeing a touch of awareness in the young woman's eye that she didn't like, looked away discomfited. 'I can see you have interesting characters, the pair of you,' the girl went on, 'and that's only at a first glance. And I'll tell you what else I know as well. You're sisters, aren't you? From an inland town, I guess; Bury or Blackburn or Burnley. Somewhere that begins with a B at any rate, I know that. And you're here on holiday . . . You're sure you won't change your mind? I could put you wise to a thing or two.'

'I've told you, no,' said Hetty, but not quite so firmly this time.

'Then don't say you haven't been warned . . .' The gipsy girl's words petered out, unfinished, but her bold stare was enough to make Hetty's hackles rise.

'All right then,' said Hetty suddenly. 'Why not? You seem to think you're so clever, so come on, let's see what you've got to tell me.' Hetty held out her right hand, palm uppermost, in front of the

29

gipsy girl's face. 'Will me hand do, or are you going to gaze into a crystal ball or summat?'

'Your hand,' replied the girl coolly. 'I'll read your palm. But we'd best go inside. It'll be more private.' She pushed aside the red curtain that hung against the entrance to the small booth and with a haughty toss of her black curls beckoned Hetty to come inside.

'No, Hetty, don't!' cried Grace in alarm. 'We mustn't. Oh, come on. Let's go before we get too involved in it all. You know we shouldn't.'

Grace looked distraught, her brown eyes imploring her sister not to be foolish, but Hetty, now she had made up her mind, was not to be swayed. 'Oh, give over mithering, Grace,' she said, though not unkindly. 'It's only a bit of fun. Let's see what she's got to say. It'll all be a load of nonsense anyway, I don't doubt.'

The gipsy girl nodded slowly, the golden circlets hanging from her ears swinging gently to and fro. 'A bit of fun? A load of nonsense, you say? Very sure of yourself, aren't you? Well, we shall see. We shall see . . .' She gestured again for Hetty to enter the booth.

Hetty stepped inside and Grace immediately followed. 'I'm coming in as well then,' she said decidedly. 'We'll do this together, our Hetty, if we do it at all.' The fearful look had almost gone from her eyes now and, in spite of her trepidation, she looked challengingly first at her sister, then at the young gipsy girl.

The small tent appeared dark at first after the brightness of the sunshine outside. The light, diffused through the dusky red material of the

30

booth, was tinged with pink, bathing the faces of the three young women in a rosy glow. There was a folding card-table with a green baize top – on which stood a ball of translucent milky-white glass – and two bentwood chairs. The girl sat on one behind the table and pointed to the other chair where Hetty then sat. Grace stood unobtrusively near the entrance of the tent from where she could hear the laughter of the children playing on the sands and the hubbub of the adult conversation. Normal everyday sounds which were comforting; the sooner Hetty was done with this silly business the better she would like it.

Hetty held out her right hand again towards the girl. 'Come on then. Tell me the worst . . . or the best. Which is it to be? All work and worry, or a rich husband and a life of luxury?' Then she added much more seriously, all trace of laughter gone from her voice, 'You will tell me, won't you? I'd like to know, I would really, an' I promise I won't make any more rude remarks. I was only 'aving you on. I'm always ready for a bit of a laugh. Me sister'll tell you.'

The girl nodded curtly. 'Your left hand first, please, if you will.'

Obediently Hetty displayed her left hand, then, to her sister's and her own amazement, sat quietly and listened.

'The finger of Jupiter.' The gipsy lightly touched Hetty's forefinger. 'A long finger. I can tell that you want to get on in life, you love a challenge . . . and you like to be the boss?' She looked at Hetty quizzically but Hetty did not respond. 'Your thumb bears it out. It shows a forceful personality.

31

Your finger of Apollo is shorter.' She pointed to Hetty's ring finger, bare at the moment of any finery. 'That's a sign of emotional problems. Trouble with your young men, no doubt.' The girl gave a quiet throaty chuckle and Hetty tutted impatiently. 'Now, the Mount of Venus.' The girl tapped the prominent fleshy pad at the base of Hetty's thumb. 'Yes . . . oh, yes. You are certainly a girl who enjoys the company of men, or you will do, before long. And you love music. You enjoy singing, don't you?'

Hetty nodded her agreement, but she didn't speak. It was quite uncanny what the girl had told her. She knew that the gipsy had summed up her personality with amazing accuracy. Still, it could just be guesswork. She had shown, hadn't she, the forcefulness of her character by the way she had spoken to the girl in the first place.

Hetty shrugged her shoulders now. 'So what? You've only told me what I'm like. I thought as how you were going to tell me what's going to happen to me, not something as I already know.'

'It all has a bearing on it,' replied the girl quietly. 'The left hand shows your character.' She tapped now at the base of Hetty's little finger. 'You love a change, don't you? You're always wanting something different. Now, let's see if your right hand bears it out. That's the hand that will tell me what you'll make of your life. Your right hand, if you please.

'Mmm . . .' The girl nodded speculatively as she bent over Hetty's outstretched palm. 'As I thought. Changes ahead. Quite drastic changes. You'll be making a journey soon, to a new abode.

And a new job . . . two jobs, if I'm not mistaken. There's some opposition. There's trouble ahead here, but you'll stick to your guns if it's what you really want. I can see that you're very good at doing that.'

'But what about the rich husband?' asked Hetty, trying to force a light, bantering tone into her voice, but not quite succeeding. 'Isn't that what fortune-tellers always go on about?'

'I'm coming to it. Just wait your hurry,' replied the girl calmly, refusing to be rushed. 'Your line of health. You're a strong young woman, very healthy, but . . .' She paused abruptly and for a moment she was silent. Then, 'I can see a period of sickness,' she went on quickly, almost gloatingly, Hetty thought. 'Take heed. It might be serious . . .' Her voice petered out and Hetty felt a tremor of fear, just the tiniest one, grip her.

'Now, the line of the heart.' The girl spoke more forcefully now. She traced her finger along the line that led across the top of Hetty's palm. 'Yes . . . yes, there's romance. A young man, a fair young man, and marriage . . . eventually. Not without a lot of trouble, though. I can see . . . there's someone in the way. Someone . . .' Suddenly the gipsy girl dropped Hetty's hand, flinging it away from her brusquely. She stared coldly at Hetty. 'I can't tell you any more. That's all I can see.' Her lips closed together in a grim line and her black eyes flashed alarmingly as she looked at Hetty. Almost, Hetty thought, as though she hated her and as though she knew something that she was loath to impart.

But that was ridiculous. What could she know?

Hetty gave an impatient toss of her head as she turned to her sister. 'Well, that was all very clever, I must say. Not that I believe it all.' Her voice sounded less than convincing. 'Come on, Gracie. Your turn now.'

To Hetty's surprise Grace stepped forward and sat on the chair her sister had vacated, bravely thrusting forward her left hand. 'It's this hand first, isn't it?' she asked quietly.

'That's right,' said the gipsy girl thoughtfully as she looked into Grace's face, then at her palm. 'Mmm . . . A different reading here all right. You're as different as chalk and cheese, you two, aren't you?' She glanced up quickly at Grace then cast a more baleful glance at Hetty, who had taken her sister's former stance at the entrance to the booth. Hetty had heard enough now; she was anxious to be off, but she also wanted to know what the cheeky minx would have to say about Grace.

'Yes, we're different in some ways,' Grace agreed. 'Go on.' She gave a nervous little laugh. 'Tell me what you can see.'

The gipsy tapped at Grace's ring finger which, like her sister's, was free of adornment. 'Your finger of Apollo is long, almost as long as the finger of Saturn.' She pointed to the middle finger. 'I can see you are emotional, but well balanced, and you usually know just what you want. You have a quiet nature – not like your sister' – again the malevolent glance at Hetty before she looked back at Grace's palm – 'and you don't mind solitude. In fact, sometimes you welcome it. Your Mount of Apollo confirms this.' She tapped the base of the ring finger. 'You love beauty in all things, don't you? Scenery, poetry, music . . . Am I right?'

Grace nodded and gave a quiet smile as she proffered her right hand.

The gipsy bent over it. 'But there are changes for you as well. A change of abode, a change of job. I can see it all clearly . . . But you must watch your health.' The girl traced a line, a not very clear one, running at a slight angle from the base of the little finger. 'I can see that you're not very robust. A weak chest, I think. A change of air would do you good but, as I've already told you, there will be a change. An important one. And I can see someone who cares for you deeply, but it's not going to be easy for you. Don't let anyone take advantage of your kind nature. You will find that you'll have to stick up for yourself and for what you want . . .' The girl let go of Grace's hand abruptly. 'That's all I can tell you, both of you.'

'Thank you,' said Grace quietly. She reached into her handbag for her purse and Hetty, stepping forward again now, did the same.

'Cross yer palm with silver now, don't we?' said Hetty mockingly, but Grace frowned reprovingly at her sister. She had a feeling that it wouldn't be wise to vex this gipsy girl.

'Sixpence apiece will do,' replied the girl in a matter-of-fact voice as she held out her hand for the tiny silver coins that Grace and Hetty gave to her.

The sunshine was dazzling and felt warm on their faces as they stepped out of the dimness of the tent into the fresh air, and they blinked at the sudden contrast of the bright light.

'Now, how about a love potion, ladies, just to make sure those predictions come true?' The girls glanced towards the next stall, one they hadn't noticed before, whence the voice was coming. A swarthy gipsy lad was leaning against the wooden support, his black eyes flashing with amusement as he looked appraisingly at Grace and Hetty. He held up a bottle of vivid yellow liquid. 'You may not be so happy to know the future, lady,' he said, addressing his remarks to Hetty, 'but I'm sure this is an offer 'ee can't afford to miss. Just one spoonful of this in your young man's tea, and you'll have him popping the question in no time. And, from what I've overheard, there is a young man, isn't there?' He raised one eyebrow sardonically.

'How dare you listen!' snapped Hetty. 'That was a private conversation, I'll have you know. It's got nothing to do with you. Nothing at all. And no – ta very much – I don't want a love potion. The very idea!' Secretly, though, she could feel the laughter bubbling up inside her at the lad's audacity. She had never seen eyes of such a deep, dense black, like smouldering coals, or such tightly curled black hair. He wore it long, almost touching the brightly coloured kerchief which was knotted casually round his neck. She glanced from him back to the girl at the neighbouring booth, who was standing there grinning slyly, obviously enjoying the interchange. There was an unmistakable likeness, not just in the colour of their hair and swarthy complexions, but in the arrogance of both their glances. Brother and sister, Hetty guessed.

'No offence intended, I'm sure,' answered the lad coolly. 'How about some stomach medicine then? Cure your colic . . . Or headache pills . . .?'

'No, ta,' said Hetty again. 'Come on, Grace. We don't want to waste any more time wi' the likes of them. We've already been here quite long enough.'

But her sister was already on her way, walking quickly along the beach. Hetty could almost feel the piercing glance of the gipsy lad boring into her back, just between her shoulder blades, as she walked away. And when she half turned round to give a quick glance over her shoulder, he was still staring. He raised an eyebrow questioningly, his wide mouth twisting into a wry grin. Hetty tossed her ginger curls and turned quickly away, tucking her hand into her sister's arm. 'Did you ever know such cheek?' she said.

But Grace didn't answer. Hetty could tell from the silence that her sister was already regretting her decision to let the girl tell her fortune. 'Aw, come on, Gracie,' she said. 'It was just a bit of fun, that's all. Don't start worrying about it. It was all a load of rubbish, as likely as not. You'll have forgotten all about it by tomorrow, you'll see.'

'I'm not so sure about that,' Grace replied. 'I didn't like the way that young woman seemed to know all about us. You must admit, Hetty, what she told us was true. A lot of it anyroad. She was right about you always wanting a change, and me being quieter.'

'She was just guessing,' Hetty replied. 'Anyone

can see just by looking at us two that we're different. There's nowt so very clever in that.'

'All the same, I thought it was sinister.' Grace gave a shudder. 'You don't think she really knows something about us, do you?' She turned and looked at her sister, her brown eyes clouded with anxiety. 'She seemed awful sure and . . .'

'Don't talk so daft, Gracie! How could the likes of her know anything about us? That's what they all say, these fortune-tellers, "There's trouble ahead . . ." Hetty's voice took on a mocking, lugubrious tone. 'Anyroad, I've heard you dismiss it all many a time as nonsense. You know what Mr Arkwright at t'chapel says. We haven't to try to look into the future.'

'Yes, I know, and that's what's bothering me now.' Grace's voice was troubled. 'Just look what we've gone and done. Goodness knows what Mr Arkwright would say if he knew. Oh . . . I wish I'd never listened to you, our Hetty. It's wrong, listening to fortune-tellers. Only God knows the future. But I can't help wondering . . . If He knows what's going to happen to us, how can we do anything to prevent it? It's often puzzled me. You remember what that gipsy girl said at first, "I could put you wise". But what good will it do us to know, if we can't do anything about it?'

'Oh, shut up, Grace!' Hetty snapped, but not unkindly. 'That sort o' talk's all too deep for me. I say, she's really got to you, hasn't she?' She squeezed her sister's arm. 'I daresay she meant that if we knew what was coming we'd be ready for it. You know what they say, "To be forewarned is to be forearmed", or summat like that. Anyroad, there's nothing going to happen to us, love. You can rest assured on that score. It's a load of bunkum she was talking. Tek no notice. I tell you what though, Gracie. We'd best not say anything to Mam. She wouldn't approve at all.'

Grace nodded. 'No, and she'd be right, too. No, we'd best not say anything.' She felt sure, as her sister avowed, that it was a load of bunkum that the girl was talking. Nevertheless, a slight shadow had fallen across the brightness of the day.

'It was him as got my dander up,' Hetty went on. 'That lad and his talk about love potions. Cheeky monkey! I've never heard such rubbish. I'd like to have told him a thing or two. Good-looking lad though, wasn't he? Those dark eyes . . .' Hetty's own eyes grew misty.

Grace laughed. 'Yes. If looks could have killed, he'd have been stone dead on the sands. You looked real mad, Hetty, an' I don't blame you.'

Hetty grinned. She felt that she had given as good as she got with the gipsy lad. But it wasn't of the young gipsy that Hetty was thinking as they walked back towards Alice Gregson's lodging house. Her thoughts were of Albert, who had made such an impression on her. As she had said to Grace, it wasn't as if he had much go about him. She had rarely met such a diffident young man. He blushed when he spoke, he fell over his words and he fell over his feet, too, when he danced. Yet there was something about him that had appealed to Hetty. He was completely unaware of it but he had inveigled his way into her thoughts, and now she knew that she didn't want to go back home to

39

Burnley, to her boring job in the mill, and leave him. You're being ridiculous, she told herself. You've only known the lad for five minutes. You'll soon forget about him when you get back home . . . But she knew that she wouldn't forget him.

Last night, Albert had taken her and Grace to the Raikes Hall Pleasure Gardens. As he had done the night before, he had danced with each of the two girls in turn and had linked arms with both of them as they strolled round the ornamental lake. But when they arrived back at Sunnyside, Grace had tactfully gone indoors, leaving her sister and Albert to say their private goodnight on the doorstep.

He had clumsily put his arms round her and, for the first time, kissed her constrainedly and inexpertly on the lips. His mouth felt cool and dry, just the gentlest touch of his lips on hers, but Hetty felt a warmth of affection surge up inside her.

'Come here, lad,' she whispered, as she put her hand behind his head, drawing him closer to her. Their second kiss was more lingering; she felt his mouth opening under hers and noticed the look of startled surprise in his grey eyes. She gave a quiet chuckle to herself as she drew away from him. She didn't want to frighten him off so soon. 'We'd best go in,' she whispered. 'Me mam'll be lookin' for me.'

'Hetty . . . Hetty.' He grabbed hold of her hand. 'I do . . . like you. A lot, I think. Would you write to me when you get back home? Not that I'm any great shakes at writing, but it would be grand if you would.'

40

"Course I will, Albert.' She leaned across and planted a kiss on his smooth warm cheek. They were much of a height and her green eyes looked into his earnest grey ones, slightly perplexed and questioning. "Course I'll write,' she said again. 'Not that I'm much good either. I was never much of a scholar. It's our Grace that's the clever one. But I'll write . . . I promise.'

'And happen . . .' Albert put his arm round her waist again and laid his cheek next to hers. 'Happen . . . you'll come 'ere again?' he asked hesitantly. 'Next Bank Holiday, p'raps? D'you think you might, Hetty?'

'Yes . . . I'd like that,' said Hetty warmly, feeling a surge of affection again for this bumbling, inarticulate young man. It was inexplicable, but she felt that she was already halfway to loving him. Not 'falling in love'; that was something else, something romantic and mysterious, and there was nothing that was remotely fanciful in her feelings for Albert. He was not the stuff that dreams were made of, but she could sense his honesty and worthiness – which once, she was well aware, she would have condemned as dullness – and she knew that she liked him a lot.

Now, as she walked back with her sister through the Blackpool streets, thronged with visitors all heading the same way, back to their lodging houses for their midday dinner, Hetty knew that she didn't want to go home and leave Albert behind.

'Well, Mam, I reckon we'd best be getting our bits and pieces together.' Grace placed her cup on her

41

saucer – a pot of strong, well-brewed tea had been a satisfying end to the midday dinner of shepherd's pie, followed by apple tart – and looked enquiringly at her mother. Martha had been surprisingly quiet all through the meal. Maybe, Grace thought, her mother, like she and Hetty, was not looking forward to the return home, to the drudgery and sameness of it all as one day followed another in the mean, drab little street where they lived in the shadow of Baldwin's mill. The trip to Blackpool, short though it was, had been a welcome respite, an escape from the workaday toil. But all things had to come to an end . . . 'Hetty and me thought we'd have a last look at the prom before we go back, that's if we have time,' Grace went on. 'D'you want to come along with us, Mam? Which train are we catching?'

Martha picked up a teaspoon and idly traced the pattern in the white damask cloth, not speaking. Then she looked up at her daughters, first at Grace, then at Hetty, her brown eyes, usually serious, glowing with pleasure and her mouth curved in a broad smile. 'You can keep yer glad rags on a bit longer, the pair of you,' she said. 'We're stoppin' another day.'

'What?' Hetty stared unbelievingly at her mother. 'You really mean it? Eeh, that's grand, Mam. Albert'll be that thrilled. Just wait till I tell 'im.'

'Hold on a minute, our Hetty,' said Grace, hating to quell her sister's excitement, but surely Mam had forgotten something? She turned to her mother. 'We've got to go back to work tomorrow, Mam, me and Hetty. You can't have forgotten.

We'll be in a right load of trouble if we're not there when the hooter goes at six o'clock in the morning.'

'I doubt it, Grace.' Martha shook her head. 'If yer not there, yer not there, and there's nowt as Josiah Baldwin'll be able to do about it. He's not the ogre some of the lasses make him out to be, you know. Him and yer father were lads together at the same chapel, an' he always remembers that. And things have changed from what they were twenty year ago when I worked there. Josiah were always a fair sort of boss though, I'll say that for him . . . All right, you'll lose a day's pay, but you're not likely to lose your jobs. Anyroad,' she looked slyly at her daughters from beneath lowered eyelids and grinned, 'you'll not be needing yer jobs much longer.'

'Mam, you're talking in riddles.' Hetty put her elbows on the table and cupped her chin in her hands. 'What on earth are you on about? Don't you think it's time you told us?'

Grace looked suspiciously at her mother, her head on one side. She nodded slowly. 'You've been acting strangely all weekend, Mam, come to think of it. Come on, what's it all in aid of?'

Martha sighed. 'I know . . . I should have told you before, but I wanted to be sure first. Anyroad, I'll tell you now. Listen . . .'

The young women stared open-mouthed, hardly able to speak for astonishment at first as she told them the tale. They were to come and live in Blackpool, across the road, at the dilapidated, dejected-looking lodging house that was to let. Not that Martha intended it to remain in such a

43

sorry state for long. That was what she had been doing this weekend; sorting things out with Mr Butterworth, the landlord, and arranging for plumbers and joiners and decorators to make the place shipshape. That's why they were staying another day; there were still one or two things to see to.

'Mr Butterworth's a decent sort of chap,' Martha told the girls. 'Not one to give much away, mind, like all landlords, but he's agreed to see to the outside of the house – painting and fixing t'slates on t'roof an' all that. Oh, and he says we can have a new indoor water closet on the first landing. An' I'm to see to the inside – wallpapering and shelves and suchlike. So I reckon he's been fair. We'll have our work cut out, mind you, to get it all decent like, but we'll do it. Aye, we'll do it all right.'

Grace and Hetty looked at one another, a long, knowing look, each of them well aware of what the other one was thinking. That gipsy girl had said there would be changes ahead for both of them. A change of abode, a change of job . . . A slight smile played at the corners of Hetty's mouth and Grace gave an almost imperceptible nod.

Grace thought that she had rarely seen her mother so excited, not for many a long day, but she couldn't help feeling aggrieved that she and her sister hadn't been consulted. It wasn't like Mam to be so secretive.

But it was Hetty, in her usual forthright way, who voiced what they were both feeling. 'I do think you might have told us, Mam. Don't me and our Grace have some say in the matter? I take it you'll want us to work for you in this 'ere lodging house, so I should've thought we'd a right to be asked about it.' Secretly, Hetty was cock-a-hoop about the idea of moving to Blackpool – all the excitement, the crowds, the laughter and the razzle-dazzle, it all appealed to her innate sense of fun, to say nothing of being near to Albert – but she wasn't going to admit all this to her mother. Mam should have told them, not gone and done it all on her own. Hetty stared at her belligerently, determined not to be won over so easily.

'All right, all right . . . I know.' Martha raised her hands in a gesture of resignation. 'I realise I should have told you. I'm sorry . . . but I wanted to make sure as it was going to work before I said anything.' She leaned forward and looked at them both, the eagerness glowing in her eyes as she spoke. 'I wanted it so badly, you see. I was afraid to talk about it in case it didn't come off. But it has. We're comin' to live in Blackpool.' Her delight showed in her voice and in the expression on her face. Grace thought her mother looked years younger, almost like a girl again.

Martha's next words echoed her daughter's thoughts. 'I'm only young yet, just turned forty. But I'd been getting to feel old, real old . . .' She paused for a moment, her countenance serious again, before she continued. 'But this'll take years off me. I know it will. I'm sorry if you're cross with me, you two lasses, for not telling you sooner, but this was one time when I decided I was going to please meself.'

Grace knew that her mother was right. Martha

45

had spent most of her life at the beck and call of other folk. It was only fair that, for once, she should show some independence in making this momentous decision, even though it was a step that affected them all.

'We don't mind, Mam,' said Grace kindly. 'It fair took the wind out of me sails for a minute though, I must admit, but we know you only want what's best for us all. Don't we, Hetty?' She turned to her sister, giving her a meaningful glance. 'We don't mind, do we, Hetty?'

'No, 'course we don't,' said Hetty. Then, suddenly, she smiled, her face lighting up like a ray of sunshine. 'No . . . it'll be grand, Mam. Hard work though, keeping a lodging house.'

'Boarding house,' Martha interrupted. 'That's what it's going to be, Hetty. Not a lodging house . . . a boarding house.'

'What's the difference then?' asked Hetty, frowning.

'We'll provide all the meals,' Martha explained. ' "All found", they call it. I reckon nowt to cooking bits o' this and bits o' that for different folk. No, they'll all sit down to the same meal at the same time. I like cooking, so that won't be any hardship to me, though I know it's not going to be easy.'

'And what about us, Mam?' Hetty asked again. 'Are we going to work there an' all?'

Martha nodded. 'I daresay there'll be work enough for all of us, but I don't want to force you into anything.' She looked at her younger daughter, then at Grace, the faint wrinkles round her eyes becoming more pronounced as she smiled. 'It's early days yet. Let's see how it goes, shall we?

If we find there's not enough work for all of us, or if you don't like it, I reckon you could soon find a job in the town. Blackpool's growing by leaps and bounds according to Alice Gregson.'

'And when are we coming, Mam?' Hetty sounded quite excited now.

'In a week or two, as soon as I can sort things out back home. Then if we get a move on with the decorating an' all that, we should be able to open up by the next Bank Holiday, in August.' Martha looked concernedly at Grace who was sitting there in silence, abstractedly playing with the spoon in the sugar basin. 'I'm sorry about Walter, lass,' she said softly. 'I know you won't want to leave him. That's what you're thinking about, isn't it? It's been worrying me as I know you're getting fond of one another. But I daresay you'll be able to sort summat out with him, won't you?'

Grace looked up and smiled. 'Don't worry, Mam,' she said. 'It'll be all right.' What her mother said was true. She had been thinking about Walter, but not about how sorry she would be at leaving him. Grace was more concerned about what Walter's reaction would be when he found out that they were coming to live in Blackpool.

Chapter 3

Donnelly's High-Class Draper's prided itself on being one of the most influential businesses in the town. It was so much more than merely a draper's shop, though that was the name by which it was commonly called – Donnelly's Draper's. It had been started back in 1865 by George Donnelly, in a modest way at first as a small lock-up shop, but it had now grown to such an extent that it occupied one of the premier positions in Blackpool, a corner site near to the Tower, and from its top windows the sea could be glimpsed, some fifty yards away. This top floor had recently been opened by the present owner, Mr William Donnelly, as an elegant tea and luncheon room, in co-operation with his great friend, Mr Frederick Whitehead, who owned an equally influential business at the south end of the town, Whitehead's High-Class Confectioner's.

The windows of Donnelly's Draper's were a delight to the eye as Grace and Hetty found as they stood, like a couple of excited children, with their noses pressed flat against the vast expanse of plate glass. One window was arranged as for a wedding, the full-busted dummy in the centre displaying an elegant ivory satin wedding dress with long tapering sleeves and a half bustle and train. Other less conspicuous dummies surrounding it wore garments suitable for the guests or bride's mother, elaborate befrilled creations in turquoise or lemon, and travelling costumes in darker shades of maroon and sage green. Nearer to the floor of the window were hats, such hats as Grace and Hetty had never seen in the streets of Burnley or in the weekly market, huge extravaganzas with wide brims, bedecked with all manner of imitation fruits and flowers and birds of paradise, and overflowing with lace and ribbon and ruched tulle.

In the next window was an assortment of smaller items, not quite so skilfully arranged; a conglomeration of corsets and hosiery, gloves, leather goods and imitation jewellery. They passed by the third window, uninterested as they were in gentlemen's clothing – trousers and jackets, boots and shoes, shirts and collars, and hats, ranging from silk toppers to flat woollen caps.

'Ooh, Grace. Look!' It was the next display that was claiming Hetty's attention. 'Just look at all them cloths. Have you ever seen such colours?' The window held an eye-catching array of materials, bale upon bale of them, many of them unfolded to flow in streaming cascades from floor to ceiling, revealing in all their glory their shimmering textures and rainbow-bright colours. Silks, satins and velvets, more serviceable stuffs such as tweeds, velours and velveteen, and delicate, diaphanous arrangements of lace, muslin and tulle.

'Lovely, aren't they?' Grace gave a little laugh as her eyes scanned every corner of the window. 'You'd've thought we'd seen enough materials to last us a lifetime, wouldn't you, Hetty? I reckon we must be gluttons for punishment.'

'Not like this though,' said Hetty, longingly. 'We don't see stuff like this.' The girls were concerned with only one operation in the manufacture of the cotton cloth, tending the loom and watching the shuttle as it flew back and forth, and they saw little of the finished product. 'Don't you wish we were rich, Gracie?' Hetty went on. 'I'd have a dress made of satin, like that there . . .' She pointed to a shining apple-green fabric in the centre of the window. 'An' a parasol, an' white kid boots . . .'

'Go on, yer daft thing.' Grace gave her a playful push. 'When would you wear a dress like that? I can just see you turning up at chapel, all done up like a dog's dinner . . .'

'There's other places besides chapel, our Grace.' Hetty's green eyes flashed defiantly as she glared at her sister. 'That's all I ever hear from you and our mam. I'm fed up of hearing about chapel. An' I'm telling you, one day I will have a posh dress – a wardrobe full of 'em – an' shoes an' hats and goodness knows what. So there!'

'All right, love. All right.' Grace looked anxiously at her sister. 'You know I was only joking.' She had seen that look of defiance on her sister's face before, the aggressive tilt of her pointed chin and the determined set of her mouth in a grim little line. Hetty was a volatile creature, as changeable as the spring weather, but Grace

51

knew that soon the brightness of her smile would appear from behind the lowering grey cloud that furrowed her brow, and the sun would shine again. 'There's no reason why we shouldn't treat ourselves if we want to,' Grace went on placatingly. 'You're right, Hetty. Why should it be just the rich folk as has nice clothes? I'm going to treat meself to some stuff for a blouse. What about you? Shall we, Hetty? I know you've got a bob or two saved up, same as I have.'

Hetty turned a delighted face towards her and grinned, with not even a trace of her former petulance. 'Yes, why not? Come on. Let's go in.' She reached out a hand to push open the huge swing door, then she paused. 'I dunno though, Grace. We could happen pick up a remnant on Burnley market for a few pence. Seems a bit extravagant like.'

Grace gave a hoot of laughter. 'Honestly, Hetty. You are the limit! One minute you're on about fancy togs, silk and satin an' all that, and the next minute you're talking about rooting for a bargain in Burnley market. Make up yer mind.'

Hetty laughed then, a joyous sound which made a few passers-by turn and smile good-naturedly at her. 'You're right, Gracie. If I'm going to act like the gentry I'd best start now. Come on. We'll go in.'

They both paused on the threshold of the big department store, not speaking, but each aware of what the other was thinking. Was this place really for the likes of them? The thick-pile carpet, the solid mahogany counters with brass fittings and the tempting displays of all manner of merchandise; it was like another world. They could see other young women in the store though, just like themselves, dressed ordinarily enough in black skirts and cotton blouses, some with shopping bags over their arms. They grinned excitedly at one another and went in.

Inside, Donnelly's Draper's was a delight, not only to the eye, but to all the other senses as well. Their feet sank into the lush pile of the maroon carpet as they made their way up the wide staircase to the haberdashery department, that section of the store which provided not only materials but every other requirement – buttons, braid, elastic, hooks and eyes, needles and pins – for the seamstress. Martha had, a couple of years previously, bought a Singer sewing-machine, an expensive item, but one for which she had saved for a long time. Ready-made clothes were costly, far out of the reach of ordinary folk, and to pay a dressmaker, as the gentry and middle class could afford to do, was also out of the question. Working-class folk usually had to make do with second-hand or even third-hand clothes, but some, industrious women like Martha, were able to make their own. Grace and Hetty were adequate seamstresses too, Grace being the slightly more proficient.

The girls could not make up their minds when confronted with the hundreds of fabrics, a myriad of design and colour and texture. Grace, aware of the eagle eye of the black-dressed saleswoman, tentatively ran her finger along a lustrous swathe of rich brown satin, gently touching the silky smoothness, imagining how it would feel against her skin.

'Not brown again, Grace,' said her sister, frowning slightly. 'Why d'you always go for dark colours? Choose something brighter, for goodness' sake! What about that?' She pointed to a roll of buttercup-yellow crêpe de Chine. 'That would look real lovely with your brown hair and brown eyes. Proper cheerful it is.'

'Mmm . . .' Grace pursed her lips. She was confused, completely at a loss amidst such bounty. 'Perhaps . . . What about you, Hetty? What do you fancy?'

Hetty's choice was sparkling white muslin, sprigged with delicate flowers of cornflower blue, despite her earlier craving for silk and satin. The material felt crisp and fresh between her fingers. She could just imagine it made up into a high-necked blouse with possibly some lace at the collar and huge puffed sleeves. And yet . . . she was not sure. She liked that apple-green satin – the one she had pointed out to Grace in the window – but it was a bit sumptuous-looking. As her sister said, it was hardly the thing to wear at chapel, and Hetty knew, despite her protestations, that there was little call for either of them to wear fancy clothes. They would be moving to Blackpool soon though. There might be more opportunity here for wearing something more stylish.

'Oh . . . I can't make up me mind.' Hetty shook her head impatiently. 'It's no use, Grace, I just can't decide. I tell you what. Let's go up to t'top floor and have a cup of coffee. Then we can come back later when we've had a think about it.'

'All right then. I can't decide either.' Grace

tucked her arm companionably into her sister's as they walked away.

The saleswoman looked down her long nose and sniffed. She might have known there would be no sale there. They looked like a couple of mill girls.

On the top floor of Donnelly's store an appetising aroma of roasted coffee beans and freshly brewed tea greeted the two young women. Here, too, they were spoiled for choice, unable to decide between the variety of delicious-looking cakes – Madeira, sultana, seed cake, almond tartlets, feather-light sponges – temptingly arrayed on ornate glass stands on the marble-topped counter. A waitress in a white frilled apron and cap served them and they sat sipping their coffee and nibbling, as they knew well-bred ladies would do, stopping occasionally to dab their mouths with a serviette. This was the life, to be enjoyed to the full just for today. Tomorrow, with the return to the mill, would be soon enough for them to come back to reality.

They stared around at their luxurious surroundings and at the women at the neighbouring tables, like themselves sipping coffee or tea. Some were dressed ordinarily enough, but a few were more elegant. There was a beautifully dressed young woman walking towards the restaurant now, from the far end of the store.

Hetty nudged her sister. 'Look, Grace. Just look at that dress. What wouldn't I give to have a dress like that.'

The young woman, slim and stately, with shining pale-blonde hair, was clad in a shimmering gown of blue silk. Nothing fancy or elaborate –

very plain really – but obviously expensive.

Grace nodded. 'Gosh, yes! I'll bet that cost a bob or two.'

'She looks a haughty madam though, doesn't she?' said Hetty. 'Looks as though she owns the place.'

'Perhaps she does,' replied Grace. 'Perhaps she's the owner's daughter. Do you think she might be?'

'I don't know and I don't really care,' said Hetty. 'But I'll tell you what, Grace, I wouldn't like to be on the wrong side of that one. Anyway, never mind about her. Let's make the most of the time we've got left. We'll be going home this afternoon. Hurry up and finish your coffee, then we'll go and choose that material.'

Edwin Donnelly, from his table at the rear of the tea-room, surreptitiously watched the two girls. In his mind he was comparing them with Constance, for whom he was waiting at this moment. Constance was never on time. He seemed to spend much of his life waiting for her. What pleasant, happy – ordinary – girls those two seemed to be, obviously enjoying life to the full, revelling in what appeared to be the unaccustomed delight of partaking of coffee and cakes in luxurious surroundings. The ginger-haired one had hardly stopped talking as she stared excitedly around, her eyes taking in the oak-panelled walls and gilded ceiling and dark-green velvet curtains. His father and Mr Whitehead – Constance's father – had spared no expense in making this what they intended it to be, the most elegant and the most popular tea-room in town. Stylish – yes – but also within the reach of the pocket of the ordinary shopper. Like those two girls . . .

The brown-haired one seemed quieter, talking much less, just nodding and smiling, agreeing with her friend. Or perhaps it was her sister? Edwin thought he could see a faint family resemblance. He found himself wondering about them as he waited for Constance. What a contrast they were to her, both of them, although it was the quieter one, the brown-haired one, to whom Edwin's thoughts were drawn. She seemed, even at just a first casual glance, to be receiving so much enjoyment from life, but Edwin knew instinctively as he watched her that this girl would not just be a taker, but a giver as well. A gentle kindliness seemed to shine from her as she nodded and conversed quietly with her companion. He guessed that this little interlude in the tea-room was a rare treat for them, that money was scarce and that luxuries were few and far between.

Constance, now . . . She only seemed to be happy when she was spending money, acquiring yet more gowns and jewellery, finery and frippery, with which to bedeck her already elegantly clothed figure. Possessions . . . it seemed as though these were the only thing that would make Constance's usually cold blue eyes sparkle with a hidden fire. Acquisitiveness was Constance's besetting sin, he feared; a desire to possess not only material goods but, he knew to his dismay, himself as well. He had seen, many times, that provocative gleam in her eyes as she watched him, warily, like a cat ready to pounce. But his

57

ardour could not match hers and so his kisses and embraces – given reluctantly, to his secret shame, because he knew they were expected of him – remained chaste and undemanding. Constance would give willingly whatever he asked of her. She was his for the taking, her eyes told him, but her fervour was not reciprocated. She failed to reach that inner core of him. He could find no warmth in Constance to kindle the spark of feeling – a friendly, brotherly feeling – that he had for her into a flame.

They had been friends for many years. As far back as he could remember Constance had been there, the pretty, petted, overindulged youngest daughter of his father's closest friend, Frederick Whitehead. The two of them, though Edwin was a few years older, had played together as children until he had gone away to school and consequently had seen little of her for several years. More recently he had been her escort to concerts and dances and to the social gatherings frequently held by the close-knit circle of friends to which both their families belonged.

In their business dealings, too, he saw her most days. Edwin was now his father's right-hand man, reared and trained to take over the family business when William Donnelly retired. Not that that would be for many years yet; William was only fifty, and a very sprightly-looking fifty at that. Edwin could foresee many years waiting in the wings, so to speak. Like the Prince of Wales, Albert Edward – Bertie – who also was serving a long apprenticeship, with no sign as yet of stepping into his mother's shoes, and leading his wife a merry dance in the meantime, if all the rumours were to be believed. Edwin, like Bertie, chafed at the bit sometimes, perplexed as to how he had come to be in this position. Because it was expected of him, he supposed. His two elder brothers, to his father's deep disappointment, had shown no aptitude or inclination towards the family business. 'The shop on the corner', his brother Giles had sneeringly called it. Giles had become a great deal 'too big for his boots', to quote William's words, especially since he had married a girl from London and was living down there making quite a profitable living as a lawyer. Charles, the second son, had moved away from Blackpool too when he married, and now worked as an estate agent in the nearby town of Preston. And so the mantle of Donnelly's Draper's would eventually fall on Edwin's shoulders.

Constance also worked for her father, if it could be given the pretentious title of work. She was employed in the office, in charge of the book-keeping at Whitehead's Confectioner's at the south end of the town, but she seemed to spend most of her time partaking of morning coffee or afternoon tea and cakes with her friends. Once a day she popped into Donnelly's, ostensibly to keep an eye on the running of the tea-room, but Edwin knew that her real reason was to seek him out. He had arranged to meet her today though, it being a special day. It was her birthday, her twenty-first . . .

He could see her coming now from the far end of the floor, tall and regal, seeming to drift – like an elegant sailing-ship borne along by a gentle breeze – rather than walk between the white-clothed tables. Her sapphire-blue gown, which exactly matched the shade of her eyes, was expertly cut in flowing lines, moulded to her slender figure, accentuating her tiny waist and slim hips and her tantalisingly pointed breasts. Her long hair, silver blonde, was drawn back into a loose knot at the nape of her neck, fastened with a jewelled comb. Her hair was heavy – he had seen it flowing over her shoulders almost to her waist, straight and gleaming, when she was a little girl – and the weight of it caused her head to tilt in a superior manner, emphasising the long line of her neck and her perfectly chiselled, aristocratic nose. Constance was beautiful, there was no doubt about that, but it was a cold beauty that left Edwin strangely unmoved. He regretted, now, the experimental kisses he had given to Constance, knowing that so much more was expected of him, not only by Constance, but by their respective families as well. He knew, with a shudder of foreboding, that there would be all hell to pay, later that evening, when his birthday gift to her did not come up to all their expectations.

'Good morning, Edwin.' Her voice was casual, belying the little smile of self-satisfaction that played round her lips. She arranged her skirts elegantly round the legs of the bentwood chair. 'A lovely morning for a birthday. I feel as though nothing can possibly go wrong on a day like this.'

'I hadn't forgotten, my dear.' Edwin raised his eyebrows and his lips twisted in an amused grin. Constance was never the most subtle of people. 'I don't need reminding that it's your birthday.' He rose and walked to the other side of the table, then bent and kissed her petal-smooth cheek. 'Happy birthday, Connie, my love.' He used the diminutive form of her name occasionally, when he was feeling particularly indulgent towards her. And, he had to admit, she had never looked lovelier. Her excitement at her coming-of-age – she had no doubt been showered with all manner of extravagant gifts and effusive greetings by her adoring family – was barely concealed by the habitual arrogance of her expression. He smiled at her fondly because, in spite of everything, he was fond of her. 'You'll have to wait till tonight, though, for your present.'

'I can hardly wait, Edwin. And I know it will be the most wonderful present of all.' She smiled at him coquettishly and he could see again the gleam of ardour in her blue eyes. Her voice was cold though, brittle, like ice clinking against cut glass. 'You'll come early, won't you, Edwin? Before the others. The guests are coming for nine o'clock, but I thought it would be nice if we could have some time together first . . . on our own.'

He could feel the panic rising in his throat – what a fool he had been to get himself into such a situation – but he answered her calmly enough. 'I'll come early, Constance. Don't worry. About eight thirty. I would like to see you on your own.' If he could give her a hint, now, not to expect too much, maybe the inevitable disappointment which would come later would be lessened.

His present to her was exquisite, though not what she was expecting. It was a brooch, a sapphire to match the colour of her eyes and the gowns she often wore, surrounded by seed pearls in a gold filigree setting. It had cost him a pretty penny, as she would no doubt realise, but what would that matter when she had been expecting an engagement ring?

'I'll give you a clue,' he said lightly, desperately seeking for a way to diminish the distress he was about to cause her. 'I chose it to match your eyes.' He narrowed his own eyes thoughtfully as he smiled at her across the table. 'I can just see it pinned on the collar of that dress you're wearing . . . Oh, damn!' He put his hand to his mouth in mock horror. 'I fear I've said too much. I've nearly given the game away, and I know how you love surprises.' He hoped she would think about his words for the rest of the day and realise what he was trying to tell her. Their engagement was not to be announced.

She looked at him quizzically. He could see the beginnings of a suspicious fear in her eyes. 'You are a funny one, Edwin,' she said casually. 'I'm sure I don't know what on earth you're talking about.'

They chatted idly for a few moments before she left him, about the guests who were expected this evening, and her family and their gifts to her. What a selfish young woman she was, he thought. No, that was too strong a word; more self-indulgent, narcissistic, but she was only what her family had made her. Possibly this would be the first time that Constance had failed to get exactly what she wanted.

Edwin gazed across the room, above the heads of the mid-morning shoppers. Through the window he could glimpse the azure-blue sky strewn with fleecy white clouds reflected in the deep turquoise of the sea. The sea in Blackpool was often grey; today it was a deep blue. A lovely morning, as Constance had said. 'Nothing can possibly go wrong . . .' Edwin hated to spoil it for her, he was so fond of the girl. But fondness was not love. They who travel fastest travel alone, Edwin thought to himself, and Constance's feelings had by far outdistanced his own. He was sorry for her and he cursed himself for not having had the courage to make things clear to her much sooner. He feared that in some ways he was weak, preferring often to take the line of least resistance rather than to stand up for himself.

He sighed after Constance had left him, airily blowing him a kiss as though she couldn't have cared less about him, but he had been aware of the slight hint of tension in her vivid blue glance. Edwin's sigh came from the heart; he was depressed, aware of his vulnerability when faced with the combined force of the Donnelly and Whitehead families. The evil moment may have been postponed – Edwin had been damned if he was going to produce an engagement ring, like a conjuror fetching a rabbit from a hat, just because it was the girl's coming-of-age – but he knew that eventually his resistance would be broken down. So much was expected of him, not just with regard to the business, but in his personal life as well. The Donnellys were Roman Catholics, as were the Whiteheads, and like married like. They always had done and – according to the precepts of both the families – always would do. Anything else was unthinkable.

Grace still couldn't decide, when they returned to the haberdashery department, between the hundreds of fabrics confronting her. She was mesmerised, bewildered by the dazzling array of colours and, she had to admit, was losing interest. She had a slight headache, just a faint throbbing at the moment between her eyes, the beginnings of a stomach cramp – she knew only too well what that heralded – and a tightness in her chest. She had felt so well all the time they had been in Blackpool, but now she feared that very soon a bout of coughing would seize her. She leaned against the solid mahogany counter for support, willing the aches and pains to go away, just until she could get back to the safety of their lodgings, and allowed herself to be led along by Hetty's enthusiasm.

'Yes, I think I'll have the yellow crêpe de Chine after all,' she said, trying to force a shade of eagerness into her voice. 'Like you say, Hetty, it's bright and cheerful-looking.' Hetty's purchase was already chosen and folded at the side of the counter waiting to be wrapped. She had changed her mind again – Hetty was like that – deciding finally upon a silky voile in a delicate springtime green. Grace stared as though hypnotised as the saleswoman, more friendly now that she was making a sale, deftly measured out the required two yards and cut confidently across the material, her huge scissors snapping like tiger's fangs as they bit into the fabric. The money for their purchases was put into a round metal container and whizzed across the shop on overhead wires to the cash desk.

Grace was feeling dreadful. She hoped their change wouldn't be long in coming, then they could get out of this claustrophic place. A breath of fresh air maybe would bring her round, but she really felt as though she wanted the comfort of a feather bed. Suddenly the tightness in her chest became unbearable and she began to cough. The tears streamed from her eyes and she clung blindly to her sister's arm, feeling that any moment she might fall to the floor in a faint.

'Sit down, my dear.' The saleswoman, full of concern, produced a low chair from behind the counter. 'Oh dear . . . D'you think she's going to be all right?' she asked Hetty. Grace had turned as white as a sheet.

'I think so. She's been like this before. It doesn't usually last long once she's got over her coughing fit.' Hetty put a comforting arm round her sister's shoulders as they shook with the paroxysm of her coughing. 'Come on, Gracie. Lean against me. You'll be better in a minute.'

Grace closed her eyes for a moment, leaning against the solid warmth of her sister. The tightness in her chest had eased a little now as the phlegm had loosened, but she felt light-headed and the pain in her stomach was getting worse. When she opened her eyes again she looked up, not into her sister's green eyes, but into a pair of concerned brown ones. That was the first thing she noticed about him; his eyes, warm and kind, hazel brown with golden flecks, an exact match with the golden brown of his hair.

'Just sit there a moment, my dear . . . Don't move,' said the young man, as Grace made to rise to her feet. This was obviously a personage of some importance in the store, from the cut of his black suit and his air of breeding. The manager, perhaps? He turned to the assistant. 'Miss Walters . . . Some brandy, I think.'

After a few quiet words and nods the saleswoman disappeared, returning a minute or two later with a small bottle and a glass tumbler. The young man poured out a good half-inch or so and pressed the glass into Grace's hands. 'There . . . Drink that. It'll do you good.'

Grace obediently sipped at the fiery golden liquid. It was the first time she had tasted brandy; her mother adhered strictly to the dictums of her Methodist upbringing and expected her daughters to do the same. She grimaced slightly – it was certainly strong – but she could feel its warmth easing her throat and trickling down to alleviate the cramp in her stomach. She smiled gratefully as she handed the glass back to him. 'Thank you. I'm feeling better already.'

The young man's fine features crinkled into a smile. Grace guessed that his normal expression was a serious one, but the smile transformed his face, wrinkling the faint lines round his eyes and accentuating the two deeper clefts which led from his nose to his chin. He was handsome in a gaunt way, and tall, or maybe he appeared taller because he was standing, bending towards her in a concerned way, while she was sitting.

He held out a smooth, well-manicured hand.

'I'm Edwin Donnelly,' he said. 'I noticed you upstairs having your coffee. You both seemed to be enjoying yourselves.' He paused. ' . . . I don't think I've seen you in here before. You don't live locally, I suppose?'

'No,' said Grace.

'Yes,' said Hetty. They looked at each other and laughed.

Edwin Donnelly laughed too. 'Well, which is it? Do you live here . . . or not?'

Hetty did the explaining. She told him that they lived in Burnley but were moving to Blackpool. 'I'm Hetty,' she told him. 'And this is my sister Grace. And you're . . . Mr Donnelly? The owner of the shop?' Hetty's green eyes widened with awe.

'His son,' Edwin replied casually. 'William Donnelly's my father . . . Now, you must let me get you a cab to take you back to your lodgings. No . . . I insist,' he said, tapping the edge of the counter with a long finger as Grace opened her mouth to protest. 'You still look very pale. I wouldn't dream of letting you walk back. Miss Walters . . .'

Again, after a whispered consultation, the assistant was sent to do his bidding, and a few moments later Grace was leaning back against the leather upholstery of the cab, listening to the rhythmic clip-clop of the horse's hooves and feeling as though it was all a dream. The son of the owner, no less, and how kind and considerate he had been. When he had said that he was glad they were coming to live here he looked as though he really meant it. Or had she just imagined that his golden-hazel eyes had glowed with a special warmth as he looked at her? No . . . Hetty had noticed it too.

'Gosh! Did you see the way he looked at you?' her sister remarked. 'Fair sent shivers down me spine, it did. I reckon it was worth being ill to meet that young Mr Donnelly. You poor thing, though,' she said, more seriously. 'You did look bad, Gracie. You had me proper worried. Feeling better now, are you?'

Grace nodded weakly. 'A bit better. It wasn't just the cough though. It was . . . you know.' She pointed to her stomach, looking embarrassed. Grace suffered badly when it was 'that time of the month', but it was not a thing that you could discuss openly, not even with a sister.

Edwin Donnelly couldn't get over the feeling of elation he had experienced when he found out that the young woman would be coming to live in Blackpool. Both of them, of course – Grace and Hetty – but it was Grace to whom he had felt so drawn. Grace . . . He whispered her name softly to himself. A lovely name – it sounded like a benediction – for a very lovely young lady. With her dark-brown eyes, so tranquil and trusting, and that cloud of dark-brown hair, glinting with golden lights, that curled prettily round her neck and framed her delicate face, Edwin had thought her quite beautiful. So gentle and serene and . . . gracious. How well her name suited her. He realised with a start that he didn't even know her surname. He didn't know the first thing about her. He only knew that somewhere, somehow he must see her again.

In the meantime there was . . . Constance. He sighed as he changed into his evening suit, then placed the small gift-wrapped package elegantly tied with gold cord into his pocket. For two pins he would not go at all. He would walk as far as he could in the other direction; walk and walk until he had eased the muddle and depression that was clouding his mind; walk and walk until it was too late to turn up at the party. But the wrath of his parents, and Constance's parents too, if he were to absent himself would be too dreadful to be imagined. Edwin knew that he would go. It was expected of him.

Chapter 4

'What d'you mean, you're going to live in Blackpool?' Walter's pale-grey eyes narrowed resentfully, and Grace could feel a reciprocal anger boiling up inside her as she saw again the glint of possessiveness in their steely depths. Who did Walter Clayton think he was, for goodness' sake? He was beginning to think that he owned her.

'I've told you before. You're my girl, Grace Turnbull.' His voice was peevish, whining almost, quite unlike the booming, authoritative tones that the chapel Bible class were used to hearing when Walter Clayton got on his soapbox. 'I knew that no good would come of it when you went gallivanting off to Blackpool. I had a funny feeling about it all along and I was right, wasn't I, Grace? I knew you'd be up to all sorts of nonsense as soon as you turned your back on me.' He turned to glare at her as they walked along the street that led away from the town, walking stiffly and keeping a distance from her, refusing to take her arm as he usually did.

'You can hardly blame me,' Grace's eyes, normally so serene, also flashed with annoyance. 'I've been trying to tell you, only you won't listen. It's

Mam's idea. She's taking a boarding house and me and our Hetty have to go and help her. You can't expect us to leave her to do all the work on her own. Anyroad, she's me mam, isn't she, and I have to do as she says.'

'You'll do as *I* say, Grace Turnbull, never mind your mother. You're not going to Blackpool . . .' Walter had found his 'sermon' voice again, and his sepulchral tones echoed loudly in the early-evening quietness of the street. 'You're going to stay here and marry me, like you promised.'

'But I didn't promise, Walter,' Grace persisted. 'We're not engaged. You know we're not. I've not got your ring or anything.' She held out her left hand, bare of any finery, red with work and the chap-marks left behind after a hard winter. Clean though; Grace made sure, after she returned home from the mill each day, that the telltale grease marks were scrubbed away from under her nails. 'You've no right to say we're engaged.'

'What money have I got to throw away on rings and suchlike?' Walter's feet, shod in shiny black boots, kicked impatiently at the cobblestones. 'You don't need no ring to show that you're mine. Folks know that you are. We've been keeping company for ages now. There's been an understanding between us and you can't deny it, ring or no ring.'

Grace didn't answer immediately. She sighed, trying to make sense of what Walter was saying. Yes, she supposed there had been an understanding of sorts, but it was one that had never been put into words. Walter had assumed, in his arrogant, egocentric way, that she would marry him.

Because he had kissed her, because they went to the same chapel and because folks had seen them together it was assumed that they were courting. But how did she, Grace, feel about it? She knew that such relationships within their circle usually led to marriage. But she had already begun to feel an annoyance about Walter's proprietorial manner towards her, and when, during the short holiday to Blackpool, she had realised that she wasn't even missing him, she had known then that she wasn't at all sure that she wanted to marry him.

What she had said about her mother wasn't strictly true. Grace knew only too well that should she decide to stay here and marry Walter, instead of going to Blackpool, Martha would willingly give them her blessing. Because he was sober and upright and went to chapel, Martha considered him an ideal partner for her elder daughter. And Grace had liked him well enough too, though she and Hetty had often giggled together about his pompous piety in the pulpit. Grace had liked him – had even thought that she loved him – because she hadn't known anything different. She would have married him because he was ... well, because he just happened to be there.

Now she knew that that wasn't enough. Grace knew that there had always been something missing in their relationship. She had never been able to put her finger on quite what it was; now she knew that Walter had failed to ignite in her that vital spark that was the prelude to falling in love, the spark that she had felt when she had met that young man in Donnelly's store.

There had flashed into her mind several times that day the memory of a pair of golden-hazel eyes looking so earnestly into her own, exuding kindliness and warmth. She knew, of course, that the likes of Edwin Donnelly were not for her. She and those of his ilk were poles apart but, nevertheless, the remembrance of his kindly glance stayed with her. She had thought she had seen more than mere kindliness there, but that could have been just her imagination. But the memory gave rise to the thought deep within her that she had failed to evoke a similar response in Walter. Walter's gaze spoke of possession, of covetousness – of desire, sometimes – but it was never a kindly gaze.

'Anyroad, it isn't as if Blackpool were a million miles away,' said Grace casually. 'You'll be able to come and see us. Stay for the weekend, maybe.' Grace was hoping against hope that he wouldn't come to see her, that once she was out of the way he would forget her and find another girl to occupy his thoughts and his time. But she had to say something – anything – to ease this tension between them. Grace hated to be at variance with anyone, especially Walter, who could turn quite nasty when he had a fit of the sulks.

'Think I'm made of money, do you?' he mumbled crossly. 'I'm making no trips to Blackpool, I can tell you. A wicked, Godforsaken place it is from all accounts.' A sanctimonious note crept into his voice. 'You'd be well advised to steer clear of it.' He stopped suddenly in his tracks and turned abruptly, grasping hold of her arms so tightly that she could feel his strong fingers bruising her flesh. 'Don't go, Grace. Stay here.

We'll get married straight away. Next week if you like. You can't go and leave me.' His tone was a wheedling one that she hadn't heard him use before; he was hurting her and his grip on her arms was frightening her.

'Leave go,' she said, shrugging him away. 'Not here, Walter. You don't know who's watching.' She glanced fearfully round, imagining scores of prying eyes peeping from behind lace curtains. 'Come on. Let's walk up to t'top and we'll talk about it.' She could not stay here and marry him, she was sure about that, and she was equally determined that she would go to Blackpool, but to refuse him outright when he was in a mood like this would be asking for trouble. She would have to play him along for a bit, to prevaricate, although it was against her nature to do so.

'I'll have to go with me mam and Hetty,' she said, reaching for his hand in a friendly, conciliatory gesture. 'Surely you can see that, Walter. There'll be a heck of a lot to do, getting the boarding house ready for visitors. But I'll write to you. An' I'll come back here and see you if you don't want to come to Blackpool. Then p'raps by next spring me mam'll be able to manage . . .'

Perhaps by next spring Walter would have found other fish to fry, but, for the moment, his anger seemed to have been assuaged.

'You are my girl then?' He put his arm round her shoulder, more gently now, but his look still held the same intensity.

'Yes, Walter,' she answered quietly. If you say so, she added to herself.

He pulled her towards him and kissed her

roughly on the cheek. 'An' we'll get wed next spring then . . .?'

'Next spring, Walter.' But next spring was a long time away.

'There was no end of talk, I can tell you, when you and your sister didn't turn up for work on Tuesday morning.' Walter's voice had taken on its preaching quality again. He often referred to Hetty as 'your sister'. Grace knew that he didn't care for the younger girl very much, probably aware that she was laughing at him and encouraging her sister to do the same. 'You know what they always say, that it's favouritism because Josiah Baldwin used to be friendly with your father. If it were anyone else they'd be sacked. An' they're quite right an' all,' he added self-righteously. 'He does show favouritism. It isn't fair to the other workers . . .'

Grace had been well aware of the aggrieved glances of her fellow weavers when she and Hetty had taken their places at the loom early that morning. But they had come round a bit when they had heard the reason for the girls' absence and what the future held for them.

'Blackpool? Well, I never did! You lucky beggars . . .'

'We'd best start savin' up our pennies, girls . . .'

'There'll be a chara' load of us comin' to see you next Wakes week . . .'

'Mek sure there's no bugs in t'beds, mind . . .'

The conversation was conducted to the background of the incessant clatter of the Lancashire looms, surely the noisiest machinery ever invented, not by raising their voices – they would

76

not have been able to make themselves heard if they had tried to do so – but by an exaggerated mouthing of the words and lip-reading, known as mee-mawing. Most of the remarks had been addressed to Hetty. It was she who had done most of the explaining and it was Hetty who was the more popular of the two sisters at the mill. Grace, with her gentle, withdrawn manner, they found difficult to understand. Some of them considered her superior, thinking herself a cut above the rest; others realised that she was quiet, not possessing the same natural ebullience as her sister. But Hetty they could get along with. She was one of the crowd.

Grace understood their resentment at the mill owner's preferential treatment of her and Hetty, although he tried not to make it too obvious. Josiah Baldwin and the girls' father, Fred Turn-bull, had been great friends when the two of them were lads, attending the same school and chapel, and the friendship had continued, although to a lesser degree, into their teens and twenties. For Josiah had come on in the world, whereas Fred had remained just one of the employees in the weaving shed. Josiah had visited Fred, though, the week before he died, and he had promised that he would always see to it that Martha didn't go short and that he would keep an eye on the girls. And all his workers had to admit that Josiah was a decent sort of boss.

They started work at six o'clock in the morning, as all mill workers did, but at least they were allowed reasonable breaks for meals and for visits to the lavatory, nor were the factory gates automatically shut in their faces if they should turn up a couple of minutes late. This was the practice at many mills in the area, latecomers having to stay outside until eight o'clock, thus losing two hours' precious pay. At Baldwin's, excuses for lateness were listened to and weighed in the balance and, more often than not, the latecomer was allowed to enter. And Josiah Baldwin had never allowed the deplorable practice of 'steaming' in his mill, whereby steam was introduced to the weaving sheds to keep the humidity high, a procedure which was good for the cotton, but torture for the workers.

Yes, all told, conditions were bearable if not ideal, but Grace had been unable to quell the feeling of gladness that had seized her when she had heard the rattle of the knocker-up's pole against their window at five o'clock that morning. Gladness, and relief, that this life would not continue for much longer. It was not too bad on a spring morning, like it was now, to surface from sleep in the depths of the flock mattress she shared with Hetty and face the rigours of another day at the mill. At least it was coming light now, but in the middle of winter it could be sheer hell. Stumbling around by the light of a candle in the overcrowded bedroom – the massive brass bedstead took up most of the room – and gritting your teeth before you faced the dreaded morning wash in freezing-cold water. Some mornings the cold was so intense that ice had formed on the surface and had to be broken by a kettle full of boiling water heated on the kitchen range. But, of course, before you could do that the fire had to be lit.

Grace had the sense to know that life in a Blackpool lodging house would not be luxurious. It would be 'bloomin' hard work', as Alice Gregson had warned her mother, but it would be a totally different kind of hard work, and surely the day would not begin quite so early? And – Grace harboured the thought guiltily – it would be an escape from Walter. Maybe they would both change their minds after a period of separation – out of sight, out of mind, as the saying went – or maybe she would realise that, after all, she did want to marry him, as she had only a few moments earlier half promised to do. At all events it would be a breathing space.

Their evening stroll took them away from the cobbled streets that surrounded the mills, up a hill and on to the moors overlooking the town. From the bottom of the valley the sun was rarely visible during the working week, obscured by the thick grey smoke from the belching chimneys. Only on a Sunday, when the mills closed for the day, could the brightness of the sun be enjoyed, and during Wakes week when the factories closed down for a longer period, then the air was sparkling and clean again and the sun could shine uninhibited, in all its splendour. But by then the place was half empty, the mill workers enjoying a well-deserved rest at the seaside, missing the chance to see their home town free from its enveloping grey shroud.

From here, up at 't'top', as they called it, they looked down on a forest of mill chimneys with the wispy remnants of smoke still drifting on the still evening air, and, in the shadow of the mills, the tiny terraced houses, row upon row of them, huddled together as if for warmth and protection in the bleakness of their surroundings. Ahead of them stretched the moors, treeless and some thought comfortless in their stark beauty, but Grace knew that this was one thing that she would miss when she moved to the seaside. She loved the vast openness of the moors, green and brown now, but purple when the heather bloomed, broken by outcrops of rock. Here you could feel at peace, untrammelled by the daily worries of the world down below.

Grace held on to Walter's hand as they walked, silently now, across the springy grass, feeling more content within herself. Problems had a way of working out if left to themselves and, for the moment, this glorious evening was theirs to enjoy. It was grand to see the sun, setting now, tingeing the edges of the clouds with gold and disappearing beyond the horizon in a blaze of crimson and orange. Grace recalled the sunset at Blackpool. There the sun had vanished behind the sea; over there, beyond the hills, beyond the towns that lay between, was the seaside, the place that would soon be her new home. It was at that moment that Grace again thought of Edwin Donnelly. She remembered his golden-brown eyes looking so kindly at her, and his serious face breaking into a smile that transformed his lean features into an ascetic handsomeness. She was excited at the prospect of a new life in Blackpool, but knew that it would be unwise to say too much. Walter was revealing a peevishness in his nature which, deep down, she had suspected, but hadn't perceived in such a marked degree until this evening.

He appeared calmer now, though very quiet, and when they reached a sheltered patch of turf behind a rock he took off his tweed jacket and placed it on the ground for her to sit on. They had often stopped at such a place, sitting quietly hand in hand, talking and occasionally kissing and watching the yellow glow of the gas lamps appearing one by one in the valley below as the lamplighter went on his rounds. The evening was warm, though dusk was falling, and Walter didn't appear to feel at all cold in his shirtsleeves, rolled up to reveal strong sinewy arms covered with a down of fine black hair. Grace noticed that, though his hands were clean, his arms still held traces of oil from the machinery. The thought passed through her mind, unbidden, that Walter wasn't as particular as he might be. She remembered her own father washing himself down thoroughly at the slop-stone in the kitchen after a day at the mill, puffing and blowing and scattering drops of water far and wide. Walter, obviously, was not quite so scrupulous; below the surface Walter was, in fact, not all that he appeared to be. It was strange that she hadn't noticed it until now.

As soon as he sat down he put his arm round her shoulders and pulled her towards him. His first kiss was gentle, though Grace was aware that he wasn't looking at her; his eyes were fixed unseeingly on some point on the horizon. Then he put both arms round her, holding her tightly, uncomfortably, in a vice-like grip, and his mouth came down demandingly on hers. She felt his teeth bruising her lips then, with a faint shock of revulsion, she felt his tongue probing, forcing itself into her mouth. This was a Walter she hadn't known before; usually his kisses had been what she termed 'normal'. She knew about these other sorts of kisses, of course. She had heard some of the girls discussing such things at work when the overseer's back was turned.

Grace knew, in theory, what went on between a man and a woman, what might lead to a baby, although she wasn't sure just how she knew. Such knowledge was partly based on hearsay, and partly on intuition. And she knew where kisses such as this could lead, but, she told herself, when all was said and done Walter had never tried anything on before, and she trusted him sufficiently to know that he would not do so now. Anyway, the thought flashed through her mind, she was quite safe because it was that time of the month.

She was startled therefore when Walter pushed her roughly to the ground. She felt the weight of his body upon hers and it was even more of a shock when she felt his hand on her breast, fondling and squeezing. Then she was aware of his fingers opening the buttons of her blouse, feeling beneath her underwear. She felt her nipple harden at his touch as he rolled it between his thumb and finger, then she was aware of his other hand on her thigh gradually pulling up her skirt.

It was then that she struggled free. She put both her hands flat against his chest and pushed at him. 'No, Walter. Don't . . . We can't . . . You know that we mustn't.' She pushed her skirt back over her knees and with trembling fingers tried to fasten the buttons of her blouse. She felt so embarrassed she hardly dared to look at Walter. He would be angry, she was sure, to be repulsed like that, judging by his possessive behaviour earlier that evening. But enough was enough and she couldn't allow him to take such liberties.

To her surprise he reached across and squeezed her hand. 'Sorry, Gracie,' he said. 'Don't know what came over me. I know I shouldn't have.' He gently stroked her face, her eyebrows, her cheeks, the line of her chin, with the tip of his forefinger. 'I love you, Grace. You know I do . . . an' I want to marry you.' His voice was low and husky. 'I can't bear to think of you all them miles away in Blackpool.'

'It's only just over there, Walter,' Grace replied, trying to give a light-hearted laugh. 'Just over there where the sun's going down.' She pointed to where the sun had almost disappeared now, just the red rim showing above the bank of black cloud, but the sky above shot with glowing streaks of gold and silver and pink in an amethyst background. It was so lovely that Grace could not help but stare for a moment in wonder, in spite of the turmoil inside her. She realised, with a slight start, that Walter had said that he loved her, the first time he had ever told her so in so many words. But she couldn't say the same words to him. Even though she had half promised to marry him she wasn't sure that she loved him. She had thought she did, once. But not now; she wasn't at all sure now.

'An' we'll be wed, Gracie, won't we? Next spring . . .' Walter said, again putting his arm round her. 'Promise you'll marry me. Don't forget about me when you get over yonder.' He waved his hand dismissively in the direction of the setting sun. His eyes looked black in the fast-deepening twilight, his look intense and his voice gruff with emotion.

'Yes . . .' said Grace for the second time that evening. She knew that she was virtually promising to marry him but, just as she couldn't bring herself to say 'I love you, Walter', no more could she utter the definite words, 'I'll marry you, Walter'. She rose to her feet and brushed the specks of dry grass from her skirt. Then she started to walk briskly across the moor, leaving Walter to follow behind her. 'Come on,' she said. 'We'd best be going. It's a fair way down to the town and it's nearly dark already.'

Walter put on his jacket and hurried after her. Almost apologetically he put his arm through hers, but she didn't look at him. They spoke little as they walked down the hill and back into the cobbled streets of the town. But the thoughts of both of them would have been revealing if the other could only have read them.

Walter, too, had been startled to find his hand upon Grace's breast. It was the first time he had ever gone so far with her, but not the first time that he had been tempted. He had been so angry when he had heard that she was leaving the town and her job at the mill – going to live in Blackpool, of all places – and she had angered him again with her reaction when he had told her that they would get married at once. Not only had she refused, she

84

had prevaricated in her response to his further suggestion that they should be married next spring. Although she had said yes, he was aware of her reluctance to commit herself fully. And he was determined that he would have Grace Turnbull at all costs. She would marry him. There was no doubt in his mind about that.

It would have been easy, in the aftermath of his anger, to take her there and then on the moor that evening and, for a moment, he had been tempted to lift her skirts and force himself upon her. Then she would have had to marry him. Even if the encounter had not led to pregnancy, the shame of it would have been too great for a girl such as Grace. Once they had made love, 'gone the whole way', to quote the parlance of the girls at the mill, Grace would have been forced to become his wife. But that wasn't what Walter wanted. Not for Grace. Determined as he was that she would marry him, he was equally determined that she would go to their marriage bed a virgin. He looked forward to being the first with her, to initiating her in nuptial delights. Grace was pure and lovely, all that a woman should be, and Walter knew that he loved her. He knew also, to his secret shame, that he lusted after her. He longed to possess her, to see her glorious brown hair spread across the pillow and to stroke the milky- white loveliness of her naked body. Yes . . . he desired her, but he would wait until they were married. The prize would be all the more valuable for the waiting and there were other ways of alleviating the desires of the flesh. Walter knew that once he had said goodnight to Grace his footsteps would take him, inevitably, to the other end of town.

He obeyed implicitly the ten commandments – well, most of them – making no graven images and keeping holy the Sabbath Day. He wasn't quite sure, though, about the one that said he should honour his parents. His mother, yes; Walter had the greatest admiration for her and loved her deeply, but not so his father. For Ralph Clayton treated his wife as little more than a slave and hardly ever had Walter seen him show her any affection. If this was what marriage became after the first few years, then Walter felt that he would be better to remain single. He wanted Grace – dear God, how he wanted her – but he knew that his marriage, when it occurred, must be perfect, a thing of beauty, not the meaningless sham that his father had made of his own marriage. This was one of the reasons, Walter told himself, why he sought his pleasures now, whilst he was single. And, to come back to the ten commandments, it wasn't really adultery, was it, what he was doing? Adultery, surely, meant taking someone else's wife? Maggie wasn't someone's wife . . . she was a widow.

Maggie Sykes lived at the far end of town, so it wasn't likely that he would be seen on his occasional visits there, neither did she work at the same mill. She was really a friend of his mother's; they had been weavers together as young women and she was far nearer to his mother's age than to Walter's. When she had been left a widow at thirty-five, the young Walter, then aged seventeen, polite and anxious to observe the conventions, had called round the week after the funeral to offer his condolences. Maggie Sykes had been more than ready for consolation. When he had woken several hours later in her commodious feather bed Walter had realised that this had not happened merely by chance. He admitted to himself then why he had come to see her. Even before her husband's untimely death Walter had known that she had her eye on him, and he had not been impervious to the allure of her voluptuous hips and overflowing bosom. The questioning glance in her round blue eyes had met an affirmative response in his own, and this encounter was the inevitable result.

That was five years ago, and Walter had found an unconstrained delight in her embraces ever since. Not that they had any illusions about one another. Maggie knew all about Grace, though she had never met the girl. Walter, too, knew that he was not the only one to receive her favours. Maggie was a generous and full-blooded woman who missed the delights of the marriage bed. He was only surprised that she hadn't married again before now.

But it was Grace that he was thinking of as he crossed the town and made his way up Maggie's cobbled street, similar to the ones that surrounded his own place of work. He was frightened – more frightened than he liked to admit – that Grace would forget him when she was surrounded by the dubious delights of Blackpool. This mustn't happen. Despite his aversion to the place – an unfair one because he had never even been there – and despite what he had said to the contrary, he knew that he would go there and seek her out. He might even go and live there . . . He was a more than competent 'tackler' and felt sure that he would be able to tackle any sort of employment, and lodgings should be easy enough to find in a town with a thousand and one lodging houses. The fact that it was a den of iniquity – or so he had been told – with all its pubs and pleasure palaces, might even be a bonus. There would be sure to be souls waiting to be saved and chapel congregations desirous of hearing the word of the Lord as expounded by Walter Clayton. Yes . . . that was what he would do. He would give Grace a few months to settle in, then he would go and surprise her.

His mind made up, he knocked on Maggie's front door.

Chapter 5

To say that it had been hard work was putting it mildly – it had been exhausting, backbreaking – but they had done it, and the sense of achievement experienced by Martha and her daughters when the first visitors began to arrive for the August Bank Holiday weekend made it all worthwhile. For the moment they forgot their aching limbs and sore feet, and hands roughened by the endless washing and scrubbing, in their delight at welcoming their first paying guests. They were in business now. This was their very own boarding house and these were their very own visitors. Hetty grinned delightedly as she came back from North Station with the first family she had procured. She had maintained that she didn't mind at all 'touting' for custom at the station. Somebody had to do it if they were to make a living, and she would be in good company. Albert was still similarly employed for his mother and together they would make a good team.

Not that all their visitors were to be acquired by touting, not by a long chalk. Quite a few folk from their home town of Burnley had promised to come, and some had even gone so far as to write and book their rooms weeks in advance. It was with quiet pride that Martha looked at the framed notice by her front door, 'Welcome Rest, Martha Turnbull, Burnley'. Folks would certainly be welcome here – she and her girls would make sure of that – and would go back home feeling the benefit of a well-deserved rest.

Martha's heart had sunk right to the bottom of her boots at first, though, when they had moved in and she had realised what a gargantuan task faced them. She had known that the house was run down – Alice had told her that it had been uninhabited for several months – but her first cursory glance had not taken in the extent of the decrepitude. She knew that she had deliberately refused to notice many of the worst features, so determined had she been that they were going to make a fresh start in Blackpool and that this was the house she wanted. And it was still what she wanted, she had told herself decidedly, trying to ignore the cracked paintwork and peeling wallpaper, the mouse droppings in the kitchen, the layers of grease on the skirting boards and cooking range and the musty decaying smell that pervaded the whole house. Martha was not afraid of hard work, neither were the girls, so it was up to all of them to put their shoulders to the wheel and jolly well make a go of it.

The house was already furnished, though Martha had despaired at the sorry state of much of the furniture and the threadbare carpets and torn curtains. Visits to salerooms and second-hand shops had provided them with essential items such as bedsteads and chairs and crockery, and, when all was said and done, those were all that was necessary; a bed to sleep in, a chair to sit on and a plate to eat from. Luxuries would have to wait. Martha badly wanted a sideboard – she had seen just the one she would like in a sale-room on Church Street – and easy chairs for her parlour but, at the moment, non-essential items such as those were out of the question.

'Anyroad, there'll be precious little time for sitting down, not till the end of the season,' she remarked to her daughters, 'and maybe by then we'll have got a bob or two put by and we'll be able to treat ourselves.'

Martha had always been thrifty and had managed to save from their meagre earnings, and it was a good job she had because from the middle of June, when they moved to Blackpool, until the beginning of August, when they opened as a going concern, there had been no money coming into the house. She and the girls had worked their fingers to the bone scrubbing out each room, polishing the paltry sticks of furniture till they shone with at least a semblance of care, and redecorating several of the bedrooms.

'This is where we could do with a chap to help us,' Martha had said, surveying the torn and faded wallpaper which had once sported a design of pink roses. 'Ne'er mind,' she added cheerfully, taking hold of a corner and ripping it from the wall. It came off easily, bringing with it a shower of dust and plaster. 'We haven't got a chap, have we, girls, so we'll have to mek do without.'

Albert though, finding the three women up to their elbows in paste – and, as far as Hetty was concerned, with more on her face and clothes than on the paper – had taken pity on them. With his willing help the job had been finished in less than half the time. And the Singer sewing-machine, too, had more than earned its keep as the women ran up sheets and curtains, and cushion covers to disguise the worn upholstery and sagging springs.

Martha had contemplated it all with a glow of satisfaction one August afternoon, just before the Bank Holiday was due to commence.

'I think it'll do, don't you?' she said anxiously to her now bosom friend Alice Gregson. 'I know it's not Buckingham Palace or owt like that, but we've done our best, the lasses and me . . . I do want folks to be comfortable,' she added uncertainly, casting an apprehensive glance at Alice. 'The bedrooms are so small, aren't they? There's not room to swing a cat round.'

'So who wants to go swinging cats round, I ask you?' Alice chuckled as she gave her friend a comradely nudge. 'I always thought that were a daft saying, but I know what you mean, Martha. There's not much room in the bedrooms, I'll admit – mine are right poky little places an' all – but folks as come to Blackpool for their holidays aren't bothered about big bedrooms. They don't have 'em at home and they don't want 'em here either. They like to feel safe, in the sort of place as they've been used to. A home from home, you might say. And they'll certainly feel that here. You've made it real comfy, Martha. You've worked wonders, you and the lasses.'

'With a bit of help from your Albert,' replied Martha with a laugh. 'He's a grand lad, he is that, and I'm sure I don't know how we'd have managed without him. He did all the donkey-work for us. He's a dab hand at stripping walls and plastering, isn't he? Mind you, I've seen him right and given him a bob or two. He wasn't for taking it, but I made sure he did. He can't be expected to work for nowt.'

'Aye, he told me,' Alice replied. 'Like you say, he's a good lad, but I think there was summat in it for himself as well, don't you?' Alice grinned. 'He doesn't like to be away from your Hetty for long. I've never seen him so smitten with anybody. He's never had a young lady before – I allus thought he were too shy – but he seems to be proper taken with Hetty. I think she likes him too. D'you think so, Martha? I do hope she does. It would be grand if they were to make a go of it.'

Martha nodded slowly. 'I'm sure she likes him. They spend a lot of time together, don't they? But we'll have to see . . . just wait and see. They're both young and we don't want to push them into anything.'

Martha had been delighted to see the growing friendship between Hetty and Albert. If anyone could have a calming influence on the volatile young girl it would be Albert. But Martha knew her younger daughter only too well. Any hint that she was being coerced would be likely to make her turn and run in a completely different direction. Hetty could be a contrary little madam when she'd a mind. No . . . any decisions that Hetty made with regard to Albert, or to anything else for that matter, she would have to come to of her own volition. It was no use anyone trying to tell Hetty what she must or must not do. The lass had a mind of her own. But Martha was glad that her new friend seemed suited with the budding romance and would be pleased to welcome Hetty, eventually, as a daughter-in-law, if things worked out that way. Martha knew that not everyone took so kindly to Hetty. Quite a few of their neighbours and the folks at the chapel had, she knew, considered her younger daughter to be a bit too uppity, especially for a mill girl.

'We'd best just wait and see,' Martha repeated. 'Time will tell, but I agree with you, Alice. It would be real grand if they made a go of it. We'll keep our fingers crossed, eh?'

'Mmm . . . You've made it real comfy,' said Alice Gregson again, glancing approvingly round the smallest bedroom on the top landing. 'That furniture's come up a treat with a bit of spit and polish, and I wouldn't have given you tuppence for it when I first set eyes on it. Towels an' all.' She nodded pointedly at the white towel, a trifle threadbare but dazzlingly clean, which hung on the rail at the side of the marble washstand. 'You're spoiling 'em, giving 'em towels. My lot have to bring their own . . . And that basin and jug's real bonny. I like that butterfly design.' She glanced towards the shelf at the bottom of the washstand, which was empty. 'Where's t'chamber pot. Haven't you got one to match? I reckon that's summat you can't do without.'

Martha shook her head, a little irritably, and when she answered her voice was just the slightest bit disapproving. 'My girls have quite enough to do without emptying chamber pots. Anyroad, I

don't think it's seemly, not for young lasses.'
Martha's lips closed in a prim line. 'There's a WC
on the first landing and a closet in the back yard,
so they'll just have to make do. I think it's more
important to make sure they've got nice hot water
to wash themselves in, and my lasses'll have their
hands full coping with that every morning, never
mind chamber pots.'

Alice laughed good-humouredly. 'Aye, maybe
you're right.' Personally, she thought that Martha
was making a big mistake, was striving to be too
posh for an ordinary Blackpool boarding-house
keeper, too much 'bay windows back and front',
but she didn't say so. She knew when to mind her
own business and, besides, she was already too
fond of her new neighbour to risk offending her.
All she said was, 'It'll be all trial and error at first,
you'll see, but you'll soon get the hang of it all,
Martha. And if you want any help, if there's
anything you're not sure about, you've only got to
ask. That's what friends are for.'

'There's one thing that's worrying me,' said
Martha, frowning slightly, 'and that's how on
earth I'm going to get me sheets dry. All the
washing, of course, but especially the sheets. That
back yard's so poky there's scarcely room to hang
out one sheet, let alone six or eight. How the heck
am I going to manage?'

'Same as the rest of us, I suppose.' Alice
grinned. 'It's not easy, I grant you, but we get by.
You've got a wash house, haven't you?' Martha
nodded. 'And a rack that goes up to t'ceiling?'

'Aye, we've one of them in the wash house, and
another in the back kitchen. It's grand for airing

the clothes and for drying 'em when it's raining, but it's them sheets I'm bothered about.'

'Well, you'll just have to pray for a fine wash day and dry 'em one at a time in the back yard, or else sling 'em up on the clothes rails and hope for the best. Don't worry – you'll manage. Some landladies round here take their sheets down to the sands and spread 'em out on the beach to dry, but I can't be bothered with that. It means sitting there waiting for 'em and I've a sight too much to do, I can tell you.

'You're right though, Martha, about there not being much room in these houses,' Alice went on as they sat by the kitchen range, each with a cup of tea in their lap. 'My brother, Sam Pickering, he's a joiner and builder. More of a woodworker than actual brick-building, of course, and he reckons they built these houses with poky little rooms so that they'd pay their way. There's not much that goes on in Blackpool that he doesn't know about, I'll tell you.' Alice leaned forward, speaking confidingly, her brown eyes aglow with enthusiasm. There was nothing she enjoyed more than a good gossip. 'Apparently, the Borough Surveyor's been known to say that a lodging house should have at least ten bedrooms on a site more suitable for three or four if the house is to earn its keep. And tiny little yards at the back an' all, so that they can get more houses into the space. The builders seem to get all their own way when it comes to planning, according to our Sam. Mind you, he's not complaining. He does pretty well himself, but he's straight, I'll grant him that. He does a fair job for a fair price. If ever you want a good job doing in that line, Martha, you'll know where to go.'

Martha nodded her head silently. There was a lot that still wanted doing to the house but, for the moment, she had reached her limit. The coffers were empty. It was time to start earning some money.

'Well, this'll not buy the baby a new bonnet. I'd best be on my way. I've all them teas to see to yet.' Alice rose to her feet and placed her cup and saucer on the scrubbed pine table in the middle of the kitchen. 'Thanks for the tea, Martha, and for the guided tour.' She gave a little laugh. 'I think it's real grand, and I wish you all the luck in the world.'

Martha knew that her friend meant every word that she said. Like most Northerners, Alice didn't believe in dissembling or in handing out over-effusive compliments. If she wished Martha luck then that was what she thought her friend truly deserved. When Alice had gone Martha went into the hallway. She arranged a bunch of marigolds – all that the minuscule front garden could boast in the way of flowers – in a blue earthenware jug and placed them on the hall table, then stood back to admire the effect. She felt a thrill of pride surge through her as she looked round the entrance hall of her boarding house. This was the first thing that the visitors would see when they came through the door. She wanted it to be pleasing, to give a good impression which, hopefully, would stay with them all week.

The hallway, when they had taken over the house, had been hideous beyond belief. Dark and dank and gloomy, with peeling brown wallpaper and a carpet so worn that you were continually tripping up over the loose threads, and, taking up most of the room, a huge cast-iron hall stand that towered towards the ceiling like a menacing giant. Martha had been ruthless. The cast-iron monstrosity had been replaced by a small mahogany umbrella stand and a half-moon table. There was ample room in the cupboard under the stairs for the family's outdoor garments, and the visitors could hang theirs on the peg provided on the back of each bedroom door. Martha knew that hers was quite a revolutionary idea; most hallways in the boarding houses she had entered were dingy, nondescript places dominated by the hall stand, but she wanted to create an impression of space and light. For this reason, the dark-brown wallpaper had been replaced by a delicate design of blue and yellow flowers. Martha thought that the front door was quite beautiful, with stained-glass panels in glowing shades of red, yellow and blue and, in the centre, a rustic scene of a swan on a reed-fringed river. She often stood and stared at it in wonder, not really believing that she could be living in a house with a stained-glass door. That, too, had been dull and dingy but now, thanks to Martha's loving care and a good application of elbow grease, it shone with all of its original rainbow brightness. The hall carpet, to be sure, was only a strip of blue Axminster with polished linoleum on either side and didn't match the carpeting on the stairs. But, for the moment, it would have to suffice. Martha was well pleased with the efforts of herself and her daughters. Now all that remained was to wait for the visitors to come. She sent a silent prayer heavenwards that they would do so.

Her prayers did not go unanswered. They were full for the Bank Holiday weekend, several of the visitors staying for the whole week, and there was a steady number throughout August and September to keep them ticking over. If it had been hard work before they opened, it was even harder now, but the rewards were great, to be seen in the happy faces of the holiday-makers and in the empty plates and contented sighs which followed Martha's gargantuan meals.

It was Martha's proud boast that none of her visitors would ever be able to say that they were hungry. The fare was not fancy, but wholesome and filling, typical Lancashire dishes such as she had always cooked to feed her family. Meat and potato pie; broth with dumplings, so thick that the spoon would stand up in it; suet beef puddings and, on Sundays, a roast which could be eaten cold on Monday and made into shepherd's pie on Tuesday. To follow the first course there were bread and butter puddings, spotted dick with custard, and rice pudding made in a huge enamel bowl, flavoured with nutmeg and with a rich crispy brown top. And, for high tea, Martha's speciality cakes which had earned her a well-deserved reputation on Burnley market; Eccles cakes, maids of honour, parkin and gingerbread, and oven-bottom cake spread thickly with butter.

Martha and the girls found it easier to share the work between them, all of them 'mucking in' when they saw a job that needed doing rather than each of them having their allotted tasks. Martha was delighted at how they all worked together as a team. She knew that, in the past, several of her neighbours had thought that she spoiled her daughters. She had never overburdened them with housework, considering that they were doing quite enough by working long hours at the mill, so she was more than gratified to see them tackling the household chores like a couple of Trojans.

Martha did insist, however, that they should work to a routine – a different job for each day – just as she had always done back home in Burnley and which was the way all good Lancashire housewives conducted their affairs. Monday, of course, was washing day. She was up at the crack of dawn every morning, but even earlier on a Monday to light the fire beneath the copper in the wash house. And, despite her misgivings, the sheets were nearly always dry, ready to be ironed on Tuesday – ironing day. Wednesday was baking day, when Martha's cake tins would be replenished with all her specialities. Bread, however, she did somewhat unwillingly buy ready-made – there was a limit to the number of jobs you could cram into a day – enormous two-pound loaves with a crusty top from the baker's shop at the end of the street. Thursday was the inside cleaning day when the furniture was polished, the linoleum was mopped, carpets were swept with a stiff brush, and all rugs and coconut matting were taken outside and hung on the washing line for a good beating. And, also on Thursday, the kitchen range was black-leaded. Grace took a particular pleasure in this task, delighting in the sight of the gleaming black surface after the application of the black lead mixture with a damp cloth, followed by burnishing with a soft brush. The steel fender and fire-irons and the handles on the oven were also kept bright and shining by rubbing with emery paper. A clean, sparkling cooking range was a source of pride and joy to any housewife worth her salt, and Martha was pleased to see that Grace was following in her mother's footsteps.

On Friday it was the turn of the outside. The back yard was swilled down, the downstairs windows were cleaned and the front step and sills were scrubbed and edged in white with a donkey stone. And on Saturday the beds were stripped and made up again with clean sheets for another lot of incoming visitors. It was a never-ending circle of work, week in and week out, with precious little time for relaxation.

Hetty, however, on behalf of Grace and herself, pleaded for an evening off towards the end of August.

'Please, please, Mam,' she begged. 'Let us go. We'll make up for it. We'll work twice as hard next day. Albert's managed to get tickets for us, and that's taken some doing I can tell you. He says you can't imagine the crowds that are flocking there. Just think, actually being able to see Blondin. I can hardly believe it. That's . . . if you can manage without us, Mam. Please say you can.'

Martha laughed at Hetty's anxious face. Surely the girl didn't think that she would be so hard-hearted as to refuse to let them go out and enjoy themselves for once. They had asked for few

101

favours and had worked well and willingly all summer without many jaunts or pleasure outings to relieve the routine. Hetty and Albert occasionally went out on a Saturday evening, dancing or to a music-hall show or, more often, just to walk on the promenade. Grace had been out even less – Martha often worried about the girl's solitude since they moved to Blackpool – and she was glad that Albert had now included her, along with Hetty, in the proposed outing. He was a kind-hearted lad.

And who hadn't heard of Blondin, the world-famous tightrope-walker, who had thrilled thousands with his daring escapades high up above the Niagara Falls in America? Like Hetty said, it was unbelievable that such a personage should be appearing in Blackpool, and of course the girls must go.

'Aye. I reckon I can manage without the pair of you for one evening,' said Martha, 'even though it is the middle of the week. You deserve a treat.' She was nearly knocked off her feet by Hetty's enthusiastic hug. 'Get on with yer bother!' she remonstrated. 'There's no need for all that carry-on. Just make sure you enjoy yourselves, that's all.'

The atmosphere was tense in the high-roofed building at the Royal Palace Gardens at Raikes Hall, which housed the huge panoramic picture of Niagara Falls. It had been painted by a French artist and the proprietors of the Raikes Hall Pleasure Gardens had hoped that it would be a money-spinner. They were disappointed in this; it had proved to be a flop, but now, with the visit of

102

Blondin, 'Niagara' was coming into its own. It was a reasonably good representation of the Falls and this would give some idea of the incredibility of Blondin's original feat.

The audience cheered when Blondin appeared, a slight, wiry figure who looked every year of his age of seventy-two. They watched spellbound, hardly daring to breathe, let alone to applaud as he went through his awe-inspiring performance. Firstly, dressed in knightly armour, he crossed the rope to the accompaniment of a lively march tune. Then, clad only in tights, revealing the sparse muscles of his sinewy body, he stood on his head aided by his balancing pole. The audience gasped in admiration as one daring exploit followed another. He crossed the tightrope blindfolded, he sat, then stood on a chair and – the highlight of the performance – he carried his son, himself a middle-aged man, on his back across the rope.

The audience oohed and aahed and conversed in whispers.

'Eeh . . . Have you ever seen the likes of that?'

'I'm too scared to look.' A middle-aged woman buried her face in her hands. 'Tell me when it's over, Bert.'

'An' this is nowt compared with what he did in America. Just fancy, crossing Niagara Falls . . .'

'Aye. He's a grand old fellow. He is an' all . . .'

The applause, when he had finished his routine, was thunderous. Grace and Hetty wandered out into the fresh air at the end of the performance feeling bemused, scarcely believing it all, so extraordinary had it been.

'You enjoyed it then?' Albert grinned at them both. 'Sprightly old chap, weren't he?'

'I was scared,' Grace confessed. 'It made me feel sick to watch at times, I was so frightened he was going to fall.'

'It was real marvellous,' said Hetty, putting her arm through Albert's and pulling him closer to her. 'Blackpool's so exciting. Ooh . . . I am glad we came to live here.'

Grace linked Albert's other arm and smiled fondly at her sister. The lad never made her feel that she was an outsider when the three of them were together, but Grace was glad to see the growing friendship between Hetty and Albert. The Royal Palace Gardens were a magical place at night as the moon shone on the ornamental lake and coloured fairy lights twinkled in the trees. Grace wished at times that she had someone special with whom to share moments such as this. But it wasn't of Walter that she was thinking. He hadn't been to Blackpool to see her since they moved here over two months ago, although he had promised that he would do so, and she hadn't had a letter from him for nearly three weeks. The memory of Walter was gradually fading from Grace's mind, but there were times, like now, when she felt very lonely . . .

It was with a sense of relief that the three women saw the last of their guests depart at the end of September. They collapsed thankfully into the shabby easy chairs – all that they could afford at present – in the still largely unfurnished parlour.

Hetty leaned back, closed her eyes and sighed in

an exaggerated manner. 'Phew! Thank goodness we've seen the back of that lot till next year. Working at old Baldwin's mill was nowt compared with this. You're a slave-driver, Mam, that's what you are. I hope you appreciate what your little girls are doing for you, that's all I can say. What do you say, Gracie?'

Grace knew from the tone of her sister's voice that the girl was only teasing and her mother's amused smile told her that Martha knew it too. But she went along with the good-natured banter. 'I should jolly well hope so! Now think on, Mam, we'll be wanting our breakfast in bed tomorrow morning. We've earned it, haven't we, Hetty?'

'Go on with yer bother! Breakfast in bed, indeed! I've never heard anything like it. You'd best be up at six o'clock sharp, same as you always are. I'll have you know we've three more bedrooms to decorate yet . . .' Martha paused, her eyes twinkling roguishly. 'No . . . seeing as how it's Sunday tomorrow I'll let you have a lie-in till seven, then we'll make a start with the bedrooms on Monday, how's that?'

'Ugh!' Both girls groaned. 'For pity's sake, Mam, have a heart,' said Hetty laughing.

Grace looked at her mother a trifle apprehensively. 'You don't really mean it, do you?' she asked, with just a tinge of doubt in her voice.

'Of course I don't!' Martha laughed. 'I was getting me own back on you for having me on like that. We deserve a rest, for a day or two at any rate. But you know, joking apart, girls, we've only had a short season. About eight weeks, that's all it's been. Some of the landladies have been on the

105

go since Easter. Just imagine how they must be feeling. An' it'll be the same for us next year. D'you reckon we'll be able to cope with it all?' She looked at Grace, then at Hetty. 'I'm not joking now. Do you really think we'll be able to manage? Do you think we were right to come?'

'Of course we were, Mam.' Grace smiled reassuringly at her mother. 'Don't take no notice of what me and our Hetty say. I'll admit we're tired, we're bound to be, but we've enjoyed it all, haven't we, Hetty?'

'We've loved every minute,' replied Hetty, grimacing. She spread out her hands in front of her and looked at them ruminatively. 'Never mind the blisters on me hands and the corns on me feet and the pains in me back . . . We've loved every minute!'

'Shut up, Hetty, and be serious for a change, can't you?' said Grace, laughing, nevertheless, at her sister. 'We'd do it all again, wouldn't we?'

Hetty grinned. ''Course we would. Honest, Mam.'

Grace looked anxiously at her mother. 'You're not having second thoughts, are you? Everyone who's stayed here has said they've enjoyed it, and ever so many of them want to come again. And it's bound to get easier when we get more used to it all. Next year we'll be dab hands at it, you'll see.'

'No, Grace. I'm not really having second thoughts. I'm sure we made the right decision. It's just that . . .' Martha paused, not quite sure how to word the thoughts that were in her mind. The lasses had worked so hard and they must be feeling exhausted, as she herself was. Admittedly they were many years younger and – as far as Hetty was concerned – a good deal stronger, but how was she to tell them that very soon both of them would have to find a job for the winter? They had made some money, but not enough, not by a long chalk. Martha sighed. 'The idea of most Blackpool boarding-house keepers, or lodging-house keepers or whatever they like to call themselves,' she went on, 'is to make enough in the summer to see themselves through the winter. And they usually do it. Some of them have other incomes as well. Take Alice Gregson, for instance. She's got her husband bringing in money all year round, and Albert as well, but we haven't. And, like I was saying, it's been a short season . . .' Martha's voice petered out and she didn't look at her daughters. She stared down at the pattern of faded brown leaves in the carpet, absent-mindedly folding her stiff white apron into little pleats. 'Happen we'll make a bit more next year . . .'

'You're trying to say we've not made enough money, is that it?' said Grace, speaking calmly, although she didn't feel calm. She could tell that her mother was very worried about something. Poor Mam. After all her plans and dreams. Grace did hope that she wasn't feeling too disillusioned after starting off with such high hopes. 'We can't expect to make our fortune in a few weeks,' Grace went on. 'It stands to reason, doesn't it? We've got to work it up into a real going concern. But we'll do it, don't worry, Mam. We'll do better next year.'

'It's . . . not next year as I'm worried about,' said Martha Turnball flatly. 'It's now. This winter.'

'Stop beating about the bush, Mam,' said Hetty kindly, grinning at her mother. 'I know what you're trying to tell us.' She turned to her sister. 'What Mam's trying to say is that we've got to find jobs for the winter. You and me, Grace. That's it, isn't it?' Hetty looked enquiringly at her mother, then grinned even more widely. 'If that's all that's bothering you, you can stop worrying right now, because we know that we've got to find jobs. We were talking about it the other day, weren't we, Grace?' She turned to her sister, who nodded in agreement. 'Good heavens, Mam. We know we can't be swanning around here all winter doing nowt, like as if we're gentry or summat. Surely you didn't think that was what we wanted to do?'

'No . . . of course not.' Martha's eyes softened as she looked at her daughters. They were such good lasses, both of them. She might have known they would understand. 'It's just that we've been so busy that we haven't had a chance to talk about what we'd do when there's no visitors here. And there's so much that wants doing to the house yet. Them three bedrooms need decorating, like I was saying. And . . . oh, I've all sorts of plans, girls.' Martha leaned forward, her brown eyes gleaming like a cheerful little sparrow. 'I'd like a proper bathroom with one of them baths enclosed in wood, an' a lavatory basin. I don't like you two lasses having to make do with the old zinc bathtub. It's all right for me. It's what I've been used to all me life, but I think you should have something a bit better now. A lot of the houses round here have proper bathrooms.' She smiled ruefully. 'But you can't do much without a bit o' brass, can you? Mind you, I'm not complaining. We've had a reasonable sort of season, I suppose, to say it's our first, but there's not much money left now, and that's a fact.'

'All the more reason for us to go out to work then,' said Hetty cheerfully. 'Don't you worry. We'll have our posh bathroom before you can say Jack Robinson.'

'And your nice parlour, Mam. Don't forget that,' said Grace gently. 'I know you've set your heart on a swanky parlour same as Alice Gregson's got, and you'll have it too. You deserve it.' Grace looked round at the faded wallpaper and carpet and the threadbare curtains. This was one room that they hadn't got round to renovating. It wasn't used by the visitors and therefore Martha had said that it must be low on their list of priorities. Their first concern, always, must be to provide bright, welcoming rooms for the visitors. So far there hadn't been much time for sitting around, but Grace was determined that her mother should have a pleasant room, her own private domain, in which to take her ease. 'Hetty and I'll see that you don't go short of anything. This little room'll be like Buckingham Palace before we've finished, you'll see. And we'll see about finding jobs right away.'

'I've already found one. There – what do you think about that?' Hetty laughed delightedly at her mother's and sister's surprised faces.

'What d'you mean, our Hetty?'

'You never said anything. And how can you have found a job? You haven't had time . . .'

'Well, I have, so there! At Laycock's Confectioner's, near Talbot Square. Proper posh it is an' all. They serve afternoon teas and luncheons and I'm going to be a waitress. There was a notice in the window saying they wanted one, so I called in the other day when I was in town. Well . . .' Hetty paused, her head on one side and her lips pursed speculatively. 'It's not definite yet. I've to go and see the manageress on Monday. But I'll get it. I know I will.' Hetty was ever the optimist.

'Well, I never did! You've taken the wind out of my sails good and proper,' remarked Martha. 'And d'you think you'll like it, being a waitress?'

''Course I will. I just fancy meself in a frilly cap and apron. And I enjoyed waiting on the visitors. You know I did.'

Hetty had been in her element tripping backwards and forwards between the dining room and kitchen with her laden tray, stopping to pass a cheery comment with the holiday-makers. The older visitors had found that the sprightly young lass brightened up their day, and the young men immediately felt ten feet tall when she singled them out to speak to them. None of them, though, had been able to persuade her to walk out with them. There was never the time and, of course, there was Albert to consider. Grace had preferred to stay in the background, assisting her mother with the cooking and washing-up.

'And what about you, Grace?' her mother asked now. 'Have you any idea what you would like to do? Not that I'm rushing you, don't think that,' Martha added hastily. 'You need a rest for a little while before you start again. I don't suppose you

110

fancy being a waitress like Hetty?'

'Not really.' Grace shook her head. 'But I'll find something . . .'

Martha knew that jobs were not at all that easy to come by in seaside towns. There was very little industry such as there was to be found in the cotton towns of east Lancashire, and the work was largely seasonal, concerned as it was with the boarding-house trade. Martha would have preferred her elder daughter to stay at home and have a really good rest. The few months they had already spent in Blackpool had, she felt, worked wonders for Grace. The bracing sea air and the clean, comparatively smoke-free atmosphere had practically rid Grace of her persistent cough, and the colour had returned to her pallid cheeks. The girl had worked hard and uncomplainingly all summer and although the work was not to be compared with the wearisome grind in the unhealthy surroundings of the mill it was, nevertheless, strenuous and fatiguing. Martha would have liked her at home, to enjoy her calm, restful company, but there was very little money left and it was really necessary for both girls to find employment.

Grace was looking well, her mother thought, much better than she had for years, but she was very quiet and withdrawn. Martha wondered if she was fretting about Walter. She was bound to be missing him and it was strange that the lad hadn't been over to see her. Grace said that his mother had been ill; he had told her so in his letters. But Martha didn't consider that that was much of an excuse. He surely could have made an effort and come to see the lass. Martha spent much of her time worrying about Grace – Hetty gave her no such qualms – and she didn't like to think that she was having to pester the girl to find work.

'I'll find something,' Grace said again, nodding reassuringly at her mother. 'Blackpool's a big place. There's sure to be room for little me . . .'

Grace already knew what it was she wanted to do. She had set her heart on it, but the trouble was she didn't have her sister's confidence, the boldness that Hetty possessed to forge ahead and make things happen the way that she wanted them to. But this time Grace knew that she would have to stir herself. Jobs didn't just fall into your lap by sitting and waiting for them. It would be up to her to make the first move.

Chapter 6

Grace moved through the turnstile and on to the wooden planks of North Pier, jutting out over the grey-green depths of the Irish Sea. There was a fresh breeze today. Summer was already at its end and autumn was advancing rapidly, witnessed in the lengthening shadows, the slight mistiness in the early mornings and evenings and the definite nip in the air. Grace pulled her velour hat more firmly on to her head and turned up the collar of her black woollen coat. She had dispensed with her shawl since coming to Blackpool, and her clogs too. She was no longer a mill girl and such garments seemed to be obsolete in the seaside town. She had few regrets about moving here and frequently stopped to think what a wonderful idea it had been of her mother's that they should make the break.

She had been somewhat disturbed by Martha's admission that they hadn't made as much money as she had hoped, but it was early days yet. Grace felt sure that they would be able to make Welcome Rest one of the best little boarding houses in North Shore. For the moment, though, the season was over and Blackpool, denuded of its visitors, seemed like a ghost town. But Grace found that she welcomed the change. She preferred the resort when it was quieter, without all the hectic bustle and activity of the summer months. Many residents felt the same. You would often hear the heartfelt utterance, 'Thank goodness we've seen the back of that lot for another year!' And yet such a statement was only partly true. Blackpool residents depended upon the holiday-makers for their livelihood and for the very existence of their town. Without the visitors there would be no Blackpool and so, come the spring, they would be welcomed once more with open arms.

Grace stopped halfway down the pier and leaned against the iron railings, looking back towards the town. From here you had a wonderful panoramic view of the resort. Along the length of the promenade stretched the hotels and boarding houses. It never ceased to amaze Grace how many there were, not only on the front but in the streets behind the promenade as well. Hundred upon hundred of them; you could scarcely believe that they could all be filled, and yet, in the summer months when Blackpool more than doubled its population, the familiar sign would be displayed in countless windows, 'No Vacancies'. A sign which brought a feeling of smug contentment to any boarding-house keeper who was able to show it.

Opposite the pier, in Talbot Square, the building of the new town hall had commenced and to the north, Grace could see the ongoing work of widening the promenade. Beyond Claremont Park, a select area of North Shore which maintained its exclusiveness by the existence of toll

114

gates at either end, were the cliffs, stretching towards Cleveleys and the fishing port of Fleetwood a few miles further along the coast. To the right was South Pier and in the distance, scarcely visible, Victoria Pier, for it was now Blackpool's proud boast that it had three of those structures projecting into the sea. And, a little way along the promenade from the entrance to North Pier, the resort's supreme source of pride, the Tower. One's eyes were continually drawn to it and although it had been completed only the previous year it was already beginning to be the symbol of the resort, featuring prominently on advertisements and picture postcards.

Grace stood there for a few moments, savouring the view. There was little evidence of scenic charm in the rows of hotels and the stretches of concrete promenade – Blackpool's appeal was in the vastness of its sea and sand and sky. The tide was just coming in and the wide expanse of sand was deserted save for a few lone figures here and there. Grace recalled how, in the height of the season, you could hardly pick your way between the crowds that thronged the beach, especially in the area between the North and South Piers. It was strange how they all seemed to congregate in the same spot while the areas to the north and south remained practically deserted. The herd instinct, Grace supposed; the fear, maybe, of being alone.

Grace was glad of the solitude now. Since coming to Blackpool she had found herself, when she had a spare half hour or so – which wasn't all that often during the season – wandering on to North

Pier, breathing the salt-laden air deep into her lungs and feeling the freshness of the breeze upon her face. She knew that she was better in health already since moving here and she had no desire, ever, to return to the smoky atmosphere of the mill town. She had to admit, though, that she missed the surrounding countryside, the green hills and the wide tracts of moorland. There was very little greenery to be seen in Blackpool. The landscape here was largely grey and gold; grey sky, grey sea and mile upon mile of golden sand. In the summer the predominant hues were blue and gold, when the sun shone from an azure sky, miraculously changing the greyness of the sea to a deep turquoise shimmering with golden flecks of light. The sky was grey today, here and there interspersed with patches of silver where there was a break in the mass of cloud. Grace thought that, in all its moods, the sky here on the Fylde coast was one of its greatest beauties. There was a translucent quality to the light which you didn't see when you moved inland, away from the coast. Grace felt very small and alone as she gazed up at the vast grey expanse of sky above her, then down at the limitless grey sea lapping round the supports of the pier. Alone, but not lonely. She was already beginning to think of this place as her home, and this sky and sand and sea were all a part of it that she was fast beginning to love just as much as if she had been born here.

No, she didn't ever want to go back. And yet, if Walter were to ask her again to marry him, to return with him to Burnley, what was she to do? What was she to say? During the last few months she had been so busy that all thoughts of him had remained securely shut away at the back of her mind, save on the rare occasions when she had had a letter from him. He hadn't written as often as she had anticipated and for that she was glad. Maybe the old proverb 'out of sight, out of mind' was proving to be true, as she had hoped it might. Could Walter, perhaps, have found someone else? Grace wondered. No, she knew that she was deluding herself, that it was only wishful thinking. Walter's mother had been ill. That was the reason he hadn't been to Blackpool to see her. Florence Clayton had had a bad attack of bronchitis which had turned out to be more serious than they had at first anticipated. Walter, to give him his due, was a caring son and as he was the only one of the family still living at home he hadn't wanted to go away, even for a weekend, and leave his mother.

That was what he had told Grace and she was sure it was true, but she couldn't help hoping against hope that there might be another reason and that the longer Walter stayed away, the less inclined he would be to come at all. With every day that passed she felt safer, more able to persuade herself that their friendship was on the wane. Surely now, after so many months had elapsed, he would not hold her to a promise that she had made so unwillingly?

She recalled that early June evening on the moors – looking back on it now it seemed like years and years ago – when Walter had been so demanding both of her agreement to his proposal, and of her body. It was ages since she had allowed

117

herself to dwell upon that incident. Now, as the memory returned with clarity, she wondered what would have been the outcome if Walter had insisted, if she had been forced to succumb to his advances. He was a strong young man, not very tall but thickset, not unlike a bull terrier in build, with sturdy arms and legs. She would have been powerless against such resolute strength if Walter had been determined. Grace wondered why he had stopped. His high principles, she supposed, his religious convictions, for Walter was, undoubtedly, a very moral young man. And Grace was quite sure that he would go to his marriage bed every bit as inexperienced as she herself was.

Whatever was the matter with her? she asked herself. Why on earth was she letting her mind dwell on marriage? She had no intention of marrying him. And yet, thinking now of Walter's embraces, Grace realised with a faint start of surprise how she had begun to enjoy them, until he had startled her by trying to go further than she had wished. She thought about Hetty; Hetty and Albert and the good times they had together. Her sister would, Grace felt sure, have had more than her fair share of kisses that summer, now that Albert was, at last, coming out of his shell. And as Grace thought about them she suddenly felt lonely and, uncharacteristically, a tiny bit jealous. As she gazed into the steely-grey depths of the ocean beneath her Grace felt that she would have welcomed even Walter's kisses, knowing that she had someone who belonged to her, as Hetty did.

Don't be such a silly goose, she chided herself.

You don't really love Walter. You've hardly given him a thought these last few months. You're just feeling sorry for yourself, that's all, seeing your sister with her young man. You should be ashamed of yourself, Grace Turnbull. Now, snap out of it, for goodness' sake . . .

Grace sighed. She had come to the pier, to be on her own, to be quiet for a while to think things out; now she found that her thoughts were running away with her, leaving her more confused than she had been to start with. It was all because of Walter, drat him! For Grace knew that however much she might try to stifle all thoughts of him, to convince herself that she didn't care about him, had never cared about him, he was, nevertheless, always there at the back of her mind, an insidious image tormenting her. Grace knew that, in some uncanny way, he had a hold over her. She also knew, deep down, that she was afraid of him . . .

She shivered now, partly with apprehension as the proverbial goose walked over her grave and partly because the breeze was becoming even more chilly, and turned to walk back along the pier towards the promenade. In the block behind the Tower, the roof just visible, was Donnelly's Draper's, and it was upon this department store that Grace now centred her thoughts. She forced herself to think of the plan she had in mind rather than allowing her thoughts to wander off at a tangent in a confused muddle about Walter. Grace had told her mother that she hadn't given much thought to what she would do in the winter, but she was sure that something would turn up. But Grace, this once, hadn't been strictly honest

119

with Martha. The girl knew only too well what it was that she would like to do, what she had, in fact, set her heart on. She wanted to be a shop assistant in Donnelly's department store.

Each time she entered the shop Grace was captivated afresh by the sights and the sounds and the smells, by the whole luxuriant atmosphere of Donnelly's. And yet, though the aura of the shop was one of prosperity, it was still within the range of the ordinary middle-class and even working-class customers. The sales assistants were friendly and approachable; they had a reputation for being so and it was a well-known fact throughout the town that the owner, Mr William Donnelly, chose his staff with those qualities in mind. He was a fair-minded man and a good boss, from all accounts, and though he might be well heeled now, he had never, so it was said, forgotten his humble beginnings, how his father had started the business as a small lock-up shop at a time when the family had had scarcely two ha'pennies to rub together. William Donnelly had got where he was by sheer hard graft and was all the more admired in the town because of it. Not that you could say the same for his wife, so the rumours went. Now, there was a stuck-up piece, if ever there was one . . .

Grace had heard the gossip. Alice Gregson, good neighbour and friend though she was, liked nothing better than a good old gossip and there didn't seem to be much about the Donnelly family that she didn't know. Her brother, Samuel Pickering the joiner, was a friend of William Donnelly's and Alice loved to pass on the titbits of information that she gleaned. It was from Alice that Grace had learned of the expansion of the store, how they would soon be looking for new assistants in several departments.

If Grace had any ulterior motive in wishing to work at Donnelly's she wouldn't have admitted it to anyone, not even herself. She had, for a few weeks afterwards, harboured tender thoughts about the young man with the golden-brown hair and golden-brown eyes who had cared for her so solicitously on the day she had been taken ill, and whose smile had seemed to radiate a warmth which was for her and her alone. But she hadn't spoken to him since and by now he must, she felt sure, have forgotten all about her. The fact that she wanted to work in his father's store was purely coincidental, Grace told herself, and she firmly believed it. Although she hadn't spoken to Edwin Donnelly since that day when he had shown her such kindness, to say that she hadn't set eyes on him wouldn't be true. She had done so, twice, but on neither occasion had he noticed her and Grace wasn't the sort of girl to go out of her way to make her presence known. Not like Hetty. Grace had been glad that on the two occasions when she had caught a glimpse of Edwin Donnelly across the floor of the shop she had been on her own. Had her high-spirited sister been with her she was sure that Hetty would have insisted on going over and reintroducing themselves, which might have led only to embarrassment all round. He might not wish to be reminded of her existence, though on the other hand, from what she remembered of that young man Grace couldn't

121

help feeling – hoping – that he might not be averse to the idea of renewing their acquaintance.

These thoughts were merely half formed, fluttering incoherently like butterflies at the back of Grace's brain. When, later that evening, she went across the road to approach Alice Gregson about the matter, Edwin Donnelly had no part whatsoever in her plans. Or so she convinced herself . . .

'Grace . . . How nice to see you. Is Hetty not with you?' Alice Gregson seemed surprised to see that Grace was on her own and her question was an automatic reaction. 'No, of course she isn't! Whatever am I thinking about?' Alice chuckled as she hastily corrected herself. 'I must be going daft in me old age. Your Hetty went out not half an hour ago with our Albert. Well, come on in, lass. Don't stand there on the doorstep. Henry's just taken himself off down the road for his usual,' Alice chuckled again, 'an' I was just going to make meself a nice cup of tea and take the weight off me feet. I didn't realise how tired I was till I stopped. You don't, do you, love, when you're on yer feet all day? You haven't time to stop and think how tired you are. I tell you what, Grace, I was bloomin' glad to see the back of them visitors, till next year at any road. It's nice to see 'em come, but it's even nicer to see 'em go. I expect your ma feels the same, doesn't she, or she will do when she's been at it as long as I have.'

Grace followed the older woman along the hallway to the parlour at the back of the house, Alice talking all the while, hardly stopping to take a breath. She sat in the cretonne-covered easy chair while Alice busied herself in the adjoining back kitchen making a pot of tea, and looked round appreciatively at the comfortable clutter of objects that surrounded her. She idly fingered the fringe of the heavy chenille cloth which covered the table next to her while her eyes took in the conglomeration of photographs, pottery ornaments, brassware, embroidered cushion covers and antimacassars, all lovingly displayed and well tended. The room represented a lifetime of loving and sharing, of family affection and companionship. It was an expression of Alice's own warm personality. Grace smiled and nodded to herself as she gazed around. How her own mother would love to be able to express her individuality in such a way, by having a nice parlour in which to entertain her friends. Grace was determined that Martha should be able to do so soon.

'Now . . .' Alice beamed as she sat herself down in the opposite chair with a rose-patterned china cup in her lap. 'What is it as I can do for you, young lady? I don't think it's just a social call, is it?'

'No.' Grace shook her head. 'It isn't really.' She picked up the tiny silver spoon from the saucer, admiring its lustre and the delicate scrollwork on the handle. Alice had some beautiful things, to be sure, but then she wasn't a widow, was she? There was a lot of money coming into this house, with Henry and Albert both working, and Alice had been a lodging-house keeper for many years. Grace carefully replaced the spoon and then looked uncertainly at Alice, not quite sure, now she had finally plucked up courage to come, how to broach the subject. 'I wanted to ask you a favour, Mrs Gregson, but I don't know that I should really. It might not be fair . . .'

'Well, whatever it is I'll do me best; I can't say more than that. And knowing you, Grace, I'm sure it can't be anything too dreadful. Come on, lass.' Alice leaned forward and laid her hand companionably upon Grace's. 'I'm all ears.'

And Grace found it easy, once she had started, to talk to Alice about her desire to work at Donnelly's Draper's. ' . . . I've heard you say that Mr William Donnelly's a friend of your brother's, and I wondered if he, Mr Pickering I mean, might put in a good word for me. But perhaps it isn't fair. Perhaps I should just apply on my own, same as the other girls will have to do.'

'You don't get far in this old world without a bit of push, and that's for sure.' Alice laughed knowingly. 'Our Samuel wouldn't have got where he is if he'd been backward in coming forward. Sometimes you've got to make use of the folks you know if they can help you along a bit. There's nowt wrong in that. Of course I'll help you, lass. I'll be only too pleased to. I'll tell our Samuel as you'd like to work there, then he'll be able to fix up for you to see Mr William, I'm sure. I'm glad you had the sense to ask me. I know they'll be putting an advertisement in the paper before long to say they'll be needing staff, but there's no harm in being one jump ahead, is there? I tell you what, Grace, it's a lovely shop, isn't it? I wouldn't mind a chance of working there meself if I were a few years younger.'

'Yes,' Grace replied enthusiastically. 'Hetty and I have always liked shopping there. The first time we came to Blackpool – you remember, when we stayed here that weekend? – we bought some material there, and we had a cup of coffee in that posh restaurant. We thought we were proper toffs, I can tell you. You should have seen our Hetty crooking her little finger and talking all la-di-da.' Grace laughed at the memory. 'But they make you feel real welcome at Donnelly's, as though you're important, if you know what I mean, even though you're right ordinary, like me and our Hetty are.'

'Yes, he's well known for that is Mr William.' Alice nodded in agreement. 'He certainly doesn't put on the style and he's all the more admired because of it. Our Samuel won't hear a wrong word about him. Of course, I wouldn't really say that they're all that friendly. They go to the Conservative Club together, but that's about all. They don't see each other much apart from that. William Donnelly's a Roman Catholic, you know. All the family are, of course, and that makes all the difference. Keep themselves to themselves, Catholics do.' Alice Gregson sniffed. 'They're well known for it.'

'Catholic? I didn't know he was a Catholic,' said Grace, wondering why her voice sounded so loud in her own ears, and so shocked.

'Yes, of course he is.' Alice looked at her in surprise. 'Have I never mentioned it before? I thought you knew. But don't let that worry you, lass. William Donnelly won't be biased, if that's what you're thinking. I know as they tend to stick together, but he's fair-minded and it'll not make any difference that you're not one of them. I doubt if he'll even ask you which church you go to. It's got nothing to do with serving behind a counter, has it?' She looked at Grace curiously. 'You don't need to look so alarmed, love. I've told you, it won't make a scrap of difference..' She paused, then nodded meaningfully. 'Oh aye, I reckon you're thinking about what your mam's reaction'll be, aren't you? I know she tends to be a bit intolerant of 'em. I'm pretty much the same meself to be quite honest. Methodists are,' she added cheerfully. 'We like to think as we're the only ones as know the right road to heaven. Come to think of it, there's not much to choose between us and t'Catholics for being bigoted.'

'No, I'm not really worried about what Mam'll say,' replied Grace. 'She doesn't care for them much I know, but I wasn't thinking about that.' She stopped, then went on speaking rapidly. 'I was thinking about young Mr Donnelly . . . you know, Mr Edwin.' Grace felt a telltale blush tingeing her cheeks at the mention of his name and began to wish that she hadn't blurted it out like that. But she'd started now and Alice was regarding her questioningly, so she had to go on. 'William Donnelly's son, Mr Edwin. I . . . that is . . . Hetty and I met him once when we were in the shop. I was feeling poorly and he was ever so kind. He fetched me a drop of brandy and got us a cab to bring us home an' all . . . I'd no idea he was a Catholic,' she finished lamely.

Alice hooted with laughter. 'So what's to say that Catholics can't do kind deeds same as other folk? There's no reason why the lad shouldn't be kind, is there, just because he worships at a different church? I reckon we're all heading the same way in the end, you know.'

'No . . . of course there's no reason. That's not what I meant,' said Grace falteringly. 'It's just that . . . I didn't know, that's all.' Her voice petered out.

'Well, you know now, and you can take it from me it'll not make an 'aporth of difference to Mr William what the dickens you are.' Alice leaned forward and looked at Grace confidingly. 'If you ask me there's a great deal too much made of all this religious carry-on, but don't tell yer ma I said so.' She closed one eye in a knowing wink. 'I know she goes to church a good deal more than I do and probably she's a good deal more religious than what I am. But you know, Grace, I don't think God intends us to worry our heads too much about it all. I know that He made us an' He loves us an' He wants us to love Him, and that's about all there is to it. Leastways that's what I think. So that's that. Sermon ended.' Alice laughed a little self-consciously as though all this talk of religion embarrassed her. Certainly Grace had not heard her voice her feelings about it before.

God, however, often came into Martha Turnbull's conversation which was, Grace supposed, only to be expected. Her mother had been a devout Wesleyan Methodist ever since she had been baptised into the faith as a tiny infant. There, at the chapel, she had met and married her husband, Fred, and Grace and Hetty had been baptised there too, as well as the two little boys who had died in infancy. There was scarcely a Sunday throughout her life that Martha hadn't been to worship, twice a day sometimes. But even Martha had found since coming to Blackpool, as Alice Gregson had warned her she might, that Sunday worship wasn't always possible. The demands of a boarding house full of visitors had had to come first.

All the same, Martha was what one would call a religious woman. Her large black Bible was well thumbed, and Grace was quite sure that her mother knelt at her bedside every night to say her prayers, not gabbling them from within the warmth of the blankets as she, Grace, tended to do, or quite often not even saying them at all. It was surprising, therefore, that someone so religious and so tolerant in other respects – for Martha had never been dictatorial with Grace and Hetty – should be so intolerant of Roman Catholics who were, after all, fellow Christians. Yes, Martha may very well, when she found out, have something to say about Grace going to work for one of 'them Papists', which was how she sometimes referred to them. But Grace was determined that she wasn't going to let her mother's attitude make any difference, if all worked according to plan and Mr Donnelly agreed to give her a job.

It was strange that she hadn't known before about the family's religious convictions, Grace mused, as she walked back across the road to her home, that she had only just discovered, after being in the town for several months, that Edwin Donnelly was a Catholic. But what difference did it make what he was? she asked herself. What did it matter, even, if he was a Hindu or a Hottentot?

He was nothing to her – was he? – so why should she be so disturbed to find out that he worshipped at a different church . . .?

Grace knew that she was, to a large extent, ignorant of the principles and doctrine of the Roman Catholic religion. Such vague ideas as she did hold were inclined to be influenced by her mother's prejudice and by an experience that she, Grace, had had when she was a child. She found herself thinking now about Veronica, the little girl who had sat next to her in school; they must have been about eight years old at the time. Veronica's grandmother was seriously ill, dying, the little girl had told Grace somewhat lugubriously, her blue eyes opening wide as she confided in her friend.

'An' I'm going to light a candle for her on me way home from school. I've got me penny here, in me pocket.' Veronica had patted her stiffly starched white apron which the girls had always worn in school over their dark dresses. 'Will you come with me, Gracie? It's dark inside an' I'm a bit scared to go in on me own, but I've got to do it. I don't want Gran to die.'

Grace had been unsure. She had seen the church that Veronica attended. St Bartholomew's was a forbidding-looking, soot-ingrained building on the main road and she knew instinctively, though she couldn't have known the reason, that her mother would not have wanted her to go inside the church. To Martha Turnbull, Grace thought now in retrospect, to set foot inside such a place was to take the first step along the road to hell. But at the time Grace had only sensed that

129

her mother would disapprove, and such misgivings as she had were soon overcome because she felt so sorry for poor Veronica whose gran was dying. And so she had gone along with her friend.

The interior of the church, as Veronica had said, was every bit as dingy and gloomy as the exterior, and there was a sweet, sickly, flowery smell, as though something was burning. To the small child it was like being in a huge mysterious cavern. Who could tell what weird creatures might lurk in those deep, dark pools of shadow? At the far end of the church, above the altar, was a lifesize effigy of Christ on the cross. Grace knew that it was Jesus, but this Jesus bore no resemblance to the kind and gentle Saviour of Grace's imaginings, pictures of whom she had seen in her mother's illustrated Bible and who featured in the two stained-glass windows in their own chapel. In one of them he was depicted with a crowd of children surrounding him, and he was gazing at them fondly as he laid his hand on the head of the nearest child. 'Suffer the little children to come unto me', read the text in fancy black writing beneath the picture. And in the other he was the good shepherd leading a flock of sheep and lambs. A familiar, friendly Jesus, completely at variance with the tormented, suffering being who hung from the cross in St Bartholomew's Church. His face was twisted in the throes of agony as the crown of thorns, pressed upon his brow, caused thin rivulets of blood to trickle down his face. And from his side there gushed a stream of bright red blood. Grace had stared in fascinated horror and the figure on the cross had recurred in her dreams the next few nights. But she hadn't dared to tell her mother the cause of her nightmares.

By contrast the Salem chapel that the Turnbull family attended had seemed, in Grace's mind, to be a bright and pleasant place. The wooden cross which stood on the communion table was plain and unadorned and the clear glass in the windows let in what little sunlight there was in the smoky mill town. Salem boasted only two stained-glass windows, donated in memory of loved ones who had passed on. In St Bartholomew's Church there was an abundance of stained glass in rich deep colours through which only the faintest light was diffused.

And yet it was not all darkness inside that church. Grace recalled areas of quite startling beauty. In one secluded corner there was a statue of a lady – Grace knew without being told that it was Mary, the mother of Jesus – with the loveliest face she had ever seen, and a gown as blue as the bowl of sweet-smelling blue hyacinths that had been placed in front of her. Grace felt herself smiling happily as she looked at that lady, and the lady appeared to be smiling back at her.

And in another corner there were the candles, dozens of them, some large and some small, some unlit and others flickering like tiny glow-worms in the darkness. That was why Veronica had come, and the child placed her penny in a wooden box and took a taper and lit a small candle. Grace thought that the yellow flame must be a prayer going up to heaven. She watched as her friend knelt down and closed her eyes, then Grace did the same. She knelt on the hard wooden floor and said silently inside her head, 'Please, God, help Veronica's gran to get well again.'

The next day the old lady had taken a turn for the better and by the following week she was fully recovered. Grace felt awe-struck as she recalled the incident, just as she had all those years ago. But she still knew next to nothing about the Catholics, only that they prayed to Mary, the mother of Jesus, they said their prayers in Latin and they confessed their sins to the priest.

Chapter 7

'I'm forever blowing bubbles,
Pretty bubbles in the air . . .'

Many heads turned to look curiously at the girl whose sweet, penetrating voice could be heard clearly above the murmur of conversation, chink of glasses and occasional bursts of laughter in Tilda's Tavern. And, of course, above the voices of the other singers. When they realised which young lady it was, amongst the crowds that thronged round the tables, that was singing out so melodiously and so unreservedly their eyes lingered on her with good-humoured interest. They saw a bright-eyed, ginger-haired lass of about eighteen or so, whose apple-green blouse and green feather curling jauntily round the brim of her hat exactly matched the colour of her eyes. They smiled tolerantly in her direction, but a few couldn't help but notice the discomfiture of the young man who was sitting next to her.

'Hetty . . . Hetty, for goodness' sake, pipe down a bit!' The frowning young man anxiously tapped her arm as the chorus of voices, Hetty's

133

predominating, reached the end of the verse. 'People are staring at you.'

'Then let them! Why should I care?' The girl looked at him exasperatedly, her eyes flashing with annoyance. 'For heaven's sake, Albert, don't be such a fusspot. You're like an old woman sometimes, mithering away at me. What's the matter with you lately? You're getting to be a proper spoilsport, forever telling me I shouldn't do this an' I shouldn't do that.'

'I don't like to see you making an exhibition of yourself, that's all, love.' Albert's grey eyes clouded with anxiety as he reached across and covered Hetty's small hand with his own. 'Aw, come on, Hetty. Don't be mad with me. I promised yer mam as I'd take care of you, an' I don't like to see folks staring at you . . . Especially other fellows,' he added, gazing moodily into the amber depths of the liquid in the tankard in front of him.

'Oh, so that's what it is! Jealous, are you?' Hetty's green eyes narrowed speculatively and there was a hint of mockery in her voice. 'You don't like to see other fellows fancying me.' She tossed her head, the ginger curls dancing on her brow, looking away from Albert towards the next table. A group of lads were obviously enjoying the squabble that was going on near to them, though they may not have been able to hear all the words. They grinned at her and one of them winked, and she raised her eyebrows and looked at them disdainfully before turning back to Albert. 'Then happen you should take a bit more notice of me yourself. Take me for granted you do, Albert Gregson.'

'Aw, Hetty. That's not fair! You know it's not fair.' Albert sounded hurt and there was a glint in his eyes now that hinted of anger rather than anxiety. 'I've been taking notice of you ever since we met. I've never even looked at another lass. You know I wouldn't, Hetty. I've never wanted any other girl but you. And we've gone about together all over the place, specially since all the visitors went back. There's hardly a night I don't see you. You've no right to say I take you for granted. It's not true and you know it!'

Hetty looked at his flushed countenance and the grim set of his mouth and realised that she had gone too far. She had never seen Albert so cross before and she knew that it was all her fault. She didn't know what had got into her, but she had wanted to rile him, to make him react, and now she was sorry. She felt a rush of tenderness as she looked at him and she knew that she couldn't carry on with this game any longer. Because she knew that that was what it was. She had been playing a game with him, trying to provoke his anger. And it had worked, only too well. It was Hetty's turn now to be anxious about the raised voice – Albert's voice this time – because, once again, people were turning to look interestedly in their direction.

'I'm sorry, Albert,' she said in a small voice, sounding contrite and feeling so as well, for she hadn't really intended to hurt him. 'It wasn't true, what I said. I didn't mean it. You're ever so good to me. You are, really. I was just mad with you for trying to make me shut up . . . I like singing,' she added wistfully, smiling at him.

135

'I know you do, love.' Albert grinned at her, his good humour almost restored. 'I know you like to enjoy yourself when you come here. It's getting to be one of your favourite places, isn't it?' Hetty nodded eagerly in agreement. 'But . . . I don't know . . . I'm daft, I suppose. I get all hot under the collar.' Albert ran his finger now round the inside of the starched white collar which protruded above his tweed jacket, causing him to hold his head in a stiff, unnatural position. 'I get all embarrassed like, when I think that folks are looking at us.'

'You're too bothered about what people'll think.' Hetty took a sip of her ginger beer, then she shrugged. 'I suppose I don't really care very much. Anyroad, that's why folks come here, isn't it, to have a jolly good sing?'

Tilda's Tavern was fast becoming one of the most popular places in Blackpool for a get-together and a drink and a singsong. All highly respectable, of course. If it hadn't been Hetty wouldn't have dreamed of setting foot inside the place and Albert certainly wouldn't have taken her. For in spite of her protestations about not caring what people would think, Hetty did, in fact, care about what some people thought. Her mother, for instance. Hetty would never knowingly do anything that would upset her mother.

Martha Turnbull had raised her eyebrows in horror in the first place when Hetty said that she and Albert were going to one of those singing-rooms. Many public houses set aside a room for singing and dancing and for the occasional music hall type of act, but it was Martha's opinion that such places were not to be frequented by well-brought-up girls.

'It's all right, Mrs Turnbull, honestly it is,' Albert had assured her. 'You know I wouldn't take your Hetty anywhere that wasn't decent and respectable. You ask my Uncle Sam. He'll tell you as how Joss Jenkinson won't stand for any nonsense. Any rowdiness or owt like that and old Joss'll have 'em out on t'street before you can say Jack Robinson, I'll tell you.'

Joshua Jenkinson – or Joss as he was commonly called – was the proprietor of the Victoria Inn on the promenade, midway between the North and South Piers. The name of the inn wasn't highly original, but many establishments were named after the Queen, that venerable old lady now only two years away from her Diamond Jubilee. Tilda's Tavern was a big room at the back, largely under the control of Joshua's wife, Matilda, after whom it was named. The couple had earned a well-deserved reputation in the town for running an establishment which was not only popular with both visitors and residents, but was also eminently respectable. Martha Turnbull, truly, need have no fears for her daughter in such a place. Both Joss and Matilda, though they wanted their patrons to enjoy themselves, were agreed that there was to be no undue rowdiness or vulgarity such as they knew was rife in some entertainment rooms. Any sign of such untoward behaviour and, as Albert had assured Martha, the culprits were immediately asked to leave.

Tilda's Tavern served drinks, of course, such as were served in the main bar of the Victoria Inn, but tea and coffee, also, were available for those of their customers – and there were quite a few – whose religious scruples or their adherence to the Temperance Movement would not allow them to touch alcoholic beverages. Indeed, it was surprising how many men, and women too, of such persuasion visited Tilda's Tavern when they found out, by hearsay and later by first-hand experience, that it was not the den of iniquity that they had supposed all such places to be. Matilda Jenkinson provided a real good supper, hotpots and cow-heel pies that couldn't be bettered anywhere along the Fylde coast, and now that the visitors had all gone and the town was quieter the atmosphere in Tilda's Tavern was more intimate and friendly. Joss and Matilda welcomed a clientele of regulars, including several lodging-house keepers rejoicing in their end-of-season freedom, who met there, maybe only once, or perhaps two or three times a week to partake of a drink and a bite to eat, and to enjoy a good old singsong and an entertaining turn on the stage at the end of the room.

Hetty had been here a few times with Albert and enjoyed it all immensely. The noise and laughter and good-humoured merriment – the people here were all so jolly and friendly – and, most of all, the singing. Hetty had always loved singing. Quite a few years ago, when she was still at school, they had had a piano in their little house in Burnley. There had hardly been space for it, squeezed up in a corner against the sideboard so that there was scarcely room to open the door. She had never questioned how it had come to be there in the first place. Pianos were a luxury in households such as theirs. Mam, she recalled, had been able to strum a few tunes, mainly from the Moody and Sankey hymn book and from a few old tattered song sheets that they had acquired. And Grace had even begun to have piano lessons from an old lady who lived down the street. It had been a struggle for Mam to scrape together the pennies that were needed, but she had been determined that her daughters were going to have the chance to do something apart from working in the mill. It would be Hetty's turn to learn in a year or two but, in the meantime, Hetty could sing.

She remembered Grace picking out the tune, 'Won't You Buy My Pretty Flowers?' and herself and Mam singing together of the 'little fragile girl' who sold flowers to the passers-by. And Mam's favourite hymns, 'The old Rugged Cross' and 'Blessed Assurance'. They had had some happy times round the old piano, Dad joining in as well sometimes in his deep bass voice. Then Dad had died, so very suddenly, and there had been no money for music lessons. Hardly any money at all for a while, and the piano had had to be sold.

So Hetty's love of singing had been hidden deep within her, only given free rein once a week in Sunday worship at the chapel. Folk sitting near to her in the congregation would turn and smile at her, feeling moved by the melodious clarity of her voice and by the enthusiasm and sincerity she brought to the words of the familiar hymns. Nobody there had nudged her to keep quiet or had seemed in the slightest bit embarrassed by her exuberance. They were well accustomed to singing out with gusto and this was the part of the service that Hetty loved more than any other. The only part, if she were truthful, as she often found the prayers and the sermon tedious.

So she was delighted to find another place, besides the chapel, where she could sing to her heart's content. It was a very different kind of singing, to be sure, at Tilda's Tavern, but one that Hetty enjoyed just as much. More, in fact. She sometimes felt annoyed with Albert for telling her to be quiet. Why should she? You came here to enjoy yourself and that was what she was jolly well going to do and be hanged to Albert Gregson. She had been finding him more than a bit tiresome lately, as though he were bent on spoiling her fun. Forever reminding her that her mother wouldn't like her to drink anything stronger than ginger beer and insisting, old fusspot that he was, that she must get back home long before midnight, as though she were likely to lose her glass slipper and find her glad rags changed into tatters. Her mother would worry, he nagged at her, if she were to be late home. As if she would do anything to upset Mam; he should know her better than that.

But, she supposed, he was only being protective, trying to make sure that she came to no harm. She was well aware, from hints that Alice had dropped, that this was the first time that Albert had walked out with a young lady, and she knew that he was trying specially hard, therefore, to create a good impression with her own mother. And he was succeeding too. Martha thought the sun shone out of him. Hetty linked arms with him now, pulling him closer towards her and resting her cheek against the rough tweed of his jacket. Dear old Albert. She really was very fond of him. If only he were a bit more . . . exciting.

It was time for the performance now and the audience showed its appreciation of the juggler and of the tap-dancing brothers – two baby-faced young men with sleek black hair and beaming smiles – by cheering and applauding loudly. Then everyone listened sympathetically to the plaintive plea of the pretty girl in the frilly pink crinoline who insisted, in somewhat shrill tones, that she didn't want to leave her little wooden hut 'for you-oo'. And they joined in vociferously with the chorus of her next song when she coyly promised, 'I'll be your sweetheart, if you will be mine'.

Hetty turned to Albert, her eyes alight with happiness. 'Good, isn't she? I think she looks right pretty with the lights shining on her hair, and she sings real nice an' all.'

'Not half as good as you,' Albert whispered back. 'She's not as pretty and she can't sing as well neither. She's not a patch on you, Hetty.'

'Oh, fancy that!' Hetty widened her eyes as she wagged her head at Albert. 'I thought you didn't like me singing. Changed yer mind now, have you?'

'I never said I didn't like it, Hetty. I only said it was a bit, well, loud. But I reckon you could do as well as her if you got up there, better in fact.'

Hetty nodded, thinking how nice it would be, indeed, if it were her standing up there in a pretty frock, singing away for all the world to hear. Then she giggled to herself at the thought of Albert's

141

reaction if she were to do so. He would be more embarrassed than ever, poor lad.

'Oh, I do like to be beside the seaside . . .' Hetty heard the pianist and violinist strumming out the opening bars, then everyone joined in the chorus of what was Blackpool's unofficial signature tune, made famous by the one and only Marie Lloyd.

'There are lots of girls besides
I should like to be beside,
Beside the seaside, beside the sea.'

Hetty trilled away joyously, clinging on to Albert's arm. He looked at her lovingly as he joined in with the singing, a little less exuberantly than Hetty, but thinking to himself that the words of the song were not really true. For him there was only one girl that he wanted to be beside, and there she was, right next to him. Sometimes Albert Gregson could scarcely believe his luck.

'My goodness, you're in fine voice tonight, young lady!'

Hetty looked round to see the proprietor, Joss Jenkinson, standing next to them. She smiled back at him; she knew him by sight, of course, but had never spoken to him.

'Well, hello there, Albert,' he went on, as he noticed Hetty's companion. 'Is this your young lady then? I hadn't realised she was with you, in fact I hadn't recognised you till you turned round. I came over to see who it was trilling out like that. Talk about a bird in a gilded cage . . .' Joss laughed out loud, his fat cheeks wobbling with merriment. 'You've got a grand voice and no mistake, young lady. You have that.' He beamed at them both, then sat down on a vacant stool. 'I think I'll take the weight off me feet for a while, if you don't mind me joining you?'

Joss Jenkinson's corpulent figure, ruddy cheeks and blue-tinged bulbous nose might suggest that he was perhaps overpartial himself to the beverages he sold, but this was not the case. He enjoyed his food, and his wife's pies and puddings had proved irresistible to many a stronger-willed man, so what chance did Joss have when he lived with the woman? he would laughingly ask. But he was an abstemious man when it came to the drink, partaking only of the occasional pint to be sociable, and his florid complexion was due solely to a circulatory problem.

Hetty had been surprised when, after speaking to her, he addressed Albert by name, not realising that he knew the young man personally. Albert knew Joss, of course, as Joss was a friend of his Uncle Sam – there seemed to be very few people in Blackpool, Hetty thought, who didn't claim friendship with Samuel Pickering! – but she hadn't realised that Joss knew Albert so well.

Albert was obviously well pleased to have been singled out by such an important personage. 'Of course we don't mind you joining us, do we, Hetty?' he said. His cheeks were flushed with pride as he turned to Hetty and then to Joss. 'Mr Jenkinson, allow me to introduce Hetty. Hetty Turnbull, my . . . er, my young lady.' His cheeks turned even pinker. 'Hetty, this is Mr Jenkinson.'

Hetty bit her lip to suppress a giggle at the sound of Albert talking as though he had a plum in his mouth. Allow me to introduce, indeed! Who did he think he was? The Prince of Wales or sumat? But she smiled charmingly as Joss Jenkinson took her outstretched hand and bent towards her in a courtly manner. 'Pleased to meet you, Mr Jenkinson,' she said.

'And I'm very pleased to meet *you*, I'm sure,' Joss replied. 'My word, you're a dark horse, young Albert. I didn't know you'd got a lady friend like this tucked up your sleeve.'

Albert just nodded, at a loss for words.

'Like I was saying, my dear,' Joss continued, leaning towards Hetty, 'I came over to see who was singing so beautifully. I could hear you from the other side of the room . . .'

A tiny frown creased Albert's brow and he gave a brief nod of censure in Hetty's direction, as if to say, I told you so. But Joss appeared not to notice.

' . . . And I thought to myself, that's a fine voice if ever I've heard one. I wonder whoever that can be? Well, you could have knocked me down with a feather when I discovered it was Albert's young lady. Where've you been hiding her, Albert?'

'I don't know that I have, Mr Jenkinson. We've been here a few times lately, Hetty and me, but you've been busy, or else you've been in the other bar. I suppose you just didn't notice us.'

'Aye, I reckon that's right. I usually leave this place to Matilda – I just pop in a couple of times a night to make sure everything's as it should be – but she's indisposed this evening. A cold coming on, I think, so I thought I'd better give a hand in here. Quite a crowd in tonight.' Joss looked round appreciatively. 'But I've noticed you now, all right,' he added, turning back to the young couple. He leaned closer to them, but it was Hetty he was addressing. 'Would you be interested in a job here, Miss Turnbull?' He spoke in a low voice so that the folks around wouldn't hear, but nobody appeared to be taking much notice.

'I . . . er, I don't know . . .' Hetty sounded surprised.

'I don't mean behind the bar or owt like that,' Joss went on hurriedly. 'I meant as one of the performers. How would you like to come and sing for us?'

'Oh . . . oh . . .' Hetty could hardly speak for astonishment. 'To sing for you? D'you really mean it?' Then she grinned at him. 'You're having me on, aren't you?'

'Indeed I'm not having you on. Joss Jenkinson isn't in the habit of saying things he doesn't mean. Leads to trouble, that does. No . . . I really mean it. Of course, I don't know what else you might do for a living, but this would be just in the evenings. Two or three times a week, maybe?'

'I'm . . . I'm a waitress, at Laycock's Confectioner's, near Talbot Square.' Hetty found herself stumbling over her words. 'But that's only during the day, and during the summer I was helping me mam in the boarding house. I'm free every evening though and . . . oh . . . it would be . . . real grand.' She shook her head bemusedly and her voice was just a whisper. 'I can't believe it . . .' She turned to Albert. 'Did you hear what Mr Jenkinson was saying, Albert? He wants me to sing for him, here at Tilda's Tavern. Isn't it wonderful?'

Albert didn't answer. Hetty knew that he had heard all right, but he was just sitting there as though he had been struck dumb, with a stupefied expression on his face.

'D'you know, Mr Jenkinson,' Hetty went on, casting a mischievous glance in Albert's direction, 'Albert was only saying, when that young lady was singing, that he could just see me up there on the stage. Weren't you, Albert?' She grinned impishly at him. 'Of course, I don't suppose he ever thought you would ask me, but it started me thinking how nice it would be, and then the next minute it's all coming true. Oh . . . it's just like a dream.'

Hetty knew perfectly well that Albert's comment about her singing on the stage had been just a casual remark, and that he would, in fact, run a mile at the mere thought of it. She knew, too, that she was being a tiny bit naughty in provoking him in this way. But she couldn't help it. He was such a stuffy old thing at times and a mischievous streak that she found hard to control made her want to rile him. She wondered what he was going to say about it all, when he finally stopped goggling at her and Joss and found his tongue.

'Oh, do close your mouth, Albert,' she whispered, a trifle waspishly. 'You look just like a goldfish.' Then, more loudly for the benefit of Joss and because she really thought it was about time Albert made an observation of some sort, 'What do you think about it, Albert? Don't you feel proud of me?'

'I . . . er . . . well, I don't rightly know, Hetty.' Albert ran his finger round the inside of his collar

146

again as beads of perspiration began to form on his forehead. 'It's all a bit of a surprise, like. An' I can't help wondering what your mother'll have to say about it when she finds out. You know how she didn't like you coming here in the first place. She doesn't care for places like this.'

Joss looked at Albert, then at Hetty, his face serious. 'Why? A bit strait-laced, is she, your mother? Well, I can assure you there would be nothing . . .'

'Yes.' Albert nodded vehemently. 'She's a strict Methodist is Mrs Turnbull. She doesn't hold with . . .'

'No!' shouted Hetty. 'Me mam's all right. Honestly, she is. Anyway, I know how to get round her.'

Joss looked at them both and laughed. 'There seems to be some disagreement about what Mother will say. But she need have no fear that you will come to any harm, my dear, not while you're working for me.' He smiled at Hetty and patted her hand. 'It's a very decent sort of place we run here, Albert.' Joss turned towards the young man, raising his eyebrows in an admonitory glance. 'We'll have no truck with hooligans or troublemakers, I can tell you, so you don't need to worry about your young lady. I'll take good care of her.'

'Oh, I know that, Mr Jenkinson.' Albert was covered with confusion. 'I wasn't trying to suggest . . .'

'All right, lad,' said Joss, more kindly. 'I know what you meant, and all the more credit to you for being concerned about young Hetty here. I may

147

call you Hetty, I hope, my dear?' Hetty smiled in agreement. 'Well then, if it'll make you both feel any better I'll call round and see Mrs Turnbull. Set her mind at rest. How's that?'

Hetty nodded. 'Yes, thank you. That'ud be grand.'

Albert nodded too, but less confidently.

'Well, Hetty my dear . . .' Joss placed a glass of ginger beer, that he had ordered from a passing waitress, in front of her and a tankard of foaming ale in front of Albert. 'There you are. Have a drink on me, and the very best of health and happiness to the pair of you.' He raised his own half-pint glass. 'Cheers . . . Now then, we seem to be jumping the gun a bit, don't we? It's my wife, Matilda, that's in charge of this place, so we'll have to wait and see what she says about it all.'

He looked at Hetty's crestfallen face and smiled. 'Not to worry, though. She usually leaves it to me to fix up the acts and I'm sure you'll go down a treat with the folks here. A lot of 'em know you already. I could see 'em all listening to you singing. Now, how would it be if you come round tomorrow evening, early like – say seven o'clock – before we open, for a bit of an audition? Show us what you can do.'

'Yes, I'd love to,' Hetty replied. 'I finish work at six tomorrow, so that would be fine.'

'Good. Now, what sort of songs do you like to sing? Can you give me some idea, then I can have a word with the pianist. He's got a good repertoire, has our Bill. I'm sure he'll be able to fix you up.'

'Oh . . . all kinds of things.' An assortment of melodies had been running through Hetty's mind

148

while Joss had been speaking. Songs of Marie Lloyd; choruses from the Methodist Hymnal – but those would hardly be suitable; the airs of Gilbert and Sullivan . . . Those were her favourite. 'Gilbert and Sullivan,' she said, suddenly feeling very excited at the thought of it all. 'That's what I'd like to sing. Songs from *The Pirates of Penzance* and *HMS Pinafore* and all that. That's what I'd really like.'

The heyday of the Gilbert and Sullivan operas at the Savoy Theatre in London had ended with the 1880s, but the melodies were still extremely popular. They were sung by choirs and amateur operatic societies, played by brass bands in the parks, thumped out on pianos in many an entertainment place and whistled by errand boys and workmen as they went about their labours. Hetty had seen *The Pirates of Penzance* put on by an amateur group in Burnley and heard the songs many times at chapel concerts. She had even, on one such occasion, sung them herself and she still had at home several well-used copies purchased from song booths, dating from the time when they had had their piano.

'Gilbert and Sullivan,' Joss repeated thoughtfully. 'Yes . . . that's not a bad idea. Not a bad idea at all. It's a good while since we had anybody on the stage singing their numbers . . . Take a pair of sparkling eyes, la-la laa, la-laa, la-laa . . .' he sang quietly, wagging his head in time to the rhythm. 'I forget the words, but that was always one of my favourites. And I know that Bill's got a good stock of their music. You can read music, can you, my dear?'

'Mmm . . . Sort of.' Hetty pursed her lips. 'At least I can tell whether the notes are going up or down and I can pick out a tune with one finger. My sister was learning me, that was ages ago though, before we had to sell the piano. But once I've heard a tune I don't forget it.'

'Champion! I'm sure you'll do real well.' Joss stood up, smoothing down the white apron that covered his rotund figure. 'I'd best be moving myself now, or else the barmaids'll be accusing me of shirking my duties. See you tomorrow then, Hetty?'

Hetty nodded happily, finding it hard to believe that this was all really happening.

'Cheerio then, Albert. Be seeing you. And mind you take good care of Hetty there. It's been a pleasure talking to the pair of you. A real pleasure.' Joss placed a dozen or so glasses on an empty tray, then wove deftly through the crowd, holding the tray high above his head. For such a large man he was extremely nimble on his feet.

Hetty watched his retreating back with a feeling of unreality then glanced towards Albert. He was staring morosely into his beer.

He was quiet on the way home, too, until Hetty finally lost patience with him. 'For heaven's sake, Albert, stop sulking, you great baby!' she scolded as they walked arm in arm along the seafront. The electric lights – installed a few years ago, but still a source of wonder to such as Hetty who hadn't seen their like before – shone down on the sea and promenade, bathing everything in a soft radiance that highlighted the colours of clothing and the contours of faces. A vivid contrast to the more familiar gaslight which, by comparison, now appeared to have a brassy, yellowish hue. But Hetty was oblivious, this evening, to the beauty of the light, so vexed was she with Albert.

'I feel real embarrassed,' she rebuked him, 'you going on at Mr Jenkinson like that about such places not being respectable. And after you telling me mam how proper it all was. I could hardly believe my ears. He looked that mad with you, an' I don't blame him either.'

'I didn't say they weren't respectable,' Albert replied moodily. 'Not his place anyroad.'

'Well, that's what you were hinting at. Just because you were mad at him for offering me a job. I should think you ought to be pleased about it instead of being so . . . so childish.'

'But you've got a job, Hetty. You're a waitress now, and you've been saying how much you enjoy it an' all working at Laycock's. I reckon you've enough to do without all this . . . this singing lark.'

'It's my affair what I do with my time,' Hetty snapped. 'It's got nothing to do with you, Albert Gregson. Besides, the money'll help out a bit at home. There's all sorts of things that want doing yet in the boarding house. Mam wants her nice parlour . . . We might even manage to get her a piano again. That would be grand . . .' Her voice grew soft and she smiled at the thought of it.

'Be blowed to the piano! It's not your mother that you're thinking of at all. It's yourself. Fancying yerself as a singer, all dolled up on t'stage. I'm sorry I ever took you there in the first place, I am that!'

151

Hetty felt hurt by Albert's remarks. She hadn't just been thinking of herself . . . well, not entirely. It would be nice for Mam to have a piano again. All the same, she knew that his angry outburst stemmed mainly from jealousy. He didn't want to share her with anyone else. And she remembered, too, that she had been pretty nasty with him herself earlier this evening. She squeezed his arm. 'Aw, come on, Albert. Don't let's fall out about it. What does it matter anyway? Just a song or two on the stage a couple of times a week. It'll be a bit of fun. And you said yourself that I sing nicely.'

'I suppose so,' muttered Albert grudgingly. 'You'll have to see what your mother says about it though, won't you? I can't see her being any too pleased.'

'I can twist Mam round me little finger,' said Hetty, laughing. 'Besides, your Uncle Sam'll tell her it's all right, won't he? She sets a lot of store by what the great Sam Pickering says, I can tell you.'

Albert didn't answer, although he had previously upheld that august gentleman as the oracle on all things appertaining to Blackpool. Now his words were rebounding on him and Hetty smiled mischievously at his discomfiture.

'I'm sorry, Hetty,' said Albert in a small voice. He leaned across and pecked at her cheek. 'I suppose it's right what you said earlier on, about me being jealous. You're my girl, Hetty love, and I don't like the idea of folks goggling at you, no matter how nicely you sing. But . . . well, I know I'm being selfish, so if it's really what you want to do then I'll go along with it. Can't say I like it, mind, but I reckon I'll just have to put up with it.'

'You're a love, Albert. You are really,' said Hetty softly. She turned to kiss his cheek, but he turned at the same time and their lips met, gently at first, then more lingeringly as he put his arms round her. They stopped by the promenade railings, looking out across the sea.

'You are my girl, aren't you, love?' Albert whispered. 'I haven't said much about it, about us getting wed, like. I can't, 'cos I'm not earning enough at the moment. But . . . I want to buy you a ring . . . soon, Hetty. As soon as I can afford it. Then, perhaps, one day . . .' He paused, his thoughts unspoken, but Hetty knew what he meant by 'one day'. 'I do love you.' He nuzzled into the ginger curls that lay round the nape of her neck. 'You love me, don't you, Hetty?'

Hetty didn't answer straightaway. She wasn't sure if she loved Albert. She put her head on one side and smiled at him, then she threw her arms round him. 'What do you think?' she said with a roguish grin. 'Come on. We'd best go home or else Mam'll be worried.'

Hetty couldn't help but be fond of Albert. He was good and kind and affectionate. So trusting too. She would never dream of letting him down. Albert would make a good husband, just as his father, Henry, had been a good husband to Alice. But, in the meantime, Hetty wanted some fun and Albert, though she cared for him a good deal, was not a young man that you could describe as full of fun. Albert was . . . ordinary. He was, in fact, just the tiniest bit dreary.

★　★　★

Martha, surprisingly, didn't go off the deep end, as Hetty had suspected that she might, when she heard the news about her younger daughter's proposed début on the stage. Hetty had insisted to Albert that her mother wouldn't mind but, all the same, it had been with some trepidation that she had broached the subject the next morning as they washed up the breakfast pots.

Martha looked horrified for a moment. 'Singing . . . on the stage? In a place where they sell . . . beer?'

'And tea and coffee as well, Mam,' Hetty hastily assured her. 'And Mr Jenkinson is very well thought of. A real gentleman, he is. You'd like him, Mam. He says he'll call round to see you, in case you're worried about anything. Now, he can't say fairer than that, can he?'

'No . . . I suppose not.' Martha grinned ruefully. 'Times are changing, I daresay, and I'm having to change with 'em. I know you've always been a grand little singer. D'you remember, love, how we used to sing round t'piano? You and me and Gracie and yer dad an' all.' Her eyes softened at the memory. 'Aye, well,' she nodded. 'I suppose you can do it if you've a mind . . .'

Hetty flung down her pot towel and threw her arms round her mother, almost causing her to drop the big brown teapot she was rinsing. 'Oh, Mam! I knew you'd say yes. Oh, thank you, Mam, thank you . . . Oh, it's all going to be lovely. I know it is.'

'Never mind all that silly nonsense.' Martha pushed her away, but her face broke in a smile. 'You great daft thing! It's about time you started

154

behaving like a proper young lady, not a lumbering carthorse. You'll have to, you know, if you're going on t'stage. Now, like I was saying, you can do it, but it's all to be decent, proper like. There's to be no showing your . . . er . . . bosom, or owt like that. If you're going to stand up on t'stage for everybody to look at you, you've to make sure as they don't see owt as they're not supposed to see. Have you thought what you're going to wear? You'll be wanting a new frock, I suppose? I could easily run you one up on the machine.'

'Mmm . . . I daresay I will. I haven't given much thought to what I'll wear, I was just so excited about Mr Jenkinson asking me.' Hetty was somewhat bemused at her mother's compliance with the situation; she hadn't expected her to agree so readily. For Martha to be actually taking an interest in the clothes she would wear was more than she had dared to hope for. 'We'd best not cross our bridges, Mam,' she said. 'It's not really definite yet. Joss has to hear me sing, on me own. He might not like me.'

'Of course he'll like you,' Martha retorted. 'You've got a grand little voice. I've always thought so. D'you remember when we saw *The Pirates of Penzance*, back in Burnley? That were a lovely dress that Mabel wore. Summat like that would suit you real well, and Grace'll help me to run it up for you. I know she will. D'you know? I'm getting quite excited.'

Hetty remembered the dress of the girl who had played Mabel in the amateur production. Yes, the shawl neckline and prettily gathered skirt and long sleeves were modest enough even for her

155

mother's stringent ideas, she thought amusedly. And how wonderful it was that Martha should be so co-operative about it all.

Hetty had told Grace about it last night, in excited whispers before they went to sleep. Her sister had hugged her and said how grand it was and hoped that Mam wouldn't be too difficult. Grace seemed to be preoccupied, though, and had gone off to work this morning – she started an hour earlier than Hetty did – with a half-smile on her lips and a thoughtful expression on her face. Hetty felt sure she could guess what was going on in her sister's mind, secretive thing that she was, going off and getting a job like that, and at Donnelly's of all places. But Grace hadn't confided in her, not yet, and Hetty was determined not to ask. Grace could be very close-lipped when she wanted to be.

Joss was delighted with Hetty's singing. She stood by the piano, feeling far more nervous than she had thought she would be, and sang 'Poor Wandering One' and 'When Maiden Loves' in a voice which was a little less strident than the tones she had used the night before when Joss had first heard her.

But he seemed well pleased. 'Champion! That's grand!' he proclaimed. 'But don't be afraid to sing out, my dear. Now, let me see . . .' He rubbed his chin thoughtfully. 'It's the third week in October now. How would it be if you started at the beginning of November? That'll give you time to have one or two practices with Bill here and to brush up on a few numbers.'

'Yes, that'll be fine,' Hetty eagerly agreed.

'Now, what shall we call you. Your name's Hetty, is it? Not that there's owt wrong with it,' Joss added hurriedly, 'but it doesn't sound . . . well, it hasn't got enough of a ring to it, if you know what I mean.'

'It's Henrietta really, but nobody ever calls me that.' Hetty laughed. 'It's a bit of a mouthful.'

'Henrietta . . . that's champion!' said Joss, slapping his thigh. He looked at Hetty, at her smiling face, at her lovely green eyes shining with excitement. 'Henrietta, the Girl with the Sparkling Eyes. That's what we'll call you. That's one of my favourites, you know, "A Pair of Sparkling Eyes". It's a song for a fellow to sing really, but I daresay you could manage it. Yes . . . champion! Couldn't be better. Henrietta, the Girl with the Sparkling Eyes . . .'

Chapter 8

Grace felt happy as she walked along Bank Hey Street towards Donnelly's, now her place of employment. There was a spring in her step and a light in her eyes that sprang from joyful anticipation. Perhaps she would see him again today. Maybe he would even stop and speak to her for a few moments as he had done yesterday.

She could still scarcely believe her good fortune at being offered a job at one of the leading stores in Blackpool but, thanks to the co-operation of Alice Gregson and her brother, it had all been so easy. Not that she imagined that William Donnelly had given her the job just at their request; she had had an interview with him and he had seemed suitably impressed with her.

Her first glimpse of him, seated behind the imposing mahogany desk in his office on the top floor, had made her give an involuntary start of surprise. He was so much like his son. For a moment she had almost thought it was Edwin sitting there, until she looked more closely. The similarity was very noticeable, but this man was obviously older. His hair must, at one time, have been the same golden-brown as his son's, but now it was streaked with silver. He was thin-featured, like Edwin, with deep clefts running from nose to chin, but it was in his eyes that Grace noticed the most startling resemblance. Hazel brown with golden flecks, as she remembered from that day in early summer that his son's had been. Edwin's glance had been so full of kindliness and now his father was looking at her with the self-same expression in his eyes, but with, perhaps, a little less intensity. There was a hint of something there, though, that she couldn't quite define. A touch of sadness, maybe?

'So you'd like to come and work for us, Miss Turnbull?' William Donnelly glanced at the piece of paper in front of him where he had hastily scribbled down the few particulars that Sam Pickering had given him. He was only too pleased to be able to do a favour for a friend and he could see already that this young woman seemed eminently suitable for employment at Donnelly's. Modestly attired – but then, he guessed, she couldn't afford to be anything else – her black coat looked a little shabby, the nap worn from the fabric in odd places here and there, and the black velour hat was obviously renovated with a red silk ribbon and small red feathers at the side. It looked pretty, though, and her brown curls peeped demurely from under the brim. Her whole demeanour was one of modesty, which was an admirable attribute for a sales assistant, but she would need to be outgoing as well, able to converse with the customers and persuade them to make a purchase. He hoped she wouldn't be too shy.

'Have you had any experience of shop work?' He smiled at her, encouragingly, he hoped.

'No, I'm afraid not. I worked at the mill – Baldwin's cotton mill in Burnley – till we came to Blackpool. And since then I've been helping me mam . . . my mother,' she hastily corrected herself, 'in the boarding house. But I'd like to work here. It's what I've always wanted, to work in a big shop.'

Her voice was low-pitched and melodious, and though it held more than a trace of the accent of mid-Lancashire, the girl was clearly trying to remedy this. Not that she needed to bother unduly about it. William Donnelly wasn't averse to hearing people speak in their native accent and idiom. It showed that they weren't trying to be something that they were not. William hated people to 'put on the style'. His own wife, as he knew to his sorrow, was an example in point. It set his teeth on edge to hear her talking in that pseudo-refined accent, as if she had never been a common or garden shop assistant, as she was when he first met her. Clara, however, was very good at forgetting her humble beginnings. Something that he felt sure this girl in front of him would never do. He felt himself warming to her already. She said she had never worked in a shop before, though; experience always helped, but he was willing to forgo that. There were other qualities that counted for more than experience.

'Mmm . . .' He drummed his fingers on the desk top as though deep in thought. He didn't want to give the impression that he had already decided. 'It would have helped, Miss Turnbull, if you had

161

had some experience of shop work. But I'm willing to give you a try.'

'Oh, thank you, sir.' Her eyes shone with pleasure. Such a pretty girl she was. William couldn't help thinking how much more attractive she would look if she were dressed in a light, bright colour, or even a warm brown to match her eyes and hair, instead of that fusty black.

'We need an extra pair of hands in our haberdashery department,' he said. 'Miss Walters will be rushed off her feet in there soon with the season for balls and parties coming up. All the ladies will be coming in to choose their materials. At least I hope they will.' He gave a little laugh. If his own wife was anything to go by they would. She had recently seen her dressmaker about a new gown for the annual Catholic Ball, to be held in a couple of months' time, as if she hadn't already got a wardrobe full of suitable dresses. But, it seemed, one couldn't appear in the same dress twice.

'Yes, I think we'll start you off in there, Miss Turnbull,' he went on. 'You already know something about materials with working in the . . . er, cotton industry, and I'm sure you'll get along very well with Miss Walters. Don't be intimidated by her.' He lowered his head, speaking confidingly. 'She may appear to be a little – how can I put it? – starchy, but she's really very kind. And helpful too. She's had a lot of experience in shop work, and she'll give you a good training.'

'Yes, I've already met her,' said Grace shyly. 'I remember her being very kind.'

'Oh?' William Donnelly raised his eyebrows

questioningly. 'When was that?'

'Last summer, when my sister and me – and I –
came in the shop. I was feeling poorly,' William
noticed that the girl blushed slightly at the
remembrance, 'and Miss Walters was ever so kind
to me.'

'That's fine then. You know her already, so
that's the first obstacle over and done with.'
William smiled at her again. 'We'll go down and
meet her in a few minutes and then, if it's agreeable to you, you can start here on Monday? Will
that be convenient, Miss Turnbull?'

'Oh, yes. Thank you, sir.'

William thought that he had seldom seen a pair
of such expressive eyes, positively glowing with
happiness.

'That's fine then,' he said again. 'Now, perhaps
we could have a little chat. I like to get to know
my assistants . . . and, Miss Turnbull, you must
never feel afraid to ask me anything. If you ever
feel worried, about anything at all, I want you to
know that you can come and talk to me. I like to
feel that we're a big, happy family here . . . Now,
how does your mother like it, being a boarding-
house keeper? She's settled down now, has she, in
Blackpool?'

'Oh yes, sir. We all have. We think it's a
wonderful place. And we've had a fair sort of
season, to say it's our first. Me mam . . . Mother's
hoping we'll do a bit better next year though.'

'Yes . . . yes. It's always difficult at first.'
William placed his fingers together, making a
steeple of his hands. He looked over them at the
eager face of the girl opposite him. She wasn't so

163

shy when you got to know her. She was chatting away quite animatedly now, once she had been set at her ease. William liked his employees to feel comfortable in his presence. 'I'm sure your mother will do splendidly with her business as time goes on. She must be a very courageous woman, starting out on a new venture like that, especially when she has no husband to back her up. She's a widow, I believe?'

'Yes.' Grace nodded. 'My father died about eight years ago. But Mam's never been short of courage.'

'And she used to have a stall on Burnley market, I understand, selling her own produce?'

'Yes, that's right.' Grace looked at William Donnelly in surprise. 'But how on earth? I mean . . .'

William smiled to himself. The girl had been about to say 'How on earth did you know?', but then had tried to retract her words, believing them, perhaps, to be impertinent. She was looking a little discomfited, as though she had overstepped the mark into familiarity. He came to her rescue.

'How did I know? Because good news travels fast, as the old saying goes, and I'm hoping that it might be good news for me. Sam Pickering told me, as a matter of fact.' William Donnelly picked up a silver pencil, absent-mindedly twisting it round in his fingers as he spoke. 'You see, Miss Turnbull, I'm looking out for someone to help with the supplies for our restaurant. Cakes and pastries and pies . . . all that sort of thing. One of our suppliers has let me down badly, and I wondered if your mother would be willing to help me out. I couldn't have asked her during the season, I know, but perhaps now that business has slackened off, do you think she might consider it?' William looked at her quizzically, one eyebrow raised in an engaging manner which made him, for a moment, appear younger than he was.

'Yes . . .' Grace replied slowly. 'I do believe she might, Mr Donnelly. Of course, I can't answer for Mother. It wouldn't be right for me to speak for her.'

'Of course not. I understand that. I'll call round and have a chat with her about it myself. But, if you could perhaps give her some idea as to what I have in mind? She had a very good reputation in Burnley, I believe, for the excellence of her produce?'

'Yes, she certainly did,' Grace replied eagerly, 'and I'm sure she'll be very flattered that you've asked her.'

'Good, that's fine then.' William placed his hands flat on the table in a gesture of finality. 'Now, let's go and find Miss Walters . . .'

Grace had walked home feeling bemused. She hoped that her mother wouldn't be annoyed with her for giving William Donnelly the impression that she would accept his invitation to bake for the shop. A few days ago Grace would have expected her mother's answer to be a vehement refusal; now, she felt that Martha might be better disposed to the idea. She had been surprisingly agreeable when Grace had told her that she wanted to work at Donnelly's, that she had, in

165

fact, been granted an interview with William Donnelly himself, and Martha had made no reference to that gentleman's religious persuasion. It was possible, Grace thought, that her mother didn't know, but not very likely considering that she had Alice Gregson, who was a well-known busybody – though a good-natured one – as a bosom friend.

Now, on hearing Grace's news about her culinary reputation, her mother's overriding thought seemed to be that she had no decent room in which to entertain her august visitor. 'How can I show a posh gentleman like that into my shabby parlour?' she remonstrated with Grace. 'You'd no business inviting him round here, our Gracie. Whatever were you thinking of?'

'I didn't invite him, Mam,' Grace replied. 'It was his idea. Anyroad, he won't be looking at the state of your parlour. It's just a business call. I thought you might be pleased,' she added, a trifle petulantly, 'at the thought of earning some more money. You were only saying the other week about how hard up we were.'

'Oh, I am pleased, lass. I am. I just got a bit flustered, like, at the thought of him coming here. It isn't often we have the gentry calling.' She gave a nervous little laugh.

'Mr Donnelly's not gentry, Mam. He's what you might call "in trade". The real gentry look down their noses at such as him.'

'Oh aye, I know that. But he's a good deal posher than us when all's said and done, and I was always brought up to know me place. Oh well, ne'er mind.' Martha sighed. 'P'raps if if I earn a bit

166

more brass I'll be having my posh parlour sooner than I think. Then I'll be able to hold up my head with the best of them.'

'That's right, Mam. That's the spirit,' replied Grace, smiling at her mother. 'And I'm sure you'll like Mr Donnelly. He didn't act as if he were any different from us, for all his money.'

But, all the same, he is different and don't you forget it, Grace tried to tell herself. They're all different, the Donnellys, the whole lot of them. It was strange, Grace thought to herself, that Mr Donnelly hadn't mentioned his son, Edwin, at the interview, especially with him being his father's right-hand man. But, on the other hand, why should he mention him? He wasn't aware that she had ever met the young man and the meeting between Grace and Edwin had been, when all was said and done, just a momentary thing. By now Edwin Donnelly must have forgotten all about her, or so Grace tried to convince herself, but as she pushed open the swing doors on her first day at Donnelly's the thought of those kindly golden-brown eyes still lingered on the periphery of her mind.

She didn't see Edwin for a few days. She was beginning to think that he might have left his father's employment, but she didn't dare to ask. Then Miss Walters remarked casually at the end of the week that young Mr Edwin should be back soon. He had been on a business trip to Manchester, seeing how things were done in the big department stores there. Grace felt her heart miss a beat and she grasped more firmly the big steel scissors she was holding. She had very nearly let

167

them slip across the smooth satin fabric that she was cutting, an order for an influential customer. Thankfully, though, Miss Walters hadn't seemed to notice.

'Oh, yes, young Mr Edwin,' Grace remarked casually. 'I remember him. I was wondering where he was.'

Edwin noticed her as soon as he entered the haberdashery department on the Monday morning that he returned to work. Another new assistant, he thought. His father had employed a few girls during his absence and one was certainly needed here. Miss Walters wasn't getting any younger and was inclined to become flustered when the shop got busy. Not that it was busy at the moment; half past nine on a Monday morning was always a quiet time.

He watched the girl for a moment or two from behind a display of materials. Her head was bent industriously over the big ledger in front of her and Edwin could see that her hair was a rich brown, inclined to curl and shining with cleanliness. Not all the shop assistants were so particular, he feared. Edwin had been brought up to believe that cleanliness was next to godliness, but he realised that it wasn't so easy, in large households where money was scarce, to be always sparklingly fresh and immaculately turned out. This girl looked neat and tidy, and diligent too; a very good start.

It wasn't until she raised her head that he recognised her. He gave a start of delighted surprise as he saw again the warm brown eyes and the gentle features of the girl he had met so briefly in the store, in this same department, earlier in the year. He hadn't forgotten her; the thought of her had always been there at the fringes of his consciousness, but other matters had crowded into his mind since that day and the memory of her had been submerged in a welter of other thoughts. Now, he recalled how she had said that they were coming to live in Blackpool very soon, she and her mother and sister, and how he had decided at the time that he had to see her again. But he had been so busy all summer and, besides, he would have had no idea how to get in touch with her. He had realised soon after their meeting that he didn't even know her surname. But now, here she was; he could scarcely believe his eyes. It seemed like a miracle.

He hurried across the floor and as he did so the girl glanced across and saw him. He was aware that she gave a start, as he had done, then a joyous smile lit up her face. Edwin moved towards her, his hand outstretched. 'Well, what a surprise. How lovely to see you again.' He grasped hold of her hand, feeling the fragility of her fingers beneath his own. She was very slight, he noticed; of medium height, but possibly a shade too thin, and her eyes appeared over-large in the smallness of her face. Such lovely eyes, though, so richly brown and luminous. 'It's Grace, isn't it? I'm sorry, I'm afraid I don't know your other name. But I know you told me that you were called Grace.'

'Yes, that's right,' she answered in the softly spoken voice that he remembered. 'Grace Turnbull.

And it's lovely to see you again too, Mr Donnelly.'

'Grace . . . Turnbull?' Edwin's brow furrowed in perplexity. 'Then you must be . . . My father was telling me that he had employed a young lady for the store and that her mother, Mrs Turnbull, was going to supply cakes for us. Then it must be your mother?'

'Yes, it is.' Grace laughed. 'We both started last week, me working here and Mam . . . my mother working at home.'

'Well, what a surprise,' said Edwin again. 'I'd no idea it was your family that my father was talking about.' He scarcely knew what to say to the girl with Miss Walters hovering pointedly in the background. He knew he mustn't keep her from her work; he, too, had a thousand and one things to see to, now he had returned, but he couldn't bear to dash away from her so quickly, now he had found her again. 'And you like it here, do you, Miss Turnbull?' This, the use of her surname, for the benefit of Miss Walters who, he felt sure, was all ears. 'You think you'll be happy here?'

'Oh yes. I know I will, Mr Donnelly. Your father and everyone, they've all been so kind.'

'Good . . . good. My father likes everyone to feel at home here.' Edwin smiled and nodded, aware that his words sounded trite and that he was grinning fatuously. Damn that Miss Walters! She was making him feel distinctly uncomfortable. He could almost feel her gimlet-sharp eyes boring into his back as she bustled around moving things that didn't need moving, and he could imagine her unspoken inference, 'Some of us have work to do round here.' Be hanged to her, though. Why shouldn't he speak to the girl if he wanted to? It was his duty to make her feel welcome, and it was his shop – well, his father's at any rate – when all was said and done.

Edwin continued. 'And what about your sister? Hetty, isn't it? Is she working too?'

He listened intently as Grace told him that her sister now worked as a waitress, after they had both helped their mother in the boarding house during the summer. Then he knew he really must be moving on. Miss Walters was likely to burst with apoplexy at any moment and he didn't want Grace to get into trouble on his account. But how wonderful that he had met her again after all this time. Edwin made up his mind to seek her out again very soon. It was easy, now that he knew where to find her, but perhaps next time they could find somewhere more private to have a chat.

Edwin's thoughts drifted back, as he went about his work that morning, to the day when he had first met Grace. It had been the day, he recalled, of Constance's twenty-first birthday, the day when he had startled both families, the Donnellys and the Whiteheads, with his decision not to marry Constance. Not that he had made any pronouncement to this effect; it had been made apparent to them all in the paltriness of his birthday gift to Constance, if sapphires and seed pearls could be termed paltry. The brooch had cost him 'a bob or two', to quote the Lancashire parlance that he often heard around him and which his mother sometimes slipped into when she was off her guard. But the gift had seemed paltry to Constance, when she had been expecting so much more, and he had heard her dismiss it as such to her mother later that evening. He had taken cover in the library to escape from the aggrieved expression on Constance's lovely face and the recriminatory glances of both mothers. He had been wondering whether he should cut loose and run out of the front door, up the road and along to his own home, away from them all, when he had heard their voices.

'Don't upset yourself, Connie love. I know you're disappointed. Your father and I are too. We had hoped . . . But there are more fish in the sea than Edwin Donnelly when all's said and done, and that's what you'll have to tell yourself, my love.'

'I've never been so humiliated. A paltry brooch!'

'Shhh, love! Keep your voice down. You don't want all the guests knowing how upset you are. Just pretend that you don't care. I wouldn't give him the satisfaction . . .'

Mrs Whitehead's voice was low and Edwin couldn't catch all the words, neither did he really want to hear them. He hadn't intended to eavesdrop. The two women had, he gathered, escaped from the throng of guests in the main reception room of the house because poor dear Constance was feeling so upset. It didn't make Edwin feel any better knowing that he had behaved less than gallantly. He slumped lower in the leather armchair, praying that they wouldn't come into the library, not knowing who he hated most, himself or the whole Whitehead clan. No, he didn't hate

Constance, but he couldn't – wouldn't – marry her, and this had seemed the only way to let her know. She had proved impervious to all his previous hints.

'Hardly paltry though, dear,' Mrs Whitehead went on. 'It's a lovely brooch. Expensive too, one can see that. It really looks quite pretty, pinned on your shoulder. I'm surprised you're wearing it, seeing that . . .'

'I can't very well do anything else, can I?' Edwin could hear Constance's fretful tones and he could imagine the petulant expression on her face. 'I felt like flinging it in his face, I can tell you, but I know what you've always said, Mother, about breeding. About behaving like a lady. And he seemed as pleased as Punch too, as though he hadn't a care in the world. I could have spit in his eyes.'

'Now come along, love. This won't do at all, will it? I hate to see my little girl being so upset.' Mrs Whitehead's soothing syrupy tones were the sort one might use to a child who had broken her best doll. But then that was what Constance always had been and still was; a child bent on getting her own way.

'Dry your eyes, my love, then we'll go back to the party. They'll all be wondering where you are.'

There was a moment's silence, then Edwin heard Constance's brittle tones. 'I'm quite all right now, Mother. We'll go back. As you say, there are more fish in the sea.'

Edwin had wandered, soon afterwards, into the large drawing room where the party was being held. Just to keep up appearances; he couldn't let himself and his family down by absenting himself entirely. His absence would be sure to be noticed; it was more than likely that relations and close friends had observed already that he wasn't spending as much time with Constance as he usually did. And Edwin felt a sinking sensation deep in the pit of his stomach as he anticipated the wrath of his mother when he had to face her the next morning. But first things first. At the moment he must put on some sort of front for the benefit of the guests.

The room was almost a carbon copy of the drawing room in his own home in Whitegate Lane, just a few minutes' walk away from the Whiteheads' home here in Park Road. Edwin glanced round at its understated elegance – the intricate plasterwork of flowers and leaves on the cream walls and ceiling; the stylish plum-coloured velvet curtains and the matching deep-buttoned sofa and easy chairs; the gilt-framed mirrors and oil paintings and the spindly occasional tables dotted here and there – his eyes not really seeing it as he scanned the room for Constance. She was at the far end of the room with a group of friends, both men and women, a crystal sherry glass in her hand. Her head was thrown back and she was laughing, a tinkling, merry sound which, though it may have been somewhat forced, persuaded Edwin that she wasn't grieving unduly over his perfidy.

He smiled and nodded at her, but she turned her back as though she hadn't noticed him, continuing to laugh and talk loudly. Edwin didn't join her group, but attached himself to another small circle of acquaintances. He listened to the small talk, joining in occasionally, until people started to drift away in ones and twos. Never had an evening seemed so interminable.

His goodbye to Constance was casual – there was no point in carrying on the pretence any longer – and hers was frigidly polite. Edwin felt that he would remember that glacial blue stare for many a long day.

The dreaded confrontation with his mother at the breakfast table was unpleasant, but mercifully very short. Edwin had, in a somewhat cowardly manner, made sure that it would be brief by arriving for breakfast after both his parents had finished their meal. The dining room was empty when Edwin entered. He ignored the silver serving dishes of bacon and scrambled egg on the sideboard – he wasn't hungry – and nibbled moodily at a piece of toast and marmalade. It tasted like cardboard.

His mother started the moment she re-entered the room, as he knew she would. 'Edwin, how could you? That poor girl! She must have felt so humiliated. I've never been so embarrassed in all my life. I just didn't know where to put myself. Promising her an engagement ring, then having the damned nerve to give her a brooch.'

'Hold on a minute, Mother.' Edwin's tone was indignant. 'There have been no promises . . .'

'Don't you tell me to hold on in that tone of voice. You're lucky I don't give you a clout round the ear'ole, and it's what Constance should have done an' all.' Clara Donnelly's expressions, when

175

she was heated, were often down-to-earth, not quite what one would expect from a well-bred lady. But then Clara, to her chagrin, was not well bred. 'That poor lass. I felt right sorry for her. And whatever Mr Whitehead'll say I can't imagine. Your father and he . . .'

'Be hanged to Mr Whitehead!' Edwin was determined not to be browbeaten. 'And I'm telling you, Mother, there were no promises, whatever you may like to think. It's all been a figment of your imagination, yours and Mrs Whitehead's. I'm twenty-six now. I'm old enough to make up my own mind, and I've decided that I don't want to marry Constance. And now, if you'll excuse me . . .' He rose from the table, carefully folding his serviette and replacing it in the silver ring. 'I had better be on my way or I'll be late at the shop. Father has already gone, I take it?'

'Yes . . . Oh, for heaven's sake, girl, get off back to the kitchen.' This to the maid who was hovering near the door. Clara Donnelly turned again to Edwin, her glance so cold and disdainful that he was reminded for a moment of Constance. Now he came to think of it, they were somewhat similar in appearance. The same well-sculptured, but chilling, features and long aristocratic-looking nose, but whereas Constance was fair his mother was dark. 'Yes, your father set off a quarter of an hour ago,' his mother told him reprovingly. 'He's very little to say for himself either this morning, but he's not too pleased, I can tell you that. He's not pleased at all.'

She looked at the half-eaten piece of toast on her son's plate, and his half-empty coffee cup.

'You've eaten next to nothing, lad. You need a good breakfast inside you, Edwin, to do a good day's work.' Her tone was more placatory now and her eyes softened just a touch as she looked at him. Clara's anger was usually of short duration but, like Constance, she was fond of her own way.

'I've had quite sufficient, thank you.' Edwin's tone was still cool, but then he, too, relented a little as he saw the pensive look in his mother's eye. 'Come on, Mother. Cheer up. I know you're disappointed, but you'll get over it. Constance isn't the right girl for me, and you wouldn't want us to be unhappy, would you?' He was gone before she could answer.

Edwin had seen little of Constance throughout the summer, save when they met at church or at social functions they were both forced to attend. The frigid politeness between them gradually gave way to a casual companionship. Constance had at last, it seemed, got the message and Edwin was pleased to see that she had other admirers. Twice he had seen her in the company of Herbert Mallinson, the chief cashier at Whitehead's, her father's confectionery business.

Edwin worked long hours at the shop and, when he was not working, he kept himself busy in other ways. He was determined to break free from Constance and to make a life of his own away from the restricting confines of the church and the social clique to which he had formerly belonged. Occasionally he went to the Conservative Club with his father and an easy camaraderie grew up between the two of them. William Donnelly made

177

very little reference to the matter of Edwin and Constance, despite Clara's hints as to his displeasure.

'I expect you know what you are doing, son,' was all he had said. 'Your mother's peeved, of course, but she'll come round.' William had grinned wryly, used as he was to dealing with his wife's fits of pique.

Edwin had also joined a literary society which met weekly at one of the seafront hotels. There, a group of like-minded men and women discussed notable authors – Trollope; the Brontë sisters; the contemporary writer, Oscar Wilde; Charles Dickens, of course; and Edwin's favourite, Thomas Hardy – and read aloud passages from their works. And Sunday afternoons, after his routine attendance at Mass, would find Edwin cycling along the country lanes of the Fylde, to Poulton or Blowing Sands, or further afield to St Michael's on Wyre, with a local bicycling club.

His encounters with young women were very few, except for the odd bluestocking types who attended the literary society, and the heroines that he met in the pages of the books he read. He was beginning to feel that he preferred these to the real, flesh-and-blood creatures – they were far less trouble. Then, in the autumn, he met Grace Turnbull again . . .

She seemed ill at ease at first when Edwin took to waiting for her to come out of the back entrance of the store – she was usually alone – and insisted on walking part of the way home with her. It was easier than trying to talk to her in the shop, under the watchful eye of Miss Walters, and gradually her embarrassment lessened and she began to talk to him more freely. After he had waylaid her a few times Edwin was pleased to note that she no longer seemed startled to see him, and a smile of pleasure would light up her gentle features. He decided to delay no further. *The Importance of Being Earnest* by Oscar Wilde was to be performed at the Grand Theatre during the second week of November, and Edwin decided to ask Grace to accompany him.

Oscar Wilde was, at that moment, languishing in prison after being convicted of 'gross indecency'. An unpleasant, sordid affair, Edwin thought, not the sort of thing that one could discuss with a charming young woman like Grace, but there was no reason why the subject should be mentioned and it certainly didn't detract from the brilliance of Mr Wilde's works. Edwin had seen *Lady Windermere's Fan* — described by Wilde himself as 'one of those modern drawing-room plays with pink lampshades' — the previous year and the latest play promised to be just as entertaining. Poor Oscar Wilde. It was said that he had declared, years ago, 'Somehow or other I'll be famous and if not famous, I'll be notorious.' He's turned out to be both, poor chap, thought Edwin.

He was delighted when Grace shyly accepted his invitation. He arranged to call for her in a cab half an hour before the performance was due to start. Thoughts of Constance were the

179

furthest thing from his mind now. Nor did he consider for one moment what his mother would think of this outing. Grace, dear, lovely Grace, had agreed to go to the theatre with him and he felt the happiest man alive.

Chapter 9

'Edwin Donnelly's asked you to go to the theatre with him?' Martha stared at Grace with an expression of wide-eyed alarm. 'But . . . but you can't! It's . . . well, it's out of the question.' She looked down at the piece of sewing in her hands, a blouse that she was renovating with a new lace collar and cuffs, and continued stitching furiously, as though her life depended on it. 'It's just not right,' she muttered as her needle flashed in and out. 'It wouldn't do at all.'

Grace felt her heart sink right to the bottom of her high-buttoned boots. 'Why not, Mam? Why isn't it right? I think it was real kind of him to ask me. I can't see why you're being so . . . so difficult about it all.' To her dismay Grace felt tears of disappointment begin to well up in her eyes. She had been so looking forward to her theatre visit with Edwin and had accepted his invitation without even considering what her mother's reaction would be. Now it seemed as though Martha was going to spoil it all.

'Why isn't it right?' repeated Martha, looking grimly at her daughter. 'You just think about it for a moment, my girl, instead of acting all starry-eyed, and you'll soon see why it isn't right.' Martha's lips closed tightly in a thin line of displeasure and Grace knew that it boded ill when her mother called her 'my girl' in such significant tones. It wasn't often that Martha spoke so sternly. 'It's all very well working for the Donnellys,' she went on, 'and don't think I'm not grateful to 'em, Grace, because I am. But it's quite another matter when it comes to fraternising with 'em. No, it won't do. I know my place an' I always have, and I thought I'd brought you up to know yours an' all. Young Mr Edwin's your boss. You can't start walking out with him.'

'You can't call it walking out, Mam,' argued Grace. 'It's only a visit to the theatre. Besides, I thought you liked the Donnellys. You said how friendly Mr William was when he called, how you found you were chatting twenty to the dozen with him. And Edwin . . . Mr Edwin's just the same. He's ever so friendly, Mam.'

'I haven't said I don't like them, Grace. I do. I liked Mr William very much, a lot more than I thought I would considering he's a . . . well, he's a Catholic, isn't he? And his son's one an' all. And that's another reason why it won't do. Protestants and Catholics don't mix. They never have and they never will. It's like oil and water. It's no use.'

She looked down at her sewing again and for a few moments there was silence, save for a loud ticking of the wooden clock and Martha's heavy breathing. Grace knew that was a sure sign that her mother was upset; she only breathed in that laboured way when she was disturbed about something. Grace stared disconsolately into the

182

fire. She didn't want to openly defy her mother; she couldn't remember a time in her life when she had ever had reason to do so, but she felt that Martha was being unreasonable and she was determined not to give way in the face of her mother's querulous criticisms.

'Anyroad, you've got a young man, haven't you?' Martha continued. 'That's summat else that wouldn't be right. The way I see it you don't go walking out with one young man when you've already got another fellow waiting for you.'

'I've told you, Mam, it's not walking out. He's asked me to go to the theatre, that's all. Oh, what's the use?' Grace's voice was sharp and much louder than her normal soft-spoken tones. She was beginning to feel exasperated and thoroughly out of patience with her mother, a state of affairs she could never recall happening before. 'And if it's Walter that you're talking about,' she went on angrily, 'you can hardly call him my young man. He hasn't written to me for nearly a month. For all I know he may never write to me again.' And I hope he doesn't, she added silently to herself. 'So I don't think I need to consider Walter Clayton. He's certainly not considering me very much.'

'It's hardly the lad's fault that his mother's been ill,' said Martha brusquely. 'That's why he hasn't written lately. I'm sure he would write to you if he could find time. Anyroad, what do silly letters matter? You know the lad's fond of you and you've no business to go seeing another fellow while you're still walking out with Walter.'

'A fat lot of walking out we're doing with him in

183

Burnley and me here,' Grace retorted. 'Anyway, you've changed your tune, haven't you, Mam? You were saying only last week that it was time I was hearing from him. Carrying on something awful you were about him not writing to me.'

'Aye, happen I was; I can't deny it. But he's a good steady lad is Walter Clayton. He's our sort, Grace. He works at t'mill and he's a Methodist and he's the right sort of fellow for you. I don't want you getting any fancy ideas about Edwin Donnelly. I've told you, it just won't do.' Martha's tone was reproachful, but as she looked up from her sewing and saw the tears brimming in her daughter's eyes she sighed and shook her head. 'Eh, deary me! Whatever's happening to us, Gracie? You and me falling out. I can't ever remember us shouting at one another like this.'

She put the blouse she was stitching on the floor beside her, carefully replaced the needle in the pincushion and leaned forward, her eyes full of concern. 'I didn't meant to upset you, lass. I don't know as I've ever refused you anything in your life. Not that you've ever asked for anything out of the ordinary. You've always been such a good lass and contented like.' She paused, then nodded slowly. 'Aye, well, I suppose you can go if you've a mind. Come to think of it, it wouldn't be right to go offending the Donnellys. Happen it's just his way of saying thank you. I know you work hard in that shop. Mr William was saying when he called last week as how they're right pleased with you. And I know he's grateful for all the cakes and suchlike as I'm making for him. Aye, I reckon you'd better go. Now, come on, dry your eyes.

There's no call to go getting all upset.'

'Thanks, Mam,' said Grace softly. She sniffed back her tears and hastily wiped her eyes with her handkerchief. She didn't often weep and she felt annoyed with herself, but her tears had welled up as much at her mother's harsh words as at her disappointment. As Mam said, it wasn't often that the pair of them fell out. She gave a little smile. 'Like you say, I expect Mr Edwin just wants to say thank you.'

'Mmm, happen he does.' Martha nodded thoughtfully. 'But, Grace . . .' She looked keenly at her daughter. 'You won't start getting any silly ideas now, will you?'

'No, Mam.' Grace shook her head. 'You don't need to worry about me. I've got my head screwed on the right way.'

But Grace knew, even as she spoke, that she was already more than halfway to falling in love with Edwin Donnelly and there was nothing that she could do about it. There was nothing that she wanted to do about it. And, judging from the way that he looked at her, his golden-brown eyes alight with admiration, she was pretty sure that Edwin felt the same way.

'My goodness, Grace! I bet you're tickled pink, aren't you?' Alice Gregson's eyes opened wide with excitement. 'Going to the theatre with young Mr Edwin! Eeh, I tell you what, lass. If I were twenty years younger I wouldn't mind being in your shoes.' She gave a throaty chuckle.

Grace smiled at her. She quite often popped over the road to have a chat with Alice. She found that she enjoyed the older woman's company and Alice, though she loved to gossip, was full of common sense. You could trust her to give you a sensible, unvarnished view of things. Neither was she as intolerant as Grace knew her own mother, though she loved her very much, could be at times. 'My mother wasn't all that pleased, I can tell you,' Grace told Alice now. 'So play it down, will you, Mrs Gregson, if she talks to you about it? She thinks I'm stepping out of my class or something, apart from the fact that he's a Catholic, of course. I think that's really what's getting to her.'

Alice nodded. 'Aye, it would. She can't seem to see much good in 'em, although she's taken to Mr William, I must admit. But, talking about stepping out of your class, that's just what Clara Donnelly did when she got wed to Mr William. She were a shop assistant like you are, Grace. But that's not all . . .' Alice leaned forward, ready, as ever, to indulge in a nice bit of gossip. 'She was one of a big family. Ten of 'em there were, I've heard tell. Lived in a cottage on Marton Moss, real scruffy hovel it were an' all, from all accounts. Stepped up in the world did Clara Riley – that's what she were called afore she got wed – and now she's so la-di-da that she'll hardly give you the time of day. Of course, she were a Catholic, and I suppose that made all the difference.'

'Yes,' said Grace reflectively. 'I suppose it would.'

There was an edge to her voice and Alice looked at her keenly. 'So you'll be looking forward to it, I daresay?' she went on quickly. 'What are you going to wear? Have you got something nice? It's proper posh at the Grand Theatre. Not that it matters what you wear,' she added hastily as she noticed that Grace was looking a little crestfallen. 'You always look real pretty, Grace.'

'No,' Grace sighed. 'I can't say that I've anything special to wear. It'll be my black coat, I suppose, but I've got that yellow blouse that I made. That always looks nice, and maybe I could trim my black hat with some yellow ribbon and feathers instead of the red, so as it'll match.'

'Mmm . . .' Alice looked at her thoughtfully. 'D'you know, Grace, I've got something in my wardrobe that would suit you down to the ground. It's a brown coat with a little fur collar. Not expensive fur, mind you; I daresay it's only rabbit fur, but it looks nice. I bought it a couple of year back, but it's a bit tight on me now.' Alice laughed as she patted her hips. 'Getting a bit broad round the beam, I am. Come on upstairs with me and we'll have a look at it. That's if you don't mind wearing my cast-offs?'

'Of course I don't mind,' Grace replied eagerly. 'It's real kind of you, Mrs Gregson. I'm only too glad to have something different to wear. It's ages since I had a new coat.' She looked at herself appraisingly in Alice's dressing-table mirror. The brown coat fitted perfectly.

Alice cried out in delight. 'My goodness, Grace. You look a real bobby-dazzler in that!' She clasped her hands together in pleasure. 'Now, wait a minute. I've got a hat to match an' all. A little fur one.' She pulled a round hatbox from the top of the wardrobe and took out a little hat, an exact match for the warm brown fur on the coat collar.

'There . . .' She placed it on top of Grace's brown curls and pulled it well down over her ears. 'It fits you a treat. It might have been made for you.' She beamed at Grace in the mirror and Grace smiled back.

'It really is awfully kind of you, Mrs Gregson. I just don't know what to say.' Grace turned and placed a kiss on Alice's rosy cheek.

'Don't mention it, lass.' Alice squeezed her arm. 'Just you have a good time at the theatre, that's all. You don't think your Hetty will be annoyed, do you? With her being our Albert's young lady, I mean. She'll happen think as it should be her as I'm giving the coat to. Not that she seems a jealous sort of girl.'

'No.' Grace shook her head. 'Hetty'll not mind. Anyway, she can always borrow it if she wants to. We often wear one another's clothes with us being about the same size. No, I reckon Hetty's got enough on her mind at the moment what with being a waitress and then singing at that Tilda's Tavern. She hardly has time to sit down to have her tea these days.'

'Aye, our Albert says she's doing real well.' Alice nodded approvingly. 'He weren't right pleased about it at first though – he's a bit stuffy at times is our Albert – but he's proud of her now all right. Like a dog with two tails, he is. Have you been to listen to her, Grace?'

Grace shook her head. 'No, not yet. I'd like to, but it's not the sort of place you can wander into on your own.'

'Happen we'll all go along one evening.' Alice chuckled. 'Me and Henry and you, Grace, and perhaps your mother'll come an' all.'

'I don't know about Mam.' Grace was pensive
for a moment. She took off the coat and hat and
put them over her arm, lovingly stroking the fur
collar. 'I think Mam feels that things are getting a
bit out of control. What with Hetty singing and
Mam and me both working for the Donnellys.
When Edwin . . . Mr Edwin asked me to go to the
theatre it fair took the wind out of her sails.' She
looked at Alice, her face serious and her brown
eyes clouded with anxiety. 'Don't say too much
about it to her, will you? I'm afraid we had words
about it. She's frightened in case I start getting
what she calls "silly ideas". You know what I
mean, about Mr Edwin.'

'Of course you won't, Grace. You're far too
sensible a girl to do that, aren't you? All the same,
it's nice that he's asked you. You just have a good
time and make sure you come and tell me all
about it.' Alice chuckled again. 'I shall be watching behind t'curtains when he comes to pick you
up in that there cab. Don't worry though. I'll not
let him see me. Just enjoy yourself, lass.'

'Yes, I will. And thanks again, Mrs Gregson.'

'Don't mention it, love. It's a real pleasure.' As
Alice looked at Grace's unusually flushed cheeks
and the over-brightness of her eyes she felt a
tremor of apprehension. Maybe the girl's mother
had cause to be anxious.

The Grand Theatre in Church Street, designed by
the architect Frank Matcham, had been opened
the previous year and was already being referred
to as 'Matcham's masterpiece'. It was a cosy,

intimate little place and from her seat in the circle Grace looked round in wide-eyed wonder at the ornate plasterwork on the ceiling, the gilded boxes, the red velvet seats and the heavy curtain with its deep tasselled fringe. It was the first time she had been in a real theatre – the amateur productions she had attended in Burnley had always been in church halls – and she was finding it all very fascinating.

Edwin watched her fondly, touched by her innocence and her ingenuous delight in all that she saw around her. He thought she looked like a bright little squirrel this evening, with her brown hair peeping out prettily from under her fur hat and the fur collar framing her tiny face. Her eyes were shining like two radiant stars as she gazed excitedly at the scene around her.

The Importance of Being Earnest was a triumph, as Edwin had thought it would be, sparkling with brilliant conversation and the dazzling wit that one had come to expect of Oscar Wilde. Grace laughed delightedly at the antics of the two bachelors, Jack and Algernon, and the hilarious Lady Bracknell who dominated the action.

'I can see you're enjoying it,' Edwin remarked as the curtain fell for the interval. He reached over and touched her hand. 'I thought you would.'

'Oh, yes, I am,' Grace replied eagerly. 'It's so funny. I can't remember when I laughed so much, and it's so clever too. I can't wait to see how it all sorts out.'

'Come along.' Edwin put his arm beneath her elbow. 'We'll go and have a drink while we're waiting. Don't worry,' he added, noting the look of disquiet that momentarily flickered across her face. 'You can have a lemonade or a ginger beer. And lots of ladies go in the bar, I can assure you.' He laughed indulgently. 'You'll be in good company.'

Grace sipped at her lemonade and smiled at Edwin across the little round table. 'Thank you over so much for bringing me, Mr . . . Edwin,' she said. 'I'm having a lovely time.'

'I'm glad.' Edwin smiled, then looked at her with a glance that was half laughing, half reproving. 'Do you think you could remember, *Miss* Grace, that I'm Edwin? Not Mr Edwin or Mr Donnelly. Just Edwin.'

Grace laughed. He had asked her before when he had walked home with her from the shop to call him by his Christian name. She wanted to – oh, she wanted to so much – but it didn't always come easily. 'I'll try . . . Edwin,' she said, her eyes twinkling at him. 'But it's something as I've not been used to, calling the boss by his first name.'

He reached across and took hold of her hand, his thumb rubbing gently, caressingly against her palm. 'Then it's something you will have to get used to, won't you?' His eyes were caressing too and his voice was warm, like deep dark velvet. Grace felt a tremor of longing run through her as she looked into the depths of his golden-flecked eyes.

He squeezed her hand and then let it go. 'Now, tell me about your sister. I was so interested to hear that she had started singing. At Tilda's Tavern, you say? Is she enjoying it?'

'Yes, she's thrilled to bits. I can't believe it, our

191

Hetty being on stage, although she's always loved singing.' Grace laughed. 'She's always liked showing off a bit, too. No – I don't mean that exactly. That sounds unkind. But she's always been better at pushing herself forward than what I am. More of an, an . . .

'Extrovert,' said Edwin.

'Yes, that's the word,' replied Grace. 'Extrovert. That's our Hetty exactly.'

Edwin smiled. 'I thought she was the first time I set eyes on her. And I'm sure she'll do very well at Tilda's Tavern. It's a grand little place. I've been there once or twice and it's highly respectable. Your mother need have no qualms about Hetty performing there. She was rather worried at first, I gather?'

'Yes, she was,' Grace agreed. 'She seems to have got used to the idea now, though. But I can't persuade her to go and listen, though Hetty's singing Gilbert and Sullivan songs. They're Mam's favourites, and mine as well.'

'And mine.' Edwin nodded in agreement. 'I'll take you, Grace,' he said decidedly. 'We'll go there one night next week and hear Hetty sing. How would you like that?'

'I'd like it very much.' Grace nodded happily.

'Right. That's settled then. Tilda's Tavern next week.' Edwin rose and reached out a hand. 'Come on. We'd better be going back or we'll miss the second act.'

'That was wonderful. Really wonderful.' Grace smiled up at Edwin as they stood on the pavement outside the Grand Theatre.

The whole evening had seemed like a dream to her, completely out of the realm of anything she had experienced before; the elegant splendour of the theatre, the scintillating wit and humour of the play itself and, above all, the nearness of Edwin Donnelly, the touch of his hand upon hers and the gentleness and admiration that shone from his golden-brown eyes as he looked at her. She was aware of his closeness as he guided her from their seats in the circle at the end of the performance, his hand tucked beneath her elbow in a proprietorial manner as they moved with the crowd towards the exit. Grace was filled with a quiet exultation at the sounds and the scents that surrounded her; it was all so thrilling. Now and again she felt the softness of fur against her face as an elegantly clothed woman brushed against her. She smelled the aroma of expensive perfume, and the more commonplace, though not unpleasant, smell of camphor. All around her was the murmur of conversation as the departing audience discussed the play, some in quiet cultured voices, others in more strident tones resounding across the heads of the crowd.

'Another triumph for Mr Wilde.'

'Yes, poor man. Not that he's in any position to appreciate it.'

'The least said about that the better, my dear.'

'Years ahead of his time, of course. Such a brilliant writer.'

'And it all ended so happily.'

That was what Grace remarked to Edwin now as she smiled up at him. 'I'm so glad it ended like that. I wondered how it was all going to sort out, it seemed so complicated. But it had a happy ending.' She nodded contentedly. 'I do like stories to have a happy ending.'

'So do I, Grace. So do I.' Edwin's eyes were serious as he looked down at her, then he reached out and stroked her cheek, so very gently, with the tip of his forefinger.

'And I'm having a lovely time. Thank you for bringing me, Edwin.' Grace was discomfited for a moment by the grave, unfathomable expression on his face, especially as he had seemed so light-hearted all evening. But his seriousness was of short duration. Just as suddenly he grinned at her again.

'The evening's not over yet,' he whispered, leaning closer to her and putting his arm protectively round her shoulders. 'Come on. Let's see if we can get a cab.'

There were a couple of hansom cabs on the far side of the road, together with one of the more preponderant four-wheeled 'growlers' and a few smaller carriages belonging to private individuals. Grace shook her head as Edwin tried to steer her through the crowds towards them. 'No, I'd much rather walk, that's if you don't mind. It's such a lovely evening.'

'That's fine with me,' Edwin replied. 'I just thought you might like to go home in style, but I agree with you. It's a shame to waste God's good fresh air by shutting ourselves up in a stuffy cab.'

It was, indeed, a glorious evening, cold, but crisp and clear, the sky a backcloth of dark-blue velvet pinpointed with stars glittering like silver sequins. Grace didn't want it to end, which was why she had suggested, somewhat diffidently, that they should walk. The crowd of theatre-goers thinned out as they walked up Church Street and turned left into Abingdon Street on their way to North Shore. Edwin took her hand and tucked it into the crook of his arm. It felt just right there and he adjusted his long stride to keep time with her shorter steps. She had been aware before when walking beside him, on the occasions he had accompanied her home from the shop, of the thrusting eagerness of his gait and she had some-times almost had to run to keep up with him. Now, tonight, they seemed perfectly attuned, their footfalls echoing back in unison across the concrete pavements.

'I've only just thought,' she said suddenly, 'how selfish of me to suggest we should walk. You'll have to walk all the way home again, won't you? And it's such a long way, the opposite direction altogether from where I live. Oh dear. I'm sorry, Edwin. I should have thought.'

'Now don't you go worrying about that.' Edwin smiled as he saw the look of consternation on her face and the concern in her deep brown eyes. And all over such a little matter. Goodness, she was so lovely. Not just her face and her dainty figure, but the whole of her. All of the attributes, the physical and the mental, and the spiritual aspect, too, he guessed, that added together made up the person of Grace Turnbull. She was a truly lovely girl and Edwin felt himself give a sudden involuntary gasp as he looked at her. He knew in that moment that he had fallen in love with her. Teasingly he touched the tip of her nose with his finger as though to make light of the stupendous realisation that had just dawned upon him.

'Don't you go worrying your pretty head about that,' he said again. 'I can always get a cab if I feel like it. But I've told you, I enjoy walking. I walk to the shop every morning and home again at night, and I think nothing of going for a five-mile walk along the promenade when the mood takes me. I must admit, though, I haven't done that very much lately, not since I took up bicycling.'

'You have a bicycle, Edwin?' said Grace eagerly. 'How wonderful.'

'Yes. I bought it about a year ago,' he told her. 'One of the new safety bicycles by Raleigh, but I didn't use it very much until this summer when I joined the cycling club.' He went on to tell her about their Sunday jaunts along the coast, south to St Annes or north to Cleveleys and Fleetwood. 'But I prefer it when we go inland,' he told her, 'along the banks of the Wyre, or towards the Trough of Bowland and the Bleasedale Fells. Blackpool's a marvellous place – believe me, there's no other place to compare with it in my book – but I have to admit that it's not beautiful. I like to see a bit of greenery for a change, fields and trees and hedgerows. I'm afraid you don't see much of that in dear old Blackpool, much as I love it.'

'Do you know, that's just what I think,' said Grace, delighted that the two of them should be so much in agreement. 'I love it here in Blackpool. I've been so happy since we moved here. The air's so fresh and clean, it seems to sparkle with newness. You can't say that about Burnley, where we lived before. A dirty, smoky place it is, but you can soon get away from it, up on to the moors. Yes . . .' Grace sighed. 'I must admit I do miss the trees and the fields and the green grass. And the hills, of course. I miss the hills. It's so flat in Blackpool.'

'Flat as a pancake,' Edwin agreed. He grinned at her. 'Ideal for cycling, though. You see any amount of cyclists around the Fylde. Women, too, as well as men these days, although our club is strictly for men.'

'Yes, I know a lot of women seem to be taking up cycling,' said Grace. 'Even our Hetty and I were thinking of getting bicycles. It was Hetty's idea, not mine, you might know,' Grace laughed, 'but I think I'd like to have a try. Perhaps when it's spring again. But I have heard how skirts can get tangled up in the wheels. I shouldn't like to fall off.'

'Some women hitch them up,' Edwin told her, amused to see a look of embarrassment cross her face. She lowered her eyes demurely. 'And some of the more daring women are even wearing knickerbockers like the men.'

'Good gracious! I don't think I should like that,' said Grace in some alarm. 'And I'm quite sure Mam wouldn't approve.' She gave a little laugh. 'Come to think of it, though, it's just the sort of thing our Hetty would do. But I don't know whether I'd ever be able to do it. Ride a bicycle, I mean. How do you manage to keep it upright? Doesn't it wobble about all over the place?'

Edwin laughed. 'You might be a bit wobbly at first, but you'd soon get the hang of it. And there's

197

no finer place than Blackpool for learning to ride a bicycle. Miles and miles of promenade, it's just made for bicycling. You just need somebody to hold on to the saddle at first to keep you steady, then before you know where you are you're bowling along on your own. It's a wonderful feeling. Yes, you get a bicycle, Grace, as soon as you can. Then when it's spring we can go for rides, just you and me, into the countryside.'

The street was quiet and deserted and Edwin put his arm around her, drawing her closer to him. 'There are some beautiful spots, not very far away. Fields and trees and a little stream – all the things you're missing, Grace. And I know a wood where there's a carpet of bluebells in the springtime. I'll take you there. We'll enjoy it together. Would you like that, Grace . . .?' Edwin let his voice linger on the sound of her name. Such a beautiful name – he loved repeating it over and over – for such a sweet, graceful young woman.

'I would love that, Edwin.' Her voice was the merest whisper and, as she smiled up at him again, the stars in the dark-blue velvet sky were not as bright as the twin stars that were Grace's eyes.

Close to the high wall that surrounded North Station he drew her into a pool of shadow and gathered her into his arms. He held her close for a moment, not speaking, feeling the softness of her hair and that dear little fur hat against his cheek, smelling the fresh, clean, lavender-tinged scent of her skin, aware of the stillness and quietness and serenity that was Grace. His beloved Grace, for now he knew without any shadow of a doubt that he loved her. Cupping her face between his hands, he bent down until his lips rested gently upon hers. They felt soft and cool beneath his own and as he heard her faint gasp of surprise Edwin put his arms round her again. He felt her lips part as the intensity of his kiss increased and her arms went round him, clinging to him, clinging as though she couldn't bear to let him go.

'Grace . . . my Grace. You're so lovely,' he murmured into the softness of her hair and her fur collar. She did not speak, but he was aware of her happiness and contentment as she snuggled against him, and when she raised her head and looked up at him, her delicate little face upturned as a flower to the sun, the smile she gave him was one of unmistakable joy.

'Thank you, Edwin,' she breathed, and he laughed out loud for sheer delight at her, the happy sound echoing back from the high brick walls.

'Oh, Grace . . . Grace,' he whispered, surprised by the sound of his own laughter in the dark stillness of the street. 'Whatever are you thanking me for? I should be thanking you. And I do thank you, my darling Grace, for making me so happy.'

His lips closed upon hers again in a kiss that told more of a sweet, gentle promise than of passion. He felt her response to him, full of the anticipation of blossoming love, of as yet undiscovered delights, of the pleasures they would share together as winter gave way to spring. For Edwin knew that when springtime came round he wanted to share it with Grace. He felt his senses and his body aroused at the nearness of her, but it was a very gentle arousal. He knew that with this quiet, rather shy girl he would need to proceed carefully. Passion and the desires of his body would have to wait awhile. But, for the moment, Edwin was content. He loved Grace and, from the way she looked at him, he felt sure that she loved him in return.

'I'm happy too . . . darling,' she murmured now, her voice faltering a little uncertainly on the last word. Edwin felt as though his heart would burst with happiness. She had said it. She had called him 'darling'. No longer was he Mr Edwin or even Edwin; he was 'darling', an endearment reserved just for lovers.

He felt the laughter bubbling up inside him again like a wellspring as he kissed her once more, teasingly this time on her lips then on the tip of her pointed little nose. 'Come along,' he said gently. 'I'd better take you home now. It wouldn't do for us to be too late, not the first time, or else I'll be in your mother's bad books.'

They walked the rest of the way in a companionable silence, their arms round one another and Grace's head nestling softly against the astrakhan collar of Edwin's greatcoat. At the gate of Welcome Rest they paused and Edwin took her face in his hands and kissed her again tenderly, almost reverently.

'Goodnight, Grace. My dear Grace,' he said softly. 'I'll look forward to next week. Tilda's Tavern, mmm?'

'Mmm . . .' Grace smiled her agreement. 'I'll look forward to it as well. Goodnight, Edwin.' She stood on tiptoe and placed a kiss, as soft as the

200

touch of a butterfly's wing, on his cheek. And then she was gone.

Edwin walked the couple of miles to his home as easily as if it were but a few yards. He felt as though he were bursting with life, as fresh as the morning, and never could he remember feeling so happy. The sweet thoughts of her were in his mind as he laid his head on the pillow and he fell asleep with the sound of her name on his lips. 'Grace . . . my lovely Grace.'

'Well, who is she then, Edwin?' Clara Donnelly put down her embroidery frame on the chintz sofa where she was sitting, as soon as her son entered the room. Her irascible glance and her hectoring tone warned him that she would stand for no nonsense or prevarication and, in spite of the euphoria of the last couple of days, Edwin felt his heart sink.

Yes, he might have known; it would be Mrs Prescott. When he had caught sight of her and her husband the other night at the Grand Theatre he had wondered how long it would be before the tale drifted back to his mother. He hadn't been sure that she had seen him; their seats had been right at the other side of the circle and when, at the interval, he had accompanied Grace to the bar he had been careful not to look in their direction. But it was obvious to him now that he had been spotted by the hawk-like eyes of Emily Prescott, one of their fellow parishioners at St Joseph's and a bosom friend of Clara Donnelly.

He seated himself in one of the armchairs at the side of the fire and nonchalantly crossed his long legs. 'I beg your pardon, Mother?' he said in a polite voice, putting his head on one side quizzically. 'Who . . .? I'm not sure that I know what you mean.'

'Don't play games with me, Edwin. You know perfectly well what I'm talking about. That young woman you took to the theatre on Tuesday. Who was she?'

Edwin didn't answer. Idly he swung one foot and drummed his fingers casually on the chair arm, a half-smile playing round his lips. He stared into the fire, not at his mother.

'Come along, I'm waiting. What's her name and who is she? I want to know.'

'I don't really see that her name matters, Mother.' Edwin's tone, though cool, was still polite. 'She's a friend of mine, someone that I have met at the shop, and that's all that you need to know. She's a . . . friend.'

'Friend!' Clara almost spat out the word. 'From what Emily Prescott was telling me she's a darned sight more than a friend. Making sheep's eyes at one another in t'circle for all the world to see!' Her voice rose a few decibels and in doing so lost some of its refinement. 'Who is she? Some money-grabbing little minx, I don't doubt, who's got her eye on the main chance.'

Like you had, Mother. The words formed in Edwin's mind, but he didn't give voice to them. But his mother's remarks had angered him and he found his former trepidation fast disappearing. Why shouldn't he acknowledge Grace? It wasn't as if the visit to the theatre was to be an isolated occurrence. He intended to see Grace again and to

202

go on seeing her many times, so the sooner his family knew about her the better it would be.

He threw caution to the winds. 'All right, Mother. I'll tell you, but only because I choose to do so. Whoever I take to the theatre has nothing whatsoever to do with you, but as you seem so anxious to know I may as well put you out of your misery. Her name is Grace. Grace Turnbull. She is employed at the shop in the haberdashery department.

'A shop assistant?'

Edwin had to bite back a laugh. His mother's tones were for all the world like those of Lady Bracknell in *The Importance of Being Earnest*, when she had exclaimed, 'A handbag?'

'An ordinary little shop assistant,' Clara went on, 'and you go taking her along to the best seats in the circle as though she were somebody important?'

'Yes, Mother. That's right. Grace is a shop assistant.' He smiled sardonically. 'Like you were when you met Father.'

'How dare you, Edwin!' Two bright spots of colour burned on Clara's cheeks and her pale-blue eyes flashed angrily. 'How dare you speak to me like that?'

'Because it's true, Mother. You were a shop assistant when you met Father, in the millinery department, I believe, at Donnelly's store. Grandfather's store and now Father's. And he met you and fell in love with you and married you. That's all true, isn't it, so what's wrong with saying it?'

'It was nobbut a twopenny-halfpenny place then. There were no posh carpets on the floor –

just bare boards it was then – and only a handful of assistants an' all. We had to work like blazes for our money, from dawn till dusk, and all for a few paltry shillings. Worked our fingers to the bone, we did. Those lasses today, they don't know they're born compared with what we had to put up with. Cloakrooms and washbasins and all that. Your father spoils them. And I'm telling you straight, I'm not having some jumped-up little shop assistant getting her claws into my son.'

Edwin bit his tongue, though the anger was boiling up inside him. From what he had heard, his mother – Clara Riley as she had been then – had done precious little work in the shop after she had met William Donnelly. 'Got her claws into him' was the expression Edwin had overheard more than once, the same words that Clara had used about Grace. The store, as she so rightly said, had been a very ordinary establishment then, but the potential of Donnelly's Draper's had been obvious to everyone. It wasn't just the shop assistants who had had to work hard, and Edwin knew that, contrary to his mother's complaint, their wages had always been reasonable. His father, too, and his grandfather before him had worked unflinchingly in the building up of the department store, now one of the finest shops in the town.

And his mother hadn't done too badly out of it either, Edwin thought as he glanced round the room. The morning room, his mother's private domain, although it was not morning now but early evening. Edwin had known when she had summoned him here on his return from the shop

204

that something serious was afoot and he had guessed, too, what it would be. This was where Clara liked to conduct all her affairs, both business and family matters, like the lady of the manor exercising control over her minions. This was where she interviewed her servants and gave them their orders for the day, not that there were very many of them or many orders to be given. They had only two servants, the cook-cum-housekeeper and the maid, who, between them, coped with all the work in the house and shared a room in the attic.

His mother would have loved an army of servants; kitchen maid, parlour maid, 'tweeny' and butler, to say nothing of a footman and coachman. But, to Clara's annoyance, they owned no carriage. There was a semicircular drive, though, running from the gate past the front lawn, up to the front door and out again at the other side, but it was a symbol of aspiration rather than fact. A family needed to be very wealthy to own a carriage and here William Donnelly had dug in his heels. It wasn't necessary, he maintained; it would be a needless extravagance. William, like many Northerners, was careful with his hard-earned 'brass'. He and Edwin could walk to the shop, he had said; it was only a mile or so to the centre of the town, and Clara, when she wished to go shopping or making social calls could hire a cab. Edwin had admired his father for sticking to his guns about this although in most respects Clara seemed to get her own way.

There was nothing stinted in this room in which she took such a pride. The morning room in the

Donnelly household was the equivalent of the parlour, the room so esteemed by women in comfortable working-class families. The class to which Clara really belonged, but to which she would not admit. She fancied herself as upper class or even 'gentry', and the words 'in trade' stuck in her throat, though she had done very well out of her husband's business acumen. Here, in Clara's prized morning room, the chairs and curtains were of flowered chintz with the dainty design cleverly repeated in the wallpaper. Chelsea figures, a shepherd and shepherdess, stood at either end of the Adam fireplace, and in the corner was the glass-fronted cabinet where Clara kept her ornamental china – Meissen and Dresden figures, and tea and coffee sets by Minton and Royal Worcester. When she was interviewing her servants she liked to sit at her rosewood writing desk but tonight, though the occasion was far more of an interrogation than an informal chat, she had chosen to sit on the sofa.

Edwin was glad of that. It made her just that little bit more approachable and, though he was angry with her, he had the sense to see that nothing was to be gained by losing his temper.

He tried to speak reasonably now. 'There's no question of Grace getting her claws into me, as you put it, Mother. I enjoy her company and I've taken her to the theatre, just the once. I don't see the harm in that.'

Clara sighed and tutted with exasperation. 'You've been awkward side out ever since you threw over poor Constance, and on her twenty-first birthday, too. All this cycling and book-reading instead of settling down and getting wed like any normal young fellow. And when you do start taking notice of a young woman you have to go and choose a shop assistant. We had high hopes for you, your father and I, and Mr Whitehead too. There's the business to consider, as you know very well. Donnellys and Whiteheads have a shared interest in the restaurant and you're doing your damndest to wreck it. You're plain selfish, Edwin . . .'

'Now, hold on, Mother. The restaurant has nothing to do with Constance and me, and you know it. Mr Whitehead and Father are business partners. They're not bothered two hoots about what Constance and I choose to do. It's only you and Mrs Whitehead who were so upset about it, though heaven knows why. I told you at the time, I had made no promises and I knew that Constance wasn't the right girl for me. Anyway, it seems as though she thinks so too. She's quite friendly with Herbert Mallinson now, the chief cashier at Whitehead's.'

'Hmm. So I've heard.' Clara's tone was grim. 'But nothing can come of that. He's not a Catholic. I only hope this Grace . . . whatever she's called is a Catholic. There's no good'll come of it, Edwin, if she isn't.'

'I think you're looking too far ahead, Mother. Just because I take a young lady to the theatre it doesn't mean that I intend to marry her.' But I do, Mother, I do, Edwin thought to himself. Whatever the problem, whatever heartache or dissension it might cause with his family, he intended to marry her. Eventually. 'As a matter of fact, though, she isn't a Catholic. Grace Turnbull and her family are Methodists.'

'Turnbull . . .?' said Clara, her forehead creasing in a frown. Then, 'Turnbull . . . that family,' she shouted, her voice shrill with anger. 'How could you, Edwin? How could you? It's worse than I thought. Your father's been telling me about her. Martha Turnbull – it's the woman that's baking cakes for the café, isn't it? A nice little body he says she is, I'm not denying that, but they're not our class, Edwin. Why, the woman keeps a lodging house of all things, and one of the daughters sings in a public house. And your father says that both of the lasses, the one that sings and this . . . this Grace, used to work in a mill.'

'Yes, that's right, Mother. Grace worked in the cotton mill in Burnley.'

'A mill girl!' Clara's lips curled derisively. 'And now, to make matters worse, you tell me she's a Methodist. Oh, really, Edwin! It wouldn't have been so bad if she'd been Church of England, at least that's a bit more respectable, but one of them Prim Ranters. Bible-bashers, that's what they are, the whole lot of them.'

Edwin smiled, determined not to lose his temper. 'I very much doubt it, Mother. Grace goes to church on a Sunday, the same as we do. I would have thought that that was to her credit. I don't know whether she reads the Bible or not, but if she does then I would say that that was a point in her favour as well. It's more than we do,' he added pertinently. 'But to say that she's a Prim Ranter is just ridiculous. She goes to the Wesleyan Method-

208

ist church, Springdale, the one at North Shore. As far as I know there aren't any Primitive Methodists, Prim Ranters as you call them, in that area.'

'They're all the same. All tarred with the same brush,' said Clara stubbornly, 'and I want nowt . . . nothing to do with them. And if you've any sense you'll find yourself a proper young lady, one that goes to the right sort of church, just as soon as you can.'

Her eyes softened just a touch as she looked at her son and he fancied that he could see the glimmer of a tear misting the steely pale blue of her gaze. At least her glance was more kindly now and she tried to smile. 'No good can come of it, Edwin, you take it from me. I've seen it many times. Catholics and Protestants, they're poles apart, when it comes to marrying, that is. Yes – I know I was only a shop girl when I met your father, but at least I was a Catholic and that's what made all the difference.'

'Times are changing, Mother,' said Edwin calmly. 'A few more years and we'll be in a new century. Anyway, as I've told you, it isn't as if I've asked Grace to marry me.' But I will, Mother. I will, said the voice inside his head. 'Don't worry about me. I'm a big boy now.'

'Just be sensible, love. I only want what's best for you.' Clara's tone was less harsh now. 'You've such a promising future ahead of you. Don't go throwing it all away on . . .'

Her words were interrupted by a knock at the door and the entry of the maid-of-all-work, clad in her white apron and cap, ready to wait at the table. 'Dinner is served, ma'am.' She lowered her eyes deferentially as she bobbed a curtsey.

'Thank you, Lily.'

Edwin repressed a smile as his mother preened herself and rose from the sofa like Queen Victoria from her throne.

'Don't worry, Mother,' he said, taking her arm. 'I won't do anything foolish. Trust me?'

But he was more determined than ever that, when the time was right, he would ask Grace Turnbull to marry him.

Chapter 10

From the small stage of Tilda's tavern Hetty glanced round at the audience. Her gaze rested first on one face, then on another as she sang, and all the while she was smiling so that each person who watched her felt as though the song she was singing was for them and them alone. She had proved popular from the very first night, a sensation, Joss Jenkinson had been heard to boast. And now the announcement, 'The one and only Henrietta, the Girl with the Sparkling Eyes', would be greeted by cheers and thumps on the table from her admirers, and there were many of these, increasing nightly as the tales of her popularity spread.

Hetty revelled in it all: the chatter and the laughter; the chink of glasses; the smoke drifting gently from pipes and cigars enveloping the whole scene in a misty blue haze; the mixed aroma of ale and meat pies and coffee; and, above all, the wonderful feeling that she was among friends.

All her close friends and family had been to hear her sing, well, nearly all of them. Mam, to Hetty's disappointment, was still proving obdurate in her refusal to set foot in a public house, something she had never done in all her life and something she was convinced would set her feet firmly on the road to hell and eternal damnation. Hetty was only amazed that her mother had thrown herself wholeheartedly into the preparations for her stage début, sewing for her and helping her to choose suitable songs.

Together they had gone to the Prince of Wales' Market in Bank Hey Street and rummaged through the immense stock of sheet music that was available on the book stall. Martha had previously found a few dog-eared copies of Gilbert and Sullivan songs at the back of the sideboard drawer, mementoes of happy times when they had sung together as a family and which she hadn't wanted to throw away. And Bill, the pianist at Tilda's Tavern, had come up with a few well-tried favourites. But at Mr Bannister's market stall they had found lesser-known songs which Hetty was anxious to introduce to her public after she had made her mark with the more popular pieces. 'Love is a Plaintive Song' from *Patience*, airs from *The Sorcerer* and *Princess Ida*, and 'Were I thy Bride' from *The Yeoman of the Guard* which she had chosen to sing as her final song tonight.

> 'Were I thy bride,
> Then all the world beside
> Were not too wide
> To hold my wealth of love . . .'

Hetty sang as her eyes wandered round the upturned, delighted faces of her audience.

She smiled at Albert:

'Upon thy breast
My loving head would rest
As on her nest the tender turtle dove,'

she trilled as she looked fixedly into his eyes, and
Albert winked and grinned back at her.

Hetty felt her heart warm as she watched him.
He looked as though he were positively bursting
tonight with pride and self-esteem, and Hetty
knew that that was something she had done for
him. He was sitting just a few feet from the stage
with some of his pals from work. He had risen in
their estimation, he had told Hetty, since they had
discovered what a charming young woman was
walking out with him. He had overheard some of
their comments – 'The sly old dog! Who'd have
thought it?' 'Our Albert's obviously not so green
as he's cabbage-looking' – and when his charming
companion actually started singing at Tilda's Tavern, well, their incredulity knew no bounds. Yes,
Albert was very much one of the lads these days.
And to think that, in the beginning, he had been
even worse than her mother in opposing her
singing.

Alice was here tonight with her husband,
Henry, her brother Sam Pickering, and his wife
Elinor. They were not sitting with Albert who
was with his mates, but further back on the
other side of the room. Henry was an older
version of his son, Hetty thought, as her glance
rested upon him now. The same fair hair that
flopped over his brow, and kindly grey eyes

which could hold the same apprehensive look when he felt that his wife was behaving in too gregarious a manner. Alice was the one with the spirit and gaiety, whereas Henry was more solid and sober, each complementing the other in a marriage that anyone with only half an eye could see was a happy one. Just as we would be, Hetty reflected.

She had heard it said that if a man wanted to know what the girl he intended to marry would look like by the time they had celebrated their silver wedding then all he had to do was to look at her mother. She supposed that it applied to the father as well. Albert, she was sure, would turn out to be just like his father. He was already the spitting image of him except that whereas Albert was clean-shaven Henry sported a luxuriant moustache and side-whiskers. And Albert would, no doubt, resemble his father in disposition as well. He would be a dependable, faithful husband, just as Henry was to Alice.

Not that Hetty and Albert were engaged or anything like that, but he had hinted more than once that as soon as he was earning a bit more he would buy her a ring. Then she would belong to him 'good and proper', he avowed, and Hetty had laughingly gone along with the notion. She was not averse to the idea of belonging to Albert . . . eventually. But she had wanted a bit of fun first, which was why she had been so adamant about accepting Joss Jenkinson's offer.

And how thrilling it all was, standing up there on the stage, singing away, with the audience practically eating out of her hand. Hetty couldn't ever remember feeling so happy.

> 'And all day long
> Our lives should be a song . . .'

Hetty held out the full skirt of her silky lemon
frock as she gently swayed her body and bent her
head in time to the music. There was nothing
provocative in her movements, or in her dress,
which could even be called demure, with its long
full sleeves and high neck – Mam had insisted on
that – and a frilled bodice trimmed with lace.
Martha, with some assistance from Grace, had
run it up on the Singer sewing-machine in less
than a week. Hetty had helped by offering her
suggestions and advice, and had stood impatiently
once or twice for a fitting while her mother and
sister had grovelled at her feet with pins in their
mouths and tape measures round their necks.
Hetty knew that she wasn't much good with a
needle or a sewing-machine, not compared with
Mam and Grace, so it was far better to leave the
job to those who were more capable, she had said
with a shrug and a sweet smile.

And another dress was now in the process of
being made, more daring this time, at least as far
as the colour went; a vivid emerald-green taffeta
which would bring out the colour of her eyes. The
dress was still modest – no low-cut bodice or tight
fit round the hips and bosom – but it was fashionable, with huge leg-of-mutton sleeves and scal-
loped flounces on the skirt. Hetty thought she
might wear a large hat with that dress, with a
curling ostrich feather, instead of going bare-

215

headed as she was at the moment. The audience, she was sure, would love a change of costume.

Hetty smiled beguilingly at the sea of upturned faces, feeling all warm inside as she thought of the new dress that she would wear next week. It was odd, and quite clever, too, she supposed, how she could sing and never once forget the words while, at the same time, her mind drifted in and around a medley of thoughts.

Alice Gregson was enjoying herself tonight, her cheeks all rosy with the small port and lemon in which she was indulging. Alice was not so strict a Methodist as Mam, thought Hetty with a sly inward grin. Her head was swaying slightly in time to the slow rhythm of Hetty's song and when her brother, Sam Pickering, spoke to her Alice merely nodded in reply without even turning to look at him, so entranced did she seem by the music.

Sam Pickering looked such an insignificant little man, not one, you would imagine, who could command such awe or be in control of such a big business venture. His word was revered as gospel, to the members of his own family at least, who held him in high esteem. Hetty knew that it was Samuel who had helped to procure Grace's job at Donnelly's and, likewise, it was Samuel who had helped to convince her mother that Tilda's Tavern was not the den of iniquity that she had feared. It might well be that he was the only one who would be able to persuade Martha to come and listen to her daughter sing. Hetty resolved to have a word with that eminent gentleman later in the evening.

Her eyes drifted to the back of the room, to a table near the door where a group of youths was sitting. One of them was staring at her. Well, they all were, for that matter; Hetty was used to it, but this one . . . Hetty looked again, her eyes lingering for longer than she really wished them to on his face. That swarthy complexion and black curly hair, those deep dark eyes, that half-contemptuous smile curving round his lips. Surely she had seen that lad somewhere before. But where . . .? Then Hetty remembered and, just for a second, she faltered over her words,

'The skylark's trill
Were . . . were but discordance shrill . . .'

It was that gipsy lad, the one that she and Grace had met that day on the beach when they had been told their fortunes. Fortunes that seemed, so uncannily, to be coming true. The gipsy girl had been right about the change of abode and about the two jobs for Hetty, and also about the opposition she would encounter. Mam had opposed her at first, and Albert. What else had the girl said? Something about involvement with a fair young man – that would be Albert – but not without a lot of trouble. And something about somebody being in the way. All a load of bunkum as likely as not, as she had told Grace at the time.

But would you credit it? There was that gipsy lad at the back of the room, grinning at her as bold as brass. Hetty gave a toss of her ginger curls and looked away from him, back to Albert, as her performance drew near to its end. She smiled

217

winsomely at Albert as she sang the closing words of her song,

> 'But then, of course, you see . . .
> I'm not thy bride!'

So there, her roguish glance seemed to say. For a split second there was silence as she stood, looking so small and dainty, in the centre of the stage, then tumultuous applause as the audience clapped and cheered and thumped on the tables. Hetty lowered her head demurely, then, spreading her skirts wide, she bent in a low curtsey. Her whole demeanour was one of simplicity and innocence but, in reality, there was nothing artless about Hetty's conduct. She knew only too well the impression she was making.

He came across to their table a little while later when Hetty, her performance over for the evening, was sitting enjoying a drink of ginger ale and basking in the admiration of Albert's mates.

'So, we meet again.' He inclined his head in her direction. 'I thought as how it was you when I first seed you on the stage, but I couldn't be sure, not till later. I've been hearing such a lot about Henrietta, the Girl with the Sparkling Eyes.' His own eyes sparkled as he grinned at her. 'So I had to come and hear her for myself. Fancy it being you. I could hardly believe my eyes when I seed you up there.'

'Aren't you going to introduce us, Hetty?' Albert's voice sounded strained and when she looked at him Hetty could see no hint of welcome

218

in his grey eyes. 'You've obviously met this . . . gentleman before.'

'I can't very well introduce you when I don't even know his name,' said Hetty carelessly. Oh dear, poor Albert was beginning to feel jealous again. She tossed her head indifferently in the newcomer's direction. 'It's just a lad that me and our Grace met on the beach one day last summer . . . His sister told our fortunes,' she added hurriedly, not wanting Albert to think that she was in the habit of speaking to strange gipsy lads on the sands, 'and he was with her selling . . . medicines and suchlike.' It would be as well not to mention the love potion, she thought, the laughter building up inside her at Albert's discomfiture.

'Reuben Loveday. Pleased to meet 'ee.' The gipsy lad held out his hand to Albert which that young man took, somewhat ungraciously as he muttered, 'How d'you do?'

'And you be Henrietta, of course?' Reuben held out his hand to Hetty and as he smiled at her she could see no boldness, now, in his glance, only warmth and friendliness.

'I'm Hetty,' she laughed. 'Hetty Turnbull's me name. Nobody calls me Henrietta . . . except when I'm on the stage,' she added with a touch of pride. 'And this is Albert, my . . . friend. Albert Gregson.'

Reuben reached for a stool and sat himself down at the corner of the table between Hetty and Albert without waiting for an invitation. Indeed, if he had waited for one it wouldn't have been forthcoming, not, at least, as far as Albert was concerned. 'Our Drusilla was right then, weren't

219

she?' He raised his eyebrows enquiringly at Hetty. She said as how there was a young man, a fair young man if I remember rightly.'

'You shouldn't have been listening. Anyroad,' Hetty shrugged, 'it was just a clever guess, I daresay. The sort of thing she might say to any girl. Don't tell me your sister – Drusilla, did you say she was called? – can really see into the future. I don't believe it.'

'I don't hold wi' fortune-telling and all that sort o' nonsense.' Albert's tone was emphatic and he looked the gipsy lad straight in the eyes, a keen hard stare, before he turned to Hetty. 'And it's the first I've heard of it. You didn't tell me owt about this . . . this fortune-telling lark. An' I tell you what, Hetty; I bet your mother didn't like it.'

'She didn't know about it,' Hetty retorted. 'I'm not that stupid. And you don't need to go telling her either, Albert Gregson. And, if you must know, I didn't tell you because I hardly knew you then. Anyroad, I've never given it a thought since.'

'Please, please . . .' Reuben held up a hand in remonstrance. 'Don't 'ee go falling out on my account. That'll never do. Oh dear.' He gave a rueful smile. 'I seem to have set the cat among the pigeons.' He turned to Albert. 'There's no need for 'ee to get upset about it. Some of the women in our families really are gifted with second sight. Our Drusilla is, but there's no harm in it, I promise 'ee. They ne'er tell the dark side, even if they do see it. They only tell what folks like to hear.'

'It's wrong all t'same. Trying to look into t'future. We don't know what's going to happen, none

220

of us do, and we're not supposed to know neither.' Albert's reply was brusque and his voice sounded harsh, rough almost, after the soft-spoken tones of the gipsy, although Hetty had never thought so before.

Hetty found herself fascinated by Reuben Loveday's voice and way of speaking, the like of which she had never heard before. His voice was deep, yet soft and lilting, as though he were about to burst into song at any moment, and it held traces of an accent which Hetty, who had never been outside Lancashire, was unable to place. His abode might be in Blackpool at the moment, at the gipsy encampment at South Shore more than likely, but Hetty was sure that he originated from another part of the country. A beautiful wild place of mountains and forests, she found herself thinking.

'Anyroad, that's enough about all that. I didn't mean to offend you. Now then, what are you drinking?' Hetty was glad that Albert was trying to be hospitable now, and though his words were blunt and his face was still unsmiling at least he had made the offer.

'Thank 'ee very much.' Reuben smiled. 'I'll have a cider, if 'ee don't mind.'

It sounded like 'zoider', and Hetty felt herself smiling as a wave of sheer delight washed over her. She didn't know what was the matter with her tonight. She had felt so happy up there on the stage that she hadn't thought it possible to feel any happier. But now . . . now she felt like dancing for joy.

''Ee must be proud of Henrietta,' said Reuben

with a smile in Hetty's direction, then an enquiring look at Albert. 'She be a fine singer. I've ne'er heard a better'n.' Hetty was relieved that Reuben was addressing his remarks to Albert rather than to herself. Albert's reaction to the newcomer had at first created an atmosphere that was heavy with resentment and, for a moment or two, Hetty had been anxious about the pair of them. Then Albert had seemed to see sense and a wish to show something of the hospitality for which Northerners were renowned.

'Aye,' he replied with just the trace of a grin. 'She's not doing too badly, I must admit. Folks seem to like her, anyroad. That were a new song tonight, weren't it, Hetty? I've not heard that before.' Reuben's cider had now arrived with another ginger ale for Hetty and a pint of beer for Albert himself. He was certainly splashing his money about tonight.

'Yes. I've a few new numbers up me sleeve, and a new dress an' all. You'll be hearing 'em in a week or two, when I've had a practice with Bill.' Hetty found it hard to keep the elation out of her voice, both at the thought of her new songs and at the new addition to her circle of admirers.

Reuben, though, seemed bent on not paying her too much attention. His next remark was again directed at Albert. 'Do 'ee come along with Henrietta every night? It must be costing 'ee a fair amount in shoe leather,' he laughed, 'to say nothing of ale.'

'Aye, most of the time.' Albert nodded. 'She's here two or three times a week at the moment and I try to come along with her when I can. From the way things are shaping, though, I reckon Joss and Matilda'll be wanting her more often, so I may not always be able to manage it. Sometimes I have to work late, if we've got a big job on.'

'And what is it that 'ee do?'

'Ah'm a joiner. Ah works for me uncle, Sam Pickering. He's got a big business in Blackpool, near to t'station.'

'Same sort o' line as I be in.' Reuben nodded thoughtfully. 'Well, I be more of a wood-carver really than a joiner. I carves all sorts o' bits and pieces to sell at the markets.'

'Clothes pegs?' Albert's tone was a mite sarcastic and Hetty looked sharply at him. She was surprised. It wasn't like Albert to be so cutting.

But Reuben didn't notice, or if he did he was determined not to retaliate. Hetty could see already that this lad was placid and possessed of a wisdom that could withstand the taunts of others who were not of his background. And Hetty felt sure that his tribe were not strangers to insults and ridicule.

'Clothes pegs, of course,' Reuben replied calmly. Then, with a touch of irony, 'We have to keep our womenfolk supplied with clothes pegs to sell. It be what folks expect of us, ain't it? But I makes other things besides; tools for the kitchen, stools, cradles for chavvies . . . babies,' he added, seeing their puzzled looks, 'and I carves little animals and birds . . . all kinds o' things.'

'Jolly good,' said Albert flatly. Then, after a few desultory remarks about the crowded room and the excellence of the supper provided by Matilda and her staff, the conversation seemed to wane.

Bill, the pianist, struck up with the opening chords of 'She's a Lassie from Lancashire', signalling another session of community singing, and Reuben rose to his feet.

'Well, I'll be off then, back to me own mates. They'll be wondering where I be. Thank 'ee for making me so welcome.' Hetty wasn't sure whether or not there was a hint of sarcasm in Reuben's remark, but it didn't show in his face. He grinned at Albert, then at Hetty. 'Nice to meet 'ee both. Cheerio, Albert. Thanks for the drink . . . Henrietta.' His eyes met and held hers for a few seconds. 'I'll come and hear 'ee sing again.'

''Bye, Reuben,' Hetty called cheerfully. 'Nice to see you again.' She noticed that each time he had spoken to her he had used her full name, Henrietta.

'Aye . . . Cheerio, then,' said Albert tonelessly. He gave a deep sigh as Reuben darted away through the crowd, then turned to Hetty. But she was staring round the room, anywhere, it seemed, but at Albert, a rapt expression on her face as she joined in lustily with the chorus of voices,

> 'None could be fairer,
> Or rarer than Sarah,
> My lassie from Lancasheer.'

'Yon chap thinks a lot of himself,' said Albert grumpily as the song came to an end. 'Him and his flippin' wood-carving. Too big for his boots, that 'un.'

'Aw, come on, Albert. That's not fair,' said Hetty, putting her hand on his arm. That wasn't at all the impression that she had formed of Reuben Loveday, but she realised that the green-eyed monster was again plaguing Albert. 'He had to talk about something, didn't he? Happen he thought you'd be interested, with you being a joiner yourself. Anyroad, I thought it was real nice of him to come and say he liked my singing.'

'He needn't have bothered,' said Albert gruffly. 'Making me look a fool an' all. I felt a right idiot, I'll tell you, when I didn't know owt about that fortune-telling.'

'You should have kept quiet about it then,' retorted Hetty. Then, more gently, 'Aw, come on, Albert. Don't let's fall out about it. Look, let's go and have a chat with your mam and dad. And your Uncle Sam's there an' all. I want to ask him if he'll try and persuade Mam to come and listen to me.'

Albert grudgingly agreed and when they joined the group of older people his good-humour seemed to have been restored.

Samuel Pickering readily agreed to use his powers of persuasion on Martha. He was a good-natured little man, like his sister, Alice, and with the same darting, warm brown eyes. Hetty thought again, though, as she looked at him, how very ordinary he appeared. He was small in stature, with an insignificant moustache like a furry brown caterpillar sitting on his upper lip. His face and hands were brown, giving him a monkey-like appearance, and his tweed suit seemed too small for him. Not at all like his brother-in-law, Henry, who gave such an impression of importance in his best black suit, with a watch chain dangling from

225

his waistcoat pocket and his magnificent curling moustache and side-whiskers. And yet it was Samuel who possessed the sharpness and perspicacity, who had built up his joinery business from small beginnings until now it was one of the leading concerns in the town, while Henry, in spite of all his fine looks, was but an employee.

How deceptive appearances could be, thought Hetty. She had been mistaken in her first impression of Reuben Loveday, when she had met him that day on the beach, and again earlier that evening when she had spotted him in the audience. She had thought him bold and impertinent, but she was realising how wrong she had been. She could see already that underneath his brash manner he was a warm and thoughtful person.

She found herself looking for him as she sang, two days later, but to her disappointment he wasn't there.

That November some of the worst storms for many years swept along the Fylde coast. Blackpool was no stranger to the havoc caused by high tides, particularly when combined with gales. Visitors from the inland towns had, indeed, been known to flock there in their thousands to witness the free spectacle put on by Mother Nature. It could be awe-inspiring to watch the gigantic waves hurtling towards the shore, then cascading over the sea wall and across the promenade, drenching anyone who happened to be in their path. Sometimes the tales of destruction were grossly exaggerated, and ghoulish visitors who wished to go back home with lurid stories of the storm damage could find themselves disappointed. For on a windless day the sea could be as calm as a millpond, a sheet of sparkling glass with the sun blazing forth from a sky of cloudless blue. The Irish Sea was a creature of many moods, but there was no mistaking its angry humour one night towards the end of November.

Albert was confined to his bed with a cold that had settled on his chest.

'Right sorry for himself he is, poor lad,' said Alice with a chuckle, when she came across the road to tell Hetty that he wouldn't be able to accompany her to Tilda's Tavern that evening. 'I've told him his number's not up yet, but he's sure he's at death's door. You know what fellers are like when there's owt wrong with 'em. They've not got the stamina us women have, an' that's a fact. Anyroad, I've tucked him up with a hot-water bottle and a drink of hot lemon and he'll sweat it out of him. He'll be as right as rain in a day or two. But he's bothered about you, Hetty love. It's a wild night and he's real worried about you going out on yer own.' Even as she spoke the first drops of rain were pattering against the windowpane and the wind, which had been howling round the house and down the chimney all day, seemed to be gaining in strength. 'Whatever'll you do, love?'

'Not to worry, Mrs Gregson,' said Hetty cheerfully. 'I'll not melt. A drop of rain never hurt anyone.'

'It's not the rain, Hetty, so much as the gales,' said Alice. 'You'll get swept off your feet, lass. I don't suppose you've been out in one of our

227

Blackpool gales, have you? I tell you, you won't be able to stand up against it.'

'Don't worry,' said Hetty again. 'I'm a strong lass, I am. Anyroad, I can get a cab if it's too bad.' She glanced towards the window. 'Yes, I reckon that's what I'll have to do. I'll have to be a toff tonight and get meself a cab.' She laughed. 'There's usually one at the corner of the street by the station. Tell Albert not to worry, and I hope he'll soon be better.'

'Sooner you than me,' said Martha with a sniff. 'I wouldn't like to be turning out on a night like this. I'm glad now as I went on Tuesday. I must admit you were right, Alice, you and your Sam. It's a grand little place, is Tilda's Tavern, and I feel happier about our Hetty singing there now I've seen it for meself. Thanks for taking me along with you.'

'There you are, you see. I told you as it weren't a den of vice,' said Alice. 'There's all sorts of folks go there now. Real nobs an' all. Fancy your Grace and her young man going there.'

'He's not her young man, Alice,' said Martha sharply. 'Young Mr Edwin's certainly not our Grace's young man, no matter what folks think. Aye, I know she's been out with him a time or two, but there's nowt in it.'

'No, of course not, Martha,' said Alice soothingly. 'I never thought there was. It was just a slip of the tongue, me saying her young man. I only meant as how it's grand that all them folk are going along to listen to Hetty. She'll be famous afore long.'

'Hmm . . . mebbe,' said Martha without much

enthusiasm. She turned to her daughter. 'Well, if you're going, our Hetty, you'd best cut along afore it gets any worse. Now, mind you wrap up warm. Don't go trailing through t'streets in all them fancy clothes. You'll get 'em all mucky.'

'No, I won't, Mam. I'll take 'em in a bag and change when I get there. And stop worrying. I'll be all right, honest I will. I can take care of meself.'

The crowd was a bit thin in Tilda's Tavern that evening, Hetty noticed as she sang her opening songs, and they appeared less exuberant than usual, preoccupied with their own concerns. The place seemed, for once, to be lacking in atmosphere and Hetty began to feel a little dejected. She wished that Albert were with her. In spite of her brave words she was reluctant to face the journey home on her own, although she knew that Joss and Matilda, bless them, would try to make sure that she was safe, bundling her into a cab if necessary.

> 'Poor wand'ring one,
> Though thou hast surely strayed . . .'

she sang, an old favourite from *Pirates*, as her own eyes strayed round the audience.

She wouldn't admit to herself that she was looking for *him*, and only towards the end of the song did she allow her eyes to drift to the corner by the door where he had sat on the previous occasions. She had seen him only once since that first night, and that time he had merely nodded at her, and had not come to join them again at their table. Little wonder, considering the less than cordial reception he had received from Albert. It was hardly likely that he would be here tonight, not on such an evening of rain and high wind . . .

> 'Take heart of grace,
> Thy steps retrace . . .'

At last she let her eyes drift to the corner, and there he was, Reuben Loveday.

'Poor wand'ring one.' Her song finished on a note of elation and as she swept to the floor in a deep curtsey she felt a spasm of excitement grip her.

She took off her wide-brimmed hat with the curling feather and seated herself at a small table at the side of the room. Even though Albert wasn't with her tonight she could still partake of a drink. Her throat was parched after all that singing and it wasn't, she told herself, like sitting in a pub on her own. Respectable young ladies never did that, but everyone here knew who she was. She was one of the artistes and already a few people were looking in her direction and smiling. She sat demurely, her hands clasped in her lap, waiting for the waitress to come over to her, or so she tried to convince herself. She didn't have to wait long.

'Hello, Henrietta. On your own tonight?'

She glanced up in mock astonishment. 'Hello, Reuben. How nice to see you again. Yes, I'm on my own. Poor old Albert's got a cold.'

'Oh dear, poor chap. Well, it be an ill wind, as

they say.' Reuben grinned as he pulled up a stool and sat down next to her. 'I'll join 'ee . . . if 'ee don't mind?' He raised his eyebrows. ''Ee looks lonesome.'

'No . . . no, I don't mind at all,' said Hetty, her voice trembling a little as the feeling of excitement seized her again.

The feeling didn't abate, but only intensified as she sipped at the port and lemon that Reuben had insisted she should try.

''Ee don't want to be drinking cold lemonade on a night like this,' he protested. 'Have something that'll warm 'ee up a bit.'

Hetty found that the rich ruby-red drink was indeed warming her, bringing a glow not only to her cheeks, but deep inside her, spreading right to the tips of her toes.

'I'm surprised you're here on a night like this,' she told Reuben. 'A lot of the regulars are missing tonight and I can't say I blame them.'

'Oh, it be Luke's birthday,' Reuben replied. 'One o' the lads from the tan.' She assumed he meant the gipsy encampment. 'Us likes to have a bit of a celebration now and again.'

'And now you've left them to come and sit with me?'

'They'll ne'er bother. Don't suppose they'll even miss me.'

Hetty had drunk only halfway down the glass when Joss Jenkinson dashed over to them, his ruddy face showing signs of uncharacteristic anxiety.

'We'll have to get all t'folks out or else we'll be marooned. Look.' He pointed to the back of the

231

room. 'The tide's coming in through t'door.'

Hetty and Reuben looked towards the swing doors that opened into the passage. A trickle of water was seeping underneath the closed doors, just a dribble as yet, but already creeping round the legs of the chairs and tables nearest the exit and the feet of unsuspecting customers. But it wasn't long before more and more people became aware of it and tried to dash for the swing doors and a hasty retreat.

'No, keep 'em closed,' shouted Joss, standing with his arms outstretched, barring the way. 'The passage is all awash and the front bar's flooded already. You'd best go out the back way. Sorry, folks. I'm afraid that's it for tonight. It crept up on us before we could say "Jack Robinson". I've never seen owt like it.'

Once again the capricious tide had scored a victory over the pitiful sea defences. The high granite wall and the rows of pit props were ineffectual against the fury of the wind and the waves. The tide, as it had done many times before, had swept over the sea wall, across the tram track and the wide promenade and into the ground floors of the houses and hotels opposite. Joss and Matilda had been taken unawares. So intent were they on keeping their business going, providing their customers with food and drink and entertainment, and counting the money pouring into the till – for like most Blackpool folk they were not averse to making a handsome profit – that they had overlooked the ominous weather signs. Their feeble attempts now to keep the tide at bay with sandbags and rolls of old carpet were futile. All they could do was evacuate the premises as speedily as possible, then start mopping-up operations and assess the damage.

In a few moments nearly all their patrons had gone, out of the back door not normally used by customers, through the back yard and into a narrow cobbled alley which ran behind the premises. Only a few stragglers were left, and the bar staff who would be staying behind to help to sort out the debris. Reuben was still there, hovering at Hetty's elbow, although his friends, seeing that he was otherwise occupied, had gone.

'Can I stay and help?' said Hetty anxiously to Joss and Matilda. She looked in alarm at the water which was now about an inch deep all over the room. The hem of her emerald-green dress was already sodden and clinging round the ankles of her high-buttoned boots.

'Bless you, lass, no!' said Matilda, her small pixie-like face which had been taut with anxiety relaxing for a moment as she smiled at the girl. Matilda was wielding a sweeping brush almost as tall as herself in an effort to swoosh the water out of the door and back whence it had come. But it was proving an impossible task as she now realised.

'I feel like King Canute,' she said with a chuckle as she propped the brush up against the bar. 'And I'm not managing any better than he did either. I reckon we'll do no good until the tide turns and this blessed wind drops. No, Hetty love. You'd best be getting along home. Your mam'll be worried about you.'

'All right, Mrs Jenkinson, if you're sure. I'll get meself a cab.'

'I doubt if you'll be able to do that, lass,' said Joss. 'Not on t'prom at anyroad. They'll not be able to do owt there. Happen you'd best hang on a bit and see what happens.'

'I'll see her home, Mr Jenkinson,' said Reuben, who had been standing there quietly, listening to the conversation. 'Don't 'ee worry. Henrietta'll be all right with me.'

'Are you sure, lad?' Joss looked doubtfully at Reuben. He had promised Mrs Turnbull that he would look after Hetty and he knew very little about this lad, except that he was a gipsy. It would just happen that young Albert wasn't there, tonight of all nights. Still, this lad seemed decent enough, in spite of his background. He'd been there a few times and never caused any bother. Always most polite, he was, and he seemed a thoughtful young chap. Joss allowed his common sense to prevail; he had always prided himself on his tolerance and his ability to judge every man by his merits, notwithstanding his appearance. 'Well, thanks very much,' he said now. 'I'm very grateful to you, and I know Hetty's mam will be an' all.'

'Yes, thank you, Reuben.' Hetty smiled at him. 'I'll just have to change me frock, though, or else it'll get soaked.'

She hurried into the small cloakroom where the staff kept their coats and quickly changed into her ordinary clothes. Her feeling of excitement had subsided a little by now. Her concern at the storm damage and her anxiety to be safely home and away from it all, in spite of her offer of help, had

234

taken away some of her elation. But she still felt all warm and tingly inside and a light-headed sensation was beginning to give the whole evening the semblance of a dream.

'Leave your fancy togs there,' Matilda told her, 'and I'll take them upstairs to keep them safe. You can't be bothered with carrying a bag on a night like this. You'll have enough to do to keep yourself upright.'

They went out through the back exit, keeping well away from the seafront, but from the corner of the back alley they could see the promenade awash with the swirling water, and the foam-crested waves, as high as a mountain, still cascading over the sea wall like a gigantic waterfall. It was a good half-hour's walk from the Victoria Inn to North Shore where Hetty lived and, in spite of her feeling of unreality and the congenial company, there was a tiny niggle of apprehension gnawing away inside her as to whether or not she would arrive home safely and without the pair of them being swept off their feet. Mercifully the wind had abated a little and a few streets back from the promenade it had lost much of its intensity. The rain, too, was easing off to just a slight drizzle and apart from the odd gust buffeting them whenever they reached a street corner they were able to walk with comparative ease.

'Phew!' Hetty gasped, stopping for a moment in her tracks. 'Just let me get me breath back, Reuben.' She was panting with exhaustion and there was a pain across her chest. This was her first real experience of the notorious Blackpool gales, although she had often been out in the wind and enjoyed the feeling of exhilaration it gave her. But this was something different. Gales such as this brought havoc in their wake, and danger and destruction, and there was a presentiment of hidden menace in the atmosphere. 'Goodness! I've never known a storm like this, have you?'

'I've seen one or two,' Reuben told her. 'But this be the worst storm I've seen in Blackpool.'

'You're not from these parts then?' Hetty had got her breath back now and though the wind was less strong she still hung on to Reuben's arm which he had offered to her. Indeed, at each sudden squall she was obliged to cling to him like a lifeline. 'I didn't think you came from round here. You talk – well, different like.'

Reuben laughed. 'I was born in the Forest of Dean. It be a long way from here, Henrietta.'

'I've never heard of it. Where is it?'

'Gloucestershire, getting on towards Wales. It be a lovely spot, all rushing rivers and hills and trees. I miss it, I tell 'ee, since us came here.'

'Why did you come to Blackpool then?'

Reuben shrugged. 'Oh, us Roms is always on the move. And there was some family trouble earlier this year, so us came along to sort it out.' He stopped abruptly, as though he thought he had said too much. 'But you ain't from Blackpool either. I can tell by the way 'ee talks too.'

'Not far away. We're from Burnley.' Hetty looked at him in surprise. 'How could you tell? We all sound pretty much the same to me. It's still Lancashire.'

'There be a difference though.' Reuben nodded. 'Us Roms have an ear for accents. Besides,

Drusilla said that 'eed have a move, didn't she? I guessed that 'eed only just come to live here. Drusilla were right, weren't she, Henrietta?'

'Yes . . . she was right,' said Hetty slowly, wondering what else Drusilla knew about her. She gave a little shudder of foreboding. 'Why do you keep calling me Henrietta?' she asked him, hurriedly changing the subject, away from Drusilla. 'No one else does. Me name's Hetty. I told you.'

'It suits 'ee, that's why.' Reuben's voice was quiet, almost a whisper. 'Henrietta . . .' The syllables ran off his tongue like music. 'It be a lovely name. Hetty be ordinary, and you ain't ordinary, Henrietta. You be beautiful.'

Hetty didn't answer. She didn't know *how* to answer, as she wasn't used to compliments. Albert wasn't one for flowery language, neither were the other lads that she had met at the mill or at chapel. Reuben wasn't like anyone she had ever met before, but though he spoke in admiring tones his behaviour was most circumspect. Not once did he put his arm round her or show any tendency towards the bold behaviour which he had seemed to exhibit when she had first met him.

She reminded him of that first occasion now. 'When I first saw you, you were selling medicines, but you told Albert you were a wood-carver? What do you really do then?'

'Wood-carving, same as I told 'ee, and the same job as my father does too,' he replied. 'The medicines be just a sideline for us.' He turned and smiled at her. 'A bit of holiday fun, if 'ee like.'

'It's not true then? They can't cure headaches and stomach aches . . . and all that?' She decided

237

not to mention the love potion.

'Of course they can.' Reuben sounded indignant. 'They be powerful potions. There be herbs and berries and all manner of things in 'em. But, like I told 'ee, it's just a sideline. And Mother had asked me to go along and keep an eye on Drusilla. She be a wild 'un at times, our Drusilla.'

They spoke little for the rest of the way, except when Hetty voiced her concern as to how Reuben was to get home again.

'Do 'ee think I'm made of money?' he said, pouring scorn on her suggestion that he should get a cab. 'Cabs ain't for the likes of me. No, shanks's pony be good enough for me. I'll be home afore midnight if I step on it.'

'But it's miles to South Shore,' she exclaimed. 'That's where you live, isn't it?' Reuben nodded. 'It's a good few miles along the prom to Squire's Gate, and you'll have to go the long way round. You can't walk along the prom in weather like this.'

'Now, don't 'ee go worrying about me,' said Reuben, giving her arm a squeeze for the first time. 'I be used to walking. I've walked for miles alongside the vardo when us've been movin' on.'

'Alongside the what?' Hetty looked up at him in puzzlement.

'The vardo . . . caravan, I suppose 'eed say. The waggon.' He laughed. 'I be used to talking Romany talk, but I've made friends with a few gorgios since us moved here. Non-gipsies, I mean, folks like you,' he explained, seeing her puzzled look again. 'I be thinking now that there's a lot to be said for staying in one place.' He grinned at her. 'But don't 'ee worry about me getting back. I promised Mr Jenkinson I'd see 'ee home and I be a man of my word.'

'This is where I live.' Hetty paused at the gate of Welcome Rest, glancing anxiously at the window. She hoped that Mam wasn't peering out looking for her, but the curtains were drawn, shutting out the darkness and the wild weather, and there was no sign of life there, or across the road at Albert's home. The street was deserted. 'Thank you, Reuben, for bringing me home. It was real kind of you.'

'It be a pleasure.' He nodded and his eyes glowed with warmth as he looked at her. He reached out and touched her cheek softly with his finger, then he put his hands on her shoulders and leaned towards her. Very gently his lips touched hers and she moved towards him, willing him to kiss her more fervently. His kiss remained gentle, but it held all the promise of feelings and words as yet unspoken. Reuben held her close for a moment, then released her. 'Goodnight, Henrietta,' he said. 'I'll see 'ee again. Soon, I hope.'

'Goodnight, Reuben.' Hetty's voice was breathy with longing and, for once, she was at a loss for words. He smiled at her, then he turned quickly and walked away.

Hetty felt herself bubbling with excitement as she skipped up the path. Then, as she reached the front door, a thought struck her and she shivered at the cold which, up till now, she had hardly noticed. Albert! What on earth was she to do about Albert?

Chapter 11

The annual Catholic Ball, to be held at the Tower Pavilion in the middle of December, was the social event of the year as far as Catholics were concerned. Edwin couldn't see that there would be any harm in escorting Constance to the event, just the once. The girl had been so much more pleasant lately. When they met at church or at social functions, which they did from time to time, she was always friendly and behaved in such a normal manner towards him that one could almost forget all that had gone before, the bitterness and recriminations and angry scenes that had followed his decision not to become engaged to her.

His mother had made the tentative suggestion a few weeks previously. Edwin had been surprised, considering her former displeasure about the situation between him and Constance, at just how placatory Clara had been.

'Edwin, dear . . .' she had begun, one Sunday morning towards the end of November as they were finishing their breakfast. William had already finished and had gone upstairs to get ready for their habitual attendance at Mass.

Edwin put down his half-empty coffee cup and looked at his mother in surprise. Endearments issuing from her tongue were rare, especially of late. It was not many weeks since she had castigated him so severely about his visit to the theatre with Grace. Since then her manner towards him had been distinctly cool, although she had made no further reference to his keeping company with Grace Turnbull. She was well aware of it, though. Edwin had made no secret of his visit to Tilda's Tavern with Grace, or of his Sunday afternoon walks with her along the promenade. Clara had feigned ignorance of his whereabouts, but her frigid glances and her tight-lipped indifference had been a silent rebuke to him. Yes, his mother knew perfectly well about his gentle wooing of Grace and had shown no sign of being any more resigned to it. Her conciliatory approach, therefore, took him by surprise and immediately his suspicions were aroused.

'Yes, Mother?' He raised his eyebrows and purposely did not smile as he looked at her.

'It's the Catholic Ball next month. I was wondering . . .' She hesitated. 'Do you intend going this time?'

'I haven't given it much thought, Mother,' he answered with an air of detachment. Just what was she getting at? he wondered. Was she trying to find out if he intended taking Grace with him? Edwin had, in fact, considered this. It was something he would dearly love to do. To invite her to an important social occasion such as this would be to acknowledge her fully and would, as it were, set the seal on their relationship. It would show his family and his friends, and Grace too, that his intentions were serious, that, in spite of the difficulties – and there were many – he wanted this girl, eventually, to be his wife.

But Edwin had faltered at such an enormous step. There was Grace herself to consider. She was shy, so very shy, at least with people that she didn't know very well, and she was unused to moving in such circles. He feared that she would be out of her depth in such a gathering and that, rather than furthering their relationship, it might only accentuate the gulf between them and frighten her away. Her mother, he knew, had already had plenty to say about the difference in their social standing, as had his own mother. Then, of course, there was the fact that she wasn't a Catholic. Non-Catholics were not barred from the event; they occasionally went along as the invited guests of their Catholic friends, but they were few and far between. And, here again, Edwin feared that Martha Turnbull would be so condemnatory of the idea that poor Grace would not know which way to turn. He knew that Grace set great store by what her mother said and did, and though she had made tremendous strides already by sticking up for herself and going out with Edwin there was a limit to what Mrs Turnbull would be prepared to accept. And so Edwin had balked at taking the step, knowing full well that, to some extent, his hesitancy was due to cowardice. He loved Grace and when he was with her all his doubts vanished. But when they were apart, which, of necessity, was often, the doubts began to creep back. The whole affair was so very complicated.

But if his mother was attempting to find out, now, more about his relationship with Grace, then he wasn't going to make it easy for her. 'I hadn't really thought of going to the ball this year,' he told her, keeping his voice casual. 'Why do you ask?'

'Well, to be quite honest, dear . . . it's Constance.'

In spite of the mildness of his mother's tone and the rueful smile she gave him, her head a little on one side like a penitent child, Edwin's immediate reaction was one of annoyance. He might have known. Constance again. Why couldn't the girl leave him alone? But then, he reflected in a split second's thought before he answered his mother, that was exactly what Constance had been doing lately; leaving him alone. Her disarming friendliness on the few occasions that they met held no trace of her former distress and pique at his supposed perfidy. All the same, he had no desire to get entangled with the girl again.

'Now, look here, Mother,' he said. 'You know very well how things are between me and Constance. It's over – finished.' He made a cutting movement with his hand. 'You know it and she knows it, and that's the way I want it to stay. I told you so at the time, but you don't seem to realise that I mean what I say. It's all over, long ago.'

'Yes, dear. Of course I know that,' said Clara gently. 'And Constance knows it as well. You must have noticed that she has a lot of other . . .

244

admirers now. There's Herbert Mallinson, he's very attentive. And there's a young Scotsman, apparently, who's interested in her as well. Douglas Brodie, I think he's called, a commercial traveller who often comes down this way. She sees quite a lot of him when he's in the area.'

'Mother,' said Edwin firmly, 'can't you realise that I'm not the slightest bit interested in who Constance sees and who she doesn't see? What she chooses to do is entirely up to her. It's no concern of mine. But you were saying something about the ball, weren't you? Asking me whether I was going or not?'

'Yes, that's right, dear. Like I was saying, it's Constance. She's no one to take her. And she was wondering . . . Well, no, that's not true, it wasn't her idea at all. I should have said that *I* was wondering if you could escort her? The girl can't very well go without a partner, can she? And it isn't as if you'd have to be alone with her. You know that we always go together in a crowd, us and the Whiteheads.'

Edwin was silent for a moment. He had known as soon as his mother had mentioned the girl's name what was coming, but his annoyance had subsided a little now. He idly picked up a spoon, and traced over the pattern of flowers in the white damask cloth. He was damned if he was going to give in easily, though, or with a good grace. 'Why can't one of these other admirers, as you call them, take her then? Herbert Mallinson or that Scotsman – what's he called? – Douglas Brodie. I should think they'd jump at the idea.'

'Mr Mallinson isn't a Catholic,' replied Clara

flatly. 'That's the only thing that the Whiteheads have against him. Apart from that he seems a very suitable young man. But Constance doesn't feel that she can ask him to escort her to a big "do" like that. Anyroad,' Clara's refined tones were beginning to slip a little now as they did when she was off guard, 'it isn't up to the lady to do the asking, is it?'

Edwin didn't answer what he took to be a rhetorical question, but he reflected wryly that he had never known Constance to be backward in coming forward, not when it was a matter of getting her own way. 'And what about the young Scotsman?' he asked. 'Can't he take her?'

'It's doubtful if he'll be in the area, dear. Anyway, the same thing applies, doesn't it? Constance can't very well ask him. The poor lass was quite upset when she was telling me about it. She wants to go to the ball; she's had her new dress ready for ages.'

I'll bet she has, thought Edwin, feeling, to his surprise, a tinge of affectionate amusement at the thought of Constance and her unbridled vanity.

'But she doesn't want to be on her own all evening without a partner. And I can assure you, dear, she wouldn't have dreamed of asking you herself. She's got her pride, has Constance. Besides, she knows that you've been seeing that . . . that girl from the shop.' Although his mother was displaying an unusual gentleness in her words and her manner she still couldn't bring herself, Edwin noticed, to mention Grace by name. 'She wouldn't want you to compromise yourself, not when you're seeing . . . someone else.'

Edwin almost laughed at such a glaring example of Constance's duplicity. Wasn't she herself engaged in double-dealing with, according to his mother, a couple of beaux dancing attendance on her? But Clara hadn't seemed to see the irony of her remark.

'So I promised her that I'd ask you, dear, and see what you thought about it. It would be just the once, Edwin. There would be no question of you . . .'

'All right, Mother.' Edwin sighed. 'Just the once. So long as you understand quite definitely that it's the one and only occasion.'

Edwin felt his resistance and his annoyance draining away. There could be no harm in it. It was obvious from Constance's behaviour when she met him that she no longer harboured any amorous feelings towards him. He suspected that she had regarded him, in the main, as a good catch. No, there could be no possible danger in indulging Constance just this once by escorting her to the ball. And it wouldn't do any harm to keep on the right side of his mother. Maybe she was beginning to be reconciled to the idea of his friendship with Grace; she had at least mentioned it, which must be a step in the right direction, albeit a small step. And he was so sure of his love for Grace and of her reciprocal feeling for him that nothing could possibly harm it, certainly not his spending a few brief hours in the company of another young woman.

As Edwin smiled at his mother, the first time he

247

had really smiled at her for many weeks, he felt unusually tolerant towards her. 'Yes,' he said. 'You can tell Constance that I'll take her.'

'Thank you, Edwin.' Clara looked down for a moment as she folded her damask napkin and placed it in the silver serviette ring, so her son didn't see the smug expression on her face. When she looked up again she was smiling brightly. 'But you'll be able to tell her yourself, won't you? You'll be seeing her this morning.'

Edwin did tell Constance, as they stood on the pathway outside St Joseph's church, the Donnellys and the Whiteheads and other parishioners, exchanging chitchat after the celebration of morning Mass. She was looking very elegant in a well-fitting sage-green coat with a fur collar and fur trimming down its length, and a matching green hat with a shallow brim and a cornucopia of coloured feathers and flowers atop that added inches to her height. She smiled directly at Edwin's eyes as he spoke to her.

'I believe you require an escort to the ball, Miss Whitehead,' he said in a jocular fashion. 'Will I do?'

'I suppose so. Beggars can't be choosers,' Constance replied in an equally bantering manner. 'Thank you, Mr Donnelly.' She bobbed a mock curtsey and they both laughed.

Edwin was glad to see her in such a light-hearted mood. No doubt she would have preferred one of her other swains to accompany her and he suspected that he, Edwin, was just a stopgap. If he was any judge, Constance would be married before many months had passed. He failed, however, to see the self-satisfied look on her face as she walked down the church path, like the cat who had got the canary.

The Tower Pavilion was like a summer garden, gay with a myriad of multicoloured butterflies, as the ladies twirled and pirouetted showing off their magnificent ball gowns. There were vivid colours that dazzled the eye, crimson, emerald, saffron yellow and sapphire blue, and more delicate hues, lilac, lavender and primrose or the soft pinky rose shade of the dress that Constance was wearing. The ballroom floor, constructed from more than thirty thousand separate blocks of mahogany, oak and walnut, had been laid on a base of concrete and steel to withstand the hobnailed boots of the most exuberant dancers from the Lancashire inland towns. Not that there were any hobnailed boots in evidence tonight, only dancing slippers of satin and shoes of kid and patent leather, and the intricate inlaid pattern of the floor, a kaleidoscope of rich brown, shading from glowing russet to palest fawn, could scarcely be seen between the shifting feet.

The ballroom, with its red plush-velvet chairs, gilded balconies and brightly frescoed ceiling, was quite beautiful. The supper of daintily cut sandwiches, bite-sized sausage rolls and cakes and delicious sherry trifle was excellent, and Edwin found, to his surprise, that the company was agreeable too. He had been prepared merely to tolerate the combined forces of the Donnelly and Whitehead families and others of their cronies, reminding himself, as he had reminded his mother, that it was just the once. But he found that he was enjoying the food and the fun and friendliness, all the ingredients that together made up a pleasurable evening.

He had to admit that Constance looked lovely in her delicate rose-pink gown, a change from the pale blue which she so often chose to wear. Her dress was low-cut, revealing the milky whiteness of her shoulders and the swell of her breasts, just visible beneath the frothy lace edging. The full skirt swayed alluringly as she walked and danced and her elbow-length net gloves and a pink silken rose in her hair completed the charming picture that she made. And she knows it, too, thought Edwin, regarding her with affectionate good-humour, but comparing her in his mind with his beloved Grace.

Yes, Grace would have been out of her element here. When he thought of her he pictured a fireside, a welcoming haven of warmth and love. Or a starlit night, and he and Grace walking alone through the dark streets with their arms entwined, her eyes shining more brightly than the stars in the sky as she smiled at him. Constance, he thought, as he listened to her aimless chatter and brittle laugh, was more at home in a setting such as this, amidst all the glitter and gaiety.

Edwin smiled now as he thought of Grace, listening with half an ear to the inconsequential chat going on around him. He would be seeing her again soon. On Sunday they would walk on the cliffs or on the pier if it wasn't too cold, and next week he was taking her to a performance of *The Gondoliers* at the Opera House. He had explained to her, of course, about his compulsory attendance at the ball this evening and she had smiled and nodded understandingly. But he had omitted to tell her, he reflected with a prick of conscience, that Constance would be his partner.

They were alone together very little that evening, save when they were dancing, and Edwin made sure that he didn't dance exclusively with Constance. There were several young men who were desirous of her company and Edwin, too, found that for him there was no shortage of willing partners. The last waltz, though, perforce, belonged to Constance.

Edwin felt mellow and relaxed after partaking of several whiskies, more than was his normal habit. Though not abstemious, he liked to keep a clear head, and he knew from past experience that more than a couple of drinks took the keen edge off his powers of reasoning. In business one had to keep alert and in full control of one's senses at all times, but tonight . . . well, tonight it didn't matter so much. As he drifted round the ballroom floor to the strains of a slow waltz with Constance in his arms, he felt her soft cheek against his and the silky tendrils of her pale-blonde hair escaping from her chignon and tickling his face. Edwin felt contented and at peace with the world. He gave Constance a brotherly hug as they danced, and he heard her sigh with contentment and felt her move closer to him.

In the depths of the feather bed Constance hugged herself gleefully. It had been a wonderful evening and, as far as Edwin was concerned . . . well, so far, so good. She wanted him so much. Oh, dear God, how she wanted him and – please God – she would get him too. Tonight was only the first step, and she tucked away at the back of her mind the secret knowledge of how malleable Edwin was when he had had a few drinks.

She had long since decided that anger and peevishness were not weapons to be used in her fight to win him back. She had felt angry at first, though, and humiliated at his treatment of her, so much so that she had wanted to kick him and pound him with her fists. To be made to look such a fool on her twenty-first birthday had been unforgivable. But when her fury had subsided she had realised that that was not the way. She would win him back by guile and a pseudo-friendliness and nonchalance that was totally at variance with what she was really feeling. Constance was not used to having her desires thwarted; ever since she had been a little girl she had been indulged by her parents and elder brothers and sisters, but this was one indulgence that they couldn't grant her. This time it was up to her.

Her plan had seemed, for a time, to be working. Though Edwin, admittedly, hadn't made any overtures towards her, he was, at least, more amiable and was showing no interest in any other young women, only, according to his mother, in his books and his cycling. And, as far as Constance was concerned, her own friendships with suitors such as Herbert Mallinson and Douglas Brodie were but passing whims, entered upon lightly and just as lightly to be discarded when Edwin came to his senses. As Constance was

252

determined that he would.

And then Grace Turnbull had arrived on the scene. Constance had been unable to believe her ears when Clara Donnelly had told her, or her eyes when she had seen the girl for herself. Such a mousy little creature she was, with her pale pointed face and soulful brown eyes and all that mass of curling brown hair that looked as if it needed a good cutting and styling. Little Miss Prim, was how Constance thought of her as she watched her surreptitiously from the other side of the shop, nodding deferentially at Miss Walters's requests and scuttling back and forth with bales of materials to do the bidding of her customers. Constance felt an immediate hatred for the girl. Her eyes had rested longingly for a moment on the large steel scissors that lay on the counter. How she would love to cut off all those curling brown tresses – snip, snip, snip – until the girl was as bald as a newly shorn lamb. Constance's eyes narrowed as she looked at the shining silver blades, then she shuddered at the violent drift that her thoughts were taking. There were other more subtle ways, surely, of harming the girl?

She had entertained wild notions of trying to discredit Grace in Edwin's eyes. It shouldn't be difficult, she thought, with the help of one or two knowing friends who also happened to be influential customers, to get the girl accused of dishonesty. But Constance knew in her saner moments that this scheme was impossible. Edwin was no fool, neither was his father who, apparently, was also mildly besotted with the girl, and the accusation would never be believed. Also, if it were seen that she, Constance, was at the bottom of it, Edwin would never forgive her.

It was Clara Donnelly who had convinced her that Grace Turnbull constituted no threat.

'The girl's a mere nothing, a nobody,' she had told Constance. 'Goodness knows what Edwin sees in her. He'll soon tire of her, you mark my words, especially when he sees he's getting no encouragement from me. I'd cut him off without a penny – I would an' all – if he took up with the likes of her.'

'There's no talk of marriage, surely?' said Constance in alarm. 'He's only known the girl for five minutes.'

'Not as I know of,' Clara admitted, 'but you know what fellows are like when they get their heads turned by a pretty face. There's neither rhyme nor reason in 'em. Not that I think she's all that pretty,' Clara added. 'Puny little thing I reckon she is, all eyes and hair. She's not a patch on you, Connie love. She can't hold a candle to you for looks, or for owt else either. I'm sure I don't know what our Edwin's thinking of.'

Constance smiled to herself in a superior manner as she noticed Clara slipping into the Lancashire vernacular. As her own mother had told her, Clara was no lady and it was thanks to William Donnelly that the woman was in the fortunate position she was now, mistress of a fine house on Whitegate Lane with servants to wait on her. If it wasn't for William, her saviour, Clara would still be struggling to make ends meet in a two-roomed cottage on Marton Moss. So her mother said, but Constance herself doubted it.

You had to give Clara Donnelly her due; the woman must have had guts and determination to drag herself out of the mire and procure a well-heeled husband. Clara might not be out of the top drawer, or even out of the middle drawer as Constance's own mother was – Bertha Whitehead came from a good Catholic family, connected to the Cliftons of Lytham – but she was a staunch ally to Constance in her fight to win Edwin back.

'She hasn't been here, has she?' Constance asked now.

'Of course not!' said Clara indignantly. 'The very idea! No, the lad daren't invite her here. I reckon he knows which side his bread's buttered, though he seems to be fair smitten with her at the moment. No, I've taken a peek at her when I've been in the shop, and I'm not impressed, I can tell you, Connie love.'

Constance had fallen into the habit of taking tea with Clara a couple of afternoons a week, and between them they had devised the plan to get Edwin to the Catholic Ball. As Clara had told her son, Constance hadn't openly suggested that he should partner her, but from her subtle hints and persuasive looks Clara had got the message. They were two of a kind, Constance thought, she and Clara. Both of them possessed the same streak of dogged determination and, without expressing it, each seemed to know exactly what was in the other's mind.

And I'll win, Constance whispered to herself as she lay in bed that December night. You'll see, little Miss Grace Turnbull, I'll get him back. You see if I don't. Tonight's mild flirtation was but the first step. Constance wasn't sure how or when she would manage it but, sooner or later, she knew that her chance would come.

The Opera House, at Blackpool's Winter Gardens, was another of the architect Frank Matcham's triumphs. It had opened on 10 June 1889 with a performance of *The Yeoman of the Guard*, and the D'Oyly Carte were here again tonight, the week before Christmas, performing *The Gondoliers*. From their seats in the dress circle Grace and Edwin watched the chorus of Venetian gondoliers and rose-bedecked maidens as Gilbert's complicated plot unfolded before their eyes, and listened to the lilting strains of Sullivan's music echoing round the theatre. Such delightful tunes, thought Edwin as he hummed softly to himself, and he reached out and took Grace's hand. She turned to smile at him briefly then looked back at the stage, captivated by the colourful scene, and so they sat contentedly, hand in hand, until the interval.

'It's wonderful, Edwin,' Grace said as the red velvet curtain fell at the end of the first act. 'D'you know, I think I'm enjoying it even more than *The Importance of Being Earnest*? It's with it being nearly all music, of course. I love music,' she sighed happily, 'and all that lovely singing. Not that I can sing like our Hetty can, but I like listening to it. It's nice to hear some of Hetty's songs being sung by proper singers, isn't it? Oh dear!' She put her hand to her mouth and laughed, a merry melodious sound that made Edwin's heart leap with his love for her. 'That sounds awful, doesn't it? It's a good job our Hetty

256

didn't hear me, but you know what I mean, don't you, Edwin?'

'Sung by professionals, you mean.' Edwin smiled. 'But Hetty's getting to be quite a professional herself. There's not much of the amateur about her now. I was very impressed the last time I heard her. I daresay she could hold her own even in the Opera House.' He looked round at the opulent surroundings as he spoke. 'Is it the first time you've been here, Grace?'

'Yes, I've not been to the Opera House before,' she answered. 'I've been in the Winter Gardens, though, a time or two. Real posh, isn't it?'

'Yes, Blackpool knows how to entertain its visitors all right,' Edwin agreed, 'and that's why it was built, really, for the visitors, not for the residents.' He told her how the Winter Gardens had first been started back in 1875, but that it wasn't until recently, with the advent of the present manager, Mr Bill Holland, that the Gardens had enjoyed an upsurge in popularity.

He repeated to her an anecdote that his father had told him and which had become legendary in Blackpool.

'He always insisted on the best, did Bill Holland,' said Edwin now, 'and he would think nothing of paying a hundred guineas for a carpet. And that was just what he intended to spend on one for the Winter Gardens Pavilion. But one of his friends, apparently, was horrified. "For the trippers?" he said. "Why, they'll spit on it!" Well, this tickled Bill Holland, so the story goes, and it gave him an idea for a good advertisement. He had posters made and displayed all over Blackpool,

257

"Come to the Winter Gardens and spit on Bill Holland's 100-guinea carpet".'

Grace laughed delightedly. 'And did they?'

Edwin smiled. 'Well, they came at any rate, and they've been coming ever since, but I daresay they were too impressed with all the luxury to do much spitting. Come on, Grace.' He took her arm. 'I think we've just time for a drink before the next act.'

'That's what they call our Hetty, the Girl with the Sparkling Eyes,' Grace whispered to him part-way through the second act.

Edwin listened as the young gondolier, Marco, sang about the beauties of his bride, Gianetta.

'Take a pair of sparkling eyes
Hidden ever and anon
In a merciful eclipse . . .'

He turned to look at his own lovely Grace and she smiled back at him. Her eyes were not so much sparkling, but glowing with warmth and – he was sure – with love for him. Soon, maybe early in the new year, he would ask her to marry him and be hanged to what anyone might think, her mother or his own mother or anyone. It was only Grace and himself that mattered. But he had, he reminded himself, only known her for a few weeks. It seemed as though he had always known her, always loved her, and he wanted her to be his wife. He wanted her right now, but he knew that it was too soon to ask. Next year, maybe, when spring came round . . .

'Live to love and love to live,' sang Marco, and

Edwin's heart echoed the sentiments. If his life were to hold nothing but his love for Grace he would still be a happy man.

Grace was at the Opera House again, less than a week later, on Christmas night. There was a concert of sacred music and the Turnbull and Gregson families had decided to make it a family outing. And what a joyous, jubilant occasion it was, Grace thought, as she listened to the orchestra and soloists and choir performing all the favourite family pieces. 'Ave Maria', 'The Holy City', 'The Lost Chord' . . . She noticed that her mother's eyes were moist and that from time to time she furtively felt for her handkerchief and dabbed the stray tears away, recalling, no doubt, the happy times they had spent round the old piano when Father was alive. But it wasn't a night for sadness and Grace felt her spirits soaring as the massed voices of the choir rose to the roof.

'Hosanna in the highest,
Hosanna to the King . . .'

Outside, it was a damp, cheerless night, but as they walked home through the dark streets, the pavements and rooftops glistening from a recent fall of rain, Grace felt that she needed only Edwin here now to make her happiness complete.

She watched Hetty and Albert walking in front of her, and was glad that things seemed to be all right between them again. Grace had been concerned about the excited look in her sister's eyes when she had told her about the gipsy at Tilda's Tavern, and she hadn't liked the way Hetty had seemed highly amused at poor Albert's jealousy. Reuben Loveday, as Hetty said he was called, had seen her home on the night of the storm and, according to Hetty, had behaved like a perfect gentleman, so there must be some good in him. But Grace was not entirely sure that she could believe her sister. Knowing Hetty, Grace couldn't help but feel a niggling disquiet when she thought about that gipsy lad. Grace smiled now as she watched Albert plant a kiss squarely on Hetty's cheek, not caring that his parents and Hetty's mother and sister were walking behind them. Grace hoped that her sister realised just how lucky she was to have the love of a decent young man like Albert.

Grace didn't feel envious or lonely as she watched them, for just the thought of Edwin was enough to warm her on a cold, miserable night, and she knew that she would be seeing him in a day or two. Christmas was a family time and tonight Edwin would be with his family as she was with hers. She couldn't tell what the future held for them both; she didn't dare to look beyond the immediate morrow, but just to be with Edwin made all her fears vanish.

There were times when she was anxious, times when she thought about Walter and how, back home in Burnley, she had been scared of his dominance and his hold over her. But the occasions when she thought of Walter now were becoming less and less frequent. His Christmas card to her had contained a brief note saying that his mother was still far from well and that it had been impossible for him to get away, even for a day. No word of love, no endearments, no declaration that he was missing her . . . Grace hoped against all hope that she had seen the last of Walter.

Chapter 12

Grace tore open the envelope which bore Walter's handwriting and drew out the two sheets of cheap lined paper. A longer letter than usual, she thought, her heart sinking as she anticipated what news it might contain. The unwelcome tidings that he was coming to see her at long last, maybe? His previous letters had amounted to merely a single page.

Her eyes scanned over the lines and she gave a gasp of dismay. 'Oh no . . .' she said softly as she sat down again at the breakfast table. She had finished her tea and toast and had been about to get ready to go to work when she heard the rattle of the letter box, but now she needed a few more minutes to take in what she was reading.

'What's up, love?' Her mother replaced the knitted tea cosy over the earthenware pot that she had just refilled with boiling water and looked curiously at her daughter. 'Not bad news, is it?'

'Yes . . . yes, I'm afraid it is,' Grace faltered. 'I'll let you read it in a minute, Mam.' She knew that the letter would contain nothing that could bring a blush to her own cheeks, let alone to her mother's, especially under the circumstances surrounding the missive. 'It's from Walter. His mother's died.'

'Eeh, deary me!' Martha exclaimed, putting the teapot down heavily. 'That poor lad, and Mr Clayton an' all. What a shock for them. I can't say poor Florence – the lass'll be out of her suffering now – but I didn't realise she was that poorly. What was it, love?'

'I'm just reading it, Mam.' Grace sounded preoccupied. 'I'll pass it over to you in a minute . . . No, I didn't know she was so ill either, but she's never been strong, you know, and she suffered with her chest every winter.'

She read the rest of the letter in silence, her frown deepening and tears pricking at her eyelids as she thought of Mrs Clayton being snatched away from life at such an early age. She was a few years older than Mam, but she couldn't be more than fifty. Grace had always felt a fondness for the little woman and she remembered her now, bustling back and forth between the stove and the table, setting piping-hot dishes in front of her husband and son. There had always been a substantial meal ready for them the minute they walked in from the mill, their slippers warming by the hearth and the fire banked up to provide plenty of hot water should either of them decide to have a bath. And that, Grace knew, had been Florence Clayton's job as well, filling up the zinc bathtub, that normally hung from a nail on the back door, with kettles of boiling water and, as likely as not, scrubbing her husband's back into the bargain.

Grace hadn't felt the same affection for Walter's

father, Ralph, a brawny, red-faced man with arms on him like ham shanks and a surly manner. His only way of communicating with his wife had been, it seemed to Grace, by grunts and gestures. Grace had always been a little afraid of him and, judging by her cowed manner, Florence had appeared to be so too. Grace had never seen her without her pinny or, surprisingly enough, without a pleasant expression on her face. One might have thought she would have looked vexed or harassed – goodness knows, she had plenty reason to – but Grace recalled now how her thin features would often relax in a sweet smile. Poor Florence; she hadn't had much of a life, to be sure. Well, as Mam said, she was released from her suffering now – a platitude that Martha always trotted out on occasions such as this – but Grace liked to think that her own life would have a little more to offer than that which had been Florence Clayton's lot. A twinge of another feeling, not sorrow, more like fear, stabbed at Grace as she read the rest of the letter.

'Here, Mam,' she said, passing it over. 'You can have a look at it now. He doesn't say a great deal, apart from all that about his mam's illness.'

Grace watched as her mother also read the letter, her lips moving silently as she pored over the words. Walter had written that the bronchitis to which Florence had succumbed in the autumn, as she did each year, had left her at a very low ebb, more so than usual. When the colder weather came in January she had been taken ill again and this time pneumonia had set in. She had died a couple of days ago, at the beginning of February, and the funeral was to be held on Friday. Walter also wrote that he hoped to see Grace before long, but as he had told her so in every letter she had stopped believing him. This time, though, it would be different. There would be nothing to stop him now, would there? The disquieting thought niggled at the back of her mind and she tried to push it away.

'Hmm.' Martha put the letter back in its envelope and passed it back to Grace. She shook her head sorrowfully. 'That poor lad,' she said again. 'However'll they manage without a woman in the house? Fellows are not much good at fending for themselves at the best of times, but from what you tell me, Gracie, that pair are worse than most.'

Grace had been wondering the same thing herself. They would be lost without Florence to fetch and carry for them, in fact she wondered how they had managed all these weeks while the woman had been ill. Perhaps, now she had gone, they would begin to appreciate her. Ralph Clayton had never shown a morsel of gratitude for all that his wife had done for him.

'Eh well. That's summat they'll have to sort out for themselves,' said Martha. 'It's surprising how you can make do when it's a question of needs must. I daresay they'll manage.' She poured out another cup of tea, frowning at the blackish-brown liquid, by now barely warm. 'I reckon this'll be stewed by now, but it'll do. It's a shame to waste half a pot of good tea.' She added a drop of milk and a spoonful of sugar, then sipped appreciatively. 'T'flavour's there even if it's a bit cold.

It's amazing how a cup of tea bucks you up of a morning . . . So happen Walter'll be over to see you now, our Grace, seeing as how his mother's gone. There's nothing to stop him now, and I reckon it's about time an' all.'

'He's said so before, Mam,' said Grace evenly. 'He's said it so many times that I've stopped taking any notice of him. And as far as I'm concerned he needn't bother,' she added with a touch of acerbity. 'You know how things are now. I've been seeing quite a lot of Edwin and . . . well, I know you've always liked Walter, but I certainly don't want him turning up now, after all this time, and spoiling things.'

'Aye, I know how you feel, lass,' Martha said softly. 'And I've got to admit that that Edwin Donnelly's a nice young fellow, when you get to know him. I've got nowt against him except . . . well, you know all that and I won't go on about it again now. But he seems a decent enough chap and I can't very well leave him standing on t'doorstep, can I, when he comes calling for you?'

Edwin was invited into the house on the occasions when he called to take Grace out and he had even sat down in the parlour, now that it was furnished in a manner which Martha considered more fitting for company. But he hadn't, so far, been invited for a meal. To encourage a young fellow to put his feet under the table was tantamount to telling him that you regarded him as a serious suitor, and Martha, as yet, could not bring herself to do that. And it was just as well she hadn't, she thought now, with the chance of Walter showing up again.

'Have you never written to tell Walter as how you've been seeing Edwin?' Martha asked now, having a good idea what the answer would be.

'No . . . no, I haven't, Mam,' Grace said slowly.

'It might have been as well if you had. I told you all along as it wasn't fair when you were supposed to be walking out with Walter.'

'Well, I haven't told him and that's all there is to it.' Grace looked vexedly at her mother, then stood up in a gesture of finality. 'And I'd best be moving now or I'll be late for work. Don't worry, Mam,' she added, more kindly. 'Walter'll find out, sooner or later.'

'Aye, I know how you feel, Grace,' Martha said again. 'Walter's not been fair to you. You've seen neither hide nor hair of him these last few months and that's no way to carry on. But I've always liked the lad. I've made no secret of it and I'll still go on saying it, no matter what you think. Walter Clayton's our sort and you can't deny it. Chapel and t'mill and born and bred in Burnley an' all, like you were. And I expect when he's got this lot behind him, poor lad, he'll show up again like a bad penny. You can't get away from your roots, Grace. I've always said so.'

Yes, Mam, you have, thought Grace, listening to her mother's words in silence. Mam could never resist sticking an oar in when it came to Walter, but as far as Grace was concerned, the chapel and the mill and her upbringing in the mean streets of Burnley had now been left far behind. But as she thought about Walter Clayton, a tiny black cloud of disquiet hovered on the horizon, and Grace felt afraid.

Grace and Hetty were very pleased with the way they looked in their new cycling outfits. As laid down in the latest fashion magazines, concerning the correct wear for this popular new sport, their costumes combined comfort and practicality with the feminine modesty which had to be observed at all times. For this reason the knickerbockers adopted by a few of the more daring women had never really caught on, and Hetty, though she had been tempted, had decided against them. Their skirts were not as full as those they normally wore, but were wide enough to allow their feet full play on the pedals, and yet not so wide as to permit the skirt to billow in the wind or get caught in the spokes of the wheels. Their double-breasted Norfolk jackets with wide reveres fitted their figures neatly, ending just below the waist. Grace's costume was fawn and Hetty's a moss-green tweed of a soft, light texture, and with them they wore high-necked blouses. Hetty daringly sported a bright-green necktie, like a man's, but Grace wore a brown satin bow as a finishing touch to her apparel. Their soft hats were made of the same material as their costumes, close-fitting so that they wouldn't blow off in the wind, and their shoes, also bought specially, were lace-ups with heavy soles.

They giggled delightedly as they surveyed themselves in the full-length wardrobe mirror in the bedroom.

'My goodness, don't we look a couple of toffs, Gracie?' said Hetty excitedly.

'What Mam would call a couple of bobbydazzlers,' said Grace, laughing as she looked admiringly at her reflection.

She wasn't one for preening herself, not like Hetty who was forever pirouetting and prancing about in front of the mirror, but she had to admit that she looked nice. Her cheeks were pink with excitement and her brown curls peeped prettily from beneath the brim of the soft hat. She hoped that Edwin would think she looked nice, too, when he saw her in her new finery tomorrow. They had planned a bicycle ride for the next day, she and Edwin, for the very first time. But tonight, a fine springlike evening in late March, Grace and Hetty were going for a short spin along the promenade before the light faded.

'Come on, Grace. We'd best get moving,' said Hetty. 'It won't be long before it goes dark.'

They had had their bicycles for a few weeks and were now becoming very proficient. Their machines were not new ones – that would have proved too expensive with all the new clothes that they needed as well – but they had managed to get two nearly new bicycles from advertisements in the local paper. They had wobbled about a lot at first, as Grace had feared they might, and in the beginning she had felt so scared that she hardly dared to mount the machine. But it was amazing how easy it was once they got the hang of it. Hetty, as was only to be expected, had taken to it like a duck to water and was very soon spinning along on her own, laughing with the sheer delight of it all. Grace had taken longer to learn, with Hetty hanging on to the saddle and Grace entreating her not to let go as they wheeled up

270

and down the quiet stretch of road outside the boarding house. Then Hetty, mischievously, had let go, and Grace had been so astounded that she was actually cycling all on her own that she almost fell off. But that was a few weeks ago, and by now the pair of them were expert cyclists.

Hetty, too, was planning a bicycle ride for the next day, with Lily Tattersall, a fellow waitress from Laycock's, who, like Hetty, was a keen bicyclist. Albert didn't share Hetty's enthusiasm for this new pastime. He had dismissed it as 'A load o' nonsense, cavorting about on two wheels when you've got a pair of legs to walk on.' He was such a stuffed shirt at times and Hetty found herself getting more and more impatient with him.

As she and Grace rode along Talbot Road towards North Pier, Hetty thought of the many points on which they disagreed. Although he was proud of her and went along with her most times to Tilda's Tavern, Hetty knew that, deep down, Albert would prefer her to be singing in the chapel choir. She hadn't forgotten the barney they had had when Joss first offered her the job, and she suspected that Albert only went along with her to make sure she didn't get into any mischief. And, thinking of chapel, that was another thing they had had words about. He thought she should be there every Sunday morning – he was even worse than her mother – and didn't believe her excuses that she had to help Mam with the Sunday dinner.

'Your mam manages to get there and cook a

dinner an' all,' he told her, 'so I reckon that's a lame excuse.'

Martha, during the winter when there were no regular visitors, had recommenced her habit of Sunday morning worship. But even our Grace doesn't go every Sunday now, thought Hetty, and I'm jolly sure I'm not going to have Albert Gregson telling me what I should and shouldn't do. We're not married yet.

And what a silly fuss he had made about Reuben turning up at Tilda's Tavern. When he had heard that the lad had seen her home that stormy night he had turned as red as a turkey cock and had looked so angry that Hetty had feared he would burst. Not that he had said very much – it wasn't Albert's way to rant and rave – and he had calmed down when she told him that it had been Joss Jenkinson's idea. But Hetty had been surprised and, she had to admit, more than a little pleased at how jealous she had made him.

Reuben had been to the tavern a few times since the night of the storm, but when he had seen that Albert was with her he had, to Hetty's annoyance, kept his distance. She often found herself thinking about Reuben. At odd moments during the day, when she was dashing about with laden trays in the café or helping Mam to wash the dishes, a picture of him would come into her mind. She remembered his smouldering black eyes, his black hair curling over his neckerchief, his red lips curved in a smile and the way he had told her, in his gentle musical voice, 'You be beautiful.' And, more than anything else, she remembered how he had kissed her on the night of the storm. Just a fleeting kiss it had been, but Hetty felt warm all over even now at the thought of it. The trouble was, Reuben appeared to have forgotten all about it.

She was thinking about him now as she and Grace turned back into Talbot Square and passed near Laycock's café. Her friend, Lily, didn't seem fussy about where they should go on their bicycle ride the next day. It shouldn't be too difficult to persuade her to fall in with her own plans.

'Come on, Grace,' Hetty shouted now, bubbling over with high spirits as she thought about it. 'Race you up Talbot Road.'

She would just have time to change out of her cycling clothes before Albert called to escort her to her Saturday evening performance at Tilda's Tavern.

Walter knew that he would not be able to stand it much longer. He had found it difficult to get on with his father at the best of times, but now that his mother, the peacemaker, had gone it was well-nigh impossible. Ralph Clayton was in every way the antithesis of his son. He was a beer-swilling, loud-mouthed boor who hadn't set foot inside a chapel since his youngest son, Walter, had been baptised there. This was how Walter was beginning to see him now, although when his mother was alive he had never given much thought to his father at all; he had just made sure that he didn't spend any more time in his company than he was forced to do. Now, of necessity, they were thrown together, just the two of them, sharing the house and mealtimes and the fireside of an evening.

Walter found the close proximity stifling without his mother to act as a buffer between them. He and his father didn't often row openly, but they were so dissimilar that they found they had very little to say to one another. Walter was missing his mother more than he had thought was possible. She had seemed to be such an insignificant little body, but now she had gone Walter realised what strength she had possessed to go on, day after day, putting up with his father's surliness and his own selfishness and disregard. He knew, now that it was too late, how much he had taken her for granted. She had never said very much on the occasions when he and his father had clashed, but her very presence had had a calming effect, ensuring that neither of them said anything they might later regret. Her just being there had created a state of quietude, but now the atmosphere was at times so tense that it was palpable, a black cloud of resentment and dislike filling the stuffy little room.

Walter had been impelled to escape from the place, away from the claustrophobic surroundings and the regretful remembrances of his little mother. At least three times a week he went to chapel, to Sunday worship, class meetings and Bible study, and on the other evenings – and sometimes on his chapel nights as well – he walked to the other side of the town to console himself on the comfortable bosom of Maggie Sykes.

When he returned, earlier than usual, one

evening in the middle of March, his father had a visitor. Mrs Ackerman, the blowsy widow from lower down the street, had at least looked guilty when Walter opened the door and surprised them, jumping to her feet and patting her dishevelled auburn hair – like a bird's nest at the best of times – and trying to fasten the telltale open button on her blouse. But his father had been unconcerned, grinning widely to reveal his blackened teeth and reaching out a not too clean hand to pat his neighbour's bottom.

'Eeh, you didn't half give us a turn, barging in like that, Walter lad. Didn't he, Jessie love?' His father's speech was slurred and the small room smelled of drink. 'You'd best remember to knock next time, lad.'

Walter felt nauseated, knowing that they had both had too much to drink, and disgusted at his father's amorous goings-on. He forgot, for the moment, that he had come straight from Maggie's bed. This was one characteristic that he and his father shared, the ability to seek and to find oblivion in the arms of a woman.

So that was the way the land was lying, thought Walter, although he had guessed as much a few weeks before. It hadn't taken Jessie Ackerman long, after the funeral, and even during his mother's illness, he recalled now, to come round with panfuls of soup and plates of apple pie, offerings which Walter had disdained, knowing the state of the house from which they had come. Well, his father was welcome to her. He, Walter, wasn't going to stick around to see him make a fool of himself over a woman twenty years his junior,

275

and an improvident slut into the bargain, or to watch someone stepping into his mother's shoes. It was high time, he decided, that he went to Blackpool to lay claim to the girl he loved, the girl who would be waiting for him.

Walter couldn't have explained, even to himself, why he hadn't done so before. The reasons he had given to Grace about his mother's illness and the fact that there was only himself and his father to look after her were, of course, true, but Walter knew that, had he made the effort, he could have gone to see her long before now. Then why had he not done so? he wondered. Partly because, with Grace many miles away, he had found himself visiting Maggie Sykes more and more often. A very accommodating woman, who satisfied his most basic needs with no questions asked and no reasons given. It was an amicable arrangement with no obligation or commitment on either side – at least that was what he had thought until recently. Now Maggie had started dropping hints, very subtle ones, about a more lasting relationship, hints from which Walter had quickly shied away. That was why he had left somewhat earlier than usual this evening and it was another reason why, now, he knew that it was time to go and claim Grace as his own.

She had become in Walter's mind, over the months of their separation, the epitome of womanhood, embracing all that was loveliest in the fairer sex. To say he desired her would, he admitted to himself, be more accurate, but because of his veneration of her he had never allowed his desire to get out of control. When they were

276

married it would be different. Walter looked forward to teaching her, as Maggie had taught him, the pleasures of lovemaking, and to being the first one to take possession of that virginal loveliness.

He had found it difficult, too, to express his love and desire for her in the written word. His letters to her had been nothing more than brief notes, comments about his mother's illness and the goings-on at chapel, revealing nothing of how he really felt about her. It was strange that it should be so, Walter thought, when he found it no problem to compose a sermon or a talk for his Bible class. But his preaching was largely extempore, a spontaneous outpouring of the spirit that was given to him when he entered the pulpit or stood at the lectern with his Bible in his hand.

'I open my mouth but it is God's words that come out,' was a favourite expression of Walter's.

But it was his own words that he needed now to woo Grace, and Walter decided not to wait a minute longer. His father he would gladly leave to his own devices, and Maggie too. She had provided a comfortable haven for him for many years, a sympathetic ear and an accommodating body, but now he no longer needed her. Not for a moment did he stop to consider what Maggie's needs might be.

He decided not to write and tell Grace that he was coming. He realised, with a stab of guilt, that it was hardly likely, after all this time, that she would believe him. No, he would just turn up and surprise her and how overjoyed she would be to see him again. Hadn't she promised – well, almost promised – that night when they had walked on the moor that she would marry him?

'Next spring,' she had said. 'P'haps by next spring me mam'll be able to manage,' was what she had told him.

Well, it was spring now and Walter was going to make sure that she kept her promise. He worked a week's notice at the mill and left Burnley, for good he hoped, the following week. His father showed little surprise or interest at his departure and, as for Maggie, he hadn't even told her. It was Grace who was filling his thoughts now, his pure and lovely Grace. He wondered, with a pang of remorse, how he could possibly have left her alone for so long. But he would make it up to her. When she saw him again she would realise just how much she had missed him, and very soon, perhaps in a month or two, they could be married.

Within a week of arriving in Blackpool, Walter had found a place to stay and a job as well. His lodgings were in High Street, near to North Station, and also near to the boarding house that Martha Turnbull had taken. Just how permanent they would be Walter wasn't sure. It might well be that Mrs Jobson, the landlady, would need his room during the summer season for short-term holiday-makers, but Walter wasn't worried. By that time he and Grace would be married and living in their own little home. Walter had, over the years, been thrifty. After he had given his mother the money for his keep, the rest of his wages had been his own. He was an abstemious young man, neither smoking nor drinking, and he now had a nice little bit put by which should enable him to put a down-payment on a small house or, failing that, to rent one.

The job he found was with Mr Herbert Henderson, a coal, lime and slate merchant. Walter knew that the work would be physically hard, humping great bags of the commodities to the builders and householders in the area, but he had never been afraid of hard work or of getting his hands dirty.

He hugged to himself, like a child anticipating the delights of a birthday, the secret knowledge that he was so near to Grace, and yet unknown to her, and that soon he would see her again. He had been tempted to sneak into Donnelly's, the big store where he knew she was employed, and watch her at work, but he decided against it. No, he would surprise her on her home ground. He would call on Sunday; she would be sure to be at home then. They might even attend chapel together.

'Are you ready, dear?' Edwin raised his eyebrows as Grace entered the room, then smiled approvingly at the sight of her in her new finery. 'My goodness! That's an elegant outfit. Just perfect for bicycling. You'll be turning a few heads on the road today, Grace.' She laughed and blushed prettily at his remarks and he turned to her mother. 'I can see you've been busy, Mrs Turnbull. Your sewing-machine must have been working twenty to the dozen making all these bicycling clothes. I believe Hetty has a new outfit as well.'

'Aye, she has that.' Martha nodded. 'She's just gone off, as pleased as Punch. Our Hetty's always happy when she's got summat new to wear. Grace has done most of the sewing you know, Mr

Edwin,' she told him with pride. 'Hetty's outfit as well as her own. I do all the cutting out – that's a tricky job if ever there was one – and Grace does the sewing. And our Hetty does the supervising,' she added with a chuckle.

'Now, be fair, Mam,' said Grace laughing. 'She sewed on all the buttons.'

'Oh aye, so she did,' Martha agreed. 'Well, you'd best be off, the pair of you, and make the most of the day. Lovely weather for March, isn't it, Mr Edwin? You could almost think it was summer.'

'It certainly is, Mrs Turnbull,' said Edwin. 'A lovely day. Come along then, Grace. Let's go and enjoy the sunshine.'

Martha watched them go with the vague feeling of unease that always crept up on her whenever Edwin Donnelly called. Not that he wasn't a charming young man; in spite of her misgivings she could see why Grace was so taken with him. And his father, too; William Donnelly was a real gentleman, not the least bit stuck-up for all his wealth and eminent position in the town. It was that wife of his, nothing but an upstart from what Alice Gregson said, who seemed to be the snake in the grass. Martha knew that Grace hadn't, as yet, been invited into the Donnelly home on Whitegate Lane although she'd been keeping company, if you could call it that, with Mr Edwin since last November. And it could only be Clara Donnelly who was preventing it, because Mr William was kindness itself.

Martha knew that her thinking about this was all cockeyed. If Edwin's mother disapproved of the friendship, surely that was all to the good? She,

Martha, didn't want anything to come of it either, but neither did she like to see her daughter slighted by a jumped-up nobody who had once not had two ha'pennies to rub together. Ah well, she consoled herself, it'll all come out in the wash. Things had a way of working out if you left 'em alone, and the good Lord was in control when all was said and done. Martha had forgotten, for the moment, what a great believer she was in the power of prayer.

It was a lovely day that had been borrowed from summer, and Grace felt the happiness singing through her veins as they cycled out of Blackpool along New Road which led past the town cemetery at Layton.

'Where shall we go, dear?' Edwin had asked when they set off, and at Grace's insistence that she wanted to see the countryside for a change instead of the sea, they turned left up Talbot Road rather than right which would have taken them down to the promenade.

'Perhaps we could see the hills,' she said now, wistfully. 'Do you remember, Edwin, we talked about it that night when you first took me out? I told you how much I missed the hills and the countryside.'

'I don't think we can cycle so far today.' Edwin laughed indulgently. 'It would be a bit far, even for me, and I'm more used to pedalling than you are. But we can at least see a bit of greenery, Grace. It'll be grand to see the trees in leaf again after the long winter. Sometimes it seems as though the sun has forgotten how to shine.'

The flat roads of the Fylde were ideal for cycling and the sun was warm on their backs as they rode out of Blackpool through Little Layton and Carlton and on towards Poulton-le-Fylde. Here the cottage gardens were gay with purple and yellow crocuses, golden daffodils and orange-eyed narcissi, and the hedgerows coming alive once more with the fresh bright green of newly opening leaves. A few miles further on, nearer the village of St Michael's, the River Wyre meandered through flat green fields where black and white cattle grazed and newborn lambs with black noses frolicked on long, spindly legs. Buttercups and dandelions made vivid splashes of gold amongst the greenery, and Grace thought what a beautiful flower the common dandelion was, like a burst of sunshine, and yet how maligned. She remembered how boys at school had made rude remarks about it, something about wetting the bed, she recalled with a smile. She felt like laughing out loud at this memory of one of the absurdities of childhood, and for sheer delight at the glorious day, the sunshine and the scenery and, above all, the joy of Edwin's company.

They stopped by a copse of beech trees, not yet in leaf, their skeletal branches forming a tracery of black lace against the azure blue of the sky.

'I think we deserve a rest, don't you?' said Edwin, as they leaned their bicycles against a stile. 'This is the bluebell wood that I told you about, Grace. There'll be no bluebells out yet, of course – it's too early – but it's a lovely spot.' He held out his hand to help Grace over.

The wood was dim and cool, a welcome contrast to the glare of the sunshine, and where the sun had not penetrated, the grass was still damp from an early-morning shower. By the side of the path pale-yellow primroses peeped from beneath clusters of dark-green leaves and golden celandines bloomed, just the same colour as the blouse that Grace was wearing. She had chosen the material, she recalled, the day that she first met Edwin. She had started to fall in love with him then, even before she knew him.

Edwin took her hand and gently squeezed her fingers. 'Oh, to be in England, Now that April's there,' he quoted. 'Well, nearly there,' he added with a laugh. 'It will be next week.'

Grace smiled, her head on one side, listening to the song of a bird in a nearby tree. 'That's the wise thrush,' she countered, answering his quotation with another from the same poem.

'He sings each song twice over,
Lest you should think he never could recapture
The first fine careless rapture!

'At least I think it's a thrush,' she added. 'Is it, Edwin?'

'I wouldn't know, my love,' he admitted laughing. 'I'm not much of a countryman. My ignorance is truly appalling. But you obviously know your Browning, Grace. Do you like poetry?'

'Some of it. The ones I can understand,' Grace replied. 'And I remember that one. It's stuck in my mind since we learned it at school. It was ridiculous, when you come to think of it, learning

283

all that stuff about blossomed pear trees and chaffinches when we lived amongst the smoky mills of Burnley. I doubt if any of us had ever seen a chaffinch or a thrush.'

'But you could soon get up on to the moors, couldn't you? You told me how you missed the hills when you first came to Blackpool, and you mentioned them again today.'

'Yes, I did. That's true.' Grace turned to smile at him. 'I missed them at first, but I don't so much now. I'm so used to living in Blackpool. I love it, Edwin. I wouldn't want to leave Blackpool now, not ever.'

Edwin put his arm round her shoulders, drawing her closer towards him as they walked along the woodland path. 'Did you go to church this morning, Grace?' he asked her.

'To chapel,' she corrected him. 'Yes.'

'Oh yes, of course, chapel,' he said quietly. 'I expect your mother makes sure you go every week, doesn't she?'

'Not really. She's been quite lenient about it since we moved to Blackpool. She doesn't always have time to go herself, you see, so she can't very well insist that we go. She did when we were little, though. Me and our Hetty always had to go to chapel and Sunday school. But I go now because I want to. I feel all wrong, somehow, if I miss more than a couple of times. Do you, Edwin?'

'To be quite honest, I don't know how I feel.' Edwin sighed. 'I just go along each week because . . . well, because I always have done, I suppose. It's a habit and I never really think very much about it one way or the other. Mother always insisted that we went, like your mother did, and she would still have a lot to say, even now, if I were to miss Mass.'

'You worry quite a lot about what your mother says, don't you, Edwin?' Edwin didn't know if he had imagined the slight acerbity in Grace's words, but if it was there then the girl was more than justified. 'Like I do,' she added, as if to soften the sharpness of her remark. 'I know I don't like doing anything to upset Mam.'

'Like going out with me?' Grace turned quickly to look at him, but Edwin was grinning. 'Oh, it's all right, Grace. I know your mother doesn't entirely approve of me. She's friendly enough now, but she's never really at her ease with me. She still insists on calling me Mr Edwin . . .'

Edwin knew that the greatest stumbling block in their otherwise blissful relationship was the attitude of their respective mothers. His own mother was proving very difficult at the moment, having taken to her bed, intermittently, with some sort of mysterious malady. Edwin wasn't entirely sure that she was shamming; he had thought so at first, but he had to admit that she looked ill, pale and listless, taking no interest in her friends and family, and picking at her food. The doctor, an old family friend, had prescribed a bottle of iron tonic and told William that it was a nervous ailment, that and 'her age'. Women of Clara's age were prone to all kinds of strange disorders, he said, due to bodily changes that occurred in mid-life.

'We'll have to try and be patient with her,' William had told his son. 'Try not to upset her . . .

Look here, son,' he had said kindly. 'I know how things are between you and Grace Turnbull, and I want you to know that I don't disapprove. She's a lovely lass. There's the problem of religion, I know, but there's nothing that couldn't be sorted out with a bit of tolerance. But it's your mother . . .'

'Yes, it's always Mother,' Edwin agreed bitterly. 'I was going to invite Grace round – God knows it's high time I did – and be hanged to what Mother says, but now she's ill, or pretending to be . . .'

'I don't think she's pretending,' William replied. 'I've known your mother a long time and, for all her faults, she's a tough customer. She had to be, the way she was brought up, but she doesn't like me mentioning that. No, I think she's poorly – perhaps not so bad as she makes out, but it wouldn't do to upset her at the moment.' He put his hand on Edwin's shoulder and patted it comfortingly. 'Things have a way of working out, and I'm on your side, you can be sure of that.'

Edwin had hoped, by now, to have asked Grace to marry him, but he knew, as his father said, that he would have to wait a little while longer. Once the girl had agreed to be his wife, as Edwin was sure she would, he would have to invite her to his home, but with his mother in her present state of health that was impossible. But at least he could try to explain some of this to Grace now.

'Yes, mothers can be a problem, can't they, love?' he said. He went on to tell her about his mother's illness and about how he and his father had to be very careful not to cause her undue distress. 'If it wasn't for Mother I would have invited you to my home long ago.'

'I know that, Edwin,' said Grace quietly. 'Please don't worry about it. And I hope she'll soon be better.'

'You're so lovely, Grace. So very lovely.' Edwin stopped by a clearing where the sun shone through the bare branches of the trees, making a patch of golden warmth on the ground. He put his arms round her and she lifted her face to his, anticipating his kiss. He had kissed her many times, each time more wondrous than the last, but there had been no opportunity for more prolonged affirmations of love. They had kissed in hansom cabs, on street corners, on the clifftop promenade, but always they had to part too soon. Now the time and the place were right. This moment had been made for them.

Edwin took off his tweed jacket and helped Grace to remove hers and he spread them on the ground in the pool of sunlight, then together they sank to the ground. He pulled off her absurd little hat and her hair sprang out, a glorious brown halo, golden-tipped where the sunlight caught it. Gently he pushed her to the ground, then his fingers were in her hair, at her throat, her breasts, tenderly caressing every part of her. Slowly he undid the pearl buttons of her blouse and pushed away the fabric that lay beneath, marvelling at her loveliness, the rounded curve of her shoulders, her petal-smooth skin and her dainty breasts.

She looked up at him and smiled and Edwin knew that she trusted him. He hadn't planned this. Dear God, no. Not for the world would he hurt her, but he wanted her so much. It was not the first time for Edwin. There had been an accommodating parlour maid, once, when he was seventeen and holidaying at a schoolfriend's home in Yorkshire. And the same friend had had a sister who had taken a fancy to the handsome Edwin, as she did to all her brother's friends. But it was the first time that he had given of himself in love, and Edwin knew that, for Grace, it was undoubtedly the first time. He must be gentle with her.

Slowly, tenderly he began to make love to her, all the while muttering words of endearment. 'Grace . . . Grace, my darling . . . I love you so much, so very much,' and he felt her responding, opening to him. Only once did she cry out, and Edwin held her close to him in his distress that he had hurt her. 'Oh, Grace, my darling. I'm sorry. I've hurt you.'

'No, Edwin. No, darling,' she whispered. 'It's . . . it's all right.' Then they were carried along on a mutual wave of ecstasy until they became as one person, glorying in their love and desire for one another.

Grace had never known such joy. She stroked Edwin's hair as he lay with his head on her breast, then softly touched each closed blue-veined eyelid. She looked up at the clear blue sky, dotted here and there with cotton-wool clouds, and at the dappled sunlight glinting through the branches of the trees, and wanted this moment to last for ever. She felt no shame, only a joyous exhilaration that she belonged to Edwin. She loved him and he loved her in return. It would always be so.

He stirred when she bent and kissed his fore-head, then he smiled lovingly. 'We'll have to go, darling. I'd like to stay here for ever, but it's getting late.' He pulled a watch from his waistcoat pocket. 'Four o'clock. It'll take us about an hour to get back. Come on, love.' He rose to his feet and reached out a hand to help Grace, then they walked back along the path with their arms round one another. They stopped by the stile and Edwin put a finger beneath Grace's chin, gently lifting her face to his. 'I love you, Grace.' His kiss was just the touch of his lips upon hers, as soft as a falling leaf.

They spoke little on the journey home and when they paused by the gate of Welcome Rest he took her hand and squeezed it.

'I love you, Grace,' he said again. His face was unsmiling and his eyes serious, but the warmth in his voice told her all she wanted to know. 'Don't forget that I love you.'

The hall was dark after the brilliance of the sunshine outside, and Grace felt as though she were stepping into another world, another life, but which one was reality and which a dream she didn't know.

Her mother flung open the parlour door, her face flushed with excitement. 'We've got company, Grace. You'll never guess who's here!'

Grace felt the colour drain from her face and her limbs turn to water as she entered the parlour and stared into the smiling face of Walter Clayton.

Chapter 13

'Where shall we go then?' asked Hetty. 'Have you any ideas, Lily?' She knew that she was on safe ground. Her friend very seldom made any suggestions, always looking to Hetty to take the lead.

'I don't mind,' Lily said now, with the little laugh that accompanied all her remarks. 'It's such a glorious day and I'm glad to be out of that stuffy café for a change. Anywhere'll be nice on a day like this. You decide, Hetty.' She looked at her friend with big blue eyes that were completely guileless and Hetty knew that it wasn't an act. Lily was as trusting as a babe in arms and her looks and mannerisms gave credence to this, her wide-eyed stare and her golden, baby-soft hair and the way she had of hanging on one's every word.

Hetty could appear innocent, too, when she wished to do so, as she did now. She pursed her lips and her forehead creased in a frown as though she were deep in thought. 'Let me see . . . It'll be lovely on the promenade on a day like this. A bit crowded at the north end though. D'you think we could ride as far as Victoria Pier? There's a funfair down there, I've heard, near the Star Inn. Hobbyhorses and skittle alleys and all that, and a switchback railway.' There was a gipsy encampment there, too, on the sand dunes, with fortune-tellers, quack doctors, phrenologists and the like, but Hetty didn't mention this. 'Have you ever been there, Lily?'

'No, I haven't,' said Lily. 'But I'd love to go. What a good idea of yours, Hetty. You always think of such exciting things to do,' she prattled happily. 'If it was up to me we probably wouldn't get any further than South Pier.'

As they cycled south towards their destination, the two girls chattered light-heartedly. When they reached the South Shore terminus of the tram track they could see ahead of them the twin attractions of the south end of Blackpool, the Victoria Pier and the funfair. Hetty and Lily dismounted from their bicycles, unable to cycle across the stretch of fine sand. It was difficult even to push their machines with the sand clogging the spokes of the wheels.

'Let's leave them here against this wall,' suggested Hetty. Her eyes scanned the broad expanse of sand dunes where she could see, dotted here and there, caravans and tents and, in the background, the undulations of the switchback railway. Already a tiny frisson of excitement was beginning to take hold of her.

'Are you sure they'll be all right?' Lily's blue eyes opened wide with anxiety. 'Supposing somebody takes them? We wouldn't be able to get home again.'

'Of course we would. We could get a tram.' Hetty laughed. 'Besides, who's going to be bothered stealing these old things? Yours is no better than mine, Lily. Anyway, I know somebody who lives here . . . I think, and if I see . . . them, they can perhaps find us somewhere safer to leave 'em for a while.'

'You know someone . . . D'you mean a gipsy, Hetty? You never said before that you knew anyone who lived here.' Even Lily sounded a mite suspicious.

'I've only just thought about it,' lied Hetty. 'It's just a lad that comes into Tilda's Tavern sometimes. Anyroad, we might not see him. Come on, Lily. The bicycles'll be all right. Let's go and have a look at the funfair.'

The season was not yet in full swing, but a goodly crowd of people had been drawn to the area by the unseasonal sunshine. Hetty and Lily wandered around, taking in every vista of the colourful scene, Lily glancing backwards every so often to the spot where they had abandoned their bicycles. There were Old Dan's Hobbyhorses, a skittle alley, a rifle saloon, ice-cream stalls and, encircling these attractions, the humps of the switchback railway. Hetty's eyes were drawn to the gipsy tents and caravans. Some were ramshackle affairs, tents made from hurdles slung with old blankets, but Hetty knew that Reuben lived in a caravan, a 'vardo' he had called it. Most of the caravans appeared clean and well kept, a contrast to the makeshift tents, and were painted in bold colours, red, green and yellow, and decorated with intricate scrollwork. The ground outside each dwelling-place looked messy, however, strewn with bowls and buckets, rags and paper, the remains of a fire, all the debris of daily living. A few gipsy folk were sitting on the steps of their caravans or wandering about in ones and twos, but there was no sign, yet, of the person that Hetty was seeking.

Fortune-teller Old Gipsy Sarah – of the famous Romany Boswell family – didn't seem to be in evidence today, which was perhaps not surprising as she was well into her nineties by now, but Hetty noticed a tent with a hoarding advertising Jennie Boswell, 'Gipsy Sarah's only clever daughter-in-law'. But it wasn't the Boswell family in whom Hetty was interested.

'Can't you see him, your friend?' said Lily, sounding a little impatient, for Hetty had hardly spoken for the last few minutes.

'No, I can't. But it doesn't matter.' Hetty shrugged. 'I'm not bothered.' She tried to sound as though she didn't care, but her disappointment was beginning to take away the edge of her enthusiasm for this adventure. She must be fair to Lily, though. After all, her friend had only come along at her suggestion. 'Never mind about him,' she said now. 'And stop worriting about the bicycles, Lily. If you keep on turning round like that you'll be turned into a pillar of salt or summat.' She giggled, in spite of her let-down feeling. 'Come on, let's go on the hobbyhorses.'

And then she saw him. She could hardly believe it at first, as though the wish had conjured up not the reality but a mirage. She gave a little start of surprise, then blinked and looked again. Yes, it was Reuben, sure enough, standing behind a large waggon with a bow-top of green canvas, chatting to a small group of friends. She recognised one of them as Luke Freeman who usually came along with Reuben when he visited Tilda's Tavern.

She grasped hold of Lily's arm. 'He's there, that lad that I know. Come on, let's go and ask him if we can leave our bicycles somewhere safe.'

'Which one? Which is your friend?' Lily sounded apprehensive, and she backed away, pulling at Hetty's arm. 'There's so many of them, Hetty.'

'There's only four of 'em. It's the tall one with the red neckerchief. He's called Reuben.' Hetty knew it was no use saying the dark one with the black hair. That would be an accurate description of all of them, but Reuben was the tallest and, to Hetty's mind, the most handsome, although she didn't add this as she pointed him out to Lily.

It was then that Reuben and the other lads, too, became aware that they were being watched. Reuben looked across, frowning slightly, at the two girls standing near the end of the waggon, then recognition dawned in his black eyes and his mouth curved in a slow smile. He moved forward to greet them.

'Well, well. If it isn't Henrietta, the Girl with the Sparkling Eyes. What a nice surprise. Whatever are 'ee doing round here, Henrietta?'

'I've a perfect right to be here if I want.' Hetty stared boldly back at him. 'As a matter of fact we've come to see the funfair, me and me friend. This is Lily Tattersall.' She waved her hand vaguely in Lily's direction. 'We've come on our bicycles and Lily's worried that somebody might walk off with them. D'you think you could put them somewhere safe for us, or else she'll be like a cat on hot bricks all afternoon?'

'Yes, I'll do that.' Reuben nodded seriously. 'You can't trust gipsies. Us be a lot of thieving varmints.'

Hetty looked at him quickly. 'I never said that.' Then she saw that he was laughing and she laughed too. 'You know I didn't mean that, Reuben, but Lily'ud feel happier if they're in a safe place.'

'Of course.' His eyes twinkled at her, then he turned to smile at Lily. 'Anything to oblige a pretty lady.' Lily blushed to the roots of her hair as she stammered her thanks.

'Come on, Luke.' Reuben turned to his friend. 'Us ain't busy this afternoon. What do 'ee say to us helping a couple of damsels in distress? Now, where are these bicycles?'

Hetty led Reuben back towards the edge of the sand dunes, leaving Lily to walk behind with Luke. She knew that her friend would be all right once she had overcome her shyness. Lily liked the company of young men as much as any girl did, but she was a bit backward in coming forward and had a tendency to blush at the slightest thing, which made her appear more nervous than ever. She would come to no harm with Luke Freeman. Hetty had found him very polite and unassuming on the couple of occasions she had met him, albeit briefly. Gipsies, she thought, seemed to have earned an unfair reputation for boldness and fraud – the ones that Hetty had met had been just the opposite.

Luke was quite short, unlike his friend, and

slightly built, with a hooked nose which Hetty thought spoiled his pleasant face and made him appear older than his years. Both he and Reuben, she knew, were in their early twenties, although he hadn't told her his exact age. Trifles such as that seemed unimportant to Reuben.

'Where's Albert this afternoon?' he asked now. 'He ain't with you, then?'

'How should I know where he is?' Hetty's tone was indifferent. 'We don't live in one another's pockets, you know. You seem to have got the wrong idea about me and Albert. We're not engaged or anything like that.'

'You seemed to be pretty thick to me, the pair of you. That's why I've kept my distance lately when I've seen you at the tavern. I didn't want to upset poor old Albert. That lad's mighty fond of 'ee, Henrietta.'

'I shouldn't worry about that if I were you. As a matter of fact . . .' Hetty hesitated for a moment, biting uncertainly at her lip. She had known for some time what she should do about Albert, but she hadn't wanted to hurt him. Now she knew that she wasn't being fair to him, carrying on seeing him and letting him believe that one day she might even marry him; she knew now that she didn't want to marry Albert. Meeting Reuben again had changed all that; she would tell Albert tonight. She would tell him all that she was now going to tell Reuben. In for a penny, in for a pound, she thought as she took a deep breath. 'As a matter of fact,' she said again, 'I've discovered that Albert's not the right lad for me. We always seem to be arguing just lately, and that's no use, is it?' She looked sideways at her companion from beneath demurely lowered eyelashes and smiled at him. 'He's an old-fashioned sort of lad, you know. Very set in his ways, and he's never really liked me singing at the tavern. And I like to have a bit of fun now and again. So that's the way it is.' She shrugged her shoulders and smiled at Reuben again. 'So you don't need to worry about Albert.'

Hetty knew that Reuben would make no further move in her direction while he thought she still belonged, as it were, to someone else. He had hinted as much to her, more than once, and if Albert was no longer on the scene . . . Hetty felt a tremor of almost uncontrollable excitement at the thought of what might happen once the magnetism between her and Reuben was unleashed. Now all that remained for her to do was to tell Albert, as she would do later tonight, that it was all over between them, and to see if Reuben now rose to the bait.

'Poor old Albert,' Reuben said again, but with a sideways grin at Hetty. 'But perhaps 'ee be right, Henrietta. He be a staid sort o' chap, more like an uncle, I reckon, than a young man. I liked him though . . . Now, what about these bicycles?'

Reuben wheeled one bicycle and Luke the other back towards the green waggon where the girls had first encountered the young men. 'Now, what do 'ee say about us taking these young ladies round the funfair?' Reuben winked at his friend, and Luke nodded and grinned in agreement.

'Good idea, Reuben.'

Lily was pink with excitement, but that didn't stop her casting an apprehensive glance in Hetty's

direction. 'It'll be all right, won't it?' she whispered
to her friend while the lads were occupied with the
bicycles, propping them up against the back of the
waggon. 'We can trust them, can't we?'

'Of course we can,' Hetty whispered back.
'They're nice lads, both of them. You shouldn't
believe all you hear about gipsies, Lily. Anyroad,
it's half past two in the afternoon, not midnight.
What harm can we come to?'

It was then that Hetty became aware of someone watching her. She couldn't have said how she
knew, because the person was standing behind
her, but suddenly she felt apprehensive, a tingling
sensation down her spine. She turned quickly.
There, on the steps of the caravan, was a tall,
straight-backed figure. Her jet-black hair was
coiled in thick shining braids round her head, not
flowing loose as it had been when Hetty had first
seen her, giving her the appearance of an Egyp-
tian princess. Her glance was regal, too, and
haughty, but at this moment there was a tiny
glimmer of doubt in her eyes as though she
couldn't quite remember . . . But Hetty knew
immediately who this was. It was the fortune-
teller from the sands, Reuben's sister, Drusilla.
Then, as recognition gradually dawned upon the
gipsy girl her eyes narrowed, becoming as cold
and hard as two black cinders. She didn't
acknowledge Hetty with so much as a nod, but
stalked down the steps, her head held high, and
disappeared round the corner of the caravan.
Hetty felt a chill of fear, as though the sun had
passed behind a cloud, although the incident had
taken but a few seconds. Lily hadn't even noticed.

Reuben came across and took her arm. 'Come along, Henrietta. Let's go and enjoy the funfair . . . What's the matter?' For Hetty was standing stock-still, her eyes glazed over with something akin to dread. 'You look as if you've seen a ghost.' He looked at her in concern. 'What is it, Henrietta?'

'Nothing.' She shook her head bemusedly. 'Nothing at all. I just felt . . . dizzy for a moment, that's all.' She smiled at him. 'I'm all right again now, honestly I am.' She turned round to grin at Lily and Luke. 'Aren't we the lucky ones, Lily, getting a couple of gentlemen to show us around? Now think on, Luke, we want to see everything.'

'Yes, ma'am. Anything you say, ma'am.' Luke touched his forehead in a mock salute and grinned back at her, while Lily blushed even pinker.

Hetty turned back to Reuben. 'Your sister doesn't look too pleased,' she remarked, trying to make her voice sound normal, although she still felt disturbed by the girl's obvious hostility. 'In fact she looked as mad as anything when she saw me and Lily here.'

'My sister?' Reuben frowned. 'Oh, I suppose you mean Drusilla.'

'Yes, Drusilla.' Hetty nodded. 'She came storming out of the caravan while we were waiting for you to see to the bicycles. She looked real angry, I can tell you.'

'Yes, I daresay she would,' said Reuben thoughtfully. He turned to smile at Hetty. 'But Drusilla's not my sister . . .'

'She's not . . .?' Hetty stared at him in astonishment. 'But you said . . .'

'No, I didn't. It was you that said so, Henrietta. Drusilla and me, we be cousins. Drusilla Loveday, she be called, same as me. Our fathers are brothers. Were brothers, I should say. Uncle Benjamin died last year.'

'You're very much alike, you and Drusilla,' said Hetty slowly, the possible reason for the gipsy girl's hostility slowly beginning to dawn on her.

'Yes, that's true. Our Drusilla's like a sister to me really, especially this last year, since we've been living up here.'

And what about Drusilla? thought Hetty. Did she think of Reuben as her brother? Hetty very much doubted it.

'Never mind about her now, Henrietta.' Reuben took hold of her arm. 'We be used to her temper tantrums. I daresay she'd had words with Ma. She often does. It's best to leave Drusilla alone to cool her heels when her gets herself in a rage. Now, how about Old Dan's Hobbyhorses? Shall us make a start here?'

The four of them climbed on to the massive steeds with the flowing manes, garishly painted in vermilion and gold, and clung tightly to the twisted poles like sticks of barley sugar, as the horses went round and round, up and down, slowly at first then faster and faster. The scenery flashed past them, caravans, tents, sand dunes, blue sky and a distant glimpse of the sea, in a whirling kaleidoscope pattern. The girls could hardly walk in a straight line when they dismounted, and they clung on to the lads' arms for support, shrieking with laughter.

'Now, what do 'ee say to us taking 'em on the

switchback railway?' Reuben's eyes gleamed roguishly, and the girls' cries of, 'Oh no! Please don't . . . I'll just die! I know I will . . .' were not heeded. Hetty and Lily, indeed, had never intended that they should be.

Their hearts were in their mouths one minute, then down at the pit of their stomachs the next, as the roller coaster hurtled them relentlessly up to the sky, then down to the ground, each undulation more terrifying than the last. Their screams, they were sure, could be heard as far as North Pier, as they hung on like grim death to the steel bar in front of them and, at each rushing descent, buried their heads against the rough tweed of their companions' jackets. Then, with a squeal of brakes and a sickening jolt, the ride was at an end.

'Never again! Never, as long as I live, shall I go on there again!' Lily didn't know whether to laugh or cry and she was afraid she was going to disgrace herself by being sick.

'I thought my last hour had come! Are you sure it hasn't? Are you sure I'm not dead?' Hetty looked to Reuben for the assurance that she didn't need because, apart from feeling dizzy and, like Lily, liable to be sick at any moment, she had never felt more alive or more wildly excited.

'You look very lively to me, Henrietta.' Reuben touched her arm and as she felt his fingers tighten round her elbow her feeling of exhilaration increased. 'Let's go and sit on the grass and get our breath back. You'll be all right when you've had a rest.'

The lads sprawled and the girls sat, more decorously, on the tussocks of tough, prickly grass that sprouted from the sand dunes. Hetty picked up a handful of the fine sand and let it trickle through her fingers. It was the same sand that bordered the Fylde coast for fifteen miles or so, from Lytham in the south to Fleetwood in the north, but here it was unwashed by the sea. It couldn't be moulded into sandpies and castles as could the coarse-grained, malleable stuff that children delighted in on the beach at Blackpool. It resembled fine gold dust, Hetty thought as she watched it running through her fingers.

She pulled off her soft tweed hat that matched her green jacket and threw it on to the sand, then shook her head to loosen the mass of auburn curls. 'I think I can do without that for a while,' she said. 'It's a warm day all right. The season'll be starting early at our boarding house if this keeps up. And we'll be busy at Laycock's an' all, eh, Lily?'

'Ugh . . . Don't remind me!' Lily gave an exaggerated groan. 'I was just enjoying meself. It'll be soon enough to think about that tomorrer, Hetty.'

'Right, girls.' Luke jumped to his feet. 'If your stomachs are back in the right place I think we'll have a drink. Lemonade do for you?'

The girls nodded their approval so Luke and Reuben went to a nearby stall and came back with four bottles of lemonade which they drank through straws.

Hetty giggled. 'It's a good job we didn't have this before the ride, or I don't think it'd have stayed put for very long.'

Lily groaned again and clutched at her stomach. 'Shut up, Hetty! I was just beginning to settle down. Don't start me off again.'

'Now don't get too settled,' Luke told her. 'You and me's going to the skittle alley, Lily. You told me you'd like to have a go. What about you two?' He turned to Hetty and Reuben. 'Coming?'

Hetty looked to her companion to answer for her. He shook his head. 'No, I think I'll show Henrietta how well I can shoot.' He pointed to the nearby rifle saloon which was advertising 'Four shots for 3d'. 'I've a feeling that this might be my lucky day, Luke. Just 'ee watch me come back with the star prize.'

'Showing off again!' Luke laughed. 'All right then. We'll leave you to it. Come on, Lily. We'll see you back here in about half an hour.'

'Yes, we mustn't be any longer, must we, Hetty?' Lily was looking anxious again. 'Don't forget we've to cycle all the way back, and I told Mother as I'd be back for tea.'

'Stop worriting, Lily.' Hetty leaned back against the cushion of sand and grass. 'We shan't be late. Just go and enjoy yerself.' Hetty didn't want to think about going home. She wished that this golden afternoon would last for ever.

'Now, don't 'ee go worrying about Drusilla,' said Reuben as the other two departed, although Hetty, at that moment, hadn't been thinking about her at all. He lounged on the sand at her side, propping himself up on one elbow. 'I think I told 'ee before that she's a wild girl. That's why us stayed on here in Blackpool, so as she'd have somebody to turn to. Ma and Pa felt responsible when she was left on her own.'

Hetty remembered now that Reuben had mentioned, on the night of the storm, that he and his parents had moved to Blackpool because of some family trouble. 'What happened to her parents?' she asked now, although she didn't really care very much.

'They both died of the fever last year,' said Reuben. 'Us had just come to Blackpool from Gloucestershire, like I told 'ee before. It was supposed to be just a visit, but when this happened Ma and Pa decided to stay here and see to Drusilla, and I stayed along with 'em.'

'There's only you then? You've no brothers or sisters?'

'I've two brothers,' Reuben replied. 'But they be in Gloucestershire, both of 'em. They had girl-friends there, y'see. They didn't want to come up north, so when us moved they stayed there. I be the youngest, like Drusilla. She be the youngest in her family, too. There were four of 'em altogether, two girls and two boys.'

'What about her brothers and sisters then? Don't they feel responsible for her?' Hetty was getting tired of the subject of Drusilla, although she had felt a pang of sympathy for the poor lass when she heard about her parents' deaths. But she could see that Reuben needed to talk about it.

'They be all married and living miles from here,' said Reuben. 'No, there was only us to see to the lass, and she needed some seeing to, I can tell 'ee, when her ma and pa died. I remember how she went berserk.' Reuben's eyes narrowed and glazed over momentarily as he stared into the distance. 'She smashed all the china and threw it around the vardo, and tore all her ma's clothes into

305

shreds. Like a wild animal, she was. It didn't matter much, though, about the damage her did because all the lot had to be burned.'

'Burned? What do you mean?'

'It be our custom, Henrietta,' Reuben said quietly. 'When somebody dies we burn the vardo and all the possessions. But most of the stuff had been destroyed anyway by the time Drusilla had finished her rampaging. Yes, she's a wild 'un and no mistake. She's calmed down a bit now, but us have to watch her like a hawk sometimes.'

'So she lives with you, then? In the same caravan?' Hetty was wondering about the sleeping arrangements.

'Yes, most of the time. But I sleeps outside in a tent. It's what us always do when there's brothers and sisters in a family.' He grinned. 'Ma and Pa are very proper, Henrietta. Most Romanies are, I can tell 'ee. But Drusilla sometimes goes to stay in her aunt's vardo now – that be her mother's sister – they settled here last year. And I think Ma's relieved to tell 'ee the truth. Drusilla can be a handful at times.'

'It sounds like it,' Hetty replied, feeling bemused by all these confidences and by a glimpse into a way of life that was entirely foreign to her.

'Anyway, that's enough about Drusilla.' Reuben stood up and stretched out a hand to pull Hetty to her feet. 'Come on. Let's see if I can win 'ee a prize. I be a good shot, like I told 'ee.'

It was no idle boast and Reuben's score at the rifle range won him one of the best prizes from the shelf at the back.

'What would 'ee like, Henrietta?' he asked

proudly, putting his arm round her shoulders. She glanced at him in admiration. He really was a marvellous shot, and she could tell that he was flushed not only with success, but with delight that he was able to give pleasure to her.

She looked at the array of gifts – vases, wooden dolls and animals, gaudily painted pottery – and she chose a Staffordshire flatback ornament, sometimes called a 'fairing', depicting a pair of lovers, a sailor in a broad-brimmed hat and blue jacket and his lady friend with black ringlets and a crimson blouse, seated in front of a red, white and blue flag. It was just the sort of thing that Mam would like for the mantelpiece of her posh parlour, but Hetty intended to keep it on her own narrow shelf in the bedroom she shared with Grace.

'Thank you, Reuben. It's lovely.' Hetty was so full of happiness and high spirits that she stood on tiptoe and placed a kiss on his cheek.

'Thank 'ee, ma'am!' Reuben grinned at her, and the look in his eyes told her how much he would like to kiss her in return, and not on her cheek, she guessed. But the fairground was crowded at this spot, so all he could do was put his arm round her as they walked back to the place where they had arranged to meet Luke and Lily.

'I can see 'ee again, can't I, Henrietta?' he asked, pulling her closer to him. 'Now that you and Albert are not . . . I be sorry about Albert, but not too sorry, mind.' His black eyes gleamed mischievously and Hetty thought again about what could happen if all that latent attraction that they felt for one another were to be released.

'You know what they say, Henrietta. It be an ill wind that blows nobody any good . . . and it's blown you to me, hasn't it . . . love?' His last word was just a whisper, but Hetty's heart leapt as she heard it. 'I'll come to Tilda's Tavern this week. You'll be there on Tuesday?'

Hetty nodded happily. 'Yes, I'll be there, Reuben.'

'And maybe you'll come here again? On your own next time? Please say 'ee will, Henrietta.'

'Yes, Reuben. I'll come again.' Hetty knew that there was nothing more certain.

'D'you know what I think?' said Lily as they cycled home.

'No, what's that?' Hetty turned to smile at her friend, thinking what a wonderful friend she was. And what a wonderful afternoon it had turned out to be. And as for Reuben, well, he was the most wonderful of all. Hetty felt as though she loved the whole wide world and everyone and everything in it.

'I think that you planned all this.' Lily nodded emphatically, like a grown-up admonishing a naughty child.

'Lily! However could you say such a thing? As if I would!' Hetty scowled at her friend, before they both collapsed into giggles and wobbled perilously near the tram track.

'And d'you know what else I think?' Lily's big blue eyes and her rosebud mouth were three round Os of delight. 'I'm ever so glad you did!'

So am I, thought Hetty. Oh, so am I. The sun was low in the sky as they pedalled back north-

wards along the promenade. Not setting just yet –
there were still a couple of hours of daylight left –
but gradually westering, a huge golden ball trans-
forming the grey sea to an expanse of shimmering
turquoise and aquamarine, shot here and there
with streaks of silver. A wondrous sight, and a
fitting end to a perfect afternoon.

'What was she doing here?' Drusilla's eyes held a
look of animosity and wariness and, Reuben
thought, of fear as well. But her stance was as
aggressive as ever as she stood on the steps of the
vardo, hands on hips and her mouth set in a thin,
straight line.

'I suppose 'ee means Henrietta Turnbull?'
Reuben's tone was casual.

'You know perfectly well who I mean. That
cheeky minx that had her fortune told last summer. What does she want to come here for, pushing her nose in where she's not wanted? I saw you
with her, Reuben Loveday, strolling round the
funfair as thick as thieves.'

It was on the tip of Reuben's tongue to tell
Drusilla to mind her own business, but he knew
better than to upset her when she was in a mood
like this. As he had told Henrietta, you always
had to be on your guard with Drusilla. 'I reckon
she came to see the funfair,' he replied. 'Why else
would she be here? It's the only reason for folk
coming down here, isn't it? And they asked us to
look after their bicycles, Henrietta and her friend.
So now 'ee knows, Drusilla. That's all there is to
it.'

Drusilla's eyes were pools of darkness in her

sallow face, stagnant with dislike and distrust. 'No good'll come of it, Reuben Loveday, mixing with gorgio girls. Your ma and pa wouldn't like it. You're playing with fire and it'll only lead to trouble. I can see it coming. I knew as soon as I set eyes on that girl that she was trouble.'

Not half as much trouble as you, Drusilla, said Reuben to himself. He realised that his cousin was in love with him, or thought she was. He had known it for a long time, if he were honest with himself, but he had tried to push the thought away. It was nothing unusual for cousins to marry; it was, indeed, often encouraged in their tribe where family ties were strong. But in this instance it would not be deemed a desirable match by his parents, even if it were to be the means of Drusilla forsaking her wild ways. And to him, Reuben, the whole idea was anathema. He had tried, unsuccessfully, to encourage one or another of his friends, Luke or Ben or Daniel, to take an interest in her, but the tale of Drusilla's hysterical frenzy at the time of her parents' death had spread like wildfire around the camp in spite of his family's attempts to quell it.

For he hadn't told Henrietta the whole of the story; how, when his father, Drusilla's uncle, had tried to restrain her she had gone for him with a knife. The injury had been only a flesh wound in his shoulder, but nasty for all that, and it had been some time before they had been able to staunch the bleeding. They had managed to keep the police out of it, dismissing it as a family fracas, but which Romany family, hearing of it, would be willing to welcome such a hoyden into their midst?

Fierce outbursts of temper were not unknown
in gipsy families. Romany women, when they got
into a rage, would often damage even their own
valuable possessions, smashing china and tearing
clothes and scattering the contents of the vardo
far and wide. But when it came to inflicting bodily
harm, that was something else. Reuben knew
that Drusilla was a young woman whom most of
his friends preferred to keep at arm's-length.

'I think 'ee be imagining things,' he told her
now, keeping his voice calm. 'The trouble's all in
your mind, Drusilla. They be nice lasses, both of
them, and Luke and me just showed them around.
No harm done, I tell 'ee.' He grinned in a cheerful
manner, but Drusilla was not to be won round so
easily. She turned on her heel and stalked into the
waggon.

Reuben sighed as he watched her, for no matter
what Drusilla thought, Reuben intended to go on
seeing Henrietta.

It had been a rum sort of teatime, Martha thought
afterwards. What with Hetty grinning to herself
like that Cheshire cat they used to read about
when they were little, and Grace looking as
though she'd lost a half-crown and found a tanner,
and Walter looking daggers at 'em all across the
tea table. Martha had felt as though she were
banging her head against a brick wall, trying to
keep the conversation going and acting as though
nothing was wrong. She was glad when they'd all
cleared off after tea so that she could have the
parlour to herself and enjoy a bit of peace.

Her parlour was looking real grand, that was

one blessing, now that there was more money coming into the house. She'd managed to get the sideboard that she'd set her heart on from the saleroom in Church Street, a walnut chiffonier with fancy carved brackets and spindles. And she and the girls, with a little help from Albert again, had varnished the door and skirting boards in the same rich brown colour as the sideboard and papered the walls in a pattern of russet leaves and orange flowers. They'd bought some new chairs, too – well, not really new, but new to them – from the saleroom, with low curved button backs. Martha felt very proud that her parlour could now equal Alice Gregson's any day of the week.

It was a good feeling that they were earning enough money between them to prevent Martha worrying about how she was going to pay the bills. The girls' wages helped, and her own catering job with Donnelly's, and now, of course, she had the lodgers.

'You'll never be able to get rid of them,' Alice had warned her, 'once they get their feet under the table.'

But Grace and Hetty had supported Martha in her belief that it would be an advantage to have steady money coming in all the year round, even if the lodgers did stay put during the summer. Martha knew that she wouldn't have the heart, in any event, to turn them out of their rooms to make room for seasonal visitors, even if the latter did pay a mite more.

So they now had two lodgers at Welcome Rest. One was Leonard Whittaker, a lad of about Hetty's age who was employed as a booking clerk at nearby North Station. His parents lived at Kirkham, which was a long way for him to travel each day, so he had decided to find himself digs in the area.

The other lodger was George Makepeace, and Martha was pleased to see that the two men got on together as though they had known one another all their lives. Poor George needed consoling after the death of his wife some nine months ago. He had struggled to keep the house going, he had told Martha, just a small terraced place – two up and two down – round the corner at the back of the station, but in the end he had been forced to admit defeat.

'It's the loneliness that I can't cope with, Mrs Turnbull,' he had explained to her. 'That awful sinking feeling I get every night when I turn the key in the lock and know that there's nobody on the other side of the door to greet me.'

Martha knew the feeling only too well. Hadn't she experienced it herself, after Fred died, and felt too, as George must be feeling now, that the grief would never lessen? But she had had the girls, and what a comfort they had been to her, whereas poor George had no family. Any thoughts Martha had about the wisdom, or otherwise, of giving up his little home she kept to herself. It was none of her business and, after all, she was wanting a lodger so it behoved her to keep quiet. But he would have, she guessed, a nice little nest egg tucked away from the sale of his property, should he ever think of starting up on his own again. For the moment, though, he seemed quite content.

'Home from home, this is,' he told her, 'and

313

young Leonard's like a son to me. I'm certainly glad Mr Pickering recommended you, Mrs Turnbull. It's one of the best days' work I ever did, moving in here.'

George worked for Samuel Pickering as a joiner, and therefore was known to Henry, Alice's husband, and to Albert. He wasn't much of a mixer, he admitted to Martha. He preferred the fireside of an evening, with a newspaper or a good book and his pipe for company, and didn't mind the solitude, just so long as he knew that there were friends within hailing distance should he need them. Martha knew exactly what he meant. Solitude was not the same thing as loneliness.

George and Leonard shared a room on the top landing. It was up in the eaves and had a sloping ceiling, but it was quite a large room and, as well as the two single beds, there was room for two easy chairs. There was also a small fireplace and George and Leonard between them saw to the carrying-up of buckets of coal and laying the fire. They ate their meals, even though there were no other visitors at the moment, at a small table in the corner of the dining room.

'They're not family, when all's said and done,' Alice told Martha. 'And if you'll take a tip from me, you'll keep 'em separate. It wouldn't do to have 'em dining with you and the lasses. You've got to respect your privacy, Martha, or else you'll never have a minute to yourself.'

Martha was glad of the homilies that Alice sent her way. She was, she felt, still green about many aspects of the boarding-house trade and was always willing to learn. She had been a Blackpool

314

landlady for less than a year, although it seemed much longer. Only a year ago the three of them had been in Burnley with no thought of moving to the seaside, and now, look at all that had happened to them since they came here . . .

Walter Clayton turning up on the doorstep had set the cat among the pigeons all right. Martha had considered, at first, on learning he had digs round the corner, asking him to come and stay at Welcome Rest. She could easily have squeezed in another lodger. Now she was jolly relieved that she hadn't mentioned it. She hadn't expected Grace to be over the moon at seeing him again – the lad hadn't played fair with her, Martha had to admit – but she hadn't been prepared for such an adverse reaction. The girl had positively recoiled from him at first, although she had struggled to regain her composure and to act with at least a semblance of normality. She had gone as white as a sheet, though, and Martha had been frightened that she was going to faint.

It was partly her own fault, the silly lass. Martha had warned her that she should tell Walter about Edwin Donnelly. No doubt that was what she'd be doing right now. The pair of them had gone for a walk on the promenade, Walter, most surprisingly, saying that he didn't want to go to chapel that evening; he wanted to talk to Grace.

And that young madam, Hetty, now what was she up to? All those secretive smiles boded no good, and Martha knew that wherever she had been this afternoon it hadn't been with Albert. Martha had seen him skulking off down the street with a real hangdog expression on his face. She fancied that things had not been right between them for some time now. Albert was a grand lad, but Martha sometimes wondered if he was, after all, quite right for Hetty. She was such a lively lass and he was so staid, more like a fellow in his forties than his twenties. And he had never really got used to her singing at the tavern. Ah well, it was up to Grace and Hetty to sort out their own affairs. Martha couldn't go on mollycoddling them all their lives. She had to let them make their own decisions, and their own mistakes, too, although it was hard at times just to sit back and watch it happen. It had been much easier, in a lot of ways, when they were still bairns.

Chapter 14

'I don't believe you, Grace. You can't do this to me.' Walter halted in his stride and swung round and took hold of Grace by the arms. His fingers, like steel bands, dug into her flesh. 'You don't mean it. Tell me you don't mean it.' His eyes were ugly with venom and his cold stare reminded Grace of a snake ready to pounce on its victim. She had seen one in the Tower menagerie not long ago and had thought it was a vile creature. It had made her shudder with loathing, and now Walter's eyes, pale grey and reptilian, were having the same effect on her.

'Don't, Walter. You're hurting me,' she cried as his grip hardened and he began to shake her backwards and forwards. She recalled his anger with her that night last summer, when they had walked together on the moors above Burnley and she had told him they were moving to Blackpool, but now his fury was much more intense. She struggled to break free and he pushed her away with such force that she staggered against the promenade railings.

He turned away from her and stared out to sea. The sky was dark now and storm clouds hovered, the earlier promise of the day having broken down with the coming of dusk. The pale moon shed a little radiance and here, on the north promenade, the newly installed electric lights bathed everything in a soft luminous glow. Grace and Walter were impervious, though, to the scene around them.

Walter's anger boiled up again and he swung round to face her. 'How dare you say that you don't want to see me any more? I've come here to marry you. I've given up me job at the mill and me home in Burnley, and all for you, Grace Turnbull. Then you have the nerve to say that it's over between us. Well, it's not over, Grace, I'm telling you. I don't give in as easily as that. I won't be cast on one side like an old coat.' He looked at her steadily, his gaze still cold and hard, then he grasped hold of her arms again, but not so fiercely this time. 'And you promised to marry me, Grace. You can't deny it. You promised.' His voice was quiet now and wheedling, the voice of a child who had failed to get his own way.

'I didn't promise, Walter.' Grace shook her head, but not too emphatically, recalling how she had given in – well, half given in – at Walter's insistence and because she had felt afraid of him. 'I admit I may have given you the impression that I'd marry you, and if you feel let down, well, I'm sorry. But I should think your treatment of me these last few months cancels out any promise I might have made.'

'What d'you mean, my treatment of you? I've wrote to you, haven't I? And you know very well how ill me mam was. I couldn't leave her and come gadding over to Blackpool to see you. I don't reckon you've any cause to complain. You knew I'd come sooner or later. And now I'm here, and what do I find? That you're walking out with another chap, a toffee-nosed one an' all. I suppose that's where you were this afternoon? Out with this Edwin Donnelly fellow. I thought your mother looked a bit flustered when she said you'd gone bicycling with a friend, but I never dreamt . . .'

'I thought Mam might have told you who I was with,' said Grace quietly.

'Well, she didn't. And why should she do your dirty work for you? At least you could have written to tell me, Grace. And I'd soon have been over, I can tell you, to put a stop to all this nonsense.'

'It's not nonsense, Walter. I've been seeing Edwin – quite a lot – and I intend to go on seeing him. And I don't care what you say. For all I knew you might have found someone else. In fact, I really thought you had.'

'There'll never be anyone else for me, Grace.' His words were just a whisper. 'And I'll not give you up. Never! D'you hear?' He banged his fist on the iron railings as his voice resumed its former hectoring tones. 'I'm staying here in Blackpool till you come to your senses. And you'll be only too glad to come crawling back to me when that Johnny-come-lately throws you over. You just see if I'm not right. I don't suppose he's asked you to marry him, has he, this Edwin Donnelly?'

'No, he hasn't,' Grace replied truthfully, but she held her head high, proudly and defiantly. 'But he

319

loves me and he will ask me. And when he does, then I'll say yes. He can't ask me at the moment. It's difficult . . . His mother's ill and . . .' Grace paused, unwilling to tell Walter any more. It wouldn't be wise, at all events, to mention their difference in religion. It would only be more fuel to his fire, and Walter would be sure to find out, sooner or later, if he remained in Blackpool, that the Donnellys were staunch Roman Catholics. And there was no need to mention Clara Donnelly's antagonism, nor that of her own mother. Why should she have to justify herself to Walter Clayton anyway? It was really none of his business.

'Oh yes, it's difficult, I don't doubt.' Walter's voice was scornful. 'It'll always be difficult. There'll always be some excuse or another. He'll not marry you, Grace. He's no intention of marrying you. The Edwin Donnellys of this world don't go marrying young lasses as work in their shop. He'll happen string you along for a while – fellows like him are good at that – but when it comes to getting wed he'll choose one of his own kind. You mark my words.'

'You know nothing at all about him, Walter. You've never met Edwin and you've not the least idea what he's like, so if I were you I'd shut up about him.' Grace's indignation was adding fire to her words and her former trepidation at Walter's anger was receding a little. She was determined that she wouldn't let him intimidate her any longer. 'I love Edwin and he loves me and . . . and I'm going to marry him,' she added firmly. He hadn't asked her yet, but she knew that it was only a matter of time. She belonged to Edwin now. They had declared their love for one another that afternoon in an unashamed commitment. Nothing could touch them now. Nobody could ever come between them. She was Edwin's, and his alone, for all time.

She turned to Walter again. 'Please believe what I say, Walter. It's no use. It's all over between you and me.' She reached out and gently touched his arm. 'I'm sorry if I've hurt you, but it would be wrong to go on seeing you. I love Edwin now.'

He didn't answer, but just continued to look at her fixedly, his pale-grey eyes seeming to probe the depths of her being, so that a tremor of fear welled up in her again. Then, 'Come on, I'll see you home,' he muttered, taking hold of her elbow.

They didn't speak during the five-minute walk back to the boarding house, and when they paused by the gate of Welcome Rest it was Grace who broke the silence.

'Thank you for seeing me home, Walter,' she said. 'It was kind of you not to let me walk back on my own. And I'm sorry. Truly I am, but I won't change my mind. I can't, not now, but you'll find someone else, Walter. I know you will . . .' Her voice died away as Walter's eyes blazed into her own.

'I won't change my mind either, Grace Turnbull. You're my girl and I shan't let you go, not ever. Goodnight, Grace. You'll be seeing me again. Soon . . . I promise . . .' His last words were a sibilant whisper, and again Grace was reminded of a snake, the creature that was so loathsome to her. She shook her head in silent disbelief at her own thoughts as she watched him stride away up the street. She didn't loathe Walter or even dislike him. How could she when they had been friends – loving friends at one time – for so long? But still the disquiet remained. It was as though Walter's presence and his chilling words, 'You'll be seeing me again . . .', had left a stain on the pristine freshness of her love for Edwin, and Grace shivered with foreboding.

'Don't take on so, Gracie.' Hetty put her arm round her sister's thin shoulders as they huddled close together in the depths of the feather bed. 'You've told Walter that it's all over between you and him, so you can't do any more. And what can he do about it? I'll tell you what he can do. Nothing! Never mind all that rubbish about not letting you go. He'll have to when he realises that you're serious about Edwin. He'll get the message, Gracie, before long. Whatever else Walter Clayton is he's not a fool, and he's got his pride an' all. He won't want to carry on chasing around after you when he sees it's no use.'

'You don't understand, Hetty.' Grace tried to sniff back her tears. 'I'm scared of him. I don't know why, and I know it's silly of me, but I can't help it. It's the way he looks at me, all creepy somehow, with those pale staring eyes. He's changed, Hetty. I never used to feel like that about him.'

'Huh! I wouldn't let a cocky little fellow like Walter Clayton frighten me. He's all talk, that one. He thinks he's cock of the midden when he gets up in t'pulpit, bashing away on his Bible. But from what I've heard he's not all he's cracked up to be, not by a long chalk.'

'What d'you mean, Hetty?' Grace sat up and looked at her sister. 'What d'you know about him?'

'Oh . . . nothing much.' Hetty was sorry she had spoken, but the words had been out before she had realised what she was saying. And when all was said and done she didn't know all that much. Only vague rumours about Walter Clayton being at the other side of town more often than was reasonable, and about a woman old enough to be his mother, but just who it was Hetty had no idea. The gossip had been circulating round the mill long before they left Burnley, but it had never reached Grace's ears. Grace had been such an innocent, trusting sort of girl – she still was – that no one had liked to mention it to her. Hetty didn't really want to disillusion her now, but neither did she want her sister to go on thinking that Walter was blameless. 'I haven't heard much, Grace, only that he was a bit . . . friendly, like, with another woman. An older woman. You know what I mean. It might not be true – you know what the lasses at the mill were like for tittle-tattling – it's just a rumour that were going round.'

'I'm sure you're wrong, Hetty.' Grace sounded horrified. 'I can't imagine Walter . . . What? To stand up and preach at folks about 'em being sinners and then to . . . Oh no, I can't believe that, our Hetty.'

'You're too trusting, Grace. That's your problem.' Hetty stared into the semidarkness towards her sister. Grace's eyes were luminous in the shadow, uncertain and bewildered. 'I always thought that he wasn't good enough for you, that Walter Clayton, but I certainly wasn't frightened of him, and no more should you be. Pompous little prig he was, he just made me want to laugh and I think he knew it an' all. He was never right smitten with me.'

'No, I remember the pair of you didn't get on too well.' Grace tried to smile. 'So you really think he'll leave me alone now, do you? He won't pester me any more? He says he's staying in Blackpool, he's got a job here and he won't let me go. Oh, Hetty . . .' Grace's voice was rising again, in a crescendo of panic.

'Steady on, Gracie.' Hetty took her sister by the arm and shook her gently. 'You really must stop all this. You're going to make yourself ill. I've told you, he can't do anything. Forget him. He's just not worth it. Anyroad, I've heard enough about silly old Walter. What about Edwin? Did you have a good time this afternoon? Where did you go?'

'Into the country. Near St Michael's.' Grace's voice held no enthusiasm. It had all been so wonderful, but now it had been tainted by Walter's reappearance. All the joy seemed to have vanished. 'Yes . . . We had a lovely time,' she went on. 'The daffodils were blooming in the gardens and the birds were singing. It was . . . grand,' she finished lamely.

'Well then!' Hetty beamed at her. 'And you were with Edwin, and you'll see him again tomorrow, and the day after, and the day after that, so what have you got to worry about?' An impish gleam came into Hetty's eyes. 'And never mind the daffodils and the birds an' all that. Tell me, did you stay on your bicycles all the time? I bet you didn't!'

Grace actually smiled. She put out a finger and touched the tip of Hetty's nose. 'Just keep that out of it, little sister. You want to know far too much.'

Hetty grinned. She was sure there wouldn't be a great deal that Grace hadn't told her. She wouldn't get up to much, not their Grace, but Hetty had succeeded in what she was trying to do. She had managed to remove the stricken look from her sister's face and make her smile again. And Hetty had problems of her own at the moment. Perhaps, now, Grace might listen to her.

Grace's next words sounded as though she had read her sister's mind. 'Well, I reckon that's enough about me. I just had to tell you though, Hetty. I was that worked up about it all. But I'll try not to worry about Walter, honest I will. You know what Mam's always saying, "It'll all come out in the wash." Now, what about you, little sister? What about that bicycle ride with Lily? From the look on your face I'd say that you've got a secret or two up your sleeve.'

'And you'd be right, Grace.' Hetty nodded, soberly for once, and when she spoke her voice was serious too. 'You're not the only one with man problems. I've got 'em an' all. It's me and Albert. It's all over, Grace.'

'No! It can't be. Whatever do you mean? Why, Hetty?' Grace seemed, momentarily, to have forgotten her own worries. Then, 'Where did you go this afternoon?' she asked, looking suspiciously at her sister. 'Has that got something to do with it?'

'You might say so.' Hetty grinned wryly. 'We went to the funfair.' Grace still continued to look at her blankly. 'You know, at South Shore . . . near the gipsy encampment,' she added with emphasis. 'Now do you see?'

'The gipsy . . .? You mean you went to see that Reuben? Oh, Hetty! And Albert found out? Well, I don't wonder he was mad with you, but I daresay he'll forgive you. I can't see Albert bearing a grudge for long. But really, you are the limit sometimes, our Hetty.'

Hetty had to smile at Grace's 'big sister' voice. But now it was her turn to say, 'You don't understand. It's not just that Albert's mad at me. It's all over between us. I'm not going to see him any more. I told him so tonight. I'm . . . well, I'm going with Reuben now. I was with him all afternoon, and he's coming to Tilda's Tavern on Tuesday, and then I'm going to the fairground to see him again. Oh, it's all so exciting, Gracie. I just can't wait!'

'And what about poor Albert?' Grace didn't sound as though she shared Hetty's excitement. 'What did he have to say about it?'

'He was a bit upset,' said Hetty in a tiny voice, her elation, for the moment, subsiding. 'But I think he understands.'

To say that Albert was 'a bit upset' was, as Hetty knew full well, a vast understatement. He had been devastated.

'Hetty? Hetty . . . love?' His eyes were full of pain, like a puppy that had been scolded, and yet

326

there was no reproach there. He kept repeating her name in disbelief. 'But, Hetty . . . I don't understand. You say you don't want to go on seeing me? But why, Hetty? You're my girl, aren't you? You've been my girl for ages now, an' I'm saving up for a ring and . . .'

'I'm sorry, Albert.' Hetty placed a hand on his arm and gave it a little squeeze. Gosh! This was proving to be much harder than she had anticipated, and he didn't know the real reason yet. He didn't know about Reuben, but she would have to tell him. If she didn't he would only find out from someone else. 'I like you a lot. I'll always like you, but I'm too young to settle down, to be engaged and to think about getting married an' all that. I want to have . . . well, I want to have a bit of fun first.'

Albert nodded soberly. 'Aye, I know I'm not what you could call a bundle of fun, Hetty. But we're as the good Lord made us, all the lot of us.' He stared morosely across the stretch of black sea, at the foam-capped waves illumined only faintly by the pale moon. There was little light on this part of the promenade save that created by God. Albert and Hetty had often walked there, delighting in the near darkness and stopping now and again to kiss. It was Albert's favourite stretch of the promenade up here, just a clifftop path really, near to Uncle Tom's Cabin. It was where he had brought Grace and Hetty that first night. Ever since she had come to Blackpool it had been Hetty, Hetty, only Hetty for Albert. She was the first girl he had ever kissed, and Albert wanted her to be the only one. He didn't want anyone but Hetty and if she wasn't with him then he would never visit this part of Blackpool again, never.

He turned to face her now. 'I know I've been hard on you lately, Hetty. We've done a lot of arguing, haven't we, love? I'm sorry – I didn't mean to be so heavy-handed with you.'

'It's not that, Albert. It's not because we fall out. All couples fall out now and again, it's only natural.'

'But I've been a bit awkward with you lately, more than a bit, I know I have.' Albert sighed. 'I'm just an ordinary sort o' chap. Dull as ditchwater compared with you, Hetty. You're like a . . . a ray of sunshine. You brighten the place up. Not like me. I'm an old stick-in-the-mud, I know that's what the chaps at work think about me. I suppose I was trying to exert my authority when I went on at you, throwing me weight about, like, so as you'd take more notice of me. Happen I've gone too far. I'm sorry, Hetty.'

'I've told you, it's not that, Albert.' Hetty knew that it was, in fact, partly the reason. She had been annoyed with Albert trying to boss her about, although she had known that he was only trying to behave as he thought a real man should, showing his dominance over the weaker sex. But she knew that she couldn't, in all fairness, allow him to take any of the blame for what had happened now. It was her fault entirely and she had to tell him so, although it was going to be one of the most difficult things she had ever done. 'Albert . . . listen. It's not your fault at all. There's . . . there's somebody else.'

'Somebody else? You mean . . . another chap?'

Hetty nodded.

Then realisation dawned in Albert's eyes and they narrowed speculatively. 'It's that gipsy lad, isn't it? That Reuben . . . what's he called? Reuben Lovelace or summat.'

'Reuben Loveday,' said Hetty quietly. 'Yes, it is.'

'I might have known. I might have bloody well known.' Hetty was astounded at Albert's words. She had never before heard him use even the mildest swearword and this one was spoken, not in anger, but in quiet resignation. 'So he's got what he wanted at last. He's been sniffing round after you ever since that first night at Tilda's Tavern.'

'Now that's not fair, Albert, and you know it. When he saw that you and me were together he kept away from us, after that first time, you know he did. He behaved like a perfect gentleman.'

'Perfect gentleman!' Albert spat out the words. 'How can one of them gippos ever be a perfect gentleman? Don't give me that, Hetty.'

'But it's true, Albert. He wouldn't ask me to . . . to see him again, because he thought I belonged to you. It was me as told him that I didn't.'

'What d'you mean?' Sudden suspicion glinted in Albert's eyes.

'We went down to the fairground this afternoon, Lily and me, and I saw Reuben there. And I told him . . .' Oh heck! This was making her sound simply awful, but Hetty knew she had to go on and tell Albert the truth. 'I told him that you and me weren't . . . weren't friendly any more. And I'm seeing him again. Next week.' There was

329

nothing of defiance in Hetty's words. How could there be at the sight of the wounded look on Albert's face?

'You mean you threw yourself at him?'

'No, it wasn't like that . . .'

'I think it was exactly like that,' said Albert grimly. 'I hope you've got what you want, you and this Reuben fellow. I wish you joy of him, Hetty. Come on, we'd best go home.'

Hetty felt like crying. It had been dreadful, telling Albert, but she had known that she mustn't hold anything back.

'I won't trouble you any more, Hetty.' They paused by the gate of the boarding house after a silent walk home, and Albert stood stiffly at a distance from her. 'I don't suppose you'll be seeing much more of me now.' The look in his eyes was fathomless and Hetty, again, was close to tears. Even more so when Albert, after a second's hesitation, leaned forward and placed a kiss on her cold cheek. 'Be happy, Hetty,' he said, before he turned and walked away.

'Do you think there'd be room for me to go and stay at Uncle Charlie's in Blackburn?' Albert sounded weary and the dark rings beneath his eyes were evidence of a restless night. Alice had known there was something wrong when he had gone straight upstairs last night after seeing Hetty, and she had heard his footsteps on the landing in the early hours.

'Do you mean you'd like to go on a visit, Albert? A little holiday?' Alice looked at her son curiously. 'Aye, I'm sure there'd be room for you at our

330

Charlie's. He's always been fond of you, and I daresay Sam'ud let you have a few days off. You've been working hard lately, lad, haven't you? Happen you're a bit tired. You could do with a change.'

'No, it's not a holiday I'm thinking of, Mam.' Albert played idly with the knife beside his breakfast plate, but the plate was empty. He hadn't attempted to eat any of the fresh toast that Alice had made for him, and his pint mug of tea, strong and with just a little milk, the way he liked it, was standing there going cold. 'What I meant was to go and stay there for good, well, for quite a while, anyroad.'

'Leave Blackpool? And your job?' Alice put her cup down heavily and the tea slopped over into the saucer. 'Whatever are you thinking of, lad?'

'I could easily get another job. I'm a qualified joiner now, and Uncle Sam'ud put in a good word for me. He says I'm doing right well.' Albert hesitated, then he looked at his mother, his eyes full of hurt. 'It's Hetty, you see, Mam.'

'Aye.' Alice nodded knowingly. 'I thought it might be summat to do with Hetty. Fallen out, have you?'

'It's more than that, Mam. It's all over. She's . . .' Albert bit his lip. 'I'll have to tell you before you find out from Mrs Turnbull. She's got another chap. She doesn't want me any more.' A hint of bitterness crept into Albert's voice.

'I see . . .' Alice didn't launch into a vehement tirade about the girl as her son might have expected her to do. She had known for a while that things were not right between them. They

331

hadn't been so since Hetty started singing at Tilda's Tavern. 'But there's no need to leave Blackpool, surely? Brazen it out, lad. Let her see that you don't care.'

'But I do care, Mam. That's the point. I care so much that I can't think of anything else. I can't just carry on as though nothing has happened, with Hetty living across the road and you being so friendly with her mother. I've got to get away.'

'She's only a young lass,' said Alice evenly. 'Try to understand, love. Happen she wants to fly her kite a bit before she settles down.'

'That's just what she said, well, summat like that.'

'And you're only young an' all, Albert. Too young, really, to be thinking of getting wed, although I've always known you were fond of the lass.'

'I'm turned twenty-one, Mam. And you weren't even that old when you married Father, were you?'

'No, you're right. But it's different when it comes to your children. You always think they're not old enough. And you're the only one as I've got left now, Albert. But don't do anything hasty. I can tell you're upset, but you might feel different in a day or two.'

'I won't, Mam. I love Hetty. I love her so much that nothing else matters.' Albert spoke simply, in a way that Alice had never heard him speak before. He had never been one to give way to his emotions. 'I know I'm not much of a one for poetry or owt like that, but some of those songs that Hetty sings, they really get to me. That one about

332

the sparkling eyes, it just reminds me of Hetty. I love her so much, Mam.'

Alice leaned across and put her hand over his work-roughened one. 'Yes, I can see you do, lad. But it'll get easier as time goes on. It won't hurt so much . . . Aye, perhaps you're right. It might not be a bad idea to leave Blackpool for a while.'

He'd got it real bad now, poor lad, and no mistake, thought Alice, but Hetty was the first girl he'd ever had. He might be able to forget her if he got away. But Alice wouldn't tell him that. He wouldn't believe her anyway. 'You never know, she might change her mind,' she added brightly. 'You know what they say. Absence makes the heart grow fonder, and if you're not here she might realise how much she misses you.'

'Pigs might fly,' said Albert moodily. 'No, she's fair smitten with this gipsy lad, I can tell.'

'The gipsy . . .? That Reuben, the lad that brought her home that night?'

'Aye, that's the one,' replied Albert flatly.

'Oh, I see . . .' was all Alice said. But oh dear, oh dear, she thought, her mind in a turmoil. That was a pretty kettle of fish all right. Hetty going with a gipsy lad. Whatever was Martha Turnbull going to say about that?

Walter had been horrified by his first glimpse of Blackpool. It was even worse than he had anticipated, and his original impression, of a real Sodom and Gomorrah of a place, only increased as the weeks passed and the season got into its full swing.

The army of touters for the lodging-house trade,

which had greeted the Turnbull family on their first visit to the town, was not so forceful when Walter first arrived at the end of March, the season having not yet started in earnest. There was just a handful of vociferous landladies hanging round the station entrance, but Walter was to see the crowd increase both in number and in volume as the season progressed. And this was but a foretaste of the cacophony of riotous sounds that welcomed visitors as they left the station and wandered into the streets of Blackpool. Nearly every café and souvenir shop and place of entertainment had its resident touter, raucously proclaiming its delights, but from a discreet position on the doorstep of the establishment in order to avoid prosecution for touting in the street.

There were itinerant musicians, too, wandering along the streets and the promenade, German bands and barrel organs, complete with monkey, and street hawkers offering a wide variety of goods for sale. By far the most popular commodity on sale was the oyster. Walter had noticed the large number of oyster stalls on the promenade and the nearby streets on his first day at work, as he was driven through the town on the coal waggon, and he commented on it to his colleague, Amos Armitage.

'Aye.' His new friend nodded. 'They reckon that they sell seventy-five thousand of 'em during the season. Would you believe it? They're shipped from America and stored at Knott End – that's the place up yonder . . .' he gestured northwards with his thumb, 'on the Wyre éstuary, in a huge oyster bed. And then each morning they're brought into Blackpool. It's getting to be quite a big industry here, selling oysters, and disposing of the shells, of course.'

'The shells? Why, what do they do with them?' asked Walter.

'Well, at one time they used to tip 'em into the sea, but now they're ground into grit and sold to the Fylde poultry farms,' Amos explained. 'I tell you, Blackpool people are always ready to seize on any way of making a few bob.'

'And what do the poultry farms use them for?' Walter was mystified.

'Feeding the poultry, of course. Hens have to eat grit to produce good eggs.'

'Oh, I see.' Walter nodded. Then he grinned. 'I wondered why me breakfast egg always tasted fishy.'

'Aye.' Amos grinned too. 'So now you know. I reckon most of the visitors notice too, but there don't seem to be many complaints. Folks come to Blackpool to enjoy themselves. They don't want to spend their time grousing.'

Walter learned many titbits of gossip like this as he settled into his job with Mr Herbert Henderson, the coal, lime and slate merchant. The work was physically hard, as he had known it would be, and dirty too. He often arrived back at his lodgings looking like a chimney sweep, and he missed the ministrations of his mother, who had always made sure that there was plenty of boiling water for him to have a good wash of an evening. And his work at the mill had been nothing like as mucky as this job. It was fortunate that Mrs Jobson, his landlady, had a bathroom, but she had

335

looked askance at him the first time she had seen him in all his grime and told him he'd have to pay extra for all the hot water he was using.

Walter was determined that he would be away from there as soon as possible and in his own little place. The fact that Grace would not be with him did not deter him. Anyway, as he had told her, he would not take no for an answer. It would be only a matter of time before she was his again. Patience, that was all that was needed; patience and perseverance . . . and prayer. Grace Turnbull would belong to him before the year was out. Walter was confident of it.

Amos Armitage, who also worked for Mr Henderson, was what you might call a kindred spirit. Walter had recognised it straight away and he hadn't been a bit surprised to learn, that first day, as he sat with Amos on the coal waggon, behind the two huge carthorses, that his workmate was a teetotaller and a non-smoker and a Methodist to boot. Walter was amazed that his new companion was able to hump the heavy bags of coal about as he did, for he was only a little fellow, short and slightly built, with a curious gnome-like face. But his forearms had a muscular strength, bulging beneath his jacket, and his shoulders were broad, out of proportion with the rest of his body.

Amos was a bachelor, some ten years older than Walter, with a small house of his own near to the town centre and the Methodist chapel he attended, close to Central Station. It wasn't long before he took Walter along with him to his place of worship and before many weeks had gone by Walter was getting to be a leading light there, as he had been back home in Burnley, taking class meetings and Bible study and, occasionally, preaching a Sunday sermon.

It wasn't the same chapel that Grace and her family attended, but Walter felt that that was all to the good. It wouldn't be wise to overdo things; he was already getting great satisfaction from watching Grace – spying on her would be nearer the truth, but Walter would never have called it that. He was just putting himself in the picture, letting her see that he was still around and that he hadn't gone back to Burnley with his tail between his legs. That Edwin Donnelly that she was knocking about with was a handsome fellow – even Walter, biased as he was, had to admit that – but it wouldn't be long before he threw her over. In the meantime Walter would just watch and wait.

He almost hugged himself with glee to see her start with surprise when he appeared round the corner at the very moment she came out of the house with Edwin Donnelly. And there was the time when she had emerged from the back entrance of Donnelly's store, with that fellow in tow again, and Walter had just happened to be driving past on the coal waggon. Very soon he came to know her movements almost as well as she knew them herself.

It was Amos Armitage who took Walter along to Tilda's Tavern, after assuring him that it was a harmless place, almost on a par with a temperance establishment.

'Joss Jenkinson does serve alcohol, I must admit,' Amos explained, 'but there's tea and coffee and soft drinks for those that prefer 'em and he doesn't allow any rowdiness or owt like that. You don't need to fear that you'll be compromising yerself, lad. I know you've got your principles – so have I – but you've got to stretch a point now and again in a place like Blackpool.'

Amos had been amused by Walter's provincial narrow-mindedness, although there was no doubt about it, the lad knew his onions all right when it came to preaching. Just what had brought him to this neck of the woods Amos wasn't sure. Trouble with a lass, as likely as not. Walter had hinted at some such thing, but on the whole the lad was inclined to be very tight-lipped about his personal affairs. Amos had felt himself in high dudgeon a time or two, though, listening to Walter's sancti-monious denunciations of Blackpool as a den of iniquity. He'd felt like telling him that if it was as bad as all that he'd best get back to where he came from. Like all true 'sand-grown 'uns' Amos wouldn't hear a wrong word about his native town, although he had to admit the place had its faults.

'Aye, it has its rowdy element,' he had been forced to agree. 'When all's said and done it's a working-class resort, catering for folks such as us, and they're not all as abstemious as thee and me, Walter lad.' Amos laughed. 'When Blackpool first got going, the idea was to make it into a select watering place catering for the toffs, but the cheap excursion trains soon put paid to that idea. And the Wakes weeks an' all. The place is fair bursting at the seams during the season with folks from the Lancashire mill towns. Of course you'll know all about that, won't you, lad, coming from Burnley?'

What was the young fellow doing here? Amos wondered again. He'd had a good job as a tackler in the mill from all accounts, and yet here he was, humping bags of coal in a place that he reckoned to despise. Well, there was nowt so queer as folks, and it wasn't really any of his business so long as the lad pulled his weight at Henderson's. And he was certainly doing that.

'You'll like it at Tilda's Tavern,' Amos told him. 'Blackpool's not all ale-houses and fallen women, you know. In fact the Temperance Movement's gaining ground now. Have you been to the South Beach Coffee Palace yet?' Walter shook his head. 'Well, that's a temperance place, owned by the British Workman Company. You can get a first-class meal there, quite cheap it is an' all, and it's very popular with trippers who are of our persuasion. I reckon Joss Jenkinson has tried to model his place on the Coffee Palace. But, like I said, he does serve alcohol. And there's some jolly good turns there, too. Music-hall type of acts, you know. There's a girl as sings there, and I'll guarantee you'll not hear any better anywhere in Blackpool. I've heard far worse at the Empire up the road. Anyway, you're welcome to come along with me, lad, and see for yourself. Let your hair down a bit. It'll do no harm.'

Walter, in spite of his misgivings, was impressed by the atmosphere at Tilda's Tavern. Blackpool folk were certainly friendly, you had to say that for them, and Amos had gone out of his way to make him feel at home in the town, thought Walter, as he sipped his lemonade and watched the variety acts taking place on the small stage. The juggler was jolly good, and so was the baritone, singing romantic ballads, and Walter applauded loudly, but he didn't much care for the tap-dancing duo with their baby faces and flashing smiles. He didn't hold with fellows prancing about like that; it wasn't manly. But what a surprise he had when the girl singer that Amos had raved about, 'Henrietta, the Girl with the Sparkling Eyes', turned out to be none other than Hetty, Grace's cheeky young sister. Now that was something that Martha Turnbull had omitted to tell him, and Walter wasn't altogether surprised. He imagined that Mrs Turnbull wouldn't be any too pleased about it. Hetty had always been a forward young madam, laughing behind her hand at him and encouraging Grace to do the same. But she could certainly sing, he'd grant her that. Walter watched through narrowed eyes as she simpered coyly and cast come hither glances at all the fellows, but if she'd seen him she wasn't letting on. Neither was he. Walter hastily looked away and let his eyes wander to the other side of the room.

His heart gave an extra beat and a smile played at the corners of his mouth as he caught sight of Grace, with Edwin Donnelly, as usual. They must have just come in, before Hetty started to sing, and Grace hadn't noticed him yet. But she would see him all right. Walter would make sure of that. He leaned forward in his seat, staring fixedly in her direction.

★ ★ ★

'Your Hetty's on top form tonight,' Edwin whispered.

'Yes, that's one of my favourites,' Grace replied as Hetty came to the final bars of 'The Moon and I'.

'Ah, pray make no mistake, We are not shy,
We're very wide awake, the moon and I.'

Hetty spread her emerald-green skirts wide as she curtseyed to her audience. And Grace, with the rest of the onlookers, applauded loudly, feeling so very proud of her sister.

But when she glanced sideways a few seconds later she gave a gasp of dismay and the glass of ginger beer she was holding spilled on to the front of her blouse. She hastily mopped at it with her handkerchief, but not before Edwin had noticed her discomfiture.

'Is there something wrong, dear?' He leaned forward and put a solicitous hand on her arm. 'You're looking worried.' A suspicious frown creased his forehead. 'It's not . . .? Don't tell me . . .?'

Grace nodded. 'Yes, I'm afraid so,' she whispered. 'It's . . . it's Walter again. Over there.'

Edwin sighed and tutted with exasperation as he looked in the same direction as Grace's fearful glance. 'Mmm . . . I can see him. It's the stocky chap with the moustache and spotted tie, isn't it?' Grace nodded again. The moustache was a recent acquisition, grown since she had left Burnley. 'But he's not looking over here, Grace. He seems very busy talking to the fellow next to him.'

'But he was looking at me,' Grace insisted.

'Well, he isn't now,' said Edwin firmly. 'And if he starts being a nuisance I'd be quick to do something about it, I can tell you. But stop worrying; you're bound to come across him occasionally, with him living in the same town.'

'But why does he stay, Edwin? What's he doing in Blackpool? I told him it was all over, but he wouldn't believe me, and now he's following me about.'

'Nonsense! You told me he had a job here, didn't you? He can't just down tools and leave again straight away. And perhaps he likes it here. There's no need for him to leave just because you've told him you don't want to see him any more.' He stopped at the look of consternation on Grace's face. 'Oh, I'm sorry, darling. I didn't mean to speak sharply, but we've gone over all this before. I think you're imagining things. Now, admit it. You have imagined it once or twice, haven't you?'

Grace was forced to nod in agreement. There had, indeed, been a couple of occasions when she had thought she had seen Walter and it had turned out to be only someone who resembled him. But he had got her into such a state that it wasn't surprising that her imagination was playing tricks on her. She was sure that that was Walter's intention, but Edwin wouldn't countenance any such thinking. And that was the worst thing of all; now Edwin was beginning to get annoyed with her, dismissing it all as an absurd fancy.

She had been truthful with Edwin, as she had

342

been with Walter, and told him the whole story. He had listened and seemed to understand, although it had been the first he had heard of the young man in Burnley.

'You're mine now,' he had said, kissing her in a proprietorial manner, 'and I would say it serves him right for not coming to see you before now. Don't worry about him, Grace.'

But Grace couldn't forget Walter's last words to her, 'You'll be seeing me again. Soon . . . I promise . . .' And he had made sure that she had seen him. The sight of him sitting up there on the coal waggon, driving past Donnelly's store, had filled her with foreboding.

'Come along, darling. Snap out of it.' Edwin patted her hand now. 'Where shall we go tomorrow? The bluebell wood?' he added coaxingly. 'Perhaps by now the bluebells really will be out. I keep telling you about them, don't I?'

'Yes . . . yes, I'd like that, Edwin,' said Grace, but not with the same confidence that she had felt a month ago.

Twice since that first March afternoon they had visited 'their' wood and both times Edwin had made love to her, so exquisitely, so gently, that all her anxieties had melted away. He had assured her that she need not fear that anything would go wrong, that he would be careful. She supposed he meant that he would make sure she didn't have a baby. She hadn't quite understood how he could prevent it, but when, on approaching a climax to their lovemaking, Edwin had turned away, then she had known what he meant.

He would make love to her again tomorrow and

343

she would respond. They would speak words of endearment and there would be nothing in the whole world but the two of them. Safe in Edwin's arms she could forget about Walter and about the other little niggling doubt that hovered at the back of her mind. Edwin's mother was still suffering from her mysterious malady, and consequently Grace had not yet been invited to the Donnellys' home. And though they now belonged to one another unreservedly, Edwin had still not spoken of marriage.

Chapter 15

Edwin gave an involuntary start as the shrill ring of the telephone echoed along the hallway. The instrument had only recently been installed, about a fortnight ago, and he was still not used to its ear-piercing jangle. He was accustomed to hearing it at the shop, of course, but at home it seemed an alien thing.

He picked up the black receiver from the stand on the wall, holding it stiffly against his ear as he spoke into the mouthpiece. 'Hello, Blackpool 357. Edwin Donnelly speaking.'

'Oh, hello, Edwin. Thank goodness it's you that answered.' The voice at the other end sounded breathy and agitated, but Edwin thought he recognised the brittle tones. The next words proved him right. 'It's Constance here . . .' There was a second's pause before she went on. 'I don't know how I dare ask you, Edwin, but I'm at my wits' end. I've got myself into a terrible state and I've nobody else to turn to. Mother and Father are away this weekend, you know.'

'Yes, I realise that, Constance.' Edwin's voice was noncommittal. She had told him earlier that day, when he had seen her at church, that her parents were away for a long weekend. They had gone to Southport to stay with her aunt and uncle and wouldn't be returning until Tuesday. 'What can I do for you?' he asked, not sounding, or feeling, too enthusiastic. 'What are you in such a state about?'

'There's a mouse in the kitchen! I saw it a few minutes ago when I went in to make a cup of tea. It scuttled under the dresser and I daren't go in again. I simply daren't!' The girl sounded almost hysterical. 'I was so frightened that I just turned and ran. I didn't even make my cup of tea.'

'And what do you want me to do about it, Constance?' Edwin's voice was cool, but he was grinning to himself. He knew very well that she was asking him to go and get rid of it for her, but there was no harm in playing her along for a little while. The trouble with Constance was that she thought you could drop everything and run to her assistance every time she snapped her fingers. 'The poor mouse is more frightened of you than you are of him. Or her, of course. Was it a male or a female, Connie? Did you notice?'

'Don't play games with me, Edwin!' Constance snapped. 'I'm really scared and all you can do is poke fun at me. I've heard all that silly nonsense before about the mouse being more scared than I am. It's what my father always says, but it doesn't make any difference. I loathe the things. Oh, Edwin . . .' Her voice was pleading. 'Could you come round? Please . . . Come and get rid of it for me. Or at least set the trap for me. I daren't even do that.'

'All right, Constance. I can't very well refuse

such an impassioned plea, can I?' He gave a little laugh. 'I know you've always been frightened of them. I'll be round in about half an hour. Now, don't worry . . . Yes . . . I'll see you soon . . . Goodbye.'

He sighed as he replaced the receiver. The girl really was a dratted nuisance, and just when he was going to settle down to another read, the umpteenth one, of *The Mayor of Casterbridge*. And where were Constance's devoted suitors? he wondered. Why hadn't they been summoned to her rescue? Douglas Brodie, no doubt, was miles away, north of the border, but what about the other one, Herbert Mallinson? Why couldn't she have asked him to help her? It was raining, too. Not the sort of night for turning out unless you really had to, but he knew that the gentleman in him wouldn't leave Constance in the lurch. He remembered that she had been scared of mice ever since she was a tiny girl. It was nothing unusual; most women of his acquaintance were, his mother, brought up as she had been in a rough-and-tumble household, being the exception.

It had been a real so-and-so of a day, he thought, as he hurried through the damp, dismal streets, and not just weather-wise, although it was the weather that had spoiled his plans. May had been a capricious month and now, after weeks of intermittent sunshine, they had had a day of persistent rain. He and Grace had planned a bicycle ride for the afternoon, to their favourite spot near St Michael's, but the inclement weather had put paid to that. Instead, they had wandered along the promenade, dodging into shelters to escape the showers, and finally abandoning the idea altogether when Grace had started to cough. The poor girl had looked dreadful; Edwin hadn't seen her look so bad since the day he first met her in Donnelly's store. Her cheeks were flushed, but with a feverish, not a healthy tinge, and her eyes were ringed with dark shadows.

He had been worried about Grace recently. She seemed to have lost much of her previous sparkle and was forever looking over her shoulder as though she were fearful of what – or, more likely, who – was lurking round the next corner. He had told her to put that former young man of hers, Walter Clayton, right out of her mind. Of course the fellow wasn't harassing her by following her around, at least not wittingly. It was a ridiculous idea and it was all in her imagination.

Edwin knew that he was partly to blame for Grace's present nervous state. If only he were to throw caution to the winds and ask her to marry him, and to invite her into his home as he knew he should, then, he felt, much of her tension would disappear. But he knew that it was impossible. His mother was still suffering, more so if anything, from her mysterious ailment, and the doctor was insisting on a second opinion if her condition didn't improve before long. Edwin was convinced that she could help herself, if only she would. In the meantime it was not only Clara who was suffering, but her family as well, and the repercussions were affecting his relationship with Grace. Knowing that he was partly at fault didn't do anything to improve matters. He was often irritable these days, even with his dear Grace whom he loved so very much. He felt guilty, too, about their relationship. She wasn't, he knew, the sort of girl to enter into intimacy lightly. She had done so because of her love for him, and because he had spoken, so many times, of his own love for her. And yet he hadn't asked her to marry him. There were times when Edwin Donnelly hated himself.

The rain was still falling, a steady drizzle that soaked you to the skin before you realised how wet you were getting. Edwin was beginning to shiver by the time he turned into Park Road where Constance lived and was starting to curse the girl for her silliness. It was ridiculous for a grown woman to be frightened of a mouse. Only as he pushed open the gate and walked up the driveway did he begin to wonder why she hadn't asked one of the servants to come to her assistance.

The door opened almost immediately at his knock and Constance ushered him into the hallway. 'It's so good of you to come. I really do appreciate it, Edwin. Oh dear . . . you're soaked through.' She brushed her fingers down the length of his sleeve and her hand came away wet. She wiped it on the skirt of the gown she was wearing, an elegant creation of midnight-blue velvet which buttoned up to the neck where there was a frill of frothy white lace.

She saw him glancing curiously at her apparel. 'I was just about to have an early night,' she said, lowering her eyes demurely. 'I love retiring early now and again with a good book . . .' It was the first Edwin had heard of it. From what he knew of her, Constance hardly ever opened a book, except for women's magazines. ' . . . So I changed into my dressing gown and popped into the kitchen to make a cup of tea. And then I saw it. Well, like I told you, Edwin, I was so scared I just turned and ran.'

'What about Rose? Or Mrs Winters? Couldn't they have helped you, or didn't you like to admit you were frightened of a mouse?'

'Oh, it's not that.' Constance's blue eyes were pools of innocence. 'It's Rose's Sunday off. And poor Mrs Winters was so worried because her mother is ill, so I said she could have the evening off as well. It was the least I could do, with Mother and Father being away. I could hardly expect her to stay here at my beck and call when she was needed elsewhere. So there's only little me, all on my owny-own.' She gave a tinkling little laugh.

'I see . . .' Edwin tapped the tips of his fingers together contemplatively. 'Well then, what about this mouse? That's what I've come for, isn't it? Lead the way, Constance.'

'You'd better take your coat off, hadn't you, Edwin, or you'll catch a chill.' Edwin divested himself of his greatcoat and Constance shook it, scattering tiny droplets of water all over the rich red carpet. 'There you are, you see. I knew you were soaked. Oh, you are a love, coming to my rescue like this.' She hung the coat over the newel post at the foot of the stairs and led the way to the back of the house.

'You go in first,' she said as she pushed open the kitchen door. She hung back timorously. 'It might jump out at me.'

Edwin grovelled on his hands and knees, steel poker at the ready to do the dreadful deed should the poor creature appear. 'There's no sign of it now, Constance,' he said, peering underneath the dresser. Still in a kneeling position he circled the kitchen, poking beneath chairs and cupboards and in the corners of the cooking range. He knelt back on his haunches. 'No, not a glimpse of him. He'll have scuttled back into his hole, you can be sure. I'm pretty certain that's the last you'll see of him, but I'll set a trap if you like. Do you have one?'

'In there.' Constance pointed towards a corner cupboard. 'Get it out for me, would you please, Edwin?' Her blue eyes were fearful and her mouth trembled. 'I don't even like touching the traps, nasty, horrible things they are.' She gave a shudder. 'Ugh!'

Far worse for the poor mouse, thought Edwin, as he placed a morsel of cheese on the cruel spike. It was a job he didn't like doing. He would much prefer to let the little thing go free, but Constance wouldn't be satisfied until the deed was done. 'There . . . I'll put it by the dresser, where you saw the mouse. So long as you don't call me in the morning to come and empty it.' He grinned at her. 'I draw the line at that.'

'Oh no. Mrs Winters will be back in the morning. And Rose. They'll see to all that for me.' Constance's voice was offhand. 'Now, I think we deserve that cup of tea. At least you do, Edwin. I've done nothing at all.' She paused with her hand on the kettle, then put her head on one side thoughtfully. 'Or . . . what about something just a

351

teeny bit stronger? Yes, why not?' She smiled radiantly. 'You've earned it, Edwin, and it will warm you up as well. Come along in here and make yourself comfortable.'

'Well, perhaps just the one. But only a small one,' said Edwin as he followed her into the drawing room.

He laid his head back against the plum-coloured velvet of the settee and sipped appreciatively at the amber liquid in the cut-glass tumbler. This was a delightful room, an almost exact copy of the drawing room of his own home, and he felt very much at ease here. He hadn't wanted to come, not at all, and had been inwardly cursing Constance for being such a nuisance, dragging him away from his fireside and the company of his book on such a dreadful evening. But now he was here he found his irritability draining away and it was pleasant to sit and chat with Constance about old times.

She sat decorously in the chair opposite him with her knees pressed together and her hands, when they were not holding the sherry glass, clasped tightly in her lap, and they talked about their relations and friends and the fun they had had together on family holidays. Constance rose to replenish the fire, handling the silver tongs as though she was afraid they might bite her. She rarely, if ever, Edwin surmised, stooped to do such menial tasks for herself. As the flames licked around the new coals Constance sat down again, this time not on the chair, but on the settee near to Edwin. But not before she had refilled his glass from the cut-glass decanter.

He demurred only slightly, placing his hand over the tumbler in a half-hearted gesture. 'No more for me, Constance. You'll have me nodding off. I'm feeling drowsy already. Oh, all right, then. If you insist . . . but only a drop.'

After several more drinks and a trip down memory lane, Edwin was feeling very relaxed, and the next time Constance topped up his glass, reaching out stealthily to lift the decanter from the occasional table near to her hand, Edwin didn't notice. His eyes were closed.

'Wake up, sleeping beauty.' Constance teasingly touched his closed eyelids with her fingertips and Edwin opened his eyes and grinned at her.

'Sorry, Connie. It's unforgivable of me, I know, to go to sleep in the presence of a lady.' He laughed as he patted her hand. 'You've heard the music-hall joke, haven't you? That's no lady, that's my old friend, Connie. I warned you what would happen if you plied me with too much whisky.'

He picked up the glass again and sipped with growing relish at the fiery liquid, feeling it trickling down his throat, into his stomach, warming every part of him. He no longer felt sleepy, only soothed and tranquillised, all his former anxieties fast disappearing in a haze of contentment. He drained the glass, tipping his head back as he drank the last drop, then placed it on the small table near him. It was a long time since he had felt so happy and free from care.

He became aware of Constance's hand on his knee, of her fingers gently stroking his thigh in an upward direction. 'Naughty, naughty . . .' he admonished her, covering her hand with his own.

She didn't answer him, but just continued to look at him, her blue eyes indecipherable. He couldn't see love there, as he had so often seen shining from Grace's trusting brown eyes – for even at this moment he thought, fleetingly, of Grace – nor even longing or desire. Just what he could perceive in Constance's eyes he wasn't sure. Mesmerised by her hypnotic stare, hardly realising what he was doing, he lifted his hand to her head, drawing her face closer to his. His fingers caught on the tortoiseshell comb that anchored her hair and he dragged it out, watching the long, pale-gold tresses ripple round her shoulders.

Then his hands were stroking down the length of her hair, lingering on the swell of her breasts where her tresses ended their cascading fall. As she leaned forward, so slowly, his lips met hers and his fingers fumbled with the fastening of her midnight-blue gown.

'I'll do it.' Constance's voice was breathy and tantalising, and Edwin watched as one bewitched as she stood in front of him, tall and statuesque, and slowly began to unfasten the buttons of her dressing gown, from the collar to the hem. Then she shrugged it off her shoulders, letting it fall to her feet in a ripple of dark-blue folds. Edwin gave a gasp of astonishment when he saw that beneath the gown she was naked. He noticed the upthrust of her breasts, pointed and firm, and the pale milky-white sheen of her long limbs as she stood there with her head upraised, like a sea goddess arising from the waves.

354

She stretched out a hand to him. 'I think we might be more comfortable upstairs, Edwin?'

'No . . . here,' was all Edwin said as he quickly divested himself of his constraining garments and seized hold of her, firmly but not roughly. She was beautiful, there was no doubt about that, and such loveliness was not something to be spoiled or handled unfeelingly. They sank to the floor and he made a carpet of the blue velvet gown beneath them.

There was little time for Edwin to dwell on the niceties and the subtle overtures to the act of love. Constance was eager and willing and Edwin noted, at the fringes of his consciousness, as he entered her that she was not a virgin. He wasn't altogether surprised, nor was he shocked, it was just something that his mind absorbed with detachment.

Constance spoke little, then or later, and by tacit agreement they both knew that it would be unwise for him to spend the night there. The servants would be back in the morning, and his own parents would question his whereabouts if he were away from home overnight.

Constance's kiss on his cheek, as she opened the door to let him out, was merely friendly. 'Thank you so much, Edwin . . . for seeing to that horrid mouse. You've saved my life. I don't know what I would have done without you.'

'My pleasure,' he replied unsmilingly. 'Goodnight, Constance.' As the cold night air reached his face, awareness was beginning to return to him. He nodded curtly at her and their eyes met and held for a few seconds, silently appraising one

355

another, before he turned and strode quickly down the path.

The rain had stopped now, but the night was still cold and cheerless. The haze of euphoria which had surrounded Edwin had just as quickly evaporated, leaving him with a headache and a feeling of regret and self-reproach. He should have refused her enticements and he knew now that if he had not been in such a stupor, induced by the whisky, he may well have done so. He cursed himself for his stupidity and, above all, for the weakness that he knew to be at the heart of his being.

What an ineffectual person he was, he thought bitterly. If only he had stood up to his mother, illness or no illness, and insisted that he intended to marry Grace, come what may. If only he had asked his dear lovely Grace to marry him, none of this would have happened. Or would it? Constance was still Constance, devious and determined upon getting her own way at all costs, as she had done with him tonight. What difference would a definite promise of marriage to Grace have made with a woman as wily as Constance?

If . . . if . . . Only a tiny word, yet so telling. But it was pointless to brood upon all the ifs. What was done was done, irrevocably and irreversibly. It would most certainly never happen again. Constance had had her way with him, Edwin thought ruefully. The term was more often used when a man seduced a helpless young girl, but it fitted here and Edwin knew that it was true. She had lured him into her arms as, no doubt, she had lured other gullible young men before him. Edwin remembered now his discovery that she was not a virgin, and had not been for some time, he guessed, judging by her sexual prowess. He had been startled by the way she had led him on to dizzier and more ecstatic heights, until the final climax had been upon him almost before he was aware of it. There hadn't been time . . . A spasm of fear seized Edwin now as he realised what he had done. Please, God, don't let there be any repercussions, he prayed silently, although he knew it was too late for prayer and that God could do nothing to undo what Edwin had done tonight.

But he would never, never be such a fool again. He knew only too well what liquor did to him. From now on he would leave it alone, like Grace and her Methodist cronies, he thought with a wry smile. His sweet, lovely Grace . . . He loved her so much, and what had happened tonight wasn't going to affect his relationship with her. She must never know, and he would make it up to her. Soon . . .

Constance stretched luxuriously, her arms above her head and her toes reaching into the depths of the feather mattress, tingling all over with self-gratification. It had been so easy. So very easy. She had known that Edwin would be unable to resist the whisky. She knew him so well and had watched for a while now the way he behaved after he had had a couple of drinks. Edwin just couldn't hold his liquor. A little went a long way with him and soon had him reeling like an inebriated stripling. But he would never learn. Edwin did not possess the strongest of moral fibre, but it didn't stop her from loving him . . . or yearning for him.

Tonight's encounter would, she was sure, bring about the result she longed for. She was midway between her periods, the most fertile time of all, she had been told, and if her desire was anything to go by then she was more than halfway there already. Ruminatively she stroked the swell of her breasts and her flat stomach, imagining how they would fill out and expand as the new life grew within her. For a fleeting moment she curled her lip in distaste. The last thing she wanted, in reality, was to be fat and ugly, nor was she particularly fond of children. Babies, she had to admit, she detested,but it would all be worth it to make Edwin hers. As he would be now; she was convinced of it.

And how clever she had been to fabricate that story about the mouse. No . . . it wasn't all invention. There had been a mouse a fortnight ago, espied by Constance on one of her infrequent visits to the kitchen, and just as hastily dispatched by the servants. And it was more than possible that the mouse had relatives . . .

Chapter 16

'Now you'll stay where you are, my girl, and no nonsense. A day or two in bed'll work wonders, you'll see.' Martha tucked the heavy quilted eiderdown around Grace's slim body, then put a hand on her forehead. 'Mmm . . . You're still a bit feverish, but not as bad as you were last night. You had me real worried, I can tell you, when you came in drenched through. And cough, cough, cough you were all evening. I thought you were never going to stop.'

'I'm feeling a lot better now, Mam. Honestly I am. I've hardly coughed at all this morning, and my headache's nearly gone.'

'You're not well enough to go to the shop, though.' Martha smiled fondly at her daughter and patted the slender hand that lay on the paisley-patterned eiderdown. 'And you won't go in all week neither, if I have my way.'

'They'll wonder where I am.' Grace gave a tiny worried frown. 'I'll have to let them know, Mam. D'you think you could . . .?'

'Now don't start worrying your head about that. Just concentrate on getting better. Yes, of course I'll let 'em know at Donnelly's. They'll be calling round anyroad after dinner for the stuff that I've baked for 'em. I'll send a message with the cab driver then. But Mr Edwin'll have guessed why, when you don't turn up. I feel like giving that young fellow a piece of my mind, I do an' all, for letting you get soaked to the skin like that.'

'It wasn't Edwin's fault that it rained, Mam. And he did get a cab to bring me back from Talbot Square. It would've been even worse if we'd gone out on our bicycles like we intended doing. There's no shelter at all on them country roads.'

'Oh, you can stop making excuses for him.' Martha sniffed. 'Aye, happen he did get you a cab, but only when it was nearly too late. You looked as though you were at death's door when you staggered into the house. And I notice he didn't show his face. Too ashamed, no doubt . . .'

'He had the cab waiting outside, Mam. He couldn't waste time coming in here.'

'Oh aye. I know, I know. You won't hear a wrong word about Edwin Donnelly. Well, you won't be seeing him this week. You can make up your mind as to that. You've got to stay put until you're well again . . . I think I'll send one of the lasses round to get Dr Ferguson from the next street. It won't do any harm for him to have a look at you.'

'Oh no, Mam. There's no need. Really there isn't. I've had these attacks before and they always pass. There's no sense in throwing good money away on doctor's bills. I'll be all right.' Grace gave a weak smile. 'And I'll do as I'm told. I'll be a good girl and stay in bed.'

'All right then, if you're sure.' Martha looked at

her daughter thoughtfully. 'Doctor's bills can be quite an item, there's no doubt about that. But if you get any worse I shan't hesitate. Well, this won't buy the baby a new bonnet . . . I'd best be getting on with me work. I'll pop up in a little while to see how you're going on. Is there anything else you want, love? There's a jug of lemon juice on the table, and you've got your hot-water bottle. D'you want a book to read, or a magazine? There's a few downstairs that the visitors have left behind.'

'No thanks, Mam. I don't feel like reading. I'll just lie here quietly and try to go back to sleep. It's surprising how tired I am and I don't know why. It isn't as if I've been working extra hard. It's you that's done all the work in the house lately, the lion's share of it, anyway. You've quite enough to do with a houseful of visitors and the two lodgers without having to fetch and carry for me as well.'

'Get on with yer bother! Hard work never killed anyone and I thrive on it, our Grace. I always have done. You know that. Besides, it's not so bad now that I've got the two lasses to help me. It was a good idea, wasn't it, getting Gladys and May over here? I knew you and our Hetty wouldn't want to give up your jobs now that you're both settled in so nicely, so it's all turned out for the best. Things usually do if you give 'em a chance.'

Martha paused thoughtfully, and though she had said that she must be getting on with her work she sat down on the edge of the bed. 'I don't know about our Hetty, though, and that gipsy fellow.' She looked down at her lap, nervously folding her flowered apron into pleats. 'Goodness

361

knows how that's all going to turn out. What d'you reckon to it, Grace?'

'He's a nice enough lad, Mam,' said Grace. 'We shouldn't be biased because he's a gipsy. I've known plenty worse fellows than Reuben Loveday. It's Hetty throwing Albert over like she did that I didn't like. I know you could say I did the same with Walter, but it wasn't really the same at all, Mam. I hadn't seen him for months.' Grace's voice was beginning to rise, a trifle hysterically, as she thought of Walter.

'No, I know that, lass. Don't start fretting about that again or you'll make yourself really poorly.' Martha squeezed her hand. 'No . . . I didn't like the way she treated Albert either. I could have given her a good hiding, I could that, when I heard what she'd done, the naughty little madam. And Albert's such a decent young fellow an' all. He thinks the world of her. Yes, I felt like smacking her.'

'That'll be the day, Mam,' said Grace smiling.

'Oh aye, I know I've never so much as lifted a finger to either of you. I don't believe in it, to tell you the truth. You can get a lot further with talking than with clouting kids around, I've always thought. But perhaps it's what our Hetty was short of. Happen I've been too soft with her all along.'

'I don't think so, Mam. She's wilful, I know, but she's got her head screwed on the right way. And perhaps she's right. Perhaps Albert hasn't enough go about him for our Hetty. Mam . . .' Grace reached out and took hold of her mother's hand. 'Why don't you ask her to bring Reuben here, then you could see for yourself? I think you'd have a surprise if you met him, I do really.'

'Happen I will, in me own time.' Martha nodded curtly. 'But I'm not going to give in too readily. She likes to have us all on a piece of string, does our Hetty. It won't do any harm to keep her on tenterhooks for a bit. Well, I really must get moving or it'll be dinnertime and nothing done.' She stroked Grace's forehead gently, pushing back the damp curls from her brow. 'Now, you try and have a sleep and don't worry about anything. I'll be up again in a little while.'

Grace sighed thankfully as her mother tiptoed out of the room. All she wanted at the moment was to be on her own and to let the rest of the world go hang. She felt she couldn't be bothered with anything or anybody, not Donnelly's, or Hetty and Reuben, or Walter . . . or even Edwin. To lie there peacefully and comfortably in her own little island away from them all was just the panacea that she needed. Maybe if she stopped thinking about all her problems they would just go away. Grace stared at the diffused pink light filtering in through the rose-patterned curtains – Mam hadn't drawn them back this morning, just as though she were a real invalid – knowing that such thoughts were defeatist ones. Grace was no quitter. Problems didn't disappear overnight because you didn't think about them, although, as her mother had said, they sometimes had a way of working out if left alone. Grace was thankful even for her present sickness if it gave her a chance of escaping from all her besetting worries for a few days.

She felt all right so long as she lay still. The feather pillow and mattress felt blissfully cosy, moulding themselves round her body, her neck and her chest and her shoulders, all the parts of her that ached when she tried to sit up. Grace knew that she had looked dreadful when she staggered into the house at teatime yesterday and, in spite of what her mother said, Edwin had been most concerned about her. It had been her fault, not his, that they had stayed out so long in the rain. She had wanted to prolong the precious time that she could spend with him and so she hadn't told him at first just how poorly she was feeling. She felt, though she couldn't have said why, that their days together were numbered. When she had eventually told him that she was feeling ill he had bundled her into a cab straight away.

It was seeing Walter again at Tilda's Tavern that had unnerved her. How had he known that she would be there? It was uncanny, the way he turned up wherever she went. And yet Grace knew, deep down, that it was merely a coincidence. Edwin insisted that all these encounters were coincidental and that she was imagining things. They had had words about it and he had been so irritable with her, unlike his usual even-tempered self. It hadn't been the first time that Edwin had snapped at her lately and he was often preoccupied. His mother was still ill, though, and that must be worrying for him, not knowing what was wrong with her . . .

Grace pushed aside her disturbing thoughts of Edwin and let her mind drift away from him and away from Walter to her own family. Her mother was happy here in Blackpool, happier than she had been for many a long year, and Grace was glad about that. The move to the seaside had brought many problems in its wake. There was Hetty and Albert, and now Reuben, and herself and Walter . . . and Edwin – always her thoughts returned to Edwin – but human relationships were always fraught with problems. It was part of the whole process of living. They were problems that would have been avoided if they had stayed in Burnley, but Grace knew that, in spite of all the difficulties, they would all – her mother and Hetty and herself – only choose to do the same again if they were given the chance.

Martha, as she had just told Grace, thrived on hard work, and the boarding house was getting quite a name in the neighbourhood for being one of the best run little places in North Shore. Grace recalled how it had looked when they had first set eyes on the house a year ago – could it really be only a year – with its peeling paintwork and grimy doorstep and its general air of dilapidation. To see it now, freshly painted in bright green, with crisp lace curtains hanging at the windows and the step scrubbed and edged in white with a donkey stone, you could hardly believe it was the same place.

Gladys and May, two young girls from their street back home in Burnley, were now working there, for the season at least. It was quite commonplace to employ girls from the mill towns for seasonal labour. The lasses found it a welcome change from being employed at the cotton mill and it was one mouth less to feed at home. It did mean, of course, that one more room was occupied and couldn't be used for visitors. Gladys and May shared an attic bedroom next door to the one shared by the two lodgers, but Martha was still, in the remaining bedrooms, able to accommodate up to twenty guests, quite enough for a house of that size and plenty for Martha and her staff to cope with.

Hetty now worked only part time as a waitress at Laycock's Confectioner's, and for the rest of the time she helped in the boarding house. Grace thought fondly what an asset her younger sister was in the dining room with her pert smile and her cheerful banter. She, Grace, was still willing to stay in the background assisting her mother with the cooking and cleaning, but her work at Donnelly's prevented her from helping out as much as she would have liked. Martha had insisted that they should both keep on with their jobs even after the season started again. They were both highly thought of at their places of employment and it seemed a shame to forfeit jobs that they enjoyed.

Yes, Grace mused, things had worked out well for Martha at Welcome Rest. Her worries at the end of last season about the shortage of money had proved to be just a temporary setback. They were doing very nicely now, what with the two lodgers, and Martha's little baking job for Donnelly's, and herself and Hetty working. To say nothing of the visitors. They had had a steady number in nearly every weekend since the season started at Easter, and now this weekend, for the first time, Martha had been able to hang in the front window that coveted sign, 'No Vacancies'.

I would just choose this week to be ill, Grace thought, with Mam rushed off her feet. Not that she ever complained, and there were the two girls to help out, and Hetty . . . Hetty was like a whirlwind these days, waitressing at home and at the restaurant and singing a few times a week at Tilda's Tavern. And bubbling over with merriment, even more so than usual, since she had started walking out with Reuben Loveday. Poor old Albert, to Grace's regret, had disappeared from the scene altogether. Alice had told her that he had gone to live in Blackburn with an aunt and uncle and had very quickly found work there as a joiner. He had been really cut up about Hetty, but Grace hoped that he would have the good sense to put her out of his mind now and find himself a nice sensible girl. Grace liked Albert, not in a romantic way of course – there could never be anything like that between herself and Albert – but she was fond of him in the way a sister was fond of a brother and she wished him well. He deserved a nice, sensible sort of girl, not a flibbertigibbet like her sister.

But when it came to love it was hard to be sensible. Hetty hadn't been very sensible, giving up Albert for that gipsy lad, and yet she seemed to love Reuben. And was she, Grace, being sensible? Had she been wise to let Edwin make love to her, without any promise as to the future? She tossed her hot head back and forth on the pillow, then she grabbed hold of it and turned it over, and sank her head thankfully into its coolness. Try as she might to prevent it, her thoughts always came back to Edwin. She had felt so sure of him.

She had told Walter that Edwin would ask her to marry him but now she feared that it was all an illusion, that her dreams were gradually dwindling away as dreams do in the cold light of morning. And yet he had told her so many times that he loved her. Edwin, oh, Edwin . . . Grace felt hot tears stinging her eyes and she quickly brushed them away. She would not cry. She would not even think of him. She would lie here comfortably and peacefully and not worry about anything, as she had promised her mother she would.

The pinky-red curtains fluttered in a gentle breeze and from outside in the street Grace could hear the footsteps and the happy voices of holiday-makers as they made their way to the beach, and the clank of an iron spade being dragged along the pavement. The rain had vanished overnight and it promised to be a sunny day. Grace closed her eyes and tried to close her ears to the sounds and her mind to the distracting thoughts. She was so tired of it all. She must try to sleep and, for a while, to forget.

'Come and meet my parents this afternoon, will 'ee, Henrietta?' Reuben put an arm round Hetty's shoulders as they strolled along the beach, southwards, away from the funfair and the gipsy encampment. 'I've told them such a lot about 'ee, and they want to meet 'ee for themselves. Please come . . .'

Hetty looked at Reuben, her green eyes serious for once. 'Oh, I don't know.' She shook her head perplexedly. 'I feel so scared somehow, of meeting your mam and dad. I know it's silly of me. I'm not usually scared of anything, but I feel all hot and bothered when I think about it. Suppose they don't like me? And then there's . . .' Hetty hesitated. 'Will your cousin . . .?'

'Now stop worrying your head about Drusilla. I've told 'ee, she's not with us at the moment. She's taken the huff it seems, and she's staying with her aunt at the other side of the camp. Good riddance is what I say. And I've told 'ee before, 'ee needn't fear Drusilla, not so long as I'm around. I won't let her do 'ee any harm.'

Hetty shuddered inwardly as she always did when she thought of Reuben's cousin, whom she had supposed for so long to be his sister. The thought of the gipsy girl with her imperious manner and her cold disdainful stare filled Hetty with dread. She had seen her only briefly during the time she had been friendly with Reuben, more than two months now, and the two girls had never exchanged words, not since Drusilla had told Hetty's fortune. But looks were enough. Hetty knew that there was resentment and dislike smouldering in those black eyes, although the girl had glanced at her only fleetingly, as though at a black beetle that had crawled from under a stone, barely worthy of her notice. But if, as Reuben promised, Drusilla would not be there, Hetty knew that it was time she met his parents.

'All right then,' she said. 'I'll come. Then perhaps next week you can come and meet me mam. Our Grace is trying to persuade her to ask you to tea, but she can be a bit awkward sometimes, can Mam.'

Her mother had not been pleased with her over her treatment of Albert, and that was putting it mildly. Hetty was still smarting from the tongue-lashing she had received from Martha, something very unusual in their household as it was very rarely that heated arguments occurred. Not that it had been an argument. Hetty had had no defence. She knew she had behaved badly over Albert and whatever her mother said to her about her being a selfish unfeeling little madam she knew she richly deserved. But it didn't make any difference. She was head over heels in love with Reuben, and he with her, and nothing could dim their joy in one another. Except Drusilla . . . The niggling thoughts of her would persist just when Hetty was beginning to forget her.

Her mother would come round, though. She always did in the end, and Grace, as always, was a great one for pouring oil on troubled waters. Martha, surprisingly, had been far more angry over Hetty's treatment of Albert than had Alice Gregson. Hetty had felt nervous of facing Alice again after what had happened, but she need not have feared. Alice hadn't even mentioned it and continued to treat Hetty as just one of the daughters of her bosom friend. And if there was more cordiality in the woman's manner towards Grace than there was towards her, Hetty, then, again, it was no more than she deserved.

Hetty and Reuben had spent as much time together as they possibly could since that day in late March when Hetty had so boldly come to seek him out. Sunday afternoon would find them strolling along the beach or across the sand dunes hand in hand or, on the more deserted stretches at South Shore, with their arms entwined round one another. Hetty occasionally came on her bicycle or sometimes rode on a tram the length of the promenade from North Pier to Squire's Gate. Lily had accompanied her only once since that first occasion and the brief friendship between her friend and Luke had dwindled away.

Not so with Hetty and Reuben. She could hardly wait for the times she would spend with him. Most evenings he would come along to hear her sing at the tavern, as Albert had used to do, and then they would walk home along the darkened streets, stopping frequently to kiss in pools of shadow, their lips lingering longer and longer each time as their desire grew. The days were lengthening now, and on the evenings when she was not at the tavern Reuben often met her from work or at a prearranged spot on the promenade.

They enjoyed their evening strolls along the clifftop paths or meandering through the streets of the town, window-gazing and mingling with the steadily increasing numbers of trippers. Hetty thought that living in Blackpool had all the advantages of being a visitor and none of the disadvantages. She didn't have to go home when the precious week came to an end, as holiday-makers did, but could stay for ever and ever in this exciting, fun-packed town that she loved more than any place on earth. Not that she had known many other places, she reminded herself, nor did she want to. Blackpool held all that she could ever wish for. She sailed through her work at home and at the restaurant without ever feeling tired, and sang the evenings away at Tilda's Tavern uplifted on a fluffy cloud of buoyancy. She had never in her life felt so happy, and at the centre of it all, at the hub of her existence, was Reuben.

They loved the crowds at the tavern and in the centre of the town, and folks seeing them together could not but share in their joyful mood and their gladsome delight in one another. The young couple were so much in love it warmed the heart just to look at them. But Hetty and Reuben welcomed the solitude too. Their favourite haunt was the wild stretch of sand dunes, south of the encampment, and it was there that they came together, joyfully and unrestrainedly, one Sunday afternoon in late spring. Hetty felt no compunction in giving herself to Reuben in this way. To do so was as natural as breathing. She felt little pain at their first encounter, so completely opened up was she to receive his love, and the feeling of wellbeing and wonder that succeeded their intimacy surpassed all other considerations. She belonged to Reuben, now and for all time, as he belonged to her.

Their lovemaking that first time was a joyous thing, as it was always to be, full of laughter and fun. Later they lay still, arms loosely thrown over one another, with the soft sand and the prickly star grass at their backs, the blue sky overhead and all around them the raucous cries of the seagulls. Hetty was concerned hardly at all with the future and what it might hold for them.

372

Today, this very moment, was of the essence, with Reuben's strong arms about her and his deep musical voice murmuring in her ear.

She lay there contentedly that summer afternoon, light-heartedly agreeing with what he was whispering, occasionally coming in with a satisfied, 'Mmm . . . that would be lovely.'

' . . . And we'll have a little cottage, Henrietta, just the two of us, right away from all this.' He waved his hand vaguely in the direction of the encampment. 'I'll have a little shed, maybe, where I can do my wood-carving. And we'll have a garden, Henrietta. We could grow tomatoes and lettuces and sell 'em at the market along with my wood-carvings. And we might even have a pony and trap to take us to market. Would 'ee like that, Henrietta?' Reuben's voice sounded boyish in his enthusiasm.

'That would be lovely, Reuben,' Hetty said again, snuggling against his shoulder. She wasn't surprised to hear Reuben say that he wanted to live in a cottage rather than in a caravan. He had often told her of his desire to settle down and spend his days in one place rather than wandering up and down the country. His family had stayed in Blackpool for about a year now and he felt that they would soon be getting itchy feet. 'But I don't know where you'd find a cottage with a garden,' she told him. 'Not in Blackpool. Most of the smaller houses open straight on to the street at the front, and there's only a little yard at the back. You could hardly call it a garden.'

'I be thinking of Marton Moss,' said Reuben. ''Tis not very far from here, a mile or so inland. I meet a lot of folks at the markets who live on the Moss. They have their own little bit of land and grow their own produce. Some even have a greenhouse. They make a tidy living, some of 'em, but they have to work hard, mind 'ee.'

'You'd have to work very hard, Reuben, to have your own pony and trap,' Hetty reminded him.

'I ain't afraid of hard work.' Reuben grinned at her. 'And I'd be doing it for 'ee, Henrietta. I'd do anything for 'ee.' He raised himself on one elbow and looked down at her, love and admiration, wonder even, shining from his dark eyes. 'You be beautiful, Henrietta,' he told her, as he had told her so many times. 'I do love 'ee.'

He lowered himself to her and their lips met again, lingeringly, not wanting to break apart. His hand felt for her breast. But there wasn't time, not now, and Hetty reluctantly struggled free. 'We can't, Reuben. Your mam'll be expecting us, won't she?' She sighed. 'If I've got to meet them I suppose I might as well get it over with. Come on.' She sat up and started to brush the fine sand from her skirt.

'Henrietta, wait.' Reuben's glance was urgent and he put his hands on her arms, holding her firmly. 'It's not just a dream, all this talk about a cottage and a garden and all that. I love 'ee, Henrietta. I want to marry 'ee. Will 'ee marry me, love?'

'Of course I will, Reuben. You know I will.' Gently Hetty stroked his lean brown cheek and his delicately arched eyebrows. For all his swarthy masculinity Reuben was fine-featured and had an almost aristocratic bearing. 'I love you too . . . so much,' she said quietly, looking at him in awe. She hadn't thought it was possible to love a man as much as this. What had started out as a bit of fun that March day when she had come to seek him out had now developed into so much more. Now she couldn't imagine her life without him. She had only been waiting for him to ask her to marry him, knowing that it was incvitable. They might not be able to marry for a while yet, but it would happen. It was as certain as night following day, summer following spring.

They walked back to the encampment with their hands clasped and their arms swinging like a couple of children.

'I've saved up quite a bit, Henrietta,' Reuben told her. 'I'm not without a bob or two, as they say round here. It be the women that takes care of the money as a rule in our families, but Ma knows how I feels about that. She lets me keep some of my profits for myself.'

'I should say it's pretty much the same where I come from,' said Hetty. 'I remember, back in Burnley, some of the women tried to keep a tight rein on the money, or else the fellows'ud have boozed it all away at the pub. Not that they always managed it, the women I mean. Some of the husbands kept the lot for themselves and their poor wives had a terrible job trying to make ends meet. I made up me mind then that I'd never let it happen to me. Me dad weren't like that, though. He always handed his pay packet over to me mam on Friday night, then they'd go through it together, setting aside a bit for this and a bit for that. I remember it well, even though I was only a little 'un at the time. It's the best way, I reckon.'

'I'm sure 'ee be right, Henrietta. There seems to be more rows about money than anything else with our lot. Some of the fellows get a bit shirty when they can't have it all their own way. But 'ee'd be surprised, most Romany fellows don't go drinking away the money like I've seen the gorgio lads doing, even when they've got it to spend. Like I've told 'ee though, it's the women that are the bankers. My ma has a canvas bag where she keeps the money. She wears it round her waist under her apron. It be safe there, safer than banks, that's what most of our folks reckon.'

'And what do you think, Reuben?' Hetty had never had a great deal to do with banks, regarding them as a prerogative of the rich. In Burnley they had never had enough money to consider a bank necessary, but now she knew that her mother had recently opened an account with a bank in Clifton Street.

Reuben shrugged. 'I've never worried too much about it either way. It's only lately I've begun to put a bit on one side. For 'ee, Henrietta.' He drew her closer to him and kissed her cheek. 'I want us to have a little place of our own, where I can be my own boss. Our women have too much to say for themselves at times. Us poor fellows be pushed around something shocking. But us'll make out, won't us, love? Us'll be happy?'

'Of course we will, love.' Hetty smiled at him. 'I'm always happy when I'm with you. But you won't tell them just yet, will you, Reuben? Your mam and dad, I mean, about us wanting to get married. I think I'd better tell my own mother first. I'm not twenty-one, you know, and she might say no. I'll be twenty in a couple of months, though, so it's not all that long.'

'I'll wait for 'ee, love. If your ma won't let us get married yet, then us'll just have to wait. And I won't say anything to Ma and Pa yet if you don't want me to. But I think they know how I feel about 'ee. They wouldn't have invited 'ee to come to the vardo if they didn't think I was serious about 'ee. And don't worry, Henrietta. They'll love 'ee, I know they will, and I'll be there to take care of 'ee.'

The Lovedays' waggon, which Hetty had, of course, seen before, was a large one constructed mainly of wood, painted in a dark shade of green, with a bow-top of stretched green canvas. Now, as she looked at it more carefully, she noticed that the door and the frame were richly decorated with painted scrollwork and flowers of red and yellow, and carved with heads of animals, deer, wolves and bears. Reuben's handiwork, she guessed.

The ground outside the waggon was, as she had noticed before, here and at the other caravans, rather untidy, littered with wood and paper and piles of rubbish. But inside the waggon she was impressed by the sparkling freshness of the place. Every surface, whether of wood or brass, gleamed with recent polishing, and she was dazzled by the array of bright colours that surrounded her. Across the settee was flung a fringed silken shawl, black with a pattern of huge red roses, and a woven rug, striped in red, blue and yellow, lay on the floor. Hetty knew that her own mother's parlour was crowded, after the fashion of the day.

Women loved to cram their rooms with their most precious possessions – photographs, china, brassware, clocks, cushions, rugs, lamps – giving scant regard to matching colour or design. Hetty's mother, especially since there was now more money coming into the house, had begun to furnish her own parlour in this way, and Grace and Hetty had teased her that it was getting so full of things that there was no room for people.

But Hetty had never seen such overcrowding as there was here in the Lovedays' caravan. There seemed to be not an inch that wasn't filled. In every corner there were cupboards, beds that fastened back to the walls, and shelves guarded by brass rails, obviously to stop their contents from falling off when the waggon was on the move. On the shelves there were brass lamps and ornaments, pottery jugs, wood-carvings of animals, and cups and saucers painted with brightly coloured flowers and with gilded rims and handles. At the small windows the lace curtains were looped back with ribbon bows in a bright shade of pink.

When they sat down to drink tea it was from the most delicate eggshell china, so fine that you could almost see through it, decorated with dainty sprigs of primroses and violets, and the silver spoon, too, in the saucer, was so exquisite that Hetty just had to hold it reverently in her hand and examine it more carefully.

Mrs Loveday saw her looking at it. 'Bonny, ain't it?' she said, smiling at the girl. 'I be very proud of my china and my silver, Henrietta. It's been in our family for . . . oh, I don't know how long. A hundred years or more, maybe. It be handed down from one generation to the next, and us takes great care of it.'

'It's beautiful, Mrs Loveday,' said Hetty. 'I hope you didn't think I was rude. I couldn't help looking at it, you see.'

'Not at all, my dear. I like folks to admire my things. Us be a houseproud lot, us Romanies.'

'And you're very honoured, Henrietta.' Reuben smiled encouragingly at her. 'The best china only comes out for special visitors, isn't that so, Ma?'

Mrs Loveday nodded. 'That's so, Reuben. And it's so nice to meet 'ee at last, Henrietta. Ain't it, Eli?'

Mr Loveday from his seat in the corner also nodded in agreement. 'Yes, Ruth. 'Tis good to meet her.' He smiled at Hetty. 'Any friend of our Reuben's is welcome here.'

There had been no doubt about the warmth of their greeting and hospitality, and Hetty had felt her fears fast disappearing, especially with Reuben there as a prop and mainstay. Mr Loveday was an older version of Reuben, his thick wavy hair now silvering and the lines on his swarthy face very pronounced. Mrs Loveday resembled her son hardly at all, being short and plump with rosy cheeks and a wide smile. There was a certain similarity in the dark eyes, though, a shrewdness and a far-seeing look which made Hetty feel that Ruth Loveday, just by looking into her eyes, could perceive all that she wanted to know about her. Hetty remembered the ability of gipsies to see into the future and wondered if Mrs Loveday, too, was possessed of the gift.

The woman wore a black dress, the colour that Hetty's own mother often wore, but apart from the colour there was little similarity. Mrs Loveday's dress, though dark in hue, was shiny and full-skirted, of satin or some such material, and over it she wore an apron embroidered with brilliant birds and butterflies. The silken shawl round her shoulders was similar to the one that covered the settee, save that the roses were yellow instead of red.

She wanted to know all about Hetty, not in a nosy, prying way but, it seemed, out of genuine interest. Hetty was surprised, looking back on the afternoon, at just how much she had told the older woman about herself. About her mother and Grace and their new venture into the boarding-house business, about Grace's employment at Donnelly's store, and her own job at the restaurant, and her singing engagements at Tilda's Tavern. Ruth Loveday had already known quite a lot about that. And about Burnley and how she had used to work in the cotton mill there, and how she loved Blackpool so much more than the inland town. Hetty wondered musingly, after that afternoon, if there could be anything about her that Ruth Loveday didn't know.

It was the end of June when Hetty knew for certain that she was carrying Reuben's child.

Chapter 17

It was during the same month that Constance knew that she was not pregnant. Her plan to entrap Edwin had not worked.

She had woken early, conscious of the familiar, dragging pain at the pit of her stomach. Oh no, she murmured to herself. It can't be. It just isn't possible. She had felt so very sure; so rapturous and fulfilling had been the act of love between herself and Edwin, that there was no doubt in her mind as to the outcome. She had already noticed a tightness in her breasts and fancied they were growing fuller, and once or twice on awakening in the mornings she had felt decidedly queasy. It couldn't, surely, have been her imagination? When she visited the bathroom and saw the telltale smear on her nightgown she had to admit that she had been wrong.

She stormed back into the bedroom and flung herself on to the bed in a paroxysm of temper. Damn, damn damn! She pounded the pillow with her fists until the feathers flew into the air, then she buried her face in its depths feeling the bitter tears of frustration seeping through her closed eyelids. What the hell was she to do now? She had lost him, there was no doubt about that, and he would go ahead and marry that milk-and-water miss, that goody-goody Grace Turnbull. Constance knew that there would not be another chance for her with Edwin. On the occasions that she had seen him lately he had reverted to his former coolness of manner towards her. Whether he regretted the episode she wasn't sure, but from his behaviour it was more than likely that he did. In some ways Edwin was such an irresolute character, lacking the courage of his convictions. And yet Constance knew that in spite of his weaknesses she loved him and she still wanted him.

Had she been pregnant, as she had hoped and as she had been so sure she was, then there was no doubt that Edwin would have done the decent thing and married her. Whatever other faults he might have Edwin was an upright young man and would not have allowed her to go through the disgrace of giving birth to an illegitimate child. And if, by some chance, he had proved difficult, Constance had known that she could rely on the help of Clara Donnelly. But now her position was worse than before. Prior to the episode of the mouse in the kitchen, which was how Constance thought of it, she and Edwin had been getting on quite well. They had been almost, she had thought, on their former footing. If it hadn't been for that dratted Grace Turnbull she and Edwin would have been engaged by now. She was convinced of it. Now he was distant towards her and frigidly polite, and Constance knew that she would have to face up to the fact that Edwin Donnelly was not for her.

She lay still for several moments in an agony of disappointment and wretchedness. And the pain gnawing at her stomach didn't help. Constance knew that she may very well have to spend the day in bed, as she often did at this time of the month, with a hot-water bottle clutched to her until the worst of the pain subsided. The only cure for the suffering one had to endure with monthly periods was, according to her married friends, childbirth.

Constance wasn't enamoured of the idea of having children, in fact she thought it was a perfectly obnoxious idea, but it would be worth it, she sometimes thought, to get rid of this monthly agony. And it would be worth it, even if it meant having a dozen children, to get Edwin. Now he could never be hers.

Unless . . . unless . . . The germ of an idea took root at the back of Constance's mind and as it began to grow she almost forgot about her pain. There was no way that Edwin could possibly know whether she was truly pregnant or not, just as he would never know when she was suffering from her monthly indisposition. It was not the sort of thing that one discussed with young gentlemen, or with anyone, for that matter. Constance's own mother was unaware when it was her daughter's time of the month. After telling her the bald facts, which Constance had already known, she had then left her daughter to cope with such matters on her own. Unlike the working classes who, Constance had heard, were often known to discuss such things quite freely. Mothers of working-class girls, such as Grace Turnbull, sometimes even knew the exact day that their daughters were due and started to worry should they be so much as a day or two late. Not so with Constance's mother. To talk about bodily functions in that way would be very much beneath her dignity. Constance decided that she would tell her mother nothing; merely, when the time came, that Edwin had changed his mind and that the two of them had decided to get married after all.

For Constance had made up her mind to ignore this monthly period. She would pretend that it had never happened – for who could prove otherwise? – and then, in a few weeks' time, she would approach Edwin, with all due modesty, and tell him that she was 'late'.

Constance leapt from the bed, her pain almost gone, so elated was she by her newly formed plan. This way it would be even better than actually being pregnant. When she and Edwin were safely married she could tell him, then, that she had been mistaken. The only difficulty that she could see was that she couldn't afford to wait too long. If the weeks and the months passed by and there was no change in Constance's face and figure, Edwin's suspicions would be sure to be aroused. But if she could persuade him that they must be married soon, by August, say . . . And she could confide in him that she was feeling very sick in the mornings. It surely wouldn't be too indelicate to admit to that. Edwin was gullible; look how he had been taken in by the incident of the mouse. Constance hugged herself with glee. It was sure to work. How could it possibly fail?

★ ★ ★

Hetty hadn't told Reuben yet, nor had she told her mother, but when she missed a second period she knew that she had no choice but to confide in Martha. She could no longer ignore the tightness in her breasts and her lack of appetite in the mornings. Once or twice she had been sick, but had made a pretence of leaving her breakfast because she was late for work. And soon her stomach would begin to swell and her waistline thicken. Grace, surely, would notice, sharing a bedroom with her. But Grace was preoccupied and didn't appear to have fully recovered from her attack of bronchitis in May. It had left her listless and pale and when you spoke to her, sometimes she didn't answer. Hetty thought that often she didn't even hear what you had said.

Hetty waited until Grace had gone to work, then she leaned her elbows on the breakfast table and looked steadily at Martha. 'Mam . . . Mam, I want to talk to you. There's something I've got to tell you.'

Martha didn't answer. She didn't even look at Hetty, but picked up the brown earthenware teapot and poured herself another cup of tea. Deliberately she added the milk and then stirred the liquid several times before, very slowly, placing the spoon in the saucer. She took a deep drink, almost draining the cup with one swallow, then she wiped her hand across her mouth. Only then did she look at her younger daughter, searchingly, but not without some affection.

'Aye, I know full well that you've got summat to tell me, lass.' Martha nodded curtly. 'You're going to have a baby.'

Hetty gasped and put her hand to her mouth. 'But how did . . .? It was our Grace, wasn't it?' Then she shook her head perplexedly. 'But I didn't even tell . . .' Hetty sighed and hung her head for a moment before she looked up and across the table at her mother. 'How did you know, Mam?' she said quietly.

'How did I know? I've been your mother, haven't I, for the last twenty years? That's how I know. There's precious little as I don't know about you, and about our Grace an' all. It's a mother's business to know these things.' Hetty noticed that her mother didn't sound angry, just resigned and a little sad. Hetty wasn't sure that the look of hurt on her mother's face didn't make her feel worse than ever. It might have been better if Martha had ranted and raved, but that was not her way.

'Aye, I've known for some time,' Martha went on. 'I knew as how you'd missed last month, and now you've missed another one, haven't you, lass?' Hetty nodded. 'And you look different an' all. There's something that shows in the face when you're carrying a bairn. I doubt if anybody else'ud notice but, like I've said, I'm your mother. Aye, I knew about it, Hetty. I was just waiting for you to tell me in your own time. I knew you'd have to sooner or later. And what about Reuben?' For the first time Hetty could see a glint of anger in her mother's eyes. 'What does he have to say about it?'

'I haven't told him, Mam.' Hetty's voice was just a whisper.

'You haven't told him? Whyever not?'

'I'm not sure. I kept thinking I'd start. You

386

know I'm not always all that regular. And then I just didn't know what to say. I don't know why I've not told him, Mam.' Hetty's voice petered out.

'Hmm. It's not like you to be at a loss for words,' said Martha drily. 'But you'd best tell him, and quick sharp an' all. He'll have to do what's right by you. I don't want him disappearing in that there caravan pretending he doesn't know owt about it. It wouldn't be the first time that a gipsy had done a moonlight flit at the first hint of trouble.'

'He's not like that, Mam. You know he's not. You said you liked him when he came here for tea. And I wish you wouldn't keep calling him a gipsy. I never even think about that now. It doesn't make any difference what he is. I . . . I love him, Mam.'

'Hmm.' Martha grunted. 'It's to be hoped you do, after you've gone and let him get you in the family way. And it's to be hoped he loves you an' all. It's only a few months back you were saying you loved Albert.'

'I don't think I ever said that, Mam.' Hetty still felt a pang of guilt when she thought about Albert. But she had never felt about him the way she felt about Reuben. 'I was fond of Albert,' she said now, 'and I'm real sorry if I hurt him, but I love Reuben. I really do, Mam. And you needn't worry about him being a gipsy. He wants to settle down and live in a house like ordinary folks do. He's always talking about finding a little cottage.'

'Talking's one thing and doing's another. Let's see if he puts his money where his mouth is. That's if he's got any money.' Martha raised her eyebrows. 'And you've got to admit, our Hetty, when all's said and done, he's still a gipsy and they're not renowned for staying in one place.'

'Reuben's different . . .'

'So you keep telling me. Let's hope he is. But just think on that you tell him . . . tonight. You'll be seeing him later, I daresay?'

'Yes . . . and . . . well, thanks, Mam.' Hetty looked down, plucking nervously at her skirt. Now that the business of telling her mother was over and done with she felt like crying, but whether from relief or happiness or sadness she wasn't sure.

'Thanks for what?'

'For . . . well, for not shouting at me. For not getting mad at me. I know a lot of mothers would have done.'

'Aye, a lot of mothers'ud have shown you the door, lass.' Martha nodded grimly. 'But I can't see any sense in that. You're me daughter and I'll stick by you, right or wrong. That's what being a mother's all about, leastways that's how I see it. I remember young Edith that lived down the street in Burnley. The same thing happened to her, but her mam and dad wouldn't let her inside the house once they found out. They were too ashamed, they reckoned. The poor lass went to live on a farm out Clitheroe way with an old aunt and uncle. I'm sure I don't know what happened to her or the bairn. She were never mentioned again. And I've known plenty more that have ended up in the workhouse.' Martha shook her head sadly. 'Aye, it's a rum world, Hetty, when parents cast off their own flesh and blood because of their pride. And that's all it is, sinful pride. You know what our Lord said about not casting the first stone . . .' Martha's voice was thoughtful as she stared unseeingly across the room.

'But you needn't think I'm pleased about it, Hetty, because I'm not.' Martha's tone changed and she looked sternly at her daughter. 'You've been a naughty girl, there's no two ways about it, and you'll have to get wed before you begin to show. And you'll tell Reuben at once, do you hear me?'

Hetty nodded. 'Yes, Mam.'

'Right, well that's that then. I'm off to see to the bedrooms, and you can clear away in the dining room, there's a good girl, and then help Gladys and May with the washing up. Work has to go on, no matter what . . .'

Reuben looked serious and contrite as he sat on the edge of the settee, twisting his cap round and round in his hands. 'I love Henrietta, I can assure 'ee. I do love her, and I'll do what's right. Us wanted to get married anyway.' He glanced at Hetty sitting next to him and smiled encouragingly at her. 'But I'm really sorry as it's happened like this.'

'Too late to be sorry, lad,' said Martha gruffly. 'The damage is done now, that's the way I see it, so the pair of you had best get wed. Anyroad, I daresay it took two.' Reuben could see just the merest glint of amusement in Martha's eyes as she looked at him, although her mouth was unsmiling. 'I daresay our Hetty had a hand in it an' all.'

389

Beneath his swarthy skin a faint blush tinged Reuben's cheeks. He looked down at the floor and so did Hetty.

'Like I said,' Martha went on, 'you'll have to get wed, and be sharp about it an' all. And it's got to be a proper wedding at the chapel, mind. We want no hole-and-corner affair and no jumping over the brush. I've heard tell as how they do that, some of you . . . Romanies.'

Reuben nodded. 'Yes, I must admit that's true, Mrs Turnbull. Some Roms jump across a broomstick or leap over a bonfire. It's a form of marriage ceremony, 'ee see, and they believe that it's what they promise to one another that matters, rather than making vows in church. But there's a lot of 'em that do get married in church,' he added hastily, 'and I don't mind that for Henrietta and me.'

'Chapel,' Martha corrected him.

'Yes, chapel then.' Reuben smiled again at Hetty and she reached out and touched his hand.

'Right then. That's that. I'll ask the minister and we'll see if we can sort something out for August. That should be soon enough.' She glanced surreptitiously at Hetty's waistline. 'I reckon you'll not be showing a lot by then. It's up to us to put a brave face on it and make the best of a bad job. And it's no use you two sitting there grinning at one another.' Martha scowled at them. 'Marriage is no laughing matter, I'll tell you. You'll realise afore long that it's not all roses round the door and happy ever after.'

Her glance softened as she looked at them sitting hand in hand, Reuben still somewhat dis-

390

comfited and Hetty abnormally subdued. 'But I reckon you'll make out, the pair of you. Aye, I daresay you'll do all right.'

'Edwin . . . Edwin, wait. I must talk to you.'

Edwin halted his brisk stride down the church path and turned to find Constance at his side. He looked at her with barely concealed impatience. 'Yes, what is it, Constance? I'm in rather a hurry. My parents and I have been invited out to lunch with the Reardons, and I'm meeting . . . someone this afternoon.'

'Your mother's feeling better then?'

'Slightly.' Edwin gave a brief nod. 'It's one of her better days. What did you want to talk to me about, Constance? Can't it wait?'

'No . . . No, it can't wait. But I can't tell you now, not here.' Constance glanced nervously at the groups of fellow church members mingling around them. 'Could I see you later today? Please, Edwin. I must see you.'

Edwin looked at her properly for the first time and could see a hint of nervousness, fear almost, in her blue eyes. A numbing fear seized him, also, as an appalling thought flashed into his mind. Oh no! Not that. It couldn't be. But he knew that he couldn't refuse to meet her. 'Very well then, Constance,' he said coolly. 'Where shall we meet? Shall I come round to your place this evening?' She nodded assent. 'About eight o'clock?' Slowly Constance lowered her head in agreement.

Edwin's eyes narrowed as he watched her, her eyes downcast, the very picture of modesty, had he not known otherwise. 'Your parents won't be out, will they?' he asked suspiciously.

'No.' A half-smile flickered across her lips, but her eyes were blank. 'Mother and Father will be at home. But I'll make sure we're not disturbed. Thank you, Edwin.' She reached out and touched his elbow and her hand lingered there for a moment. 'Thank you for saying you'll come.'

'Eight o'clock then. Goodbye, Constance.' Edwin turned and strode away quickly, wondering how he was going to get through the rest of the day, the lunch appointment with the Reardons and his meeting with his dear Grace this afternoon, with this threat hanging over him.

As eight o'clock approached Edwin was more and more sure that he knew what Constance wished to tell him, and he also had some idea as to what he would say.

Her news, therefore, came as no surprise.

'I'm expecting a child, Edwin,' she said quietly. 'Your child.'

'Are you sure?' He looked at her shrewdly. 'It's only a few weeks since . . . How can you be sure, so soon?'

'It's six weeks ago,' Constance replied. 'It was towards the end of May when we . . . when you came round that evening, and it's July now. And I'm . . . I'm late.' She looked down at the floor, as if embarrassed. 'I've missed . . . two periods now.' Her voice was barely audible.

'And that's . . . unusual?'

She nodded and when she spoke her voice was a flat monotone. 'I'm usually so regular. And besides, I'm feeling . . . poorly. I was sick yesterday and again this morning. It's getting hard to keep it from Mother.' The blue eyes that looked so steadily into his were imploring.

Edwin hardened his heart. To be forewarned was to be forearmed and he had prepared in advance what he would say. He raised his eyebrows and kept his voice casual. 'How do you know it's mine?'

He was unprepared for the effect his words had upon Constance.

'Edwin . . . Edwin, how could you? How dare you suggest . . .?' Her voice rose both in volume and in pitch, so much so that he glanced fearfully at the door of the morning room. The drawing room, where he presumed her parents were sitting, was just across the hallway. She burst into tears and a wild frenzy of sobbing seized her as she flung herself against the chintz cushion on the settee. 'I've had to cope with this . . . all by myself . . . for weeks and weeks . . . and then all you can say is . . . that . . . that it's not yours.' The face that she turned to him was anguished, the tears welling from her eyes and rolling down her cheeks, splashing on to the pale-blue bodice of her silken dress. 'And I'm so frightened. What am I going to do? How can you say it's not yours? You're the only one I've . . . been with, Edwin. There's never been anyone but you.' Her voice was imploring.

'Now, now, Constance. Come along.' In spite of himself Edwin couldn't bear to see her so distressed, and she really did seem disturbed and afraid, even though he knew that her words, about him being the only one, were not true. He

reached for his large white handkerchief and
dabbed at her eyes. 'I didn't exactly say that. I
didn't say that it wasn't mine. I said . . . how do
you know that it *is*?' He looked at her reprovingly,
though not unkindly. 'Now, come along, Constance,' he said quietly. 'I wasn't born yesterday,
you know. I know that I wasn't the first. Was I? So
it's only natural that I should wonder . . .'

'It was a long time ago, Edwin,' Constance said
contritely, hanging her head again. 'A very long
time. I'm . . . I'm almost ashamed to tell you. It
was the brother of one of my friends. I was only
seventeen. He . . . he took advantage of me. He
made me . . . I didn't know . . . that you could
tell.' She looked at him pleadingly. 'But there's not
been anyone since. Only you, Edwin. And I've
never wanted anyone but you.'

Edwin sighed inwardly, a deep sigh that
reached the depths of his being. Dear God, whatever was he to do? There was no doubt that the
girl was in trouble. Fear such as that which was
written on her face could not be feigned, neither
could those pitiful tears and sobs. And all because
of one moment of madness and forgetfulness. He
didn't speak for several moments as he sat dejectedly, his hands clasped between his knees and his
head lowered, staring unseeingly at the pattern of
roses in the carpet. His mind groped wildly for a
solution to the problem. He recalled a friend of his
who had been in a similar predicament. There was
a woman, apparently, in the Central Drive area
who would perform . . . Whatever was he thinking of? Edwin closed his mind immediately to such
wicked thoughts. His friend had not been a Cath-

olic and, besides, Constance was a well-brought-up, refined girl. He couldn't possibly subject her to such an indignity.

'What are we going to do, Edwin?'

The anxious voice near to him brought him to his senses. What else was there to do?

'I'll marry you, Constance,' he said quietly.

'Oh, thank you. Thank you, Edwin.' She put her arms around him and raised her face to his, awaiting his kiss. He rested his cheek against hers, briefly, but did not allow their lips to meet. Instead he kissed her cheek then gently pulled away from her.

'We'll get engaged, Constance. Soon. Then we can . . . get married,' he almost faltered on the words, 'later in the year.'

'It can't be too much later, darling.' Her use of the endearment didn't go unnoticed, neither did her demure glance at her waistline. 'I will begin to . . . show, before very long. We can't afford to waste too much time or Mother will find out.'

'You don't intend to tell your parents, then, that you are . . . expecting a child?'

'Oh no. Of course not.' A slight frown wrinkled Constance's brow. 'It would be better if they were to think that you've changed your mind, that you've decided to marry me after all. That you really loved me all along . . . and you've only just realised it.' The blue eyes, still tear-dimmed, that she turned to him seemed completely guileless.

'They will be suspicious if we get married too soon, Constance,' said Edwin firmly. 'Anyway, these things take time to arrange. We'll get married in September maybe, or early October. That's just over two months away. You should still be able to get away with it then without anyone knowing.' He looked at her enquiringly. 'But haven't you realised that they'll be sure to find out . . . when the child is born?'

'By that time it will be too late for them to worry.' Constance smiled happily. 'They'll all be so pleased that you and I have decided to get married at last. I knew you wouldn't let me down, Edwin.'

'All right, Constance. We'll choose a ring next week from the jewellers in Market Street.' Edwin was finding the atmosphere in the small room claustrophobic and he could feel the beads of sweat forming on his forehead. He was also feeling sick. He rose to his feet abruptly. 'Come along. Get your coat and we'll have a breath of fresh air.'

'Aren't you going to talk to my parents?' Constance paused with her hand on the drawing room door.

'Not this evening, Constance. I'll see them . . . tomorrow.'

'Very well then.' Constance opened the door and called out cheerily, 'Edwin and I are just going for a walk, Mother . . . We might have some news for you soon.'

Edwin smiled at Constance, a smile, he felt, that didn't reach his eyes, as he poked his head round the drawing room door. 'Goodnight, Mrs Whitehead, Mr Whitehead. I'll call and see you both tomorrow, if I may?'

They spoke little as they strolled round the fringes of the Royal Palace Gardens. Edwin felt sick in his heart and mind, as well as physically sick. He felt that he might keel over at any moment, but he was aware of his promise and of the loyalty that he owed to the girl who was carrying his child.

But what of his promises to Grace? Had he made her any promises? Edwin knew that he hadn't, not in so many words, but he had declared his love for her many times, not only in words but with his body as well. He loved her so very much. He couldn't bear to think of the next day when he knew he must face her with the truth, before he went to see Constance's parents. No, never the truth, he decided. He would never be able to bring himself to tell her the whole of his infidelity, that another woman was now bearing his child. That would hurt her too much. She would have to think that he had succumbed to family pressures, that Constance was the daughter of a business colleague, that he had no choice but to marry her . . .

His mind was going round in circles and he was aware that he hadn't spoken to the girl next to him for about five minutes.

'Don't worry, Constance,' he said. 'I won't let you down.'

'Grace . . . Grace, I must talk to you.' Edwin realised as soon as he had spoken that his words were an echo of what Constance had said to him on the church path yesterday. Was it possible that only a day had elapsed since that meeting when he had known, intuitively, that all his dreams about this lovely girl were to be shattered into tiny pieces?

After he had left Constance at her gate he had walked the streets till midnight, his mind in a turmoil and aware, whenever he stopped for a moment, that his limbs were trembling. He hadn't slept and he knew that the dark shadows beneath his eyes were evidence of this. He tried to smile at Grace now but his face felt frozen. And the tremor in his hands was starting again. He gripped hard on the edge of the counter to steady himself.

Grace looked at him anxiously, her lovely brown eyes filled with concern as they always were when she could see that someone was troubled. Dear, dear Grace. What a selfless person she was, always putting the worries of other people before her own. And soon he was going to hurt her very much. The thought of it was unbearable, but Edwin knew that he could not delay, not another moment.

'Whatever's the matter, Edwin? You don't look at all well, dear,' said Grace.

'No . . . A sleepless night. Just a slight indisposition.' His voice sounded strained and hoarse to his ears, not like his own voice at all, as though it were coming from far away. 'Grace, I must see you. There's something I have to tell you, before you go home this evening. We'll go for a walk . . . on the promenade, find somewhere we can talk.'

'All right, Edwin.' Grace's voice was quiet and she sounded calm, but that was no indication of how she really felt. Inside her there was a feeling of apprehension, of slowly mounting unease which increased as she stared at Edwin's unsmiling face and saw the look of blankness and despair in his eyes. Suddenly she guessed what it was he wanted to say and she felt sick with fear.

Slowly he reached out and covered her small

hand with his own. He uttered just one word, 'Grace . . .' before he left her, walking dazedly through the bales of silks and satins, aware of nothing but the ache in his heart and the emptiness inside him.

The promenade was quieter towards the end of the afternoon. Not deserted – Blackpool promenade was never deserted at the height of the season – but now the shops were closing and the visitors were trooping back to their boarding houses for high tea. Grace and Edwin were able to find a vacant seat looking out to sea. The tide was going out, leaving ridges on the sand and rock pools near to where a few sailor-suited children were scrabbling about with fishing nets. But they, too, would soon be gone, dragged away unwillingly from the delights of the sea and sand by parents whose thoughts were already fixed on the next of the day's pleasures. What would it be today? Fish and chips, maybe, or boiled ham and salad? Blackpool beach would be deserted again, an unending stretch of golden sand awaiting the influx of the crowds who would be there again next morning as soon as the sun rose.

'Grace . . . Grace, my love . . .' Edwin's voice faltered over the words, especially the last two, knowing full well that he shouldn't really be saying them, that this was the last time he would be able to do so. 'I don't know how to begin . . . I just don't know how to tell you . . .'

'Then let me help, Edwin.' Grace's voice, always quiet, was softer than usual and she did not look at him as she spoke. Her eyes were fixed on some point on the horizon where the sky met the sea, azure blue blending into a deep, dark turquoise. 'You want to tell me that . . . that you can't see me again. That your parents . . . your mother . . . doesn't want you to go on seeing me. And you have to do as you are told.'

If there was a hint of bitterness in her last words Edwin knew that he deserved it and more. Not that it was Grace's way to be bitter, and it certainly wasn't obvious in her tone of voice, but Edwin was so conscience-stricken that he was aware of the slightest nuance and shade of meaning in her words. Now she had gone part-way to revealing the truth it was somewhat easier for him.

It wasn't his mother – not really – but Edwin seized on this as a way of making things a little bit simpler, not only for himself but for Grace, and shielding her from the cataclysmic effect it could have on her were she to know the whole truth. That she would be sure to know it eventually he pushed to the back of his mind.

'You know, of course, that I'm a Roman Catholic,' he began, 'and you are . . . not. This always causes trouble in a family, Grace, especially when it comes to . . . marriage. I should have told you before, I know that. I didn't want to face up to it. I thought that things would work out. My parents have always been friendly with . . . with the Whiteheads. You know, Mr Whitehead runs the café with my father, and they have a place at South Shore.'

'Yes . . . I know.'

'It has always been assumed that . . .' Edwin

faltered, then started again. 'Mr Whitehead and my father are business partners, and they always hoped that . . . Mr Whitehead has a daughter . . .'

'Constance,' Grace said flatly.

'You . . . you know about Constance?' Edwin turned to look at Grace, for the first time since he had started speaking, in some surprise. He had never mentioned the girl to her, and yet how naive he must have been to suppose that she knew nothing of Constance Whitehead.

'Yes, I know about Constance.' Grace nodded. She had heard from Miss Walters in the haberdashery department of his father's business partner. How the families had hoped it would come to something, but that there had been a rift between the young couple. Just how Miss Walters had known all this Grace wasn't sure, but it was surprising how the sales assistants seemed to know all the gossip about their employers and their families. Miss Walters hadn't said anything recently, of course, knowing of the friendship between Grace and Edwin, an attachment of which Grace knew the woman disapproved although she hadn't actually said so.

'I know about Constance,' Grace said again. 'In fact, that was why I had some idea, Edwin, about what you wanted to tell me.' He hadn't told her yet, not all of it, but she knew only too well what was coming. 'She . . . Constance . . . came into the shop this afternoon, after you'd spoken to me. She came into our department.'

'She spoke to you? She told you . . . something?' The alarm showed in Edwin's voice and on his face.

'No, she didn't speak.' Grace recalled to herself now how the girl had appeared, tall and regal, in her ice-blue gown, the colour that she so often chose to wear. She had seen Constance several times in the store, though not recently, scrutinising her, Grace, and then walking away with her head held high. This afternoon she had just stood there, not smiling, and though Grace couldn't have said in any honesty that the girl was gloating, all the same she had known intuitively why she was there. Constance had stood for a few moments, watching, her expression impenetrable, then had disappeared as silently as she had come.

'But I knew, Edwin. I guessed when I saw her what it was that you wanted to tell me. It's you . . . and Constance, isn't it?'

Edwin nodded numbly. It was cowardly of him to be allowing Grace to do most of the talking, but the words refused to come.

'You're . . . you're going to marry her?'

Edwin nodded again. Then, 'She's a Catholic,' he said lamely, 'like I am. We've been friends for a long time, a very long time, since we were both children. You mustn't think that it's any sudden thing, Grace, between Constance and me. She's . . . she's always been there . . . I was deluding myself when I thought . . . that you and I . . . I love you, Grace, but it's just not possible.' Edwin's eyes were full of pain and Grace knew it was hurting him to say the words. But there was fear there, too, flickering in the golden-brown depths, and Grace realised that of the two of them she was the stronger.

As far as Edwin was concerned, he felt more

402

wretched and miserable than he had ever felt in his life. This dear, sweet girl, whom he loved more than anyone else in the world – and would always love – and he was causing her such hurt and anguish. But no more pain than his act of betrayal was causing to himself. For that was what it was; he had betrayed her, and all for one stupid moment of weakness with a girl who, compared to his lovely Grace, was a mere nothing. Fruitless as it was now to protest that he loved her, that was, nevertheless, what he found himself doing.

'I . . . love you, Grace,' he said hesitantly. 'I still love you. Please believe me.'

But not enough, Edwin, she said to herself. You don't love me enough, and not nearly so much as I love you. But the words remained unspoken. She felt anger welling up inside her now, rather than hurt and anguish. That might come later.

'Edwin,' she said, 'I wouldn't have thought you could do this to me. I thought you were too high-principled to lead me on the way you did and then to . . . to abandon me. I gave myself to you because I loved you. I knew what we were doing was wrong, but it didn't seem to matter because I was so sure of you. And then for you to tell me that there's someone else and that you don't want me any more . . .'

'But it isn't like that, Grace . . .'

'Isn't it? Then what is it like?'

'I do want you. I still love you, Grace – believe me, I do – but . . . it just isn't possible.'

'Very well, Edwin.' Grace's voice was calm

and she could still feel nothing but a numbness inside her. Even the burst of anger had subsided. 'I'll leave you now. There's no point in us talking any more, or even in seeing one another again.' She stood up without making any attempt to touch him. 'Goodbye, Edwin. I hope you get what you want. I hope that she will make you happy.'

'Grace, wait . . . Don't just go like this. You can't . . .'

'Goodbye, Edwin.'

Grace turned and walked away. She knew that if she stayed another moment she might say something she would regret, or else the tears would begin to fall. By the time she had finished the ten-minute walk to her home she was composed enough to face her mother and her sister. She wouldn't tell them today. Her mother had already had to face enough anguish with Hetty's momentous news without having to bear the burden of Grace's unhappiness as well. Although Grace knew, in her heart, that her mother would not be sorry that it was all over between her and Edwin Donnelly.

Grace realised as she walked home that Edwin's words had not come as a great surprise to her, not really. Grace knew now that she had only been waiting for the inevitable.

But that didn't make it any easier to bear. Alone in her room, away from Hetty and her mother, her self-control broke and she gave way to tears.

She knew that she could not bear to see him again, to work in such close proximity with him in the store. The next day she handed in her notice and the following week she found part-time employment at Mrs Amelia Marsden's Drapery in Queen's Square.

Chapter 18

'Now go easy with her, Walter lad, that's all I ask,' said Martha. 'She's had a rough time lately and she's bound to be upset. Don't go rushing her into anything. Just take your time about it, nice and steady like, and she'll happen come round to your way of thinking.' She gave a deep sigh. 'I certainly hope she will, that's for sure.'

Martha looked at Walter Clayton sitting opposite her and thought again, as she had always thought, what an ideal partner he would be for her elder daughter. Sober and industrious, and a chapel-goer – becoming one of the leading lights, in fact, of the chapel he attended in the centre of town, if what she heard was true – and obviously still potty about Grace in spite of the fact that she had given him the go-by in favour of Edwin Donnelly. He hadn't the handsome looks and the refined manner of young Mr Edwin, to be sure, but what did looks matter or posh manners when you behaved as that one had done? Handsome is as handsome does was a true maxim, Martha thought, and it had proved correct in the case of Edwin Donnelly.

She hadn't got to the bottom of it yet, as Grace

had told her very little. The girl didn't seem to want to discuss the matter at all. She had merely told her mother that she wouldn't be seeing Edwin again, that it was all over between them and, what was more, she was leaving Donnelly's store as well.

William Donnelly had seemed embarrassed about the affair when he saw Martha. He had made a point of calling round in person when the van called to collect the daily supply of baking, instead of leaving the business to the van driver.

'I'm real sorry, Mrs Turnbull,' he had muttered. 'I'd hoped that something could be sorted out between my lad and your lass. She's a grand girl, is Grace. But, well, you know how things are. It isn't always easy for me at home, or for Edwin either.' Martha didn't really know and she made no comment, but she assumed he was referring to his wife. It was no secret that she led him a merry dance and that she was now suffering from some sort of nervous ailment. It was Martha's opinion that she wanted a good shaking.

'Anyway,' Mr Donnelly went on, 'the lad seems to feel now that he can't go on seeing your Grace, that it wouldn't be fair to her . . . I don't know.' His look was shamefaced although Martha knew that it was none of his doing. 'There's the religious aspect, of course. It was bound to cause problems in the end, and Constance is a Catholic . . .'

'Don't worry, Mr Donnelly,' Martha had assured him. 'Happen it's all for the best. Our Grace is upset, I'm not denying it, but she'll get over it. I've said all along that oil and water can't mix, if you know what I mean.'

William Donnelly was a good boss and that was all that Martha wanted. She was in his employment and she was very grateful to him for the nice little baking job that he had put her way, but socially they were poles apart, and as far as religion was concerned they were too. She had never approved of Grace walking out with the boss's son, and now her chickens were coming home to roost as Martha had feared that they might all along. She was sorry that the girl was hurt and it grieved Martha to see the look of pain in Grace's eyes even though she spoke little of the matter. She was young enough, though, and, like Martha had told William Donnelly, would get over it in time. But it must have been a bitter blow to the lass when she was thrown over in favour of that Constance Whitehead, a stuck-up piece if ever there was one, from all accounts. Martha had heard the rumours and it appeared that the two of them, this Constance and Mr Edwin, had been friends since childhood and that now they were engaged and planning a wedding before very long. Martha had her own ideas as to why they were in such a hurry about it but, wisely, she kept her own counsel and wouldn't dream of voicing her suspicions to Grace. But time would tell.

And now here was Walter Clayton again. Not that a visit from him was anything unusual. He had fallen into the habit of calling to see Martha when he knew that Grace would not be there, usually on a Sunday afternoon when she was out with Edwin Donnelly, and he always made sure that he had gone before she returned home. Now it was Thursday afternoon, his half-day off from his work at Henderson's coal merchant's and Martha, as always, was ready to stop work for a little while to chat with him.

No, thought Martha, he certainly hadn't the looks of Edwin Donnelly – that one would be enough to turn any girl's head, even Grace, who had always seemed so sensible – but Walter was a pleasing enough young fellow. He wasn't very tall, but he was thickset with broad shoulders and Martha felt sure that they were shoulders that you could cry on when you were in trouble. His straight brown hair shone today as though with recent washing. It must be hard for the lad, Martha thought, to keep himself clean doing such a dirty job, especially when he was living in digs. He hadn't, she noticed, managed to remove all the grime from beneath his fingernails, but his face, broad and red-cheeked, was clean enough and his grey eyes were full of concern as he looked at Martha.

'And you say she's not working at Donnelly's store now? She's finished with that an' all, as well as with that Edwin fellow?'

'Aye. She decided to make a clean break. She's working for Amelia Marsden in Queen's Square now. It's only a little place compared with Donnelly's, a draper's shop specialising in baby clothes and knitting wools and silks and all that. But she seems happy enough there – as happy as she can be under the circumstances – and Mrs Marsden's very kind to her. She's only there afternoons and she helps me in the mornings.'

'What time does she finish?'

'Half past five.' Martha looked at Walter

steadily. 'Aye, I know what you're thinking, and it might not be a bad idea at that. Go and meet her, Walter lad. But, like I've told you, just watch your step with her. Take it nice and easy and with a bit of help from Him above . . .' Martha smiled as she glanced at the ceiling, 'you may find that things'll work out for you.'

'Yes, God works in a mysterious way at times, Mrs Turnbull.' Walter, unlike Martha, didn't smile, and Martha could see why her younger daughter thought of him as a pious Holy Joe. But Hetty had always been like that, skittish and ready to poke fun at some people. Grace was not Hetty, and Grace would be all right with Walter Clayton, once she'd come to appreciate his sterling qualities. Martha was sure of it.

'Grace . . . Grace, wait a minute.'

Grace turned at the sound of the urgent voice as she stepped through the door of Amelia Marsden's draper's shop, then her heart sank when she saw who it was. 'Walter . . . Look, just go away and leave me alone. I thought I'd made it clear to you that I didn't want to see you again.' Grace took a step away from him, but she was halted by Walter holding on to her arm.

'No, don't go. Please, Grace. I want to talk to you. Please . . .'

Grace looked into Walter's grey eyes, unwillingly, but was surprised by what she saw there. She remembered how he had used to look at her in the past, covetously, as though he had wanted to possess the very heart and soul of her. There was nothing of that in his glance now, only concern

411

and a slight puzzlement and – yes – a hint of kindliness. Grace had looked so often for that in the past, but had never seen it there. In spite of herself she stopped, but her voice when she spoke was still cool. 'Yes, what did you want to say to me?'

'Aw, come on, Grace. Don't be like that. Not with me. This is Walter, you remember, your old pal Walter from the mill? Don't go all stiff and starchy on me, love. That's not like you.'

'You haven't behaved much like an old pal, Walter.' Grace's eyes narrowed and burned with remembered anger and fear. 'What on earth did you think you were playing at, following me around like that? I'd told you it was all over, but you wouldn't leave me alone. Every time I went out with . . . with Edwin, you popped up out of the blue. You had me in a terrible state, Walter. Whatever got into you?'

'It wasn't every time, Grace.' Walter shook his head.

'Well, it seemed like it. And it upset me, I can tell you.'

'I'm sorry, Grace. Really I am.' Walter lowered his head, staring at the pavement. 'I reckon I was jealous. I don't honestly know what it was that made me behave like that. It was like rubbing salt into a wound, I suppose. I just had to see you. Even though you were with that chap, I still had to see you.' He raised his head and looked at her again. 'But it's different now, I believe? You and him, you're not . . .?'

'I don't want to talk about it, Walter. Not at all.'

'All right then. We won't talk about it.' Walter

tried to smile and his eyes, usually cold and humourless, were lit with a faint spark of gentleness which didn't go unnoticed by Grace. 'At least let me walk home with you. I'm in digs near to your place, you know, top of High Street, but I'm looking for a place of me own. Just a little place, two up and two down, but somewhere I can call me own.'

'All right then, Walter. Seeing that we're going the same way I don't suppose I can stop you.' Grace started to walk up Queen Street towards the railway station near to where they both lived, and Walter fell into step beside her.

It was strange walking with him again after all this time, and at first Grace was at a loss for words. It seemed odd to make polite conversation with someone she had known as long, and as well, as Walter, but that was what she found herself doing.

'And what do you think of Blackpool? Do you like living here?'

'Yes, I'm getting used to it now. I didn't care for it much at first though.' Walter didn't say why. 'But I reckon there's far worse places to live, and the air's nice and clean. That's a point in its favour.'

'Not like Burnley.'

'No, as you say, not like Burnley.' Walter turned to look at her, almost shyly, his eyes revealing again the unfamiliar gentleness which Grace had noticed a few minutes earlier. 'We had some good walks though, didn't we, Grace, up at t'top, away from all the muck and smoke? It were grand up there.'

'Yes . . . it was,' replied Grace slowly. 'I miss the hills. I remember saying to . . .' She stopped abruptly, biting her lip, before going on. 'I've told quite a few people that that's one of the things I miss, the hills and the greenery. It's the only thing I miss really.'

A picture flashed into Grace's mind of the moor above the mill town, purpled, as it was in late summer, with heather, the huge outcrops of rock crouching like brooding giants, and the sunlight, unhindered up there away from the smoke and grime, breaking through the clouds and highlighting the colours, the mauves and greens and browns of that vast wild landscape.

She turned to smile at Walter, unaware that she was doing so. 'Blackpool's a concrete wilderness when you compare it with the moors and the countryside around Burnley. But it isn't fair to make comparisons. They've got the sea and the sand here and that's what the visitors pay their money for when they come on their holidays. It's a good job they do or folks like my mother would go out of business. She's certainly no regrets about coming here.'

'No, so I gathered. She was telling me that she's having a good season.' Walter didn't enlarge on this statement, in fact he suddenly stopped speaking as though he was aware that he had said too much.

Grace made no comment. She had suspected that Walter had kept in touch with her mother and his words seemed to bear this out. Not that she cared much; she was still numbed from the shock of the end of her affair with Edwin, and what other people said or did affected her little. It was as much as she could do to get through each day, one endless day at a time, going through the motions of living. She was like an automaton as she helped her mother each morning with the cooking and cleaning, and served the customers each afternoon with knitting wools and sewing silks and buttons and braid and baby clothes, all the while feeling nothing inside her but a gnawing emptiness. To see Walter at her side again looking so normal and friendly and kind – unexpectedly kind – was like stepping back into the past, to a time before she had ever heard of Edwin Donnelly or even thought of coming to live in Blackpool.

Grace smiled at Walter again. 'Yes, we're having a good season. Mam was a bit worried at the end of last summer that we hadn't earned enough to make ends meet. I think she was beginning to wonder if we'd been right to make the move. But we're doing fine this year. "No Vacancies" sign in the window quite a few times, so that can't be bad.' She gave a little laugh. 'It's funny how you start talking like a boarding-house keeper when you live in Blackpool. It seems to be all they're bothered about, making a "bit of brass" as they say, but I suppose you can't blame them. It's what it's all about when all's said and done.'

'Yes, it's their livelihood,' Walter agreed. 'Mrs Jobson, my landlady, she's just the same. Always trying to work out how she can squeeze in another visitor or two, shoving beds in all over the place where there's not really room to swing a cat round. I'm surprised I've not got me marching orders before now. She could get more money for my room if she let it out to short-term visitors, but she happen doesn't like to turf me out. She's a decent sort really, and it's only a poky little room up in the attic. Anyroad, like I told you, Grace, I'm on the look-out for a place of me own. Amos Armitage, a mate of mine at Henderson's, he's got his own little place off Central Drive. Rented, I mean, he doesn't own it, but he's going to have a word with his landlord and see if he can come up with something for me.'

'That's nice, Walter,' said Grace, and then the conversation seemed to dry up.

They walked along in silence for a few moments, Grace making no attempt to think of things to say. If Walter wanted to walk home with her then that was up to him, but she certainly didn't intend to go out of her way to be chatty and friendly, not after the way he had treated her. She had to admit, though, that he seemed different, nicer and not nearly so frightening now – not frightening at all, in fact – and she began to wonder why she had ever found him so.

When he spoke again she answered him politely but without going into further details. 'Yes, Hetty's doing very well with her singing. I daresay you had a surprise, didn't you, seeing her on the stage? But she's always had a good voice if you remember.' She didn't tell him about the staggering news that Hetty had recently stunned them with, remembering how priggish he could be and that he had never cared much for her sister. She guessed that he had only enquired about Hetty out of politeness or because he was searching for something to say. He would find out soon enough

416

about Hetty's forthcoming marriage to Reuben Loveday and the reason for its haste.

They stopped by the gate of Welcome Rest and looked at one another steadily. Several seconds elapsed before Walter spoke. 'Grace . . . I've been wondering. There's a concert on Saturday night at our chapel. You know, the one I go to, in the middle of town. Would you . . . d'you think you would come with me, Grace?'

Grace didn't answer.

'Please, Grace. I'd really like you to come. At least . . . think about it, would you?'

The reason Grace didn't answer immediately was because another picture had flashed into her mind, again of Burnley . . . and Walter. She found herself thinking about concerts at the chapel they had both attended; she remembered the worn wooden floorboards and the rickety stage; the aspiring artistes – warbling sopranos and slightly off-key baritones, and little girls in their best frocks reciting, 'O Captain! my Captain! our fearful trip is done . . .' or 'It was the schooner Hesperus, That sailed the wintry sea . . .'; full-bosomed ladies wielding enormous tea-urns; the fun and the laughter and the fellowship . . . Since coming to Blackpool Grace hadn't felt part of the chapel community in the same way. She and her mother and, occasionally, Hetty attended the service on a Sunday morning, but that was all. They hadn't entered fully into the life of the place in the way they had done in Burnley.

For the last few months, of course, there had been Edwin, always Edwin. He, too, had been a member of a church, a very different one it was true, but never once had he suggested that Grace should accompany him to any of the functions. He had never asked her to share in any aspect of his social life, and that had hurt. At the time she hadn't thought it mattered. It had been sufficient for her just to be alone with Edwin. Now, looking back on it, Grace knew that it had hurt her far more than she had realised. She had wanted to share every part of his life with him and to be accepted as Edwin's young lady, and he had never invited her to do so. She wanted, now, to feel part of a happy, friendly family again.

'Yes, Walter,' she said now. 'I think I'd like to go to the concert. Thank you for asking me.' Suddenly she grinned at him. 'But I've just had a terrible thought . . . You're not singing, are you?'

He grinned back at her, then burst out laughing, one of the few times, she thought, that she had heard him break into spontaneous mirth. 'No, I'm not singing. The visitors wouldn't thank me if it started to rain, would they?'

It was only a feeble joke, but they both laughed again. It had been a source of amusement at the chapel in Burnley that Walter Clayton had a voice like a corncrake.

'I'm so pleased you'll come, Grace.' Walter's smile was full of warmth. 'I'll call for you on Saturday, seven o'clock.'

'All right, Walter. I'll be ready.'

Grace wondered afterwards why she had agreed so readily, but by going to a chapel concert with Walter she was surely not committing herself to anything, was she? And she badly needed a change of company other than her own.

418

Walter was overjoyed that Grace had agreed to accompany him to the concert. It was more than he had dared to hope for and he made up his mind that he would not lose her this time. But he remembered what Martha Turnbull had said. The girl had been badly hurt; he must take things steadily and be careful not to rush her. Walter felt that he would do anything if only he could be sure that Grace would eventually belong to him. He had been given this second chance. He mustn't spoil things this time; he couldn't risk losing her again. To think that she would be his again, his lovely Grace . . .

He couldn't imagine, now, what had got into him, why he had behaved in that dreadful way, following her around and frightening her. It was almost as if he were two different people. Walter had preached many times about the devil and all his works, how he prowled around like a roaring lion, seeking someone to devour.

'Resist the devil and he will flee from you,' Walter had often thundered from the pulpit. He knew, to his shame, that he was not always very good at practising what he preached. He had allowed the devil inside him to have the upper hand, to take control and lead him into wicked, sinful ways. He had been guilty of jealousy and spite and malice. He had hurt his lovely Grace whom he loved more than anything in the world.

But, in spite of everything, the good Lord had seen fit to lead her back into his hands. He would cherish her this time. He would take his time, slowly and steadily, but eventually she would be his. He would be the one – the first one – to know her, to possess her, to teach her what love was all about. In his mind he saw her dark-brown hair curling against the white pillow, her slender body, her tiny pointed breasts tingling at his touch.

'Resist . . . resist . . .' Walter admonished himself, trying to thrust the lustful thoughts away. If he had patience and trusted in the Lord, then Grace would be his in time.

'Now, don't you worry about a thing, Mrs Turnbull,' said George Makepeace. 'Len and I'll see to the visitors at night if they want anything. Anyroad, Gladys and May'll be here, won't they, to make a cup of tea for them? Just you go and enjoy yourself for once and leave it all to us.'

'Thank you, Mr Makepeace,' said Martha gratefully. 'It's real good of you. I don't know what I'd have done without you.'

'You'd have managed fine, same as you always do,' George replied, 'but I am here and so's Len, and that's what friends are for, to give a helping hand. So you can go to your Hetty's wedding party with a clear conscience and leave it all to us.'

Martha had never ceased to be thankful that she had made the decision to take in a couple of lodgers. George Makepeace was turning out to be a real friend in need. She watched him now, enjoying the cup of strong tea with which he always liked to finish his evening meal. He was fiftyish, she guessed, stockily built with greying hair inclined to wave and still thick and wiry, and with eyes of a startling blue. They had looked sad when she had first known him, but now he seemed to be recovering from the death of his wife over a year ago, and the light was returning to his eyes along with his renewed interest in living. Martha liked to think that she had been partially responsible for this by offering him, as she had done for the past few months, home comforts and a listening ear when he needed it. Recently she had noticed that George's conversation had tended to be less about his wife and more about her, Martha's, family and their doings. Yes, indeed, George was becoming a very good friend.

So was her other lodger, Leonard Whittaker, a somewhat shy lad whom, Martha was pleased to see, George had taken under his wing and treated like a son. Leonard was a lanky youth whose arms and legs seemed too long for him, giving him the appearance of a puppet on a string. He had a shock of straight carroty hair, freckles to match and overlarge reddish hands. His smile redeemed his otherwise unprepossessing features, for he was a pleasant lad and you couldn't help smiling yourself at the sight of his heart-warming grin.

He smiled at Martha now. 'Aye, we'll take care of it all, me and George. You just go and enjoy yerself, Mrs Turnbull, and don't worry about a thing.'

It was just like Hetty, Martha thought, to be getting married at the beginning of August, right in the middle of the holiday season when they were all so rushed off their feet that they scarcely had time to take a breath. Not that the girl had any choice as to the timing of the marriage, the way things were. They had arranged the service for next Wednesday afternoon at the Methodist chapel in North Shore, and Joss and Matilda

Jenkinson had offered to put on a 'do' at night for a few of the family and friends. It was to this that George and Leonard were referring, because Martha had been bothered about going out in the evening and leaving the visitors to see to themselves. It wasn't often that there was an emergency; sometimes visitors returning late, after the door had been locked, needed letting in or, very occasionally, someone might be feeling poorly. Now Martha knew that she could go off without any worries, leaving everything in the capable hands of her two lodgers and the two young girls, Gladys and May.

It wasn't much in Martha's line, if she were honest, having a wedding party at Tilda's Tavern, which she still thought of as a pub. Until she came to Blackpool she had never so much as set foot in a public house, believing that respectable women didn't frequent such places. Now she was, of necessity, having to change her attitude a little. Joss and Matilda had been kindness itself to Hetty, and on the couple of occasions that Martha had been to the tavern she had to admit that she had encountered no rowdiness or drunkenness or unseemly behaviour. Martha certainly hadn't time in the height of the season to cope with a wedding party, however small. But the girl had to be given a good send-off, no matter what the circumstances were, so Martha was very grateful to Joss and Matilda for their offer. Their attitude was typical of Blackpool folk, warm-hearted and friendly and always ready to lend a helping hand. But Martha knew that she would breathe a sigh of relief when the day was over and Hetty and Reuben were well and truly married.

The girl looked demure on her wedding day in her dress of deep cream silk – white would have been quite out of the question – with a deep edging of lace at the neck and sleeves. Her bonnet with the curling feather and the half-veil which just covered her eyes were unable to suppress the mass of auburn hair which peeped from under the brim and curled round the nape of her neck. She carried a small posy of rosebuds and lilies of the valley and looked, Martha thought as she wiped a tear from her eye, every inch a bride. Grace, as her bridesmaid, wore a similar style of dress, but in a lilac shade, with a matching straw hat in the tall 'postboy' style, trimmed with feathers and flowers. Both girls would make the dresses do for years to come as their 'best' dress, the style being suitable to wear on any occasion that called for something a little out of the ordinary.

It was the first time that Martha had seen Reuben's parents, and though she knew that they were unaccustomed to attending a place of worship they seemed to be quite at their ease in the chapel. Their mode of dress, however, seemed outlandish, at least to Martha's way of thinking. Ruth Loveday's dress was black, a colour that Martha herself often wore, although it wasn't the colour she would have chosen to wear at a wedding. And she certainly wouldn't have dreamed of going to chapel wearing her pinny. Over her dress Mrs Loveday wore a pleated apron, embroidered with every bright colour you could imagine, which, Martha guessed, was more for show than for cooking and cleaning in. The silk shawl round her shoulders was fastened with a brooch made from a gold crown, and earrings made from half-sovereigns dangled from her ears.

Eli Loveday also displayed evidence of his wealth on his person. Martha didn't like to peer too closely, but the buttons on his dark-green jacket looked very much like half-crowns, and the smaller buttons on his sleeves like silver shillings.

In spite of their flamboyant appearance the couple seemed nice and ordinary and Martha felt herself warming to them as she chatted with them outside the chapel after the service.

'Now, don't you be fretting about your Henrietta,' Ruth Loveday told her. 'She'll come to no harm with our Reuben. He's a good lad though I say it myself, and he'll take care of her.'

'Yes, I'm sure he will,' Martha was forced to agree. 'And they've got their little house on the Moss to move into. I'm pleased about that.'

'It ain't our way though, Mrs Turnbull,' said Eli Loveday, shaking his head. 'It ain't our way at all. We be travellers, 'ee see, always have been and always will be. Doesn't seem right for us to bide in one place too long. But Reuben, he be different. He's had this hankering for some time for a little place of his own. And since he met Henrietta the urge to settle down has been even worse with him. But we'll not stand in the lad's way. He knows what he wants.'

'And he wants Henrietta, that's for sure,' said Ruth Loveday firmly. 'And she's good for him. I can see that just by looking at the pair of them.

They'll be happy enough, Mrs Turnbull. Don't 'ee worry.'

As Martha looked into the gipsy woman's far-seeing dark eyes and saw the conviction there, some of her misgivings subsided. The woman was no fool, and what did it matter if the lad was a gipsy? He'd got a good living in his hands and he'd insisted on them having their own little home. And as for Hetty, well, she'd always been a survivor.

'Aye, I reckon they'll manage,' Martha said now. 'We've done all we can. Now it's up to them.'

Martha was glad of the company of Ruth and Eli later that evening. She had been too busy since coming to Blackpool to make many friends of her own age and, under the circumstances, she had felt that she couldn't ask her one special friend, Alice Gregson, to share in the merrymaking surrounding Hetty's marriage. Apart from herself and Reuben's parents they were mainly young folk at the wedding party at Tilda's Tavern. There was Lily Tattersall and a couple more of Hetty's waitress friends from the restaurant where she had worked, Grace and Walter, and several of Reuben's mates from the encampment. And his cousin, Drusilla.

Now *she* looked a hussy, if ever there was one, Martha thought. She had never seen a dress of such a startling crimson colour as the one the girl was wearing, nor such huge gold circlets as were dangling from her ears. But it was more her manner than her dress that drew Martha's attention to her; her haughty stance with one hand on her hip, the arrogant tilt of her head and the way

425

she tossed back her long black curls. Martha felt a tinge of foreboding as she watched her. It was strange that Hetty had never spoken to her of Drusilla.

Hetty had been worried when she knew that Drusilla was invited to the wedding party, although the girl had been far more cordial towards her just lately. The two girls had encountered one another a few times recently at the encampment and, though they had exchanged only a few words, Hetty was relieved that Drusilla was no longer treating her with cold disdain.

Now, as the party got into its swing, Drusilla came and sat down next to Hetty. 'You're my cousin now,' she said. 'Fancy that! I never thought when I told your fortune all that time ago that one day you'd be related to me.' Her words were friendly enough, but Hetty could still see in Drusilla's eyes the knowing look that never failed to unnerve her. It did so now.

She gave a nervous laugh. 'Really? I should have thought you'd have seen it all written here in me hand. That's what it's all about, isn't it? Knowing what's going to happen. I should've thought you'd have been able to see something as important as a wedding.'

'I can see some things . . .' said Drusilla slowly. She stared hard at Hetty. 'Most things, in fact.'

Hetty was never sure whether Drusilla's so-called gift was just a superb act or whether she really did have the power she professed. And even though the girl was now making some effort to be agreeable, at least on the surface, Hetty felt that

426

she would never be able to rid herself entirely of the disquiet she experienced in Drusilla's presence.

However, she forced herself to smile at the girl. 'I'm glad you could come, Drusilla,' she said.

'Oh, yes. I wouldn't have missed our Reuben's wedding, not for anything. And I know that you and I are going to be friends . . . Henrietta.' Drusilla lingered on the name. 'That's what he calls you, isn't it? Henrietta. I heard your sister call you Hetty, and your mother, too, but Henrietta's so much . . . grander, isn't it?'

Hetty laughed self-consciously, not sure if Drusilla was poking fun at her. That was the trouble with Drusilla. Hetty was never sure. 'They've always called me Hetty at home. It makes no difference, does it, what they call me?' Hetty shrugged. 'It's still me.'

'Yes, it's still you . . .' Drusilla paused. 'And, like I said, I hope we'll be friends, Henrietta, you and me. Aunt Ruth and Uncle Eli are moving on soon – did you know? – and they wanted me to go along with them. But I'm going to stay here with my Aunt Lettie. I make a nice living here in Blackpool, winter as well as summer. Besides, I want to stay near to you both, you and our Reuben. You'll be lonely, I daresay, Henrietta, when you move into your little cottage, especially with the chavvy coming.' She looked pointedly in the direction of Hetty's stomach. 'You'll be needing friends around you, and your mother and sister are at the other end of Blackpool, aren't they?'

'I'll make out,' said Hetty briefly, 'but come and

427

see us by all means. You'll be very . . . welcome.'

The two young women looked at one another appraisingly for several seconds and Hetty was relieved when Joss Jenkinson interrupted them.

'Hetty, I think it's time now. You did say you'd give us a song, didn't you? I know everyone'll be real thrilled, with you being a blushing bride an' all.' His cheerful red face beamed at her and Hetty experienced a sudden rush back to normality. She pushed all thoughts of Drusilla away.

'Yes.' She smiled at Joss. 'Of course I'll sing. I promised I would. Just the one, though, I think, tonight.'

Joss made his way to the small stage and several people banged on the tables for silence so that he could make himself heard. 'And now . . . the one and only Henrietta, the Girl with the Sparkling Eyes.' When the applause died down Joss spoke again, more confidentially. 'And I'll let you into a secret, ladies and gentlemen. Today is the little lady's wedding day.'

Hetty had no doubt of the affection in which she was held as she stood alone on the stage. She looked a demure little figure, still dressed in her wedding apparel, the cream silk dress with the bonnet and dainty half-veil, clutching in her hands her bridal posy. She could feel the warmth and love surrounding her, a palpable thing, and she felt sad knowing that this performance would be very nearly her swan song at Tilda's Tavern. She had already given up her job at Laycock's and she would no longer be able to help her mother at the boarding house. Both these places were too far from the Moss where she and Reuben would be living for her to travel each day. Besides, her condition would soon make her work as a waitress quite unseemly and the young couple had plans to work together on a bit of land that surrounded the cottage. The tavern was not so far away, but Hetty knew that her days here, too, were numbered, and the thought brought sorrow in its wake. There was joy, though, to counteract it as she looked at her new husband gazing at her with shining eyes.

When Hetty began to sing, her song was just for Reuben.

> 'When a merry maiden marries,
> Sorrow goes and pleasure tarries,
> Every sound becomes a song,
> All is right and nothing's wrong . . .'

The audience was hushed as they listened. This was a very different Henrietta tonight, not the vivacious, coquettish miss that they had been used to, but a young woman with a much more serene and sober mien, as befitted a bride on her wedding day. But the mirth was not entirely hidden, and all the joy and merriment that was part of Hetty came bubbling to the surface as she sang.

> 'All the corners of the earth
> Ring with music sweetly played,
> Worry is melodious mirth,
> Grief is joy in masquerade,

Sullen night is laughing day,
All the year is merry May . . .'

The song from *The Gondoliers* was an inspired
choice, and after a few moments' silence when
Hetty stopped singing the audience went mad,
applauding and cheering and banging on the
tables.

'More, more, Henrietta. Come on, don't be a
spoilsport . . .'

'Give us another one . . .'

'Come on, lass. One for yer wedding night . . .'

Hetty hadn't intended singing again, but she
was forced to submit and so she sang the song
which had given her the name by which she was
known at Tilda's Tavern, 'Take a Pair of Sparkling Eyes.'

Ruth Loveday's eyes were moist as she came to
sit down next to her new daughter-in-law after
her performance. 'That was kushti, my love.
Really grand. And if I didn't know before that you
and our Reuben were just right for one another I
knows it now. Here, lass . . . I'd like 'ee to have
this.' Reuben's mother unfastened the slender
chain that hung round her neck and pressed it
into Hetty's hand. 'It's the coral necklace that
belonged to my mother, and her mother before
her, and now I'd like you to have it, Henrietta.
Make sure you wears it, mind. It'll bring you luck
and ward off any evil spirits. And kushti-bok to
the pair of you, my dear. Kushti-bok.'

Hetty knew that the words meant good luck.
She wasn't sure that she believed in good-luck
charms and suchlike. They had been frowned

upon in the Methodist chapel she had attended as a child, but not for the world would she offend Reuben's mother.

'Thank you, Mrs Loveday,' she said, kissing the woman's cheek. 'It's real kind of you and I'll take good care of it. And I'll look after Reuben an' all, don't you worry.'

'I'm sure you will, my love, and he'll look after you. The pair of you'll do all right. I've no fears about that. Just think on that you share all your troubles as well as all your joys. That's what marriage is all about.'

'Shall we slip out and go for a walk, Grace?' Walter leaned across the table and took hold of Grace's hand. 'I don't think they'll miss us, do you?'

'All right, Walter.' Grace smiled at him. The noise and the heat in the room were beginning to make her head ache and she would welcome a breath of fresh sea air. She had enjoyed the wedding party, though, and had been pleased to see that even Walter had made some effort to get into the party spirit. But the young people there were Hetty and Reuben's friends and Walter had little in common with them. Neither, if Grace were honest, had she. 'Yes, let's go and have a look at the sea,' she said now. 'I always like the prom when it's quieter.'

They crossed the tram track and leaned against the railings, looking out across the midnight-blue ocean. It had been a warm sunny day for Hetty's wedding, followed by a balmy evening.

'Your Hetty's in good voice tonight,' Walter

remarked, 'and I must admit she looks lovely, almost angelic, in that dress. You'd hardly believe it was the same girl.'

Grace looked sideways at him. 'I know our Hetty's not exactly your favourite person, is she? You and she never hit it off.'

'Live and let live, Grace,' Walter replied, to Grace's surprise. She recalled a time when he would never have made a remark such as that, but Walter seemed different now. 'Yes, live and let live, that's what I'm beginning to think. Hetty seems to have changed, and it looks as though that gipsy lad might be good for her when all's said and done.'

'I hope so, Walter,' said Grace with feeling. 'I certainly hope so, and so does Mam. She's done enough heart-searching about it all on the quiet, has me mam, though she's putting on a brave face.'

Hetty wasn't the only one who had changed lately, thought Grace. The young man beside her didn't seem the same person at all as the one who had been so possessive of her in the long-ago mill-town days, or the one who had intimidated her by relentlessly pursuing her, not all that long ago. This new Walter was not so full of himself, and the bombastic, belligerent individual whom she had feared had been replaced by a much gentler and friendlier person. Grace had found herself, to her surprise, enjoying his company, and after their first outing together to the chapel concert she had agreed to see him again. She hadn't seen Edwin at all, and though his treatment of her still hurt, she tried not to think about it. When thoughts of him arose she firmly pushed them back, and gradually she found that he was no longer on her mind all the time, day and night, as he had been when they had first parted. Now there were long periods, hours at a time, when he never came to the forefront of her mind, although the memories of him still lingered in the background.

'Happen marriage'll do your Hetty good,' said Walter now. He moved closer to Grace and put his arm round her shoulder. 'Grace, there's something I want to tell you.'

Grace looked at him, sensing the excitement in his voice, like a child who'd got a new toy.

'Yes, Walter, what is it?'

'You remember I told you I was looking for a little place of me own? Well, I've got one. Amos Armitage, God bless him, has managed to pull a few strings with his landlord and he's got me a house in the next street to him. Just off Central Drive. I can move in next week if I like.'

'That's wonderful, Walter. I'm so pleased for you.' Grace did feel happy for him. She knew how difficult it was for him in lodgings, especially trying to keep clean after a day on the coal round. He may not have realised, though, that there might well be a new set of problems when he tried to cook and clean for himself and do a job of work as well. She supposed, looking back on it, that she should have anticipated what was coming next.

'There's something else as well, Grace.' Walter hesitated. 'I know I've behaved badly, love. Things haven't been right between us for a long while now, and I know it was me own fault. I should

433

never have left you on your own all that time. I should have come over to see you, but what with Mother being ill and . . .'

'Never mind all that now, Walter. What's done's done, and there's no sense in keeping on about it. It's all behind us.'

'Aye well, happen it is, but I want it to be all right between us again. Like it used to be, back in Burnley.' He pulled her closer to him. 'You don't know what it's meant to me, Grace, having you with me again these last few weeks. It's a lot more than I deserve.'

Grace thought again how much he had changed. She had agreed to go on seeing him in the beginning because she was lonely, and because she knew it would please her mother if she did so. Not a very good reason, Grace knew, for walking out with a young man against your better judgement, but Martha had been so distressed over the business with Hetty that Grace had felt she must try to make amends. Martha had put on a brave face to the world and had been stoical in the support she had given to Hetty but, beneath it all, Grace knew how much Martha was suffering. She had found her weeping in the parlour one night a few weeks ago.

'Mam . . . Mam, you mustn't upset yourself like this,' Grace had said, rushing to her side and putting her arms round her mother. 'Hetty's grown-up now and she's to lead her own life. She's made a mistake, but it'll happen turn out for the best. Reuben's a good lad and he loves her. You mustn't fret, Mam.'

'A gipsy lad though, Grace,' Martha whispered.

She turned a tear-stained face to her daughter. 'What's bred in the bone'll come out in the blood. Aye, I know I shouldn't be prejudiced, and I know he's said he'll settle down and they'll live in a house an' all that. But how do we know, Gracie? How do we know she'll be all right? When I think about that grand lad, Albert . . .'

'It's no use thinking that way, Mam,' said Grace firmly. 'She's made her choice and now it's up to her to make a go of it. Don't you worry; Hetty knows what she's doing and she'll be all right.'

Martha sighed. 'Aye, I hope so. Dear God, I hope so. At least there's one thing I'm glad about, lass, and that's you and Walter. I'm so pleased you've started seeing him again. He's a good lad, Grace.'

'Yes, I know that, Mam,' Grace said quietly. 'He's . . . well, he's different somehow now. We seem to be getting on quite well.'

Grace was glad her mother hadn't said 'I told you so', either then or later, but the look of satisfaction on Martha's face when she saw them together spoke for itself.

'Grace . . .' Walter turned towards her now. 'Look at me, Grace.' She moved her head to look into his eyes, which looked, at that moment, so regretful and pleading. 'I still love you, Grace. I've never stopped loving you. I want you to marry me . . . please, Grace. Please say you will.'

Grace wondered why she had once felt so afraid of this young man at her side, but she had. Oh yes, she had indeed. It was as though he were two different people, but the one beside her now was certainly not someone to be feared. But did she love him? Grace knew, deep down, that she could never love him in the way she had loved Edwin, that wonderful, exhilarating feeling that had filled every part of her, then left her so very, very empty after he had gone. But that was all in the past, not to be thought of now. She was growing fond of Walter, this new, different Walter and, perhaps, the fondness would develop into love.

'Yes, Walter,' Grace said quietly. 'I will marry you.'

Chapter 19

The only honeymoon that Hetty and Reuben could be said to have had, apart from the rapturous nights that they shared together in their little home, was a ride on Blackpool's newest attraction, the Big Wheel. It was opened during the third week in August, 1896, soon after Hetty and Reuben's marriage, and the young couple decided that they must be part of the excitement that everyone was feeling with regard to yet another jewel in Blackpool's already dazzling crown.

They had watched it being erected for the past year or so at the rear of the Winter Garden buildings, but that didn't take away from the thrill that they felt on seeing it, for the first time, ready to receive its hordes of excited holidaymakers. And some residents too, of course, although many of them tended to take the attractions of their own seaside town for granted.

'Gosh! Look at that. Enormous, isn't it?' Hetty exclaimed as she stood arm in arm with Reuben at the Victoria Street entrance, gazing up at the huge iron structure. It weighed 1,000 tons and rose 220 feet into the air, less than half the height of Blackpool Tower, to be sure, but impressive for all that. There were thirty carriages which would each hold thirty people, and Hetty and Reuben had to queue for about half an hour before they were admitted through the turnstile.

The ride itself was something of a disappointment, as the wheel kept stopping and starting again as each carriage in turn reached the ground, allowing passengers to alight or ascend.

Hetty listened to the comments of her fellow passengers.

'Ain't it going slow? I thought as how it'ud whizz round.'

'Aye, you'd hardly think we were moving at all.'

'Look t'other way, though. Look at the axle. It looks as though it's fair spinning round. Oh heck! It's making me feel proper dizzy.'

Hetty held on to Reuben's arm, bubbling over with happiness. No matter if the ride was slow, it was still a marvellous adventure.

'Oh look, Reuben,' she exclaimed in delight as the wheel rose higher. 'Look at the people on the top of the Tower. They're all looking down on us. And don't they look near?'

The view from the highest point was glorious, a vast panorama of sea and land. To the west was a great expanse of water, the Irish Sea, and to the east the green loveliness of the Fylde countryside with a dark background of hills in the distance.

'Burnley must be over there, somewhere,' said Hetty, pointing vaguely, 'and that town we can see with the mill chimneys, that must be Preston. Oh Reuben, isn't it all wonderful?'

They could see the River Ribble to the south, and to the north the windings of the River Wyre and the fishing port of Fleetwood with the grain elevator visible on the skyline.

And then they were almost down again, the carriages seeming to nearly touch the rooftops of the houses in Adelaide Street as they descended.

'That was wonderful,' Hetty said again as they alighted. 'Thank you for taking me, Reuben. Oh, aren't we having a lovely day?'

'It isn't over yet,' Reuben whispered with a gleam in his eye as, hand in hand, they set off to walk the couple of miles to their home.

Hetty and Reuben's home on Marton Moss was the tiniest little place, a low-ceilinged white-washed cottage with two rooms upstairs and two downstairs. The floorboards were roughly laid, and Reuben, in bed on a Sunday morning – the only day of the week when he was not up before six o'clock – could watch Hetty through the chinks between the bedroom floorboards as she prepared the breakfast in the kitchen below. And Hetty knew that if she wasn't careful when she was dusting or making the bed she was liable to put a leg right through the downstairs ceiling. The stone-flag floor was uneven, and such meagre furniture as they had stood at crazy angles. In the cottage next door, the home of the Braithwaite family, Hetty had been intrigued to see that the grandfather clock which stood in a corner had been accommodated by digging a hole in the floor. Another alternative in these low-ceilinged places, so Eliza Braithwaite told her, was to cut a hole in the bedroom ceiling. Hetty and Reuben had no grandfather clock, but Reuben, over six feet tall, had to remember to lower his head when going through the doorways and up the winding stair-case to the bedroom.

Reuben rose at an early hour each morning in order to travel with Jack Braithwaite to market in his pony trap. It was Reuben's ambition to have one of his own, and if hard work and perseverance were anything to go by, Hetty felt sure that it wouldn't be long before he realised his objective. At the moment he stood the markets, as he had done before his marriage, selling the wooden articles he made, and sometimes Hetty accompanied him, assisting him on the market stalls. But he had aspirations, too, to make a living from the small piece of land he rented, as did most of the folk of Marton Moss.

This small area of the Fylde, no more than a mile in width and six miles from north to south, was like a world apart. It was a fertile area which had been formed over thousands of years by the bark and foliage of gigantic trees, felled by hurricane winds from the nearby sea, rotting into the peaty soil; thus was the moss formed by each successive year's growth of plant life falling to decay. The folk who lived in this locality were hardy and self-sufficient and the sophistication of the nearby towns of Blackpool and, further afield, Preston, had influenced them but little. They produced most of the necessities of life in their own homes, travelled everywhere on foot – except for those, like Jack Braithwaite, who were wealthy enough to have their own conveyance – and were renowned for their sense of humour and their neighbourliness.

Hetty and Reuben hadn't been in the house many hours before they made the acquaintance of Jack and Eliza, and as the weeks went by Hetty had more and more reason to be thankful for her friendly neighbour. For Hetty, after the first excitement of making a new home with Reuben had passed, often found that she was lonely. She missed her mother and Grace and her friends at Laycock's café and Tilda's Tavern. It had not proved possible to go on singing at the tavern. It was too far to walk at night along unlit and largely unmade roads, and besides, Hetty's figure was now beginning to expand, after the first few months of pregnancy had passed, at an alarming rate. She knew that it would be unseemly, now, to appear in front of an audience.

Hetty peered at herself in the flyblown wardrobe mirror, wondering whatever had happened to the slim, coquettish miss in emerald-green silk who had pranced and pirouetted on the stage not all that long ago. This roly-poly person in the voluminous gingham dress, with her rosy-red cheeks and sun-browned hands and face, this surely couldn't be the same girl. The eyes were the same, though, as lively and as sparkling as ever, and so was the hair, its auburn curls gleaming with constant brushing.

She grinned at her reflection in the mirror and pulled a face. Come on, cheer up, she told herself. Reuben'll be home from market soon and you've to get a nice meal ready for him. Never mind feeling sorry for yourself, girl, and making out that you're lonely. You won't be lonely for long, and then there's the whole of the evening ahead of you . . . and the night. Hetty's heart leapt at the thought of seeing her husband again. They had been married for a month now and were, if it were possible, more in love than ever.

Hetty sang to herself as she gathered together the ingredients for their evening meal; bacon and sausages, which Martha had given her when they called at Welcome Rest on Sunday. Martha often helped out a little, especially if she had 'overbought' for the visitors, and Hetty knew that she would be offended if she refused her offer. Potato cakes that she had prepared earlier in the day, the way her mother had shown her, with mashed potatoes and flour and butter, browned on the griddle. And pearly-white mushrooms gathered this morning from the edge of the little wood behind the cottage. This was a new discovery pointed out to her by Eliza Braithwaite. Hetty was delighted to have made this find and knew that Reuben would share her pleasure. He believed, as all gipsies did, in making full use of the fruits of the earth which had been put there by God – O' Del, Reuben sometimes called him – for everyone to share.

Hetty was dismayed, therefore, at their mealtime, when Reuben pushed them to the side of his plate.

'Ugh! Mushrooms; I can't abide the things.' His distaste showed on his face.

'Oh, Reuben . . . I've picked them specially for you. I thought you'd be pleased.' Hetty's mouth tightened into a pout and Reuben laughed at her.

'Now, don't 'ee fret, Henrietta. And don't pull your pretty little face like that. It'll freeze.' He reached out and tweaked at her cheek. "Ee weren't to know. How could 'ee? I've never been able to abide the things, ever since I were a chavvy. They taste mouldy to me, as though I'm eating earth, although I know they're reckoned to be a great delicacy. You want to be careful an' all, Henrietta, gathering mushrooms. Sometimes they're not what they seem; some of 'em are poisonous.'

'Not these, Reuben,' Hetty assured him. 'Eliza showed me where they were growing, and she knows what she's doing. I'm real sorry you don't like them though.'

'Don't 'ee worry. I'll eat the rest of it.' Reuben tucked into the fat succulent sausages and the crispy bacon with gusto. 'And these potato cakes are just kushti!' He licked his lips. 'I've never tasted any like these before. Have 'ee made them, my love?'

'Yes, I've made them, Reuben,' Hetty said proudly.

'What a clever little wife I've got. I think that deserves a kiss.' Reuben got up and came to stand behind Hetty's chair, putting his hands on her shoulders and stooping to kiss her lips. His hands stroked her neck and felt inside her bodice, touching the curve of her breast. 'It deserves more than a kiss, I'd say,' he murmured, 'but there's all evening, isn't there, Henrietta?'

'Get on with you, Reuben.' Hetty slapped playfully at his wrist. 'Let me finish me tea in peace. And if you're not going to eat those lovely mushrooms give 'em to me. They're too nice to waste.' She picked up his plate and pushed his leavings on

443

to her own. 'There! Now get on with your meal like a good boy.'

This September evening followed the same pattern as most of their evenings together. When Hetty had washed up their dishes she lit the oil lamp and closed the curtains, then settled down in her usual spot on the clipped rag rug near to Reuben's knee. Reuben sat in the wooden rocking chair, the only comfortable chair they possessed, made so by the addition of a cushion on the hard wooden seat. Hetty leaned her head against his knee and he lovingly stroked her hair, tangling his fingers in the mass of auburn curls and playfully pulling at them. She sighed with contentment. This was the best time of the day, with just the two of them snug and happy in their own little home. She loved the feeling of quietude when the curtains were drawn, shutting out the dark and the mistiness of approaching autumn. The oil lamp cast a pool of yellow light in a corner, but the rest of the room was in shadow, except for the firelight glimmering on the steel fender and fire irons.

This room where they sat in the evenings and where they ate their meals – where, in fact, they lived – was the kitchen. It was the only downstairs room that was furnished – and that only sparsely so. The other room, the 'parlour' – or so it would be if it contained any furniture – was a minute place, which Hetty hoped, eventually, to furnish with a couple of easy chairs and a sideboard. There would be no room for anything else. The kitchen contained only the barest necessities for living; Reuben's rocking chair and three other wooden chairs – one for Hetty and two more in case they had company – a scrubbed pinewood table, and a dresser which held odds and ends of crockery, mostly given by Martha or bought second-hand from market stalls. And, of course, the kitchen range, the most important item in the room. There was a central fire and on either side of the grate there were brick-lined ovens for baking. It was hard work for Hetty – formerly undomesticated – to keep the range regularly blackleaded and to make sure the fire didn't go out. But she was becoming, to her surprise and delight, very adept at conjuring up tasty dishes by using the oven and hot-plate. The kettle on the hob was kept steaming all day, just as her mother's did at Welcome Rest. At the top of the range was a wooden mantelpiece where Hetty had displayed such treasures as she had: several of Reuben's carved wooden animals; a wooden clock; a mug depicting Queen Victoria's Golden Jubilee of 1887, which Hetty had been presented with along with all the other schoolchildren in Burnley; a colourful tin, again depicting the sovereign, which contained biscuits; and, in pride of place, the fairing which Reuben had won for her at the rifle range, depicting the sailor and his sweetheart. There was nothing that spoke of luxury or even much of comfort in the room, but Hetty was happier than she had ever dreamed was possible.

'Tell me one of your stories, Reuben,' she said now. 'One of your old Romany legends. You're so good at telling stories. A happy one though, please.'

Hetty had been surprised to discover during the

first week of their marriage that Reuben was unable to read or write, apart from his name which he had signed on the marriage certificate.

'I've never been in one place long enough to do any book learning,' he had told her with a careless shrug. 'What do it matter? I be happy as I am, and I can write me name. Ma made sure as I could do that, and that's all I need as far as I can see.'

Hetty's light-hearted attempts to teach him to read with the aid of her childhood story books had ended up with him in gales of laughter and often in kissing and cuddling. Hetty, herself, was no great scholar and they decided that reading was unimportant. What did reading matter, so long as they could talk? And Reuben, Hetty soon discovered, was a born storyteller, like many of his kin.

He had told her several of the myths about the origins of his race, often with the recurrent theme that gipsies were forever doomed to wander the earth as a punishment for the sins of their ancestors. One legend claimed that they were descended from the first murderer, Cain, while other harrowing tales said that gipsies refused to help the Virgin Mary during her flight into Egypt, and that it was a gipsy who forged the nails that were used in Christ's crucifixion.

'Oh, Reuben, how dreadful!' Hetty had cried. 'You don't really believe all that, do you?' Some of the stories had filled her with horror, but at the same time she was fascinated by the power of Reuben's storytelling.

'No, I can't say I believe it,' Reuben replied, 'but I'm just telling 'ee, Henrietta, so that 'ee'll know how our race is often reviled. In olden days it was

446

a criminal offence just to be a gipsy. It be a lot better now, but there's still a lot of prejudice, love. I can't say how happy you've made me. You never seemed to mind. It never made any difference, did it, me being a Rom?'

'Of course not, Reuben,' Hetty assured him. 'And it never will. I love you . . . I love you so very much.'

She knew that Reuben, usually so happy and seemingly carefree, had, nevertheless, a more sombre side to his nature that made him brood at times about the injustices of life and the slights which were often flung at his race. Which was why she urged him now to tell her a happy story.

'All right then, Henrietta,' said Reuben. 'A happy story it'll be. I'll tell 'ee how O' Del made the first gipsy . . .

'Thousands and thousands of years ago, when he'd made all the plants and the animals and the birds and the fishes, he decided to have a try at making a man. Well, O' Del he got hisself some chalk from the downs and he moistened it with water from the river, and he moulded it and patted it and prodded it till it were just the right shape. Then he put it into the oven to cook, but . . . O' Dordi, do 'ee know what happened?'

Hetty shook her head, her eyes wide with interest like a child's.

'Well, O'Del, he only went and forgot about it. And when he went to the oven and took out the man he'd made, what did he find? The poor thing was overcooked, as black as a lump of coal, and that was how O' Del made the first negro.

'So he decided he'd try again. Well, O' Del he got

hisself some more chalk, and he moistened it and moulded it and poked and prodded it till it were just the right shape again. Then he put it into the oven. Now, O' Del he was determined he wouldn't go wrong this time. He wasn't going to spoil another good lump of chalk. So he waited just five minutes, then he went to the oven and took out the man. And what did he find? A pasty, under-done creature as white as the lump of chalk he'd put in. And that was how O' Del made the first white man.

'So, nothing daunted, he tried again. Third time lucky, he thought. So O' Del he got hisself some more chalk . . .'

'And he moistened it and poked it and prodded it . . .' Hetty joined in with him laughing, reminded of bedtime stories with her mother and Grace, stories of the three bears and Cinderella and Red Riding Hood.

'And he put it in the oven and he waited,' Reuben continued, 'not too long and not too short a time. And when he went to the oven to take out his final attempt what did O' Del find? A nicely cooked man, as brown as a berry. "That's kushti," said O' Del. "That's just right. Not too white and not too black, but just right." And that was how O' Del made the first gipsy.'

'That's a lovely story, Reuben,' Hetty said happily. 'And d'you know what I think? What O' Del said was quite true.' She knelt up and ruffled her husband's hair, then she ran her finger musingly down the length of his lean brown cheek and over the firm line of his jaw. 'You're just right. Just right . . . my darling Reuben.' Her last words

were just a whisper and she lifted her face anticipating his kiss. He did not disappoint her . . .

Hetty knew that she had never felt happier in
all her life. Everything was perfect, at least it
would be if it wasn't for . . . Drusilla. She pushed
the intruding thoughts away. With Reuben's
strong arms about her and his lips upon hers it
was no time to be thinking of Drusilla. It would be
time enough to think about Reuben's cousin when
she next appeared.

Drusilla was a regular visitor at their home on the
Moss. It couldn't be said, in all honesty, that she
came frequently or overstayed her welcome; nevertheless, it was too often for Hetty. If she could
have been sure when the girl was coming it might
have been better, then she would have felt prepared. But as it was Drusilla appeared whenever
it took her fancy. She usually waited until Reuben
was at home, but occasionally she came during
the day when Hetty was on her own and these
were the visits that unnerved Hetty. She never
knocked at the door, but suddenly Hetty would be
aware of her presence there in the room. The back
door of the cottage was often left wide open during
the day. Though Reuben had welcomed the idea of
living in a house rather than a waggon, some of
his gipsy traits still lingered. Hetty was continually finding all the windows in the house flung
wide open, as well as the door.

'I think you were born in a barn,' she told her
husband soon after their marriage, quoting a
favourite expression of her mother's. She laughed
as she firmly closed the bedroom window to keep

out the rain and the wind which was tearing at the flimsy cotton curtains. 'I don't mind a bit of God's fresh air, but this is ridiculous. It's enough to give us pneumonia.'

Reuben laughed too. 'Maybe you're right, my love. About being born in a barn, I mean. Maybe I was. Romany women always give birth outside, 'ee knows.'

'Oh . . .' Hetty put her hand to her mouth. 'I didn't mean it, honestly. It's just a saying. Me mam says it. I only meant . . .'

'I know what 'ee meant, Henrietta,' said Reuben kindly. 'Don't take on so; I'm not offended. But it takes some getting used to, this living in a house instead of a vardo. Sometimes I feel as though I'm trapped, living inside four walls, that's why I open all the windows and doors. And I find it odd going upstairs to bed. I be used to living in just the one room, 'ee see . . . But don't 'ee worry, my love.' Reuben came and wrapped his arms round her as he always did when he could see she looked troubled. 'I be getting used to it, and I'll do anything for 'ee, Henrietta. But leave the door open during the day, love, when we're at home . . .'

And that was why Drusilla was able to appear so unexpectedly. She did so one September morning. Hetty looked up from her task of black-leading the grate to see the tall, slender figure standing in the doorway. Just one glance was enough to make her feel uncomfortable and flustered, an unusual state for Hetty, who usually didn't give a fig for what anyone thought or said. Now she was aware of her dishevelled hair, her grimy apron and her blackened hands and, of course, her less than slender figure. Drusilla looked cool and dignified, as ever, her hair wound round her head in a thick, lustrous plait and her red dress, the colour she invariably wore, covered with a black fringed shawl. Over her arm she held a basket filled with blackberries.

She held it out to Hetty. 'See, aren't they the most delicious blackberries? I won't offer them to you, Henrietta. I know you've plenty of time to pick your own, haven't you? These are for Aunt Lettie, but I'm sure our Reuben'ud love a nice blackberry pie. From what I recall he was always partial to blackberry and apple. Aunt Ruth used to make lovely ones, kushti they were, and bramble jelly too. You'll have to show Reuben what a clever little wife he's got . . . won't you?'

Hetty felt herself bristling at Drusilla's words. Reuben often told her what a clever girl she was, teasingly, making gentle fun of her newly acquired culinary skills. She basked in his admiration, but to hear Drusilla utter the same words filled her with resentment. He must have spoken them in his cousin's hearing and Drusilla was always quick to seize an opportunity to take a rise out of Hetty.

Quickly Hetty ran her hands beneath the tap and wiped them on a towel, then snatched off her dirty apron. 'I'll make us a cup of tea,' she said, reaching for the kettle which was already quietly bubbling on the hob. There was no need to invite Drusilla to sit down and make herself at home, because she had already done so. She was seated in the rocking chair, which Hetty always thought of as Reuben's chair, idly tapping her foot and swinging backwards and forwards.

'We've already had a blackberry pie,' Hetty told her, trying to sound casual. 'The hedgerows round here are full of them now, as you've obviously found.'

It was not a long way, not much more than a mile, from the gipsy encampment at Squire's Gate to Hetty and Reuben's home on Marton Moss, mainly along country lanes bordered by hedges heavy, at this time of the year, with God's bounty. 'I shall go and gather some more this afternoon. It looks as though I'd best be quick or they'll all have gone. And I'll get some more mushrooms, too. Reuben doesn't like them though,' she added, half to herself.

'No, he doesn't. He never did.' Drusilla's voice took on a proprietorial air and again Hetty felt herself bristling.

'Have some more tea,' she said flatly, rising to fill Drusilla's half-empty cup. She really must try not to let herself get so agitated by the girl. 'You've had a good season, have you, with your fortune-telling?' she asked, although she was not particularly interested. She just wanted Drusilla out of her house as soon as possible.

'Oh yes. Very profitable.' Drusilla nodded. 'I'm with my Aunt Lettie, you know, now. Aunt Ruth and Uncle Eli have moved on, but of course you'll know that. Reuben'll miss them, I daresay. He's not used to being on his own. He's always been one of a crowd, has our Reuben, surrounded by his family and friends.' Her eyes wandered speculatively round the sparsely furnished kitchen. 'He's bound to feel lonesome at times, all on his own.'

'He's not on his own,' said Hetty through clenched teeth.

'No . . . of course not.' Drusilla's lips curled in a smile. There was a few seconds' pause before she spoke again. 'You're not wearing the necklace that Aunt Ruth gave you.' Drusilla gestured towards the necklace of carved and polished coral on a fine silver chain which was lying on a corner of the dresser. 'Don't you want it? If you didn't want it you shouldn't have taken it. Aunt Ruth doesn't part with her treasures lightly, I can tell you. She wouldn't be very pleased to see that you've discarded it.'

'I haven't discarded it,' replied Hetty, feeling annoyed with Drusilla for being so nosy and also slightly guilty about not wearing the necklace. Reuben had told her she should wear it all the time. 'It's just that I'm not used to wearing jewellery except when I'm dressed up. I do wear it when we go out,' she said defensively, thinking as she said it that such times were becoming very few and far between. 'I think it was real kind of Mrs Loveday to give it to me.'

'Foolish if you ask me.' Drusilla raised her eyebrows. 'That necklace has been in the family for years and years. The least you can do if you don't want to wear it is to take care of it. Put it somewhere safe or you may find that it has . . . gone.' She waved her hands expressively. 'Anybody could walk in and take it.'

Hetty suppressed a desire to tell the girl to mind her own business. Who would want the necklace anyway? And nobody ever visited except Mam and Grace and Eliza Braithwaite from next door. 'All right then,' she said brightly. She picked up the necklace then walked across to the mantelpiece and popped it into the Golden Jubilee mug. 'There, that's away from prying eyes now. That do for yer?'

When she turned round Drusilla was looking fixedly at her, her eyes glazed over as though she were in a trance. Not for the first time, Hetty felt afraid . . .

'Reuben,' she began tentatively, later that same evening. 'What's the "Evil Eye"?'

'What do 'ee mean, Henrietta?' Reuben looked at her suspiciously.

'Just what I've said. What is it?'

'Why do 'ee ask?' Reuben's voice was wary.

'It's something I've heard about, ages ago. And I thought about it again today. It was when I saw Drusilla looking at me. She was looking at me ever so strangely, Reuben.'

'Drusilla . . . she's been here again?' Reuben's eyes narrowed and for a moment he looked worried.

'Yes . . . She called this morning. She didn't stay long but, like I said, Reuben, I didn't like the way she looked at me.'

'Aw, Henrietta, come on, love. 'Ee be imagining things.' Reuben shook his head. 'She wouldn't . . . She's been much more friendly lately, since Ma and Pa moved on. I was only thinking how much she's improved. She doesn't seem so difficult as she used to be.'

Reuben sounded convincing, but Hetty had the

impression that he was trying to convince himself as well as her. It was true that when Reuben was there Drusilla did make an extra effort to be pleasant, but when the two young women were alone together her manner was not quite so charming. Hetty knew that Drusilla was jealous of her and, though she tried to keep it hidden, it was still there, bubbling away beneath the surface. Drusilla's fondness for her cousin was something that Reuben and Hetty had never discussed, but both of them knew that the other was aware of it.

'Tell me about the "Evil Eye",' Hetty persisted. 'What is it?'

'It's a bewitchment, caused by being stared at,' said Reuben. 'That's all I can tell 'ee. Some folks believe in it, others don't. You can prevent it, though, by wearing a talisman, like that necklace Ma gave to you. I've told 'ee to wear it, Henrietta,' he said reprovingly, looking at her neck. 'but 'ee don't.'

'I've never believed in lucky charms.' Hetty shrugged. 'Mam always brought us up to believe they were nonsense. But if you really think I should wear it more often, then I will.' She recalled how Ruth Loveday had said, as she gave it to her, that it would ward off evil spirits. 'You do believe in it then, Reuben, the "Evil Eye"?'

'I didn't say that,' he replied slowly, 'and I can't really believe Drusilla wants to do 'ee any mischief, but it won't do any harm to wear the bit of coral. Wear it for me, there's a good girl.'

'Mmm . . . Your cousin seemed very interested in it an' all,' said Hetty thoughtfully. 'She seemed real surprised that your mam had given it to the likes of me.'

'Now that I can believe,' said Reuben grinning. 'Drusilla's a greedy little madam, and I wouldn't put it past her to do a bit of choring if she felt inclined . . . Stealing,' he added, seeing Hetty's puzzled look. 'It wouldn't be the first time. She's like a jackdaw when it comes to trinkets and she's had her eye on that coral necklace for a long time. Not that it would ever have gone to Drusilla. She's from Pa's side of the family and that belonged to Mam. But make sure 'ee wears it, my love, then she can't get her hands on it.'

'All right, Reuben. I'll put it on straight away.' Hetty retrieved the necklace from the Jubilee mug and handed it to Reuben. 'Fasten it for me, love.'

Doing so was an excuse to fondle Hetty's neck and the swell of her breasts, and the small task ended, as so often, with a kiss.

'Now don't 'ee worry any more about Drusilla,' said Reuben, stroking her hair. 'I'm sure she doesn't want to harm 'ee. Anyway, 'ee's safe enough here with me. What do 'ee say to a bit of a tune tonight?' He moved to the cupboard at the bottom of the dresser and took out his violin. 'I'll play and then 'ee can sing for me, Henrietta.'

It had been a great surprise and joy to Hetty to find, in the first week of their marriage, that Reuben could coax magical tunes from his old violin and that he was largely untaught. It was a gift, he told her, as it had been with his father.

'I'll tell 'ee the story about the violin,' he said now, 'and why it be the gipsy's favourite instrument. 'Tis another fearsome tale, though, so don't 'ee go taking it seriously.' He laid his hand upon her shoulder as she sat comfortably at his feet, her head resting on his lap.

'A long time ago,' Reuben began, 'so the story goes, there was a beautiful gipsy girl called Mara and she had no more sense than to fall in love with a gorgio, same as I did.' Hetty looked up at him and put out her tongue, and he ruffled her hair. 'But the difference was, 'ee see, that he didn't fall in love with her, like you did with me.' He stooped to kiss her.

'So this Mara, she decided to ask the Devil to help her, but he would only do so if she sold him the souls of her family. Well, she was so desperate for the gorgio lad to love her that she did just that. And the Devil he came and he turned her father into a sound-box, and her four brothers into strings, and her mother into a bow. And out of their six souls was born the violin. Mara learned to play this wonderful instrument, and soon the handsome gorgio – did I tell 'ee he was handsome? A few of them are . . .' Hetty turned to slap at Reuben's face and he kissed her again.

'The handsome gorgio fell in love with her. But the Devil came back and he carried them both off to hell. Mara dropped the violin and it was left behind. But one day a poor gipsy lad found it and started to play it, and he discovered that it was magic. And since that day gipsies and violins have been inseparable.

'Mmm . . . I believe the last part of it,' said Hetty. 'The way you play is magic, Reuben. Play for me now, love.'

And so Reuben began to play, melodies that she had heard before and some that she hadn't, and it was as though their small kitchen had been invaded by an exaltation of larks. Hetty closed her eyes and she could see the deep forest glades, rushing rivers and cascading waterfalls and, in the distance, purple mountains capped with fluffy white clouds.

Then Reuben started to play a different tune. Hetty recognised 'Take a Pair of Sparkling Eyes', and she looked up at her husband and smiled, her eyes dancing with merriment. Then she joined in with the words.

> 'Take a pretty little cott,
> Quite a minature affair
> Hung about with trellised vine . . .'

Reuben had given her so much happiness that she felt she was overflowing with it.

It was in the middle of the night that the first cramping pain seized hold of Hetty.

Chapter 20

'Just leave her alone, will 'ee, Drusilla? I don't want 'ee coming round when Henrietta's on her own. Do 'ee understand?' Reuben took hold of his cousin's arm and forced her to look at him. 'Just keep away, do 'ee hear me?'

Drusilla pulled away from him. 'Leave go, Reuben. You're hurting me.' She looked at him keenly before her lips curved in a travesty of a smile. 'Yes, I understand perfectly. You want me to keep away from your precious little wife. But I'm afraid I don't see your problem. She's all right. 'Tisn't as if she'd lost the chavvy.'

'She's had a bad time. It was touch and go, I can tell 'ee, and she damned nearly lost it. Anyway, she's to rest for the next couple of weeks and I don't want her upsetting . . . not by anyone.'

Drusilla shrugged her shoulders and spread out her hands. 'If you say so, cousin dear. But I'd have thought she'd have been glad of some company, all on her own in that Godforsaken place. Her own ma and sister don't see her all that often, do they? I'm only trying to be friendly, to show a bit of . . . cousinly love, shall we say? 'Tisn't my fault if she chooses to be so ungrateful.'

459

'Don't pretend that you don't know what I'm talking about. You worry her, Drusilla. You know that you do. She was real flustered when you'd been round the other day, and it was the same night that she started with the pains.'

'You're surely not trying to blame me for that?' Drusilla's tone was aggrieved.

'No . . . I don't suppose I'm really blaming you,' said Reuben slowly. He sighed. 'But you know as well as I do that the pair of you have never got on. You were daggers drawn since that day you told her fortune, before we even knew who she was.'

Drusilla raised her eyebrows. 'Was it any wonder? The cheeky little madam, answering me back and making out that I was talking a lot of nonsense. I've met her sort before and they always get my dander up, you know that, Reuben.'

'Yes, I know it doesn't take much to get 'ee in a tizzy. And you and Henrietta are a good pair, I must admit. She can usually give as good as she gets, can Henrietta.'

But she had more than met her match with Drusilla, thought Reuben. He wasn't sure how much his wife was imagining things and how much Drusilla was to blame. He knew that his cousin was jealous of Henrietta, or had been when she first came on the scene, but Drusilla had made an effort to be friendly recently and, at least when he was there, she showed no sign of her previous animosity. There was that wild streak in Drusilla though. Reuben recalled her uncontrolled frenzy when her parents died and her fierce attack upon his father. They had been inclined to forgive her at the time, believing that she had been distraught at the sudden death of both her parents and, admittedly, she had not shown such perversity of behaviour since. But scenes such as those were not quickly forgotten and Reuben was uneasy. His cousin was possessed of the gift of second sight, that was certain. She might well have other, more sinister powers. Reuben couldn't believe, in his heart, that she would want to do his wife any serious harm, but neither did he want to take any chances. However, he decided it might be advisable to adopt a more reasonable tone with Drusilla.

'I'm sorry I shouted at 'ee,' he said now, 'but I'm worried about Henrietta. We were lucky that she managed to hang on to the chavvy, but she'll have to be very careful for the rest of the time. I can't risk having her upset. So do as I ask 'ee, please, Drusilla.' He reached out and took hold of her arm again, more gently this time. 'Women get some funny ideas when a chavvy's on the way and Henrietta gets herself into a state whenever you come to see her. So don't 'ee come unless I'm there. Savvy?'

'Yes, I understand, Reuben.' Drusilla looked at him searchingly. 'I understand only too well. Now, if you will excuse me, there's work to be done.' She walked back up the steps of her aunt's waggon, then paused in the doorway and turned to look at him. 'Be sure you give my kind regards to your wife, won't you? And you can tell her she's got it wrong. Both of you are wrong.' Drusilla shook her head slowly. 'I can't harm Henrietta.'

Reuben pondered on his cousin's words as he walked back home. What exactly had she meant?

She hadn't said 'I won't harm Henrietta.' What she had said was 'I can't . . .' He wished he could trust her, but he never had been able to do so and he knew he never would. The only thing he could do was to prevent the two of them from being alone together for the time being, if possible until after the chavvy arrived.

Thank goodness for a neighbour like Eliza Braithwaite, he thought now. She had come to Henrietta's assistance in the early hours of the morning, two days ago, when the pains had started, and by her skilful ministrations she had managed to save the child. Eliza acted as unofficial midwife in that close-knit community on Marton Moss and had brought any number of babies into the world, most of them living, it was her proud boast. And at the latter end of life she was pleased to assist her neighbours with laying-out. She was looking after Henrietta now, making sure that the girl kept her feet up and didn't stir far from her bed until things had settled down. Reuben knew that he could trust his wife in Eliza's capable hands when he returned to his stand on the markets the next day. It might be as well, though, he thought, to get the doctor to look at Henrietta, just to be on the safe side. They had a few bob set on one side for emergencies and there was nothing that Reuben wouldn't do to ensure the wellbeing of his beloved wife and the child they were expecting.

Edwin Donnelly's thoughts, too, by mid-September, were centred around the child that Constance was expecting. How far on was she now? he thought to himself. She must be about three and a half months . . . It was about six weeks since she had stunned him with the devastating news, and at that time she had been only a few weeks into her pregnancy. She could only just have known for sure. Edwin was largely ignorant of such matters, but he would have thought, by now, that there might have been some outward signs of her condition, some fullness in the face and breasts, perhaps, and a slight thickening of the waistline. But Constance appeared much the same as ever. She had confided in him, shyly, that her morning sickness was now abating a little and that she was feeling much better in health.

Plans for the wedding were going on apace. The ceremony was to be at St Joseph's church in three weeks' time, celebrated with Nuptial Mass in the presence of about a hundred guests, followed by a reception at the prestigious Imperial Hotel on the North Promenade. Already wedding presents had started to arrive and Constance had had her final fitting for her wedding dress, the details of which were to be kept a secret from Edwin. His half-jovial enquiry as to whether there was sufficient room at the waistline – after all, it was a full three weeks to the wedding – had been met with a frosty look from Constance and an admonition not to be so vulgar. He couldn't joke with Constance these days, so much on edge had she become, but then, Edwin realised with a tinge of surprise, he had never been able to do so.

He had tried not to think about Grace, and the ache in his heart had lessened somewhat to a feeling of numbness. It was futile to think about

her, and that had been made easier by her decision to leave her employment at Donnelly's. At
least he didn't have to see her each day and be
reminded of how shamefully he had treated her.
He hoped she was well and that she was finding
contentment, if not happiness, in some other
sphere. He had heard nothing of her since she had
left the shop, and if his father knew anything of
Grace's movements then he was not saying.
William Donnelly was still in touch with Mrs
Turnbull, but the subject of Grace was a closed
book between Edwin and his father. Edwin was
well aware that his father disapproved of his
conduct in abandoning Grace and taking up with
Constance again so suddenly, although he hadn't
actually said so. William Donnelly, of course,
didn't as yet know the real reason for Edwin's
apparent change of heart. Whether it would be
better or worse when the family did know the
guilty secret, Edwin was not sure.

Edwin's mother now appeared to be almost
back to normal, her nervous ailment having suddenly taken a turn for the better. Edwin suspected that the news of his engagement to
Constance had had a lot to do with the improve-
ment in her condition.

He gave a deep sigh as he approached the
Whiteheads' home. He never knew what sort of a
mood Constance would be in these days. One
minute she was bubbling over with excitement as
she discussed plans with him for the forthcoming
wedding – usually a one-sided conversation – and
the next minute snapping at him peevishly. These
changes of mood, he supposed, were indicative of

her condition. Maybe she would be better when they were married and she could be sure that her child would be born in wedlock. It would be too late then to worry about what people might think. Marriage . . . Again Edwin felt his heart plummeting at the thought of the step he was taking – that he had been forced to take – but he knew that he had made his own bed, in one moment of foolishness, and now he would have to lie on it. A very apt simile when it came to the wedding night, and Edwin realised, to his consternation, that that wasn't something upon which he wished to dwell.

Constance looked at him dazedly when she met him in the hallway. 'Oh . . . hello, Edwin. You're a little earlier than I expected. I didn't realise it was that time.'

'I don't think so, dear.' Edwin pulled out his pocket watch. 'No, it's just turned eight o'clock.' He looked at her in some concern as he saw her shake her head confusedly. She looked pale too, with dark shadows under her eyes. 'What's the matter, Connie? Aren't you feeling well? Come along, you'd better sit down.'

He opened the drawing room door and took her arm and led her to the settee. She flopped down, very inelegantly for Constance, and leaned her head against the cushions. Edwin could see beads of perspiration on her forehead.

'Does your mother know that you're feeling poorly?' He took hold of her hand. 'Shall I go and tell her?'

'No . . . She doesn't know. Mother's out. She's gone to a committee meeting for the Ladies'

Fellowship. Father's in his study.' Constance's voice was quiet and she kept her eyes closed. 'It must be something I've eaten, I think. Stomach pains . . .'

'Can I get you something? A drop of brandy, perhaps? Yes, I'm sure that would help.' Edwin went to the sideboard where the cut-glass decanters stood and poured out a measure of brandy. He added a dash of soda water and took it back to Constance. 'There you are. Drink that. If it's a stomach upset it'll help to settle you down.'

'Thank you, Edwin.' Constance smiled at him briefly as she took the glass and began to sip the liquid.

'But . . . don't you think you ought to call a doctor?' Edwin looked at her solicitously as a thought occurred to him. 'It might be . . . You could be starting a . . . miscarriage. You don't want to risk . . .'

'Don't be ridiculous, Edwin!' Constance's eyes blazed angrily and her fingers clenched tightly round the stem of the brandy glass. 'How can it be a miscarriage? I mean . . . I don't think it's . . .' She stopped suddenly, her eyes glazing over with pain. 'Oh . . . Edwin, help me!'

The glass fell from her hand and dropped to the floor, its contents spilling across the deep pile of the maroon carpet, as Constance clutched hold of her stomach. 'Oh, Edwin. This pain . . . I'll have to go . . .' She rose unsteadily and staggered towards the door. She pushed Edwin away irritably as he tried to put his arm round her. 'Just leave me alone, can't you? I must get to the bathroom . . .'

Edwin decided that he could waste no more

time. He went to the study door and knocked, then opened it without waiting for an answer. 'Mr Whitehead . . . Could you come, please? It's Constance. She's feeling ill. I really think we should call the doctor.'

'Oh dear. What's the matter? Do you know?' Frederick Whitehead's eyes, behind the thick lenses of his spectacles, looked concerned but knowing as well. Edwin knew him to be a very shrewd man, a good business partner to William Donnelly and certainly no fool. Edwin definitely preferred him to Bertha Whitehead. Constance's father, though he was very fond of his daughter, was not so liable to give in to her whims and extravagances as was her mother, and Edwin knew that most of the spoiling and indulgence that had surrounded Constance had been mainly Bertha Whitehead's doing.

'I think it's a stomach upset,' Edwin said now. 'She's gone very pale and she's obviously in pain. But it would be as well to be sure . . .' Now was not the time to confide in Frederick Whitehead as to Constance's condition, but Edwin suspected that that gentleman might be only too well aware of what ailed his daughter.

'Yes, you're right, lad. It would be as well to be on the safe side.' The look he gave Edwin was meaningful, but not unkind. 'Where's Constance now?'

'She's gone to . . . She dashed upstairs.'

'Right. I'll pop up and see to her, tell her to get into bed. Bertha's out at the moment – committee meeting – but she shouldn't be long. Could you ring the doctor, Edwin? Dr Frobisher . . . Of course you know that, don't you? He's your doctor as well. His number's on the pad by the phone . . .'

Bertha Whitehead came home before the doctor had arrived and Edwin felt that his own presence was unnecessary. There was nothing he could do while Constance's mother was fussing over her, and it would prove extremely difficult to make conversation with Frederick Whitehead. But he was the girl's fiancé, strange though the idea still seemed to him, and he really should wait and find out what was wrong with Constance.

Frederick Whitehead noticed his discomfiture. 'Look, Edwin,' he said kindly. 'There's not much point in you hanging about here. Bertha's seeing to Constance – the lass seems a bit more composed now she's got into bed – and once the doctor arrives she'll be in good hands. The best, I might say. Dr Frobisher knows what he's doing. So you get yourself off home, lad, and if there's anything to tell you – anything I think you should know . . .' he paused meaningfully, 'then you can be sure I'll ring and tell you. Now don't worry.' He patted Edwin's arm reassuringly. 'Constance will be all right. I'm sure she will.'

'Thank you, Mr Whitehead,' said Edwin. 'I must admit I feel like a spare part hanging around here. Give my love to Constance and if I don't hear anything from you I'll call and see her in the morning.'

Edwin felt bewildered as he walked home. There was a sneaking little thought at the back of his mind that it might be a way out of his problem if Constance were to miscarry. Then, just as quickly, he pushed the idea away, horrified at the direction in which his thoughts were leading him. There could be no question of him abandoning Constance just because there may no longer be the necessity for them to marry. He had already cast aside one young woman . . . Oh, Grace. Dear lovely Grace. His heart gave a sudden lurch as he thought of her, something he didn't allow himself to do very often. No, his loyalties must lie with Constance now, for better, for worse, in sickness and in health, till death . . . Edwin gave an involuntary shudder as the familiar words came into his mind. No, there could be no way out for him. He would be repeating those words in a few weeks' time and he knew that it would be better if he resigned himself to the fact and made up his mind to make a go of his marriage. He owed it to Constance.

Rose, the young maid, answered his ring at the door bell the next morning. He had decided to call and see Constance before going to the shop. He had had no telephone message so he assumed that there had been no emergency and that his suspicions that Constance might be miscarrying had proved groundless. Edwin wasn't sure whether he was glad about this, or sorry.

'Good morning, Mr Edwin.' Rose bobbed a curtsey as she ushered him into the hallway. 'Mrs Whitehead's upstairs with Miss Constance. Would you like to wait in the morning room? Oh, just leaving, are you, Doctor? Here's your hat.'

Dr Frobisher, tall and distinguished-looking, with dark hair silvering at the sides and a well-trimmed moustache, took the top hat which Rose held out to him and nodded at Edwin. 'Good morning, Edwin.' The doctor was an old family friend who had ministered to the Donnellys as well as to the Whitehead family for many years. 'Your young lady is as well as can be expected, I'm pleased to say . . . Thank you, Rose, that will be all. I'll see myself out when I've had a word with Mr Donnelly.'

The doctor followed Edwin into the morning room. 'Yes, it was a nasty attack, but I'm pleased to say that she will be all right.'

'An attack . . .?' Edwin looked at him enquiringly.

'Yes, a severe gastric attack. The stomach pains she was suffering were quite intense, poor girl, and combined with the . . . er, period pains, she really must have been feeling quite poorly.'

'Period pains?' repeated Edwin, aware that he was beginning to sound like a parrot.

'Yes, she started her monthly period last night,' the doctor explained patiently, 'and that coming on top of everything else . . .'

'But . . . what about the baby?' Edwin was feeling bemused.

'The baby . . .?' Dr Frobisher stared at him in bewilderment.

'Yes . . . Has she lost it, then?'

Dr Frobisher was silent for a few moments, then, 'There is no baby, Edwin,' he said slowly.

'But she said . . .' Edwin shook his head perplexedly. 'Are you quite sure?'

Dr Frobisher nodded. 'Quite sure.' His eyes, as he looked steadily at Edwin, were kind but serious.

Edwin still couldn't take in what he was hearing. 'But you said Constance was having . . . er . . . a period. Could it not have been a . . . miscarriage?'

'No, no, no.' The doctor shook his head emphatically. 'Not at all. Just a normal period, a painful one, though. Constance always suffers with pain.' The look he gave Edwin was full of understanding. 'She told you she was pregnant then, did she?' Edwin nodded. 'She wasn't,' Dr Frobisher said briefly. 'I needed to examine her thoroughly last night – you understand? – and she is most certainly not pregnant. I'm sorry, Edwin.' He smiled sadly. 'It's an old trick, as old as the hills. I'm sorry to be the one to disillusion you, but . . .'

'Not at all, Dr Frobisher. I'm glad you told me.' Edwin's tone was resolute and a look of grim determination had come into his eyes. 'I'm only sorry that I was taken in by Constance's lies. To think that I've been such a fool . . .'

'Now, steady on, Edwin.' The doctor took hold of his arm. 'Just count to ten, there's a good fellow, before you go rampaging up there. I can see you're determined to have it out with her.'

'You can bet your life I am! The conniving, deceitful little madam. And to think that I believed her.' Edwin turned to the doctor. 'I can go and see her, can't I? She's well enough to receive visitors?'

'Oh yes, she's quite well enough this morning.' The doctor looked at him gravely. 'She was poorly though, Edwin. There's no doubt about that. However, the medicine I gave her seems to have done the trick. I thought it would, but I promised her mother that I'd call again this morning just to make sure she was all right. A pity, perhaps, that my visit coincided with yours. Constance would have no idea that her little . . . secret was going to be discovered.'

'A pity? I don't think so,' said Edwin grimly. 'I think it was fortunate. Very fortunate. Thank you, Dr Frobisher.' He gripped the doctor's outstretched hand firmly. 'Thank you for telling me. I will always be grateful to you.'

'You mean . . .' The doctor leaned forward confidentially. ' . . . You're not going to marry her?'

'No, I am most certainly not going to marry her.'

The doctor nodded curtly. 'Well, I expect you know your own business best. Just take it easy with her, though. She's still feeling a bit shaky.' Then suddenly he grinned. 'She's a tough customer though, is Constance. I don't suppose she'll go into a decline when she hears what you've got to say. I shouldn't think so for one moment.' He grasped hold of the other man's arm. 'Good luck, Edwin.'

Edwin bounded up the stairs two at a time. Rose had asked him to wait in the morning room, but he didn't intend to delay this confrontation another second.

Mrs Whitehead was just coming out of Constance's room and she stared at him in surprise. 'You're in an almighty hurry, young man.' Her tone was haughty and a trifle disapproving. How like Constance she sounded, Edwin thought. 'Of course I can understand that you're anxious to see your fiancée.' She smiled condescendingly. 'And because she is your fiancée I think you might be allowed to see her for a minute or two. Only a few minutes, mind. Constance has been very poorly, poor love, so you mustn't overstay your welcome.'

'Don't worry, Mrs Whitehead.' Edwin's tone was resolute. 'What I have to say to Constance won't take more than a few moments.' He was aware of the strange look that she gave him, but Edwin no longer cared. He turned away from her and stormed into Constance's bedroom. He was in such a rage that he didn't even care if Mrs Whitehead stayed on the landing to eavesdrop. The whole family would know soon enough that it was all over between him and their precious little girl.

Constance was propped up against a mountain of frilly pillows, a lace-trimmed bedjacket in her usual shade of pale blue draped round her shoulders. 'Edwin, how lovely.' She gave a cry of surprise when she saw him, then stopped as she noticed the look on his face. 'Why . . . Edwin. What's the matter?'

'What's the matter? What's the matter?' Edwin's voice was rising in an angry crescendo. 'You may well ask what's the matter, you deceitful hussy!'

'Edwin! How dare you speak to me like that? I've been poorly – I'm still poorly – and you have the nerve to come bursting in here and to call me a . . . a . . .'

'Hussy, Constance. That's what I said, because that's what you are. A hussy, and a deceitful one as well. You've lied to me. I know very well that

473

you're poorly, and I know why. You're having a period, Constance. Oh, you don't need to look shocked because I've mentioned the word. I know that there's not very much that could shock you, so don't pretend to be all coy and embarrassed. I'll say it again. You're having a period; you're not having a baby and you never were.'

Constance lowered her eyes, but not before Edwin noticed a flicker of alarm in them. Her lips were closed tightly together in a thin, determined line, and it was a few seconds before she spoke. 'Yes . . . I am. A very bad one.' Her voice was quiet and she didn't look at Edwin as she spoke. 'I've lost a lot of . . . blood. And so I've lost the baby as well. It was a miscarriage, Edwin, but nobody knows except . . .'

'Don't give me that, Constance! What sort of a fool do you take me for?' Edwin almost laughed and would have done so if he hadn't felt so angry at the way the crafty little minx was still determined to wriggle out of the situation. 'I met Dr Frobisher downstairs and I asked him.' For the first time Constance looked straight at him and the alarm was written all over her face. 'Yes, I asked him about the baby. There was no baby, Constance. You're not pregnant and you never were.'

'I thought I was . . . I really did. I was going to tell you . . . before we got married.'

'I don't believe, you, Constance, and I will never be able to believe you again. And, speaking of marriage, there isn't going to be one. I'm only glad that I've found out in time.'

'No marriage? But . . . you can't do that, Edwin.

This doesn't make any difference, surely. We love one another and . . .'

'No, Constance,' replied Edwin evenly. 'We don't. I don't love you. You must have realised that by now. And if you are honest you will admit that you don't really love me. Oh yes, you may imagine that you do, but it wouldn't work, Connie. You and I have never been right for one another. You must know that.'

'But all the guests have been invited, and the presents have started coming, and I've got my dress.' Constance was beginning to sound frightened. 'What will I say to everybody? What am I going to tell Mother?'

'I'm sure you'll think of something.' Looking at Constance's panic-stricken features Edwin felt a momentary pang of compassion. 'You're very good at telling . . . stories,' he said, drawing the line at saying 'lies'. 'But I would suggest you tell the truth, or something close to it. My parents will be made aware of the full facts, but what you choose to tell your family is up to you.' He looked steadily at her and almost, but not quite, smiled, although his eyes softened a touch. 'Be brave, Connie. There'll be plenty of young men falling over themselves to marry you. You chose the wrong one, that's all.'

She looked fixedly back at him and he could see some of her old fighting spirit returning, together with the realisation that this was one battle that she had lost. Even now he couldn't hate Constance and he knew that there must have been something in her that attracted him for them to have been close friends for so long. But she was not the girl for him. He only hoped that there might be some way now for him to find his way back to the girl he really loved, that it wasn't too late.

Constance pulled the sapphire ring off her slender finger and held it out to Edwin. 'You'd better have this.' Her voice was calmer now. 'You might be needing it.'

Edwin shook his head. 'Keep it, Constance. Or . . . sell it and buy yourself a new dress. I won't be wanting it.' His anger had abated a little now and he took a step nearer to the bed and held out his hand. 'Goodbye, Connie. I hope you'll soon be feeling better. And you'll find someone far more suited to you than I am. I know you will.' He squeezed her hand briefly, then turned away and left.

There was no sign of Mrs Whitehead or of the maid in the hallway so Edwin opened the door quietly and strode away down the drive. He felt as though a gigantic weight had been lifted from his shoulders, but he only hoped and prayed that the dreadful mistake he had made in abandoning Grace Turnbull could be put right.

'Edwin, whatever is going on?' Clara Donnelly met him in the hallway as soon as he returned from the shop that evening. 'Bertha Whitehead has been on the phone, and a fair old state she was in, I can tell you. She says there's not going to be a wedding and that you and Constance have both agreed . . .'

'What else did she say, Mother?' he asked. 'Did she say anything about Constance being ill?'

476

'Only that she's feeling a little better today. No, Constance doesn't seem to have said very much to her mother, except to tell her that it's all off. Mrs Whitehead's just as mystified as I am.' Clara looked enquiringly at her son. 'It's a fine time to start having second thoughts, three weeks before the wedding, that's all I can say.'

'Better before than after, Mother,' said Edwin with a wry grin. He decided that the time had come to tell the truth, and he and his mother had been getting on much better of late. 'Come in here and sit down and I'll tell you about it.'

He opened the drawing room door and followed his mother into the room. He poured out a glass of sherry for Clara and just a small one for himself – he had been more abstemious since that unforgettable incident with Constance – and then they sat down in the green velvet-upholstered chairs and Edwin began his story.

He left very little out, although he knew that by admitting that Constance had tricked him he was also admitting that he and the young woman must have had intimate relations.

His mother raised an eyebrow sardonically and gave a half-smile. 'There must have been summat going on, lad, for her to pretend that she was having a baby.'

'Yes, Mother, there had been. Just the once – only once, mind you – but I'm not very proud of myself. I suppose you might say it served me right, but there was no call for her to deceive me the way she did. I'm sorry if I've shocked you, Mother, by telling you that I made love to Constance.'

A roguish gleam came into Clara's eyes and the half-smile turned into a full one. 'Not a bit of it, lad. How d'you think I came to catch your father?'

'Do you mean that you and Father . . .?'

'Yes, Edwin, that's exactly what I mean. And you don't need to look so horrified. You youngsters didn't invent it, you know. It's always gone on. The difference is that I didn't cheat on him. I really was pregnant – I didn't have to pretend – and I told your father and he married me. Whether he would have wed me if I hadn't been I'll never know, but I like to think that he would.'

Clara put down her sherry glass on the small table at her side and pressed her fingers together in a steeple. She gazed at them contemplatively as she spoke. 'Yes, I was expecting Giles when your father and I got married. He did the decent thing, as they say, but on the whole we've been happy and I got what I wanted. I always knew what I wanted.' She rested her hands in her lap and smiled, a trifle sadly, at her son. 'Don't think I don't understand, Edwin, because I do. I understand a good deal more than you realise. I know you and I haven't seen eye to eye in the past. I was as mad as hell with you, I'll admit it, when you wouldn't get engaged to the lass that time. But I can see now that you were right. I've been watching Constance these last few weeks, and I've been watching you an' all. Your heart's not been in it, lad, and as for her – well, she's a grasping little madam if ever there was one.'

'You've changed your tune, Mother.' Edwin sounded surprised and he leaned forward in his chair, staring at her.

'Yes, maybe I have.' Clara nodded thoughtfully. 'But a lot has happened to make me think. I've been doing a lot of that these last few weeks – thinking . . .' She paused for a moment before she went on. 'You know I've been ill?' She didn't wait for an answer. 'Well there was more to it than any of you knew. I know you thought I was shamming a lot of the time and acting up because you'd got friendly with . . . Grace Turnbull. But it wasn't just that . . . It was the letters I'd been getting, Edwin. Horrible letters.'

'Letters, Mother?' Edwin was mystified.

'Yes, anonymous ones. Vile they were.' Clara gave an involuntary shudder. 'You know that I was brought up on the Moss when I was a girl?' Edwin nodded. 'A big family we were – ten of us, although several died when they were still children, and – well – I've got to admit that I've seen very little of them since I got married. Aye, I know only too well what folks think of me.' Clara nodded ruefully. 'A jumped-up nobody who had her eye on the main chance, but they didn't know the half of it, Edwin. Not the half. My father . . .' She hesitated, biting at her lip. 'Well . . . let's just say I was the eldest girl and I was quite pretty and slim, and my mother, poor soul, had got fat and old before her time and worn down with constant child-bearing. And my father had to get his pleasures somewhere . . . at least he tried.' She didn't look at Edwin, but he could see the glint of tears in her eyes. 'I had to get away, Edwin. I just had to.'

Edwin was filled with revulsion for this grandfather he had never known, and a deep pity for his mother. This was a side of her he had never seen before. 'The letters, Mother,' he said quietly. 'You were telling me about some letters.'

'Yes . . . Mam died years ago – God rest her soul – and he – my father – he started drinking. I say started, but he'd always been a drinker. Now he got that he was never sober. He'd have ended up in the workhouse if it hadn't been for our Ada. He went to live with her and her family in South Shore, and when she'd had enough of him he went to our Alfred's. And so it went on. And I'm afraid I never took my turn. Could you blame me?' The look she gave Edwin was sad but defiant. 'Anyroad, he died earlier this year – I didn't go to the funeral – then the letters started coming. What a dreadful daughter I'd been, I'd let my father damn nearly die in the gutter, I wouldn't even pass the time of day with my brothers and sisters. You can imagine the stuff they wrote, Edwin. I say they, but I never found out who it was, of course.'

'And you kept it all to yourself? Didn't you tell Father?'

'In the end I had to. And then I began to feel better straight away. Your father was wonderful, Edwin. He was so kind to me and so understanding. And that was when I started to think about . . . things. About how lucky I am, and how I want you to be happy, all of you. Giles and Charles are both married and they seem to have got what they want. But I want you to be happy too, lad.'

She paused, looking down at her hands folded in her lap for a moment or two, then she looked at Edwin, her glance candid and direct. 'I was wrong

480

about that girl, Grace Turnbull. You loved her, Edwin. I know you did.'

Edwin nodded and smiled sadly, thinking what a brave woman his mother was to admit she had made a mistake. 'Yes, I loved her, Mother. I still love her.'

'Where is she now? What is she doing? Do you know?'

'No, I have no idea.'

'Then find out, lad, quickly. Don't make any more mistakes. We've wasted enough time already between us, and I've a feeling that she's the right girl for you. I know what I've said about her job and her religion and all that, but none of it matters. It doesn't matter a scrap if you love her.'

Edwin knew that his mother was right. He had to act quickly. His mother's illness had, in the beginning, delayed the furtherance of his relationship with Grace, but in the end it was through his own stupidity that he had lost her. But none of that mattered now. The only thing that concerned him was would she still want him, did she still love him, would he dare, even, to approach her after all the hurt he had done her?

Martha Turnbull's face was a study when she answered his knock at the door. 'Why, Mr Edwin . . . Whatever . . .?' He knew she had been going to say 'Whatever are you doing here?' and no wonder either. If Martha Turnbull thought badly of him he knew he more than deserved it. 'You'd best come in,' she said briskly, standing aside to allow him to enter.

He followed her along the passage and into the

parlour. 'Grace isn't here, Mr Edwin,' she said, sitting down and gesturing to him to do the same. 'I suppose you've come to ask about Grace?'

'Yes . . . yes. I have, Mrs Turnbull.' He smiled at her. 'But please call me Edwin. I think it's time we stopped this Mr Edwin nonsense.'

Martha nodded curtly but didn't answer.

'Perhaps it's as well Grace isn't in at the moment,' said Edwin. 'It'll give me a chance to have a talk with you first. You see, Mrs Turnbull . . . I'm afraid I've treated Grace very badly.'

Martha nodded again.

'It's a long story, a very long one . . . and I can't go into it all, but I've made a big mistake. I was going to be married . . . I suppose you knew that?'

'Aye, I knew that, lad.' Martha's tone was grim.

'Yes . . . Constance Whitehead and I were to be married. It was what our families wanted for us and Constance is a Catholic and it seemed to be right. But it wasn't right. We both know it now. It wasn't right at all. It's all over between us and . . .'

'And so you want our Grace back?' Martha looked at him keenly.

'No.' Edwin shook his head. 'Of course I don't expect to take up with Grace again where I left off. I treated her badly, I know. I just want to know if she'll forgive me . . . if she'll see me again, perhaps? Would you tell her I called, Mrs Turnbull? Would you ask her if I could call again and see her?'

'No . . . Edwin.' Martha shook her head. 'I'm afraid you can't see Grace.'

'I know how you feel, Mrs Turnbull,' said

Edwin, 'and, believe me, I don't blame you. But I'm sorry, really I am, and I can't tell you how much I regret what has happened. Please, would you just tell her that I have been asking about her?'

Martha shook her head again, but her look was full of sympathy. 'No . . . It wouldn't do any good, Edwin lad. Grace is married. She married Walter Clayton last week.'

Chapter 21

Grace had insisted that they should be married without any fuss. By mid-September the holiday season was beginning to wind down. There were fewer visitors booked in at Welcome Rest and it was unlikely that there would be many people seeking rooms 'on spec' as was the case at the height of the season. Nevertheless. Grace could tell that Martha was tired, even though she didn't complain, and the girl felt that it would be unfair to expect her mother to cope with a wedding party, even a small one. Besides, Grace herself had no desire for a party and neither, she felt, had Walter.

As the third week of September approached, the date which had been set for the wedding, Grace found herself reflecting upon her reasons for marrying Walter. What she had told her mother was true; they were getting on very well together. He was amiable and chatty and at times could be almost humorous, and Grace found that she liked this new Walter. To her relief, she no longer had any reason to feel afraid of him. Indeed, it was hard to recall, now, how afraid she had been of him; Water seemed so different now. She was beginning to feel that she could depend on him, all ingredients which would help to make a successful marriage, or so Grace tried to convince herself. And Edwin, she knew, could no longer be hers. He would soon be married to Constance Whitehead. Grace didn't want to face the rest of her life alone. She wanted companionship, she longed to have a child, and most of all she wanted to be loved and cherished. And so she had told Walter that she would marry him. Perhaps it would work out all right in the end.

Martha was delighted at the way things had turned out, and if she were honest with herself, Grace would have to admit that this was possibly the main reason for her agreeing to marry Walter Clayton. Martha had suffered a great deal of heartache recently over her younger daughter's marriage, therefore she was more than satisfied that her elder daughter at last seemed to have come to her senses. And, as Grace and Walter and Martha all agreed, there was no point in a long engagement. Walter had his own little home all ready for Grace to move into, and Martha scoffed at any idea that Grace was leaving her in the lurch by getting married so soon after her sister.

'Not a bit of it,' Martha said. She added, with a laugh, 'If you're not working for me I won't have to pay you owt, will I?' Grace and Hetty had both earned a small wage, all that Martha could afford to give them, but all three of them knew that the girls were not adequately paid for the amount of backbreaking work that they had done. It was the same in boarding houses all over the town, whole families pulling together and sharing the workload and the results of their labours being ploughed back into the business.

'Nay, I'm all right, lass,' Martha assured Grace. 'You go ahead and marry your Walter and don't worry about me. I'll admit I didn't expect both me daughters to get wed one after the other like this, but that's life, isn't it? Seems to me that it's all or nowt – I've certainly had more than me fair share of upheavals lately – but it'll happen all settle down again once you're wed, Grace.

'And we've not done too badly this season.' Like all true boarding-house keepers Martha was becoming adept in the use of the understatement. Never would they admit that they were doing well; always it was 'not too bad'. 'Aye, it's not been too bad at all,' Martha went on. 'Those two lasses from Burnley have been a godsend, they have that. I shall miss 'em when they go back home at the end of the month, but there's no sense in 'em staying here all winter. There'd be nowt for them to do, but they've promised to come back next spring, God willing. And the two lodgers'll keep things ticking over money-wise till the visitors start coming again. I can look after them two fellows as easy as winking, so don't you start worrying about me. I've said it before and I'll say it again, hard work never killed anyone. I'd have given you a party, Grace, if you'd wanted one. I don't want folks thinking I'm stingy, but if you and Walter are insisting on a quiet do then it's all right with me. It's your day when all's said and done.'

It was a very small group of people who gathered together at the Methodist chapel in North

Shore for the marriage of Grace and Walter. Hetty and Reuben had stayed at the boarding house the previous night as Marton Moss was, to quote Martha, 'the back of beyond', involving a long walk to the seafront and then a tram ride the length of the promenade to North Shore.

Hetty was still looking pale and feeling very shaky from her enforced spell in bed after almost losing the child she was carrying. But she was determined to be at the wedding to stand as a witness for her sister, and even more determined that she would squeeze into the dress that she had worn at her own wedding about six weeks previously. It needed letting out at the waist and was a tight fit, but it sufficed. The half-veil on the bonnet was more suitable for a bride than a bridesmaid – or matron-of-honour, to use the correct term – so Hetty had replaced it with a spray of pink fabric roses and a trimming of deeper pink velvet ribbon.

Grace wore the dress she had previously worn as a bridesmaid. The pale-lilac silk was eminently suitable but, like her sister, Grace had changed her headdress. Now she wore a circlet of orange blossom on a lilac band, and the short veil covering her eyes and her dark curling hair just reached to her shoulders.

Martha's eyes were moist as she watched, for the second time in just a few weeks, a beloved daughter standing at the communion rail with her new husband. Two lovely daughters, she thought, and they'd made two lovely brides, but the fellows they had married were as different as chalk and cheese. God bless them both, Martha whispered, and keep them safe. And, please God, let them be happy. Martha knew that, despite her own misgivings and despite the fact that Hetty had recently nearly lost her baby, there was no doubt that her younger daughter was happy. Happiness positively radiated from Hetty, but Martha was not so sure about her elder daughter. Grace looked contented and serene, but there had not been the same sparkle in her eyes, not since that business with Edwin Donnelly. Martha hoped that she had done the right thing in encouraging Grace to marry Walter, and that was why she prayed so fervently now that God would help her to be happy.

The bridal party, consisting of Grace and Walter, Hetty and Reuben, Martha, and Amos Armitage, Walter's friend from work who had stood as witness, gathered later in the parlour of Welcome Rest to drink the health of the newly married couple. The lodgers, George and Leonard, and the girls from Burnley, Gladys and May, also joined them, as did Alice Gregson from across the road.

'Here's health and happiness to the pair of you,' said George Makepeace who, as the eldest man present, was acting as spokesman. They all raised their glasses of dark-brown sherry and ate the rich fruit cake that Martha had made, but it was a somewhat subdued gathering, a mishmash of assorted people who scarcely knew one another trying their hardest to be jovial and friendly. Martha couldn't help comparing it with the spontaneous gaiety of Hetty's wedding party a few weeks previously, and again she found herself praying silently, Please God, let them be happy.

★ ★ ★

Grace lay in bed, the paisley-patterned eiderdown drawn up to her chin, waiting for her husband. She had come up to the bedroom first and undressed hastily, scrambled out of her clothes and into her white cambric nightgown, fearful that Walter would come in while she was still half clothed. But she could hear that he was still downstairs, washing himself at the kitchen sink and singing a hymn that had been a favourite of his at the chapel in Burnley. '... Are your garments spotless, are they white as snow, are you washed in the blood of the Lamb?'

A tiny smile pulled at the corners of Grace's mouth as an amusing thought struck her. It wasn't a very appropriate song for a coalman. Walter's garments were often as black as pitch and now it would be her job, as his wife, to wash them a few times a week in the zinc dolly tub. She heard the stairs creak as he came upstairs, and she grasped hold of the sheet, wondering why she should feel so fearful. It was only Walter, now her husband, of course, but the Walter she had known for ages who was, thank God, no longer showing any signs of his former belligerence and bullying tactics. There had been a certain restraint between them since they had come to their new home a few hours ago, but that was only to be expected.

Grace almost laughed out loud at the sight of Walter in his striped nightshirt and had to bite her lip. He would not, she thought, be amused at her girlish giggling. And what she was finding so amusing anyway? She really must try to quell the

490

mirth that was building up inside her, but she knew, in her heart, that it was an antidote to the apprehension she was feeling.

Walter drew back the curtains, letting a little light stream into the room, pale moonlight and the yellowish glow from the gas lamp further down the street. He didn't blow out the candle on the chest of drawers straight away, but sat on the edge of the bed and looked at Grace. She recognised at once the lustful look in his eyes, something that she hadn't seen for a long time, and she felt a tiny frisson of the fear that she had been trying to hold in check. But when he spoke, his voice was kind, though gruff with emotion.

'Grace . . . Grace, let me look at you. Don't cower under the bedclothes like that.' He pulled away the sheet and blanket and the heavy eiderdown and began, very gently, to stroke her hair. Then his fingers fumbled at the fastening of her high-necked nightgown. 'Come on, Grace,' he whispered. 'It's only me, Walter. Come on, don't be shy, love. I'll not hurt you. I just want to look at you. You know that I love you.'

He took hold of the hem of her nightgown and pulled it up. 'Take it off, Grace.' His voice was becoming huskier, more intense, and obediently, like a small girl, Grace lifted her arms above her head while Walter tugged away the restricting cambric garment. This is my husband, she said to herself. This is Walter. I must try to love him . . .

'Oh, Grace . . . my very own Grace. You're so lovely.' His fingers traced the outline of her figure, her thighs, the curves of her breasts and buttocks, but still Grace remained passive. I must love him, she murmured to herself. I must . . . Walter paused for a moment, then in one sharp movement he pulled the nightshirt over his head and leaned over and blew out the candle.

Then his arms were round Grace, drawing her closely towards him, and his mouth was upon hers hungrily, insistently, his tongue probing, forcing its way between her teeth. Grace felt a momentary recoil of revulsion, then she thought again, this is my husband, I must love him. It wasn't as if she were a complete stranger to the act of love. But this was no time to be thinking of Edwin. She forced her mind away from him, back to Walter, back to the times on the moor above Burnley when he had kissed her in this way. She wound her arms more tightly round him and let her mouth open under his, responding to his kiss.

'I won't hurt you, Grace. Don't be afraid,' he whispered as he parted her thighs and lowered himself on to her. 'I've wanted you for so long, my lovely Grace. And now you're mine.'

In spite of her misgivings Grace found that she was almost enjoying the experience, that she would be able to enjoy it more if only she could let herself go completely. The thought also struck her that Walter knew what he was doing. This was no inexperienced lad on his wedding night, and the story that Hetty had told her about some woman in Burnley returned to her now. She felt indignant for a moment, but Walter's body pressing down on her was becoming more demanding. 'I'll try to be gentle, love,' he was murmuring. 'I'll try not to hurt you. I love you, Gracie.' She relaxed her tensed-up muscles and allowed him to enter her.

She was unprepared for his gasp of surprise. He hesitated for just a moment before he began to move inside her, roughly, savagely almost, making no attempt now to be gentle. Then he raised himself up and stared down at her, his pale-grey eyes filled with anger and something almost akin to hatred. 'Whore!' he muttered. 'You're nothing but a whore. You let him have you, that . . . that Edwin Donnelly. He wanted to play around with you, that's all he wanted. And you let him, didn't you? Didn't you?' His voice rose as he brought his face to within an inch of hers. 'Answer me, woman! You let him have you, didn't you?'

'Yes . . . yes. Edwin and I made love,' Grace whispered, the tears welling up behind her eyelids. Walter was hurting her now, and she was beginning to feel afraid of him again. 'But it doesn't matter now, Walter. I've married you . . .'

'Doesn't matter? Doesn't matter?' Walter's voice seemed to fill the tiny room. 'How dare you say it doesn't matter? You're a whore. And because you're a whore I shall treat you like one.'

The rapid movements began again and Grace lay still, submissive beneath Walter's aggressive assault on her body. Then it was all over, and roughly he pushed her away from him and turned his back on her, pulling the bedclothes tightly round him. Grace lay wide awake in the semi-darkness, feeling more wretched than she had ever felt in her life. The hot tears of misery coursed down her cheeks, but her brain felt too numb to form even one coherent thought. The

493

only phrase that she could hear in her paralysed mind was the one she had repeated only a few hours previously, '. . . till death us do part'.

Grace had been up for a couple of hours when Walter came into the kitchen the next morning. She had set the table with a blue checked cloth and put out the willow-patterned cups and saucers, a wedding present from Martha, still too miserable to be fully aware of what she was doing. She felt that food would choke her, but the hot strong tea was refreshing and she had already drunk three cups. Walter was in his working clothes and she knew that he had washed himself in the bowl on the bedroom washstand which she had filled with hot water while he was still sleeping. For this she was thankful, as she knew that usually he washed at the kitchen sink.

She looked at him warily as he entered the room, knowing that to ignore him completely, as she felt like doing, might only provoke his wrath even further.

'Grace . . . Grace, listen to me.' He stopped by her chair and put a hand on her shoulder. She felt herself stiffen at his touch. 'I shouldn't have said what I did last night . . . I shouldn't have treated you like that . . .' Walter was mumbling and Grace could hardly hear him. She felt that the words were being dragged unwillingly from him.

She didn't know how to answer. She opened her mouth but no words came out. The anger and hurt at his treatment of her were still there inside her: she felt as though they would always be there. 'I was upset, Grace. I wanted to be the first.' His voice was petulant, like a small boy who had failed to win a race. 'I've wanted you for so long. And I wanted to be the one to show you how . . . I wanted you to love me, only me. I couldn't believe it when I found out about you and . . . him.' He seized hold of her hair now and pulled it back, forcing her face upwards to look at him. His eyes held something of the fury she had seen the night before, but there was something else, a look of bewilderment and fear. She could feel her hair straining against her scalp and she tried to wriggle away, but he held her in a firm grasp. 'It was only once, wasn't it, Grace? Tell me it was only once, you and . . . him. He forced you, didn't he, Grace? Tell me he made you do it.'

'Yes . . . yes, just the once,' Grace whispered. It was a lie, but what did it matter now? Once or several times, it made no difference. She hadn't been a virgin on her wedding night as Walter had expected. What a fool she had been, she thought now, to imagine that he wouldn't know. But Grace, in her innocence, had never so much as given the matter a thought. She was tempted to retaliate by saying that it hadn't been the first time for him either, but she knew that to do so would be futile. Obviously there was one rule for women and a completely different one for men, something she had always known but only now had it come home to her.

'We only made love once,' she repeated as calmly as she could, and, to her relief, Walter let go of her and flopped down in the chair opposite her.

He leaned his elbows on the table, staring down

at the empty plate in front of him. He didn't look at Grace as he spoke. 'You've hurt me, Grace. You've hurt me badly. But I'll try to forget that you . . . deceived me. But I was horrified to find out about you and him . . .'

'All right, Walter. Let it rest now.' Grace's voice was apathetic and her face expressionless as she set about the trivial task of getting her husband's breakfast. 'I'll brew some fresh tea. This'll be stewed by now. And I'll make you some toast. Or would you like bacon?'

'No, toast'll be fine, thank you.'

They were like a couple of strangers making the minimum of polite conversation. Grace couldn't wait for Walter to finish his breakfast and get off to work, then she could have the house to herself. She wanted to be alone, but it wasn't because she wanted to think. What good would thoughts do? She only knew that their marriage had got off to a bad start – it could hardly have had a worse one – and no matter how Walter might try to make amends their wedding night, something that should have been lovely and memorable, had been besmirched. She wondered if their marriage could ever succeed after such a terrible, traumatic beginning. And she was aware that Walter hadn't said that he was sorry. All that he seemed concerned about was his own hurt feelings. The fact that she was hurt, too, didn't seem to matter to him.

Walter, too, was miserable the day after the wedding, although he tried to hide his dejection, surrounded as he was by the banter and cheerful innuendoes of his colleagues.

'Bags under the eyes this morning, Walter!'

'Start as you mean to go on. Let her know who's boss . . .'

'By heck, you'd better let me hold the reins, Walter lad, or the horse'll be rampaging all over the show. There'll be coal all over t'road.'

His disappointment was like a sickness at the core of him, making him view everything through a grey cloud of apathy. He had tried so hard during their brief courtship, after that joyous moment when she had agreed to marry him, to be kind and considerate towards Grace, to let only the better part of himself show. And it hadn't been too difficult, so elated had he been that this lovely girl had at last agreed to become his wife. The baser side of his nature, which he thought of as his own personal devil, had been subdued; the lustful thoughts and the pride and the wickedness within him that had made him want to torment Grace and frighten her. He had longed for the wedding night to come, to know that she was his and his alone. And then . . . what a bitter blow it had been for him to discover . . . His jaw clenched and his fists tightened into balls again at the thought of it. He had been unable to quell the rage inside him. He had wanted to hurt her physically, to strike out at her, to shake her till she was senseless. Instead he had been guilty of what he knew almost amounted to rape. God forgive me, he prayed silently. I'll try to love her. I'll try to forget that I wasn't the first. I'll try to forget that she cheated on me . . . But, like Grace, he wondered if their marriage could survive such a shocking start. And although he had asked for God's forgiveness it didn't occur to him that he should also ask his wife to forgive him.

They settled down into a routine, Walter departing each day at eight o'clock for his job at Henderson's and Grace busying herself with the household chores. She no longer worked at the draper's shop in Queen's Square and never, if she could help it, did she go anywhere near Donnelly's. She visited her mother a few times a week and occasionally made the journey out to Marton Moss to see her sister, and every Sunday she and Walter attended chapel. She couldn't have said that she was happy or even contented; she just existed. Walter's frenzied assault of that first night had, thankfully, not been repeated, but his lovemaking, a nightly occurrence, left her unmoved. Not that she could think of it as lovemaking; she could not use the word 'love' in connection with Walter. He no longer told her that he loved her, although his eyes roved over her body longingly, and his hands too, skilful and exploring. But he could not rouse her; she was unable to forget the brutal words that he had spoken to her that first night or the way he had used her. She was even glad for the few days' respite each month when her period started, in spite of the pain it often brought, and prayed that soon the nightly ritual, which was how she thought of it, would bear some fruit. Then, perhaps, there would be some point in it all. Grace desperately longed for a child.

Walter found solace in his preaching. He loved the intimate surroundings of the small partitioned room at the chapel, one of several similar rooms, where he conducted his weekly class meetings. He liked to be there first, to light the single gas lamp, to set out his register and hymn book and huge Bible on the red plush cloth on the table, to feel himself the sovereign of his little kingdom awaiting his loyal subjects. There were never more than about ten of them, a couple of working men – like himself – but mainly women, middle aged and sombrely dressed, escaping for an hour or so from the confines of their homes to seek a little warmth and company in different surroundings. After he had greeted each of them with a handshake they sang a hymn, usually unaccompanied, followed by a time of prayer. Anyone who felt inclined could pray out loud, bringing their petitions or their thanksgivings to the Almighty. Some always chose to remain silent. Grace couldn't help but think, on the rare occasions that she accompanied Walter, that the unspoken prayers that she was sure these taciturn members uttered in their hearts were probably the most sincere. There was no doubting the sincerity of her own prayers, ones that were far too private to be spoken out loud. Others seemed to love the sound of their own voices, praying on and on, *ad infinitum*, for their own families, for the Queen and her family, for the wider family of God, our brothers and sisters over the seas . . . and Uncle Tom Cobleigh and all, Grace found herself thinking irreverently. But other prayers she could sympathise with; the woman who asked the Lord to help her to be a good mother, or the one who prayed that her husband would bring his money home instead of spending it at the pub. At the end of each prayer Walter would repeat the same words, 'Praise the Lord. Amen to that.'

But, more than the class meetings, Walter loved the atmosphere of a full chapel on a Sunday, especially when he had been invited, as a lay preacher, to bring the word of God to the congregation. When he stood in the pulpit and looked down at the sea of upturned faces there was an awed hush and Walter knew that he held these people in the palm of his hand, that they would hang on to his every word. His sermons, like the more informal addresses that he gave to his weekly class, were usually concerned with sin and repentance.

'Repent . . . or ye shall perish.'

'Repent . . . and be converted that your sins may be blotted out.'

'Repent . . . of this thy wickedness,' he would thunder from the pulpit.

Grace found it all somewhat confusing. Repent . . . of what? she wondered. How could these ordinary folk, the soberly dressed women – boarding-house keepers, many of them, like her mother – the working men, tram drivers and penpushing clerks, plumbers and builder's mates and carpenters, be possessed of such wickedness as Walter hinted at in his powerful orations from the pulpit?

'We have all sinned and fallen short of the glory of God,' Walter told her sanctimoniously. 'There is evil at the heart of each one of us. We all need the cleansing power of the Lord. You have been guilty of sin, Grace.' He looked at her meaningfully, and she knew to what he was referring. 'And so have I . . .' he added, as if in an afterthought.

Grace couldn't accept this God that Walter proclaimed with such passion, a harsh, unrelenting being. He seemed to be a God of vengeance and anger, a God who would be more concerned with punishment than forgiveness. Yes, she had sinned, she knew, in giving herself so unreservedly to Edwin. Walter would never let her forget it. He had never mentioned it again, not in so many words, but the knowledge of her offence was there between them. She could tell by the way he looked at her sometimes, his eyes narrowed calculatingly, and in the way he used her body each night, not so roughly as that first time, but casually, as though he were satisfying his own needs and giving no thought to Grace's feelings. Her sin, if that was what it was, had happened because of her love for Edwin. And she knew in her heart that the God that she worshipped, a God of love and mercy, had already forgiven her, even if Walter never could.

Walter's moods, and his preaching too, Grace discovered, were influenced greatly by the changes in the weather. Walter loved the sudden storms that descended upon Blackpool – one of the few things about the town that he could be said to enjoy, Grace thought – the wildness of the wind and the waves and the torrential rain. He would often come home soaked to the skin after a walk on the promenade when most folks in their right minds would be safely ensconced by their cosy firesides.

The October following their marriage some of

the worst storms in living memory played havoc with the Fylde coast. This, of course, was the usual cry. 'HIGH TIDE OF 30 FEET', 'WORST STORM FOR 50 YEARS', the headlines in the local *Gazette* would proclaim whenever Blackpool suffered, as it frequently did, from the extremities of the British climate. And the oldest of the local inhabitants would gather together telling one another with ghoulish delight, 'I've never seen owt like it, not since I were knee-high to a grasshopper.'

'You should see the damage, Grace,' Walter told her, almost delightedly, after a foray on to the battered promenade. 'Oyster stalls ripped up all over the place, and the iron railings are all broken down an' all. And Claremont Park's taken a fair hammering. There must be hundreds of tons of earth fallen into the sea. They'll have to watch out for Uncle Tom's Cabin up on t'cliffs or the whole lot'll be collapsing before long.'

'Oh dear! How dreadful,' Grace replied. 'It's awful the damage that a storm can do. And whenever it happens folk always seem to be unprepared.'

'We know not the day nor the hour, Grace,' said Walter piously. 'There's a parable to be learned from that. And there's tremendous power there at the height of the storm. You can sense the authority of Almighty God in the wind and the waves.' His eyes gleamed with crusading vigour, the way they did when he was in the pulpit.

Grace didn't answer. Grace's God was the one who had quelled the storm, who had murmured, 'Peace be still.' The God who came not in the earthquake and wind and fire, but in the still

502

small voice of calm. The God who comforted her in the hours of darkness when she lay wide awake and unhappy and lonely. A very different God from the one whom Walter worshipped.

In February 1897 a son was born to Hetty and Reuben.

'We're going to call him Zachary,' said Hetty, her green eyes glowing with pride as she looked down at the tiny bundle she held in her arms. 'Zachary Frederick – that's for our father, of course.'

The birth had not been a difficult one; indeed to look at Hetty sitting up in bed, rosy-cheeked and radiant, you could hardly believe that only a few hours before she had been suffering the pangs of childbirth. I only hope I get through it as easily, thought Grace, for she now had some happy news of her own to impart. It was hardly likely, she knew, that she would give birth with such ease as her sister had done, but she would gladly suffer the pain to know that she had a tiny being she could love and cherish, a baby who might be the means of bringing her and her husband closer together. There had been no doubt about Walter's delight when she had told him and, just for a moment, she had seen his eyes glow with unfamiliar warmth as he looked at her.

Grace leaned over now and pulled back the blue blanket that enveloped the baby so that she could see his tiny face more clearly. The little clenched fists, freed from the restraining cover, punched exploringly at the air. His hair was black, clinging to his head in moist curling tendrils and, though his eyes were closed, she guessed that they, too, would be dark like his father's.

'He's beautiful, Hetty,' she whispered, kissing her sister's cheek, 'and not at all red and wrinkled either.' Little Zachary was dark-complexioned, showing every sign of being a true Loveday child. Grace looked slyly at her sister. 'I hope mine is as beautiful. Not that it matters, does it? I shall love him – or her – whatever he looks like.'

'Grace!' Hetty looked at her with wide-eyed delight. 'You mean that you are . . .?' Grace nodded. 'That's marvellous.' Hetty squeezed her sister's hand. 'I'm really thrilled for you. When is it?'

'Oh, not for ages. The middle of September or thereabouts. I've only just found out for certain.'

'And Walter's pleased, is he? Of course, he must be.'

'Yes . . . He seems to be pleased.'

Hetty looked keenly at her sister. 'You're all right, aren't you, Grace? You're quite . . . happy? I know I never cared much for Walter, but he hasn't seemed too bad lately and, after all, you married him, didn't you?' Her glance was enquiring. 'I like to think that you're happy.'

'Yes, don't worry, Hetty.' Grace smiled at her sister. 'We're . . . all right.' She had never told anyone about the disastrous start to her marriage, and now, perhaps, with the child to look forward to, things would be better. 'And the baby will help, when it arrives,' she added. 'Yes, we're quite happy.'

'Oh, I do want you to be,' said Hetty fervently. 'Reuben and I are so happy that sometimes I can't believe it all. I sometimes feel that it's . . . it's too

504

wonderful to last, that it will all disappear in a puff of smoke, or that I'll wake up and find that I've dreamt it all.'

'It's all real enough, Hetty,' said Grace smiling. 'And I'm so glad you're happy. So is Mam. It makes her feel so much better about . . . everything. And you've got it real nice in here now. It's not so spartan-looking as it was at first.'

Grace looked round admiringly at the lino which now covered the once bare floorboards, the strip of blue carpet at the side of the bed which matched the blue daisy-patterned cotton curtains at the windows, and the washstand with the jug and bowl also patterned in blue flowers. Hetty and Reuben hadn't much money, but their little cottage, though sparsely furnished, was a happy, homely place. Downstairs, too, they had made what little improvements they could afford and their tiny parlour was now furnished with a couple of second-hand easy chairs and a triangular display cabinet which stood in a corner. It didn't matter that Hetty had little to display; this item was her pride and joy and she lovingly filled it with her ordinary earthenware cups and saucers, and childhood treasures – shells and coloured stones, a favourite wax doll and a minute doll's tea set. Some day she, too, might have a china tea service as exquisite as the one that Ruth Loveday owned, but for the moment Hetty was more than content.

'Yes, we're not doing too badly now,' Hetty told her sister. 'Reuben does well at the markets with his wood-carvings, and in the spring we're going to develop our own little plot of land, like all the folks round here do. We'll grow lettuces and radishes, peas and beans an' all that. We might even grow tomatoes if we can get hold of a little greenhouse, and we'll sell 'em at the markets along with the wooden things.'

'You'll be looking forward to going to the markets with Reuben again, won't you, when the baby's a bit bigger?' said Grace. She knew how Hetty had enjoyed going along with her husband at one time, taking pride in his work and sharing the task of selling with him.

'Yes, I'll go back when the chavvy's grown up a bit.' Hetty laughed. 'Hark at me! I sound just like one of them, don't I? It just shows how like Reuben I'm getting. It won't be very long before I'm able to take this little 'un along with us.' She looked fondly at the child in her arms and bent to kiss his cheek. 'I haven't been to market very much lately, not since I had that bad do in the autumn. Reuben's made sure that I've been careful. I was very lucky to have such an easy time. The doctor came – Reuben made sure of that; he fusses over me like an old mother hen – but Eliza next door's been very good an' all. I don't know what we'd do without her.'

'You'll be having a visit from Drusilla soon, I daresay?' said Grace.

'Yes . . .' Hetty sighed. 'Reuben thought he'd better go and tell them all at the encampment this afternoon, while you and Mam are here. Yes, I expect Drusilla'll be round before long. It's funny though, Grace; I'm not so worried about her now. She's been as nice as pie ever since that time when I nearly lost the baby. I think Reuben had a few words with her then, 'cos she's never called when I've been on me own since then. I used to get in a proper state about her . . . Strange, wasn't it?'

'Women get funny ideas when they're carrying,' said Grace smiling. 'I expect my turn will come. Here's Mam with a cup of tea for us.' She nodded towards the doorway and they could hear the rattle of tea cups as Martha carefully made her way up the creaky winding staircase.

'You've told Mam, I suppose, about your good news?' said Hetty.

'Oh yes, she's tickled pink at the thought of another grandchild.' Grace smiled. 'And just think, Hetty. Both our babies will have been born in Jubilee year.'

Queen Victoria's Diamond Jubilee was celebrated in Blackpool as it was in towns and villages all over Britain. The bells of St John's church rang out early on the morning of 22 June 1897, announcing the opening of the day's festivities. It was a public holiday for workers in the town and Grace and Walter walked through the streets arm in arm, admiring the flags and streamers and red, white and blue banners that fluttered from all the main buildings. The promenade and Talbot Square were particularly splendid, as was nearby North Pier, and the pleasure steamers that left from there were all adorned in colourful bunting, likewise the bathing vans and stalls on the sands. Donnelly's store, like several others, displayed a portrait of the Queen in a main window, surrounded by red, white and blue ribbon, and the

507

men's and women's apparel on show in the windows was also in patriotic colours.

Grace and Walter stood in Talbot Square and watched the military procession led by the band of the Derbyshire volunteers. It was a sunny day; real Jubilee weather, everyone was saying. The sun glinted on the polished bayonets and the heavy guns, and the red coats of the infantrymen contrasting with the dark uniforms of the artillerymen all made up a thrilling and memorable spectacle. And, above it all, Blackpool Tower dominated, sporting on its flagstaff the flag of the blue ensign, with flags of Britain and America and other nations fluttering from the turrets.

A couple of weeks later Grace and Walter again stood looking up at the Tower, but this time the famous structure was on fire. Walter had come in with the startling news after his weekly class meeting, and the two of them stood together at the corner of Central Drive watching in horror as the red flames flickered round the top of the huge iron structure.

'Look!' Grace cried in alarm. 'There's some men up there. Can you see them?' Against the vivid orange background tiny black figures could be seen frantically trying to beat down the flames. 'Oh . . . They'll be killed. I know they will. Oh, I hardly dare to look.' Grace was terrified and hid her eyes as the sound of crackling woodwork reached their ears and sparks from the fire were carried away in glittering showers by the west wind.

'Don't worry. They know what they're doing all right. Aye, it looks as though the fire brigade have arrived now.' Walter sounded excited and when Grace looked at him she could see that his eyes were alight, just as they had been when he told her of the storm damage, just as they were when he stood in the pulpit.

'Come on, Walter. Let's go home,' said Grace. She pulled at his arm. 'I don't want to see any more.'

'All right . . . I'm coming.' But Walter was reluctant to leave and his eyes kept straying back to the scene of the disaster. Grace felt that there were many things about her husband that she would never understand.

Sarah Florence Clayton was born on 25 September 1897, and as Grace looked down at the child lying in her arms she felt that the misery of the early days of her marriage was now vindicated. This beautiful child to love and to live for made everything worthwhile. She had agreed with Walter that they should call the little girl Florence, after his mother, for one of her names, but Sarah had been Grace's idea and he seemed well pleased with the choice.

'Well chosen, Grace,' he said. 'Yes, we shall call her Sarah.' He clasped his hands together and nodded his head earnestly. 'A fine Biblical name.'

'Yes, maybe it is,' said Grace, smiling at him. 'Sarah was Abraham's wife, wasn't she? A greedy, grasping sort of woman, I always thought,' she added boldly. 'That isn't why I chose it, I can assure you. I just happen to like it, and it also means "princess". And that's what she is. A real little princess. I'll bet Queen Victoria wasn't as

509

proud of any of her brood as I am of our little Sarah.'

Grace tenderly touched the baby's dark curling hair, so like her own, and put her finger in the little palm, thrilling to feel the tiny fingers clutching hold of her. She smiled again at Walter, not wanting him to feel left out. Yes, little Sarah would prove to be a very rich blessing, she was sure.

Chapter 22

Drusilla cowered behind the hawthorn hedge from where she could see, between the fresh green leaves and the white blossoms, the row of white-washed cottages opposite. This was the third time this week that she had waited here, starting her vigil before the sun had begun to warm the earth and while the grass was still wet with early-morning dew. And twice she had been foiled in her plan; both times Henrietta had stayed at home with the chavvy and Reuben had set off in the trap with Jack Braithwaite, his next-door neigh-bour. Perhaps today it would be a case of 'third time lucky'.

Drusilla had known for some time that she was unable to do any harm to Henrietta by the Evil Eye alone. She had tried and, to a point, she knew she had succeeded. The girl had been afraid of her – Reuben had admitted it – and Drusilla knew that Henrietta's near miscarriage had not been brought about because she had overworked when they first moved into the cottage, not entirely. She, Drusilla, had had a hand in it too. But her power was not strong enough. What she had told Reuben once was true; she wasn't able to harm the girl. Her undoubted power in the art of evil wishing was not sufficient to withstand the forces that were aligned against her; the force of Reuben and Henrietta's love for one another. Love was the greatest force on earth and Drusilla knew that the love that these two had for one another could never be broken. She knew it intuitively when she looked at them, and it filled her with an unspeakable rage and hatred for the girl who had taken her cousin away from her.

If it hadn't been for Hetty Turnbull, Reuben would have been hers by now. That was the name by which she still thought of the girl. Never, never, never would she think of her as a Loveday. She was not worthy of the name. Reuben had been beginning to warm towards her, Drusilla, to be more chatty and friendly and once or twice she was certain she had seen a flicker of desire in his eyes . . . before that girl came along. Drusilla knew, of course, that she had blotted her copybook by her extreme behaviour when her parents had died. But her aunt and uncle had forgiven her – after all, it was not uncommon for Romany women to behave in that fashion – and she had known that if she watched her step and behaved as decorously as someone of her volatile nature was able to do then before long Reuben would be hers. He was her cousin, and Romanies liked marriages to take place within the family whenever possible. Reuben had been ripe for marriage and so had she . . . Then Hetty Turnbull had come on the scene.

And now there was another little Loveday to cement their relationship even further. Drusilla was not particularly fond of children, but she had to admit that little Zachary was a handsome child, a real heart-stealer with his black curly hair and his luminous dark eyes. He was over a year old now and growing more like his father every day. There didn't appear to be much of his mother in him, Drusilla thought with satisfied malice, but Hetty was the child's mother and besotted with him from all appearances. Drusilla's jealousy grew apace as she watched the three of them together, a happy family unit with herself in the role of the visiting aunt, the outsider looking in.

She had disguised her envy very well, so much so that Hetty appeared almost relaxed in her company now. Drusilla visited them about once a week, often bearing some little gift – a ball or a rattle or a few coloured building bricks – for the chavvy, or wild flowers from the fields and hedgerows for Hetty to display in a jug and brighten up their meagre home. And all the time Drusilla had been watching and waiting, listening so that she would know about their every movement, carefully devising her plan.

At one time, soon after the child was born, her hatred had reached such a frenzy that she had been tempted to set fire to the place, to creep there at dead of night when they were all peacefully sleeping in their beds and set a match to some dry tinder, then to watch the whole lot go up in flames. But that would have harmed Reuben and the chavvy, too, and that was not what she wanted. Only Henrietta . . . she alone was the target for Drusilla's enmity and her evil plan.

The girl had been protected, from evil wishing

at least, by wearing the coral necklace. Drusilla knew, to her chagrin, that she was largely responsible for this. She cursed the day when, in an unguarded moment, she had rebuked her cousin's wife for not wearing it. When she had seen Hetty pop it casually into the Jubilee mug on the mantelpiece Drusilla had been overjoyed. Now she knew the hiding-place it shouldn't prove difficult, on one of her visits, to secrete the coveted necklace in her hand, then to transfer it to her apron pocket and make away with it. But the dratted girl had never had it off her neck since that day.

'Reuben says you're right,' Hetty had told her cheerfully. 'I've got to wear the necklace to keep me safe, so I'm doing as I'm told, see?' Laughingly she had displayed the pieces of carved coral glowing on her neck beneath the collar of her blouse, and Drusilla had felt an almost uncontrollable urge to put her hands round that slender white column and squeeze . . . But it was not the time. She had to wait and to simulate friendship with Henrietta, so that when the time came she would be taken unawares and Drusilla would never be suspected.

Anxiously she watched now for some sign of life at the cottage. They wouldn't come out of the front door – that, she knew, was rarely used – but at any moment they should appear from round the back, with luck all three of them. She held her breath and waited . . . In a few moments she heard the distant sound of a door slamming, then she saw Reuben coming round the corner of the cottage. Was he on his own again? Drusilla could feel the muscles in her neck and shoulders begin

514

to tighten with anxiety and she bit frenziedly at her lip. Then a moment later Hetty followed with the child in her arms. Drusilla could hear him chortling and could see him pulling at his mother's auburn curls, and her heart contracted with the force of her hatred, but also with relief that her plan was, at last, working. Drusilla knew that it would be several hours before they returned. She waited until she saw Jack Braithwaite emerge from his own cottage, then all four of them piled into the trap and Jack took hold of the reins and the pony clip-clopped off down the lane with the trap bouncing and swaying behind him.

Drusilla watched from her hiding-place but didn't creep out until the trap was well out of sight; she had to be very sure they had gone. Then she gloatingly patted at the small basket that hung over her arm and hurried round to the back door. With a bit of luck it would be open. Hetty sometimes followed the gorgio habit of locking the door, but often she left it open. After all, as Drusilla had heard her say laughingly, they had nothing to steal. But if by some chance today was a day that she had decided to be extra careful, then Drusilla knew where a spare key was always kept, under a bucket near the privy at the end of the garden. Drusilla looked round furtively to make sure she wasn't being observed then she turned the door knob. The door opened at once and she knew she was in luck.

She hurried into the kitchen and placed her small basket on the pine table, then, with a malicious smile, she drew out the contents and held them triumphantly in her hands. There were three of them; that should be more than sufficient for her purposes. She examined them carefully now; flesh of a pearly whiteness, but at the centre of each one the telltale tinge of yellowish-green, obvious to someone steeped in the lore of the fields, woods and hedgerows and the plants and fungi that grew there, but a detail which would go unnoticed by a greenhorn such as Henrietta. Drusilla glanced round now to make sure that the main component of her plan was there in the kitchen; if not then it would all be useless. Yes, luck was certainly with her today. There, on a shelf in the pantry, just a small alcove in a corner of the kitchen, was a basket of mushrooms, one of Hetty's favourite ingredients for a meal and one which Reuben detested.

Drusilla had stored away this knowledge at the back of her mind ages ago and gradually her plan had come to fruition. This was a sure way of harming the girl without affecting Reuben. She lifted up the three deadly mushrooms and bent her head to sniff at them. She wrinkled her nose; yes, there was a slightly unpleasant smell, but Hetty would never notice that when they were mixed in with the harmless field mushrooms.

Drusilla remembered how, at first, Reuben had made a fuss about his wife gathering mushrooms, saying, quite rightly, that she didn't know what she was doing and that fungi were not always what they seemed. Then Eliza Braithwaite, the woman next door, had started cultivating her own, and these were the ones that Hetty always used now. She generally had a basket of them to hand and Drusilla had been almost certain that today would be no exception. She put the three death cap mushrooms, as they were commonly called, on the table and looked at them, her eyes narrowing with venom. She knew what would happen if they were eaten; Romany friends had told her a long time ago, and this knowledge, too, had remained locked in a secret compartment of her mind. Then, one day in her wanderings round the countryside near Marton Moss, she had found a place where they grew, a secluded spot at the edge of a wood. They would cause vomiting and gastric pain and sweating, and could prove fatal if the person was not treated quickly. And the beauty of them, so she had been told, was that any apparent recovery was only an illusion. The symptoms often recurred, leading to death.

Drusilla's eyes, darting like a kingfisher, scanned the room, her glance resting on each object that Hetty cherished with such loving care. But she would not be cherishing them for much longer, thought Drusilla vengefully . . . There was that fairing of the sailor and his sweetheart that Reuben had won for her at the rifle range. Drusilla was tempted to fling it into the hearth and see it smash into pieces, but she knew that she must leave no clue that she had been here. And there were the brass candlesticks and the blue jug that Martha Turnbull had given her daughter to make the place look more homely. That was another, more minor reason for Drusilla's uncontrollable jealousy of the girl; a loving mother who made a fuss of her and to whom she could always turn in time of trouble, while Drusilla's own mother had been so cruelly snatched away from her in the prime of her life.

Her eyes rested now on the Jubilee mug, the hiding place at one time of the coral necklace that Drusilla coveted so much, but now Hetty wore it constantly. There was no harm in looking though. Drusilla hurried across to the mantelpiece, picked up the mug and put her hand inside. To her surprise and unbelievable joy she felt her fingers caressing the fine silver chain and the fragments of carved coral. With a cry of delight she drew it out and held it up, watching the light play on the pinky-orange pieces and the glittering silver chain on which they were suspended. So mesmerised was she by the precious necklace that she had coveted for so long and which was now in her grasp that she didn't hear the door open behind her.

'Drusilla!' The unexpected voice sounded like a gunshot in the room.

She gave a gasp of astonishment and turned quickly. 'Reuben!' Her mouth dropped open in horror. 'Whatever are you doing here?'

He took a few steps towards her, his eyes narrowing with suspicion. 'Shouldn't it be me that's asking that? I live here, don't I? What are you doing here, Drusilla, that's more to the point?' Her hand had gone quickly behind her back, but he pulled at her arm, then prised open the clenched fingers. 'You be choring, you thieving little minx! I might have known!'

She saw his eyes glint with anger and she began to feel afraid. It was all going wrong and, what was more, the deadly mushrooms were lying on the table. She must try to sneak them back into her basket and get away as soon as possible. There was no hope now of carrying out her plan today. What a thing to happen and when it had all been going so well.

Peevishly she flung the necklace to the floor. 'Take it then and give it back to your precious wife! Not that she deserves it. She doesn't deserve it one bit. She ain't even wearing it. A fat lot she cares, I must say, for your mother's prized possession.' All the time she was speaking she had been moving backwards till she now stood in front of the table, hiding the mushrooms from her cousin's view.

'It was broken, that's why Henrietta wasn't wearing it,' said Reuben as he stooped to retrieve the necklace from the floor. He held it up, examining it, speaking quietly as if to himself. 'Little Zachary pulled at it and the catch came loose . . . I mended it for her last night when she'd gone to bed, then I popped it in the mug to keep it safe. And she went and forgot it this morning. That's what I came back for . . . Not that it's any of your business,' he added angrily, 'but that's what I'm doing here, Drusilla. I've come to pick up my wife's necklace, and it's a damn good job I did an' all, you thieving hussy. Now get out before I do something I might regret.' He pointed towards the door. 'Do 'ee hear me, Drusilla? Get out . . . now!'

Drusilla hesitated, her hands behind her back, trying to feel for the mushrooms. 'D'you mean to say you've come back just to get a necklace? Couldn't she have managed without it for one day?' She was stalling for time, aware that Reuben was looking at her suspiciously.

'I don't like her to be without it at all, 'ee knows that. No, as a matter of fact I came back to lock the door an' all. Henrietta forgot this morning and she feels better if she knows the place is secure. And she was right, wasn't she, with thieves like you around? I shall be more careful to lock the door in future, I'll tell 'ee. Now, Jack Braithwaite's waiting for me at the end of the lane, so get out, Drusilla, before I have to throw you out.' He took a step towards her, his arm upraised. 'Go on, move yerself. Now . . .'

He looked at her distrustfully as she still made no move towards the door. 'What the hell are you playing at, Drusilla? What's that behind your back?' He grabbed hold of her and fiercely pushed her to one side. 'What the hell . . .? He stared at the three large mushrooms on the table, then at Drusilla, then back again at the mushrooms. He picked them up in his hands and turned them round, then bent his head to sniff at them. 'You . . . you . . . wicked scheming bitch!' He threw the mushrooms to the floor then seized hold of Drusilla by the shoulders, shaking her back and forth till her head lolled from side to side like a rag doll. 'You were trying . . . to poison her . . . You wicked . . . depraved creature. Henrietta was right all along . . . You were trying to . . .'

Suddenly he let go of her and the force of his movement sent her staggering across the room. She banged into the dresser and a blue-rimmed plate fell to the ground, smashing into pieces on the stone-flagged floor. With one fierce swoop Reuben picked up the mushrooms and flung them into the open fire in the centre of the range, which

Hetty had banked up that morning before they left. They sizzled and spat, then a noxious brown juice ran out and began to trickle over the coals.

'That's the end of that little scheme . . .' Reuben put his hand out and leaned it against the side of the range to steady himself. His head drooped dejectedly and he shook it slowly backwards and forwards, staring at the hearth, not speaking for several moments. When he did his voice was unbelieving, but less angry now, more puzzled. 'But why, Drusilla? For God's sake . . . why? The lass has never done you any harm. For you to hate her like that . . .'

'Yes . . . I hate her!' Drusilla had recovered from her momentary fright now and she stood in the centre of the room in her customary stance, hands on her hips, her head tilted defiantly and her eyes blazing as she stared at her cousin. 'I've always hated her. She's no business to be here at all, marrying into good Romany stock. I warned you at the start that no good could come of it, but you wouldn't listen. She's nothing but gorgio trash . . .'

'Don't you dare speak about my wife like that! I love her. Do 'ee hear me? I love her.' Reuben took hold of Drusilla by the shoulders, his fingers digging hard into her flesh as he forced her to look at him. 'She's all I ever wanted, and all I ever will want, so there. Oh yes . . . I know what 'ee wanted, Drusilla. But let me tell 'ee this; even if I hadn't met Henrietta I'd never, never, have wed 'ee, not in a thousand years.'

'Leave go of me then. Get away from me.' Drusilla shrugged herself free from her cousin's grip and pushed at him with both hands. 'Go to your trashy, good-for-nothing wife then, and may the pair of you rot in hell. Cheap little upstart that she is . . .'

'How dare you? How dare you . . .?' Reuben lunged at her wildly, but she jumped sideways out of his reach. His foot caught on the corner of the clipped rag rug and he stumbled. There was nothing in his path to break his fall and he fell heavily to the ground. There was a sickening crack as his head struck the corner of the steel fender, then he rolled over and lay motionless on the stone floor.

'Reuben . . . Reuben . . .' Drusilla dashed across to him and knelt by the side of his inert form. His head was twisted at a strange angle and she could see blood trickling from a wound on his temple. Panic-stricken now, she leaned over him and took hold of his head in both her hands. 'Reuben . . . Reuben, love . . . I'm sorry. I didn't mean it. I love you, Reuben . . . Reuben . . .' Her voice diminished to a whisper, then suddenly changed to a horrified scream. 'Oh, Reuben! Oh, dear God, no . . .!' as his head lolled back like a broken doll and his sightless eyes stared up at her.

'Oh . . . Dordi, Dordi . . . He can't be . . . He can't be . . .' She shook him now and pummelled him, her hands beating wildly on his chest, frantically trying to bring back some movement into his lifeless form. Then she put her ear to his breast and listened . . . He couldn't be . . . It just wasn't possible. All he had done was to fall and bang his head. One minute he had been alive and shouting at her, and the next minute he was . . . She shook her head in bewilderment, all the while murmuring, 'Reuben . . . Oh, Reuben, speak to me.' How could he be . . . dead so quickly? He couldn't be. But she knew that the force of his rage had made him fall heavily and she could hear again in her mind that stomach-turning crack as his head had struck the fender.

There was nothing to be done. Reuben was past any help now. 'Oh, my God! What have I done?' Drusilla sat back on her haunches as the terrified whisper issued from her lips. She grabbed hold of his hand and held it to her mouth, but it slid from her grasp and fell to his side with a chilling thud.

I must go. I must get out. Now. Before she comes back. Drusilla was frightened out of her wits, but even at the height of her terror she knew that she mustn't leave any clue that she had been here. She snatched the empty basket from the table and ran, out of the door, down the side of the house and into the lane. She had no coherent plan in mind. All she knew was that she had to get away from here before Henrietta came back. She would be back before long, surely, wondering what had happened to Reuben. Drusilla ran until she was well clear of the row of cottages, then she was forced to slow down by the pain in her side and her heart thumping madly against her ribs. She leaned against a hawthorn hedge gasping for breath, but she knew that there was no time to lose. She must get right away from here, and away from the encampment, too, before Reuben came looking for her. No . . . whatever was she thinking about? It was because of Reuben that she had to go. Reuben was . . . Even now her brain couldn't grasp the dreadful thought. But she knew that she must escape, before they came to get her . . .

'He's an awful long time, Jack,' said Hetty, after they had been waiting at the end of the lane for about a quarter of an hour. 'He said he'd only be a few minutes.'

'Aye, I was just thinking the same thing meself, lass.' Jack looked at her concernedly. 'And I'm afraid I won't be able to wait much longer. We got an early start this morning, that's why I suggested that Reuben should go back, but it's a fair stretch to Kirkham and I'm not going to get there in time if I don't get a move on.'

'What d'you suppose has happened to him, Jack?'

'Nowt much, lass, I don't suppose. Don't start fretting yerself.' Jack smiled at her and patted her hand, but his shrewd blue eyes looked anxious. 'But happen you'd better get off home and find out. I'd best come along with you. A few minutes'll not make much difference now.'

'No, you mustn't, Jack. You're late enough already. It'll only take me five minutes to walk back down the lane. That's why I can't understand Reuben taking so long. Perhaps he's feeling ill, or he's fallen and twisted his ankle . . .'

'Or more like he's chatting to someone.' Jack grinned. 'Don't start imagining things, Hetty love. Now, are you sure you can manage, lass? The bairn's getting a bit heavy for carrying, ain't he?'

'He'll walk alongside of me, won't you, Zachary, love?' Hetty jumped down from the trap, then lifted the child down and took hold of his hand. 'Come on. Let's go and see what's keeping Dada. Thanks, Jack, for waiting, but I can't hold you up any longer. Seems as though the Lovedays'll have to give Kirkham a miss today.' She frowned. 'There must be something up. He'd have been back by now . . .'

Her screams could be heard through the thin walls of the adjoining cottage, and Eliza Braithwaite came running immediately on hearing them.

'Now, what's up, lovey?' She poked her cheerful red face round the kitchen door, then stopped dead in her tracks. 'Oh, dear God in heaven! Whatever's happened?'

Her eyes took in the scene at a glance. Hetty kneeling by the prostrate form of her husband, holding on to his hand and sobbing and screaming, but him, poor lad, well beyond the sound of any mortal voice, and the child sitting on the clipped hearthrug playing unconcernedly with the silver and coral necklace, the one that Hetty usually wore.

'Oh, my God!' Eliza closed her eyes in disbelief, but not for more than a few seconds. This poor lass needed her help. She went and knelt down beside her. 'Hetty . . . Hetty, love. Leave him. Come on now, there's a good girl. He's . . . gone, love.' She put an arm round the still sobbing girl and led her into the parlour. 'Come on, sit yerself down, and I'll see to the bairn. The poor little mite, we'd best get him out of here.'

She went quickly back into the kitchen.

'Zachary love, come on to Auntie Liza.' She stooped and picked up the child in her arms. 'I'll take him over to Mary Boardman. He'll be all right with her for an hour or two while we get ourselves sorted out. Now, stay there, Hetty, there's a good lass, and I'll be back in a tick.'

Eliza was fearful of leaving Hetty, even for a minute, but there was nothing else she could do. She had to get the child out of the way and at least the lass had stopped screaming. She was staring at Eliza now as though she couldn't take in what she was saying. It was the shock, of course. It was to be hoped that it dulled her senses for a while, because it was a tragedy of such huge proportions that Eliza herself could hardly believe it, and she'd seen some upsets in her time. It would be a terrible facer for the lass, and no mistake, when the awful truth hit her. Eliza knew that she would have to take care of her for the next few hours to make sure that the poor lass didn't go out of her mind. Her mother and sister were miles away at the other end of Blackpool and would have to be contacted before long, but first things first.

Mary Boardman, a good neighbour, agreed to look after the child with her own large family for as long as need be, while Eliza got on with all the necessary tasks. As unofficial midwife and layer-out in that small community it was her job to see to the routine business of getting the doctor and the undertaker, but never had there been a more tragic case than this one.

Hetty knew that she would never have managed to get through that dreadful day without Eliza Braithwaite. It was Eliza who saw to the laying-out of her beloved Reuben, dressing him, as was the gipsy custom, in his best clothes. Not that Reuben possessed anything very stylish, but Eliza dressed him in his dark-green suit with the silver buttons and the red neckerchief which he had been wearing when Hetty first met him and which, to her, personified Reuben.

'But why, Eliza, why?' Hetty cried out to her friend at intervals throughout that awful day as they sat drinking endless cups of tea. 'Why did it happen? How did it happen? It just doesn't make sense.'

'We'll never know, my love,' Eliza replied, holding the girl closely to her comfortable bosom. 'It was an accident. It must have been . . . just a terrible accident.'

'But why? It isn't like Reuben to be so careless. To fall like that . . . over nothing.'

'He may have had a dizzy spell. That's what the doctor thought, didn't he, love?'

'But Reuben never felt dizzy,' Hetty protested. 'He was as fit as a fiddle.' She stared round the kitchen again. Her husband's body had been removed to the small parlour where he would lie awaiting the visit of his friends from the encampment. They would be here soon, Hetty knew, once they heard the dreadful news. Her eyes scanned the kitchen once more, wondering . . . She had felt uneasy as soon as she came near the house, before she made the shocking discovery. She knew that there had been someone else there. There was a feeling of a malign presence, of hatred and jealousy . . . Her thoughts flew to Drusilla. Had the girl been here?

She asked again, as she had asked several times already, 'You're sure you didn't hear anything, Eliza. You didn't hear anybody shouting . . . any fighting?'

'No, I've told you, love.' Eliza shook her head sadly. 'I was down the garden, right at t'other end. I went there as soon as Jack left, and I'd only just come back when I heard you shouting. I couldn't have heard owt. Anyroad, you know what the doctor said, love. There was no sign of a struggle. The poor lad banged his head, that's for sure.' There had been traces of blood found on one of the knobs on the fender, but she didn't mention that now. 'Most likely he tripped up over the rag rug. It was all rucked up and he was in a hurry, wasn't he, to get back to Jack?'

'Yes . . . and that's all my fault.' Hetty turned a tear-stained face towards her friend. 'If he hadn't gone back to get the necklace this wouldn't have happened. He told me I'd always to wear it, and I forgot. He was right, wasn't he? It would have stopped all this from happening. If only I'd remembered this morning to put it on . . .'

'It's no use saying if, lovey. If this, if that . . . It's the most useless word there is, if . . . You'll have to try and think of the good things, in a little while, I mean. About how happy you and Reuben were . . .'

'But we were married such a short time, Eliza. Less than two years. It just isn't fair . . .'

'I know that, love.' Eliza sighed. 'There's very little that's fair about life at times. But I know one thing; you and Reuben had more happiness in that short time than most people have in a lifetime together. And you've got that grand little lad. I know it's very little consolation at the moment, but he'll be a blessing to you, Hetty. It was just an accident, love. A terrible accident.'

Hetty shook her head dazedly. She still wasn't convinced. There was that plate that had fallen off the dresser, smashed on the floor, and that was right at the other side of the room. Someone else had been there, she knew it, but she would never be able to prove it. The doctor was certain it had been an accident.

The coroner, too, the next day, was of the same opinion. Reuben Loveday had lost his life as the result of a very tragic accident. He expressed his sympathy to the young widow and her child, but he had no hesitation in granting a verdict of misadventure.

Hetty had wanted the funeral to be a very quiet one at the nearest churchyard, but she knew that she couldn't prevent Reuben's friends from the encampment from turning up in full force. She had agreed, too, with his friend, Luke Freeman, that they should postpone the burial for a day or two until Reuben's parents could be contacted and given the chance to attend. Drusilla, Luke told her, had vanished. She had been talking quite a lot recently about joining some of her other relations in another part of the country, so no one had been surprised – or sorry – to find that she had gone. Nor did they seem to think that there was anything coincidental about her being missing now. They had other more serious matters to think about. Reuben had been a friend who was highly regarded at the camp, whereas Drusilla had never been popular. But Hetty found that her suspicions were aroused even further by the young woman's absence . . .

Hetty knew a little, from what Reuben had told her, about Romany funeral customs, how gipsies didn't like to bury their dead during daylight hours. But, as his widow, she insisted on a Christian burial for Reuben. He had lived in a house, she insisted; he was well on the way to becoming a gorgio as well as a Romany. She had already gone along part-way with their customs by having him buried in his suit rather than in a shroud, and by placing in his coffin certain of his possessions, his knife and chisel and several of his wood-carvings. But she drew the line at his violin; it had been precious to Reuben and now it was a reminder to her of her beloved husband. Besides – who could tell? – one day little Zachary might find that he had inherited his father's gift.

Luke Freeman, a staunch friend to Reuben, and now a very necessary mainstay to Hetty, supported her with his arm and with the warmth of his sympathy as the coffin was lowered into the ground and the clods of earth fell heavily on the lid. There were very few of Hetty's own family and friends there. Martha, though devastated by the news of the tragedy, had nevertheless to cope with an influx of spring visitors at Welcome Rest, and Grace was looking after little Zachary. Jack Braithwaite was there, and Walter Clayton and Joss Jenkinson – just the three of them – so Hetty was grateful for the support of Reuben's Romany friends. Ruth and Eli Loveday had been brought back from the West Country. They were both white-faced and sombre and obviously shaken by the death of their beloved son, but they shed no tears at the graveside. Hetty knew that death, to the Romanies, was a very private matter and never would they allow themselves to show sorrow, especially should there be gorgios present. Their grief, Hetty felt sure, would come later, as would her own, when she was alone in her little cottage with her child, the fruit of the love that she would always have for Reuben.

The mourners dispersed after the simple burial service. Hetty hadn't the heart to ask them back to the house for a traditional funeral feast, and neither did they seem to expect it. Only Ruth and Eli came back with her, and Luke Freeman, and together they performed the last ritual that they could do for Reuben, the customary burning of his possessions. It was usual to set fire to the vardo of a dead gipsy, so that his spirit would not become jealous of anyone who might live there and come back and haunt them. Reuben hadn't lived in a caravan since his marriage, but Hetty felt that the least she could do was to humour his parents in this one macabre request.

As she watched his possessions being consumed by the flames – his suits and shirts and neckerchieves, his woodworking tools and much of the labour of his hands – Hetty felt as though her life, too, was coming to an end. What was the point of life without Reuben? But she knew that she had to put on a brave face for the moment in front of Reuben's parents and friend. They had their own grief to bear without having to feel responsible for her as well.

'What will 'ee do now?' they asked her. 'Where will 'ee go?'

'I'll stay here, of course,' she replied. 'This is my home now, and Zachary'll be with me. Grace will be bringing him back soon, and Eliza, my neighbour, is very good to me. Don't worry. I'll be . . . all right.'

'If you ever need anything, you know where to find me,' Luke assured her, 'and I'll come and see you, Henrietta, often. Don't worry, we won't forget you.'

Hetty knew that what he said was true. Luke was a great friend, he was reliable and trustworthy and strong . . . but he wasn't Reuben.

When Grace brought Zachary home, Hetty assured her sister that she would be fine; Grace had her own family to see to and she must get back to them. She put Zachary to bed and told Eliza that she would be all right on her own now. There was no need for her to keep her company any longer . . . Yes, she would shout if she needed anything.

Then Hetty found that she was completely on her own for the first time for several days. Eliza had even insisted on staying the nights with her. The only sounds were the ticking of the clock and the creaking of the rocking chair as Hetty mindlessly rocked back and forth, back and forth . . . As she sat in the familiar wooden chair, Reuben's chair, with Reuben's violin on her lap, at last the tears fell, splashing on to the rosewood case, and convulsive sobs shook her body, bringing, after a while, a certain release from the indescribable pain inside her.

She didn't know how long she sat there; it must have been all night and as dawn broke she heard the child crying out in his cot upstairs. Automatically she dressed and fed him and placed him on the rug with some toys to play with. She was still sitting in the rocking chair when her mother came in a few hours later.

'I've come to fetch you home, love,' said Martha, her heart contracting with pain as she saw the desolation in her daughter's eyes. 'Come on, it's the best thing to do, Hetty, love. You can't stay here, not on your own. Come home with me.'

'This is my home, Mam,' said Hetty impassively. 'I'm not on my own. Zachary's here and . . . I'll be all right. I'll manage.'

'You can't manage, lass.' Martha sighed. 'You'll have no money coming in, and you're miles from anywhere, and the landlord'll be wanting his rent at the end of the month . . . Come on, there's a good girl, it'll be for the best, you'll see.'

Hetty stared indifferently at her mother. She supposed that what she said was true. And what did it matter where she lived now that Reuben wasn't here? Nothing mattered any more . . .

'All right, Mam,' she said. 'I'll come . . . home.'

Chapter 23

Edwin Donnelly was feeling restless as he walked home along Whitegate Lane. It was not an unusual occurrence; oftentimes now he felt a stirring in his blood, a desire to be anywhere in the world except here in Blackpool, walking back to his parents' home, where he still resided, from his employment at his father's store.

It could be something to do with spring in the air. The tall trees that graced each side of Whitegate Lane were bursting into leaf, and the flower-beds in the nearby Royal Palace Gardens were gay with colourful springtime blooms. This street where Edwin's family lived was one of the most elegant in the town and many, he knew, envied his free and easy lifestyle; no ties, no wife and children dependent upon him, and the way in which he was able to come and go as he pleased with a doting mother to pander to him and servants to wait on him hand and foot.

The relationship he had with his mother was much more cordial these days, and for that he was thankful. It seemed hard to recall, now, the time when they had been daggers drawn, when everything that Edwin did had seemed to be wrong in

Clara's eyes. It had been mostly due to Constance, of course, and her artful tricks and schemes. Once that young woman was out of the way their life had taken on a much more even tenor. Within a few weeks she had disappeared north of the border with the young commercial traveller, Douglas Brodie, and the next time her family back in Lancashire heard from her, the pair of them were already married. Now, from all accounts, she was living in Edinburgh and her husband no longer visited the Blackpool area on his travels. As far as Edwin was concerned, the less he heard about her the better. She had messed up his life good and proper with her Machiavellian schemes, and he wished Douglas Brodie joy of her.

Not that he, Edwin, had been entirely blameless. The mix-up and muddle that he had found himself in over Constance had been largely of his own making . . . and his mother's. Clara, though, to give credit where it was due, had very quickly tried to make amends. She had admitted that she had been wrong – and what courage that must have taken – and persuaded him to go after Grace. Edwin recalled the chilling shock he had received, and the wave of misery that had engulfed him when Martha Turnbull had told him that Grace was married. He was too late; he had lost her through his own stupidity.

He knew now, with hindsight, what he should have done. He should have taken notice of nothing and nobody but the dictates of his own heart and head. In his heart he had known that he loved her; his head, too, had told him that Grace was the right girl for him despite all the problems sur-

rounding them. He should have ignored the protestations of his mother and Grace's mother and
gone ahead and married her, but Edwin knew
that his chief fault had been, and still was, his
ambivalence, his inability to come to a decision
and stick to it. Always he tried to see a problem
from every angle, to weigh up the pros and cons,
and all the while time was going on and events
were moving out of his control.

One small grain of comfort to be gained from all
this sorry mess was his growing friendship with
his mother. He could hardly believe the change in
Clara. It all seemed to have grown from the time
when she had unburdened herself to him, telling
him about her father – Edwin had been horrified
at the treatment she must have suffered at his
hands – the poverty of her early life on the Moss,
and the poison-pen letters. That confession of
Clara's had acted as a catharsis, there was no
doubt about that, and now she was a completely
different woman. Edwin found that he enjoyed
her company. Her absurd pretensions and illusions of grandeur were now things of the past and
she had developed, too, that rare quality, the
ability to see her own faults and to laugh at
herself. His father, also, was much happier with
this new Clara. The strain and tension had disappeared from his eyes and they seemed to be more
contented now than they had been at any time in
their married life.

Edwin had kept in touch with Grace's mother,
too, and found that he was able to converse with
her much more easily now that she had stopped
all that silly business of calling him Mr Edwin.

Not that he overdid his visits to Welcome Rest; he didn't want Martha to think that he was fawning and, besides, there was always the danger that he would choose to call at a time when Grace was there. So he limited his visits, just calling occasionally when the van went there to collect Martha's steady supply of cakes and pastries and making sure that she knew just how much her efforts were appreciated. Martha had done wonders for the restaurant side of the business and now, more than ever, Donnelly's café was one of the most popular rendezvous in the town for morning coffee or afternoon tea.

Through Martha he was able to keep in touch with Grace's doings, although her mother was very guarded and Edwin knew that there was a lot that she didn't tell him. He was glad that Grace no longer avoided him, though, as she had done at first. He hadn't blamed her when she had terminated her employment at Donnelly's – he would have done the same in her shoes – and he had known that she had been most careful not to go anywhere where there was the slightest chance of them meeting. But that was now a thing of the past. Now he quite often saw Grace with her sister and their two children as they shopped in Blackpool and, occasionally, took morning coffee in Donnelly's restaurant. He had seen them there this morning, which was why he found himself thinking of them now. He and Grace always exchanged a few words when they met. No one would guess that, once, they had been lovers and that they had meant all the world to one another. Only Edwin knew, in his heart, that he still cared deeply for her and, occasionally, he perceived a wistful, almost longing, glance in Grace's lovely brown eyes which made him believe that she still retained a fondness for him.

It was now three years since he had lost Grace and she had made a new life for herself. Who could blame her? Walter Clayton, from the little that Martha had told him, seemed to be a good husband to her; he had always wanted her, Edwin was sure of that. And little Sarah was an adorable child. She must be about eighteen or nineteen months old by now, Edwin guessed, and though he had little to do with children he always felt a surge of joy whenever he saw the pretty little girl. Probably because she was so much like her mother; her pointed elfin face and her brown eyes were just like Grace's, and she always looked so appealing, dressed in the smocked and pleated frocks that he knew her mother made for her, with her dark curling hair – Grace's again – framed by a large sunbonnet.

Hetty's little one, too, was a handsome child, several months older than little Sarah, but he favoured his father, Reuben Loveday, more than the Turnbull side of the family. Now that was a tragedy if ever there was one, that poor girl losing her husband in such a shocking way after they had been married for less than two years. Hetty was back with her mother now, helping in the boarding house, which, as Martha had told Edwin, had seemed the best thing for her to do. She was as pretty as ever, although the widow's black that she had been wearing for the past year dictated that she was no longer quite so fashionable in her attire. And though she always smiled and laughed with everyone she met there was a sadness in her eyes that she couldn't disguise. Edwin had thought, as he watched the child with her this morning, that so long as little Zachary was with her Hetty would never be able to forget Reuben Loveday.

He was sorry for the girl, but it was still Grace who dominated his thoughts. He had been reminded when he saw them in the café of that other occasion when he had seen them there, the very first time he had set eyes on them, laughing and joking together, enjoying the unaccustomed freedom of a visit to Blackpool. It had been Grace who had caught his attention then, and it was still Grace who held that special place in his heart and mind. Edwin thought now, with a sigh, that she always would.

But he knew that life had to go on. The burning question was which direction was his life to take? Possibly the first thing he must do was to move away from his parents' residence into a little place of his own. He was very comfortable at home and there were few restrictions on him, but Edwin knew that so long as he lived there he was not entirely his own master. He always felt ill at ease entertaining his friends there, particularly lady friends. There had been a few young women who had flitted into his life, and then, just as casually, flitted out again. None of them had touched him deeply. But Edwin was approaching thirty. He knew that it was time that he seriously considered taking a wife, and Grace, alas, was far beyond his reach now. The birth of her child had, somehow, seemed to mark the point of no return to Edwin. He had known then that she could never be his, but he hadn't met anyone else who could compare with her. Marriage would be, for Edwin, largely a matter of convenience and suitability. There were several young women of his acquaintance who would fit the bill. Edwin decided, as he had done so many times, that he would try to form an attachment. And he would start looking for a suitable house as well as a suitable wife, possibly in one of the streets near Raikes Parade, close to the centre of town and a much sought-after residential area.

There could well be changes at work, too. His father had been talking for some time of opening another store at South Shore and putting Edwin in as manager there. He was just waiting for a suitable site to become available. And, unknown as yet to William Donnelly, or to Clara, and still just a vague idea on the fringes of his mind, the New World was beckoning to Edwin. An old school friend of his, Tom Murphy, had emigrated to America a few years ago and his occasional letters to Edwin were full of the opportunities to be had there. Tom, also, was in the retail trade; he had opened a clothing store in New York and was now thinking of starting a second one. Cunard steamships were now crossing the Atlantic in record-breaking time. Distances were all the while becoming shorter and very soon they would be in a new century. In a few months' time it would be 1900. Edwin had heard it said that the new century wouldn't officially start until 1901, but it was near enough for him. The nineteen hundreds, the dawning of a new age. And, more than likely, it would be a century of even greater change than this one had been. Edwin was determined that there must be changes for him, too.

'Hetty . . . Hetty, love. There's someone to see you.'

Hetty looked up from the magazine she was reading at the knock on her door. Then her mother came in. 'Come on, lass. Never mind them silly love stories now. Put that book down and come and see who's here.'

Hetty frowned slightly. 'Who is it, Mam?'

Martha laughed. 'Come downstairs and then you'll know. I'll take the bairn with me. Come on, Zachary love. Come with Gran.' She held out her hand and the little boy quickly abandoned the building bricks he was playing with and took hold of his grandmother's hand. It always pleased Hetty to see the affinity between the two of them. It was the same with little Sarah as well. Martha took a great delight in her grandchildren, and they loved her in return.

'All right, Mam. I'll be down in a minute.'

Hetty rose to her feet as soon as her mother left the room and walked over to the mirror above the mantelpiece. She must make sure she was looking her best, whoever the mysterious visitor was. She picked up a comb and ran it through the mass of auburn curls. Her hair was getting rather long and untidy-looking; she would have to ask Grace to get busy with her scissors and trim a bit off for her. She pressed her lips tightly together to bring colour to them and straightened the collar of her blouse.

She could guess who it would be, though. Joss Jenkinson, more than likely. It was his usual time for calling, early on a Sunday afternoon. He called occasionally to see how she was going on and to try to persuade her to make a comeback at Tilda's Tavern. It was almost three years since she had last sung there, but to Hetty it seemed far longer than that. It was a different existence and the girl who had pranced and pirouetted so light-heartedly on the stage had been a completely different being. She had been a carefree girl; now Hetty was a woman. So much had happened to bring her to maturity, and Hetty was sure that those faraway days when Henrietta, the Girl with the Sparkling Eyes, had been the darling of the audience could never be recaptured. Tilda's Tavern held too many poignant memories for her, first of Albert, then of Reuben, and Hetty felt that it would be too painful for her to return there. So she had always refused Joss Jenkinson's suggestion and he hadn't pressed her unduly. His invitation was, she thought, a tentative one, as though he knew she wouldn't really agree. It was obvious to anyone who met her that there had been a big change in Hetty. The girl who had married Reuben Loveday had now grown up.

She had recovered to a certain extent from her terrible loss. It was true, as well-meaning friends had assured her, that time was a great healer and that every day the pain would hurt a little less. And her own cheerful personality had helped. Hetty was naturally of an optimistic disposition;

in her happy-go-lucky girlhood days she had never been able to remain downhearted for long, and this inbred trait came to the fore now, after the first few months of grieving had passed. Nobody wanted to know you if you were miserable, she told herself, and she often hid her still-aching heart behind a bright smile. Her memories of Reuben were all happy ones and no one would ever be able to take them away from her. She had believed that their love would last for ever, that their mutual rapture would stand the test of time, but she knew now that the passing years would have taken their toll. The hair would have silvered, the eyes become less bright, the figure thickened, the gait slowed down and the ardour diminished. But Reuben, in her memory, would be forever young, his hair always black as ebony and his eyes bright and clear, glowing with his love for her.

And her little son would always be a reminder to her of her husband. Hetty was thankful that she had this living proof of their love and she was, on the whole, contented. Her mother had insisted, when Hetty returned to the boarding house, that she and the child should have their own rooms where they could be alone together. Hetty's sitting room was on the first-floor landing, and there she was able to entertain her friends and to enjoy a little solitude in the evenings if she so wished, while Zachary slept in the room next door. Hetty had argued that her mother couldn't possibly spare two rooms which could be filled at the height of the season with paying guests. But Martha had been adamant. The needs of her own kith and kin came first; besides, the business was doing very nicely and though she was by no means affluent Martha found that her bank balance was in a more healthy state than it had ever been. The boarding-house trade could be a lucrative one if you were prepared to put your back into it and work nearly every hour that God sent. Very soon they would be doing just that. Next weekend it would be Whitsuntide, the first big holiday weekend of the season, and already Martha was almost fully booked with 'regulars'.

Hetty gave a gasp of surprise as she entered Martha's parlour and the tall young man rose to meet her. She hadn't remembered him as being particularly tall, but he seemed so now and broader too. His fair hair was still the same, but now there was a growth of hair on his upper lip too, a bushy moustache which made him resemble, more than ever, his father. His eyes, kind and grey – he had always, Hetty recalled, been so very kind – were appraising her; no longer, though, diffident and self-effacing but glowing with a new-found confidence.

'Albert, how lovely to see you again,' Hetty exclaimed as she walked towards his outstretched hand. And, indeed, it was lovely to see him. 'What a surprise.'

'Hetty . . .' He spoke just the one word as he squeezed her hand, but his eyes and the whole of his face lit up in a heart-warming smile.

'What a surprise,' said Hetty again, feeling, for a moment, at a loss for words. 'How long are you staying?'

'I'm back for good now, Hetty,' said Albert as

they sat down in the easy chairs on either side of the fire. 'I had to work a month's notice in Blackburn, but I thought it was time I came . . . home.'

'But . . . what about your job? You used to work at Pickering's . . .'

'And that's where I'll be working again. Uncle Sam has agreed to let me have my job back. He was only too glad, I can tell you. There's a building boom in Blackpool at present, and he can't get enough carpenters. Yes . . . I reckon the seaside called me back, Hetty. Once you've lived near the coast it's hard to live away from it. And, of course I missed . . . everybody.' His eyes held hers for a moment and Hetty thought again how very glad she was to see him.

It was three years now since Albert had left Blackpool to go and live with his aunt and uncle in Blackburn and find employment there. He had been home now and again on short visits, but Hetty had seen him only briefly. He had written a letter of condolence when Reuben died, but this was the first time that he had sought her out to have any conversation with her.

The emotive silence was broken by Zachary coming in from the kitchen with his grandmother. Hetty had noticed that Martha had absented herself, and now she entered the parlour with a pot of tea and crockery on a tray.

'There you are . . . Now you can see to yourselves. I've some jobs to get on with in t'kitchen.' Martha set out the cups and saucers on the table, then disappeared again just as quickly. Hetty couldn't imagine what the jobs were. They had finished washing the dinner pots ages ago, and

Martha usually liked to take her ease, as much as she could, on a Sunday. She smiled to herself at her mother's vanishing act. Trust Mam . . .

'The little lad's like his father,' Albert remarked, smiling at Zachary, then at Hetty. But his eyes were serious as he went on to say, 'I was sorry to hear about Reuben. Real sorry . . . You hadn't been married all that long, had you, Hetty?'

'No . . . Less than two years. It was a terrible shock. And there seemed to be no explanation.' She shook her head. 'We never found out what caused it. Still . . . life has to go on, as they say, and I can't brood for long with this scamp around, I'll tell you.' Fondly she ruffled her son's black curls and he grinned up at her.

'And you were happy, Hetty? You and . . . Reuben, you were happy together?'

'Yes . . . Very happy. I couldn't have had a better husband,' said Hetty simply.

'I'm glad about that. I like to think that he was good to you. But, like you say, Hetty, life has to go on . . .'

She could feel Albert's eyes upon her and Hetty looked across at him. They regarded one another gravely for a few seconds. Then, 'I hope we can be friends again, Hetty,' said Albert.

He made no move towards her, but his eyes glowed with warmth and Hetty felt a reciprocal glow come into her own eyes. And her heart, which for the last year had felt like a block of ice, began, at last, to thaw and to stir into life again.

'Yes . . . I'm sure we can be friends, Albert,' she said as she smiled at him.

547

It had been an inspired sermon that he had preached that morning and Walter was still buoyed up with the thoughts of it as he walked across the tram track to the sea side of the promenade. It was a blustery early autumn day, with the promise of a storm before much longer – just the sort of day that he liked – and already Walter could see the high waves crashing against the sea wall and sending silver sprays over the iron railings, drenching anyone foolish enough to stand in their way. For Walter was not alone in his love of the stormy weather; on any day such as this many foolhardy people were to be seen on the promenade, deliberately going out of their way, so it seemed, to invite a soaking and glorying in the free spectacle of high wind and towering waves which Mother Nature frequently put on for their enjoyment. There was just time now, Walter thought, for a brisk walk as far as North Pier and back before he went home to partake of the Sunday dinner that Grace would be preparing for him.

Grace . . . his dear Grace. He felt his heart warm now at the thought at her. And Sarah, his beloved little daughter. Things had been better between the two of them since the child had been born, and there were times when Walter could almost forget the traumatic start to their marriage. He hoped that Grace had forgotten it as well. There were still occasions, though, when a fit of jealousy would seize him as he thought of Grace in someone else's arms, even though it was now three years since their marriage. But he had forgiven Grace, long since, and he hoped that she had forgiven him for his deplorable treatment of her that first night. The memory of it was still there, tormenting him like a hair shirt on his back, and he wished that he could rid himself of it.

'The blood of the Lord Jesus Christ will cleanse you from every sin,' he told his Bible class, knowing as he spoke that there were secret sins within himself that at times gave him no peace. He was quite sure that the Lord had forgiven him for his despicable behaviour on his wedding night, but Walter knew that he should ask his wife for her forgiveness as well; he should, indeed, have asked her long ago. Was it trumped-up pride within him, he wondered, that made it so difficult for him to humble himself before the woman he loved and ask her to forgive him? Women, of course, were meant to be subservient creatures. Didn't it say so, frequently, in the Bible? St Paul said that man was made in the image of God, but woman was created for man; women, therefore, should keep silent, subordinate to their husbands, reliant upon them for everything. Walter was a typical product of his age, the undisputed master of his hearth and home, and he had little time for forward-thinking women and their liberal views. His Grace, thank goodness, was not that kind of a woman, and she had been a good wife to him in so many ways. She was still not as eager as he would have wished regarding the physical side of marriage, but that, Walter told himself, was more due to her natural reticence than because his harsh treatment of her still rankled. Yes, Grace was of a modest disposition, as befitted a woman, and he was more than ever sure now that what had happened between her and Edwin Donnelly had come about because the fellow had forced himself upon her.

The thought was returning to torment him again, but he quelled it, as he was often able to do, by thinking of something else. He thought now of his prowess as a preacher. Yes, he had been inspired all right this morning, and he was sure that the hearts and minds of his congregation had been stirred up as they listened to him.

'I can do all things through Christ who strengthens me,' he had told his eager listeners, exhorting them to share with him his belief in an invincible God. And then they had sung, 'Throw Out the Life-line', the chorus of exultant voices nearly raising the roof as they had joined in praise of the Almighty.

Walter found himself singing the words inside his head now, and his lips silently forming the words as he strode along the spray-drenched promenade near to North Pier.

'Throw out the life-line across the dark wave,
There is a brother whom someone should save;
Somebody's brother, oh who then will dare
To throw out the life-line his peril to share.'

An appropriate choice of hymn for such a morning as this, with the wind and waves steadily increasing in force. There were a few people at the top of the flight of steps leading down to the beach, though now the chain was across because the tide was in. Walter could hear agitated voices as he drew near.

'The foolish lad. He'll never get him out . . .'

'Aye, it would have been as well to let him go, but you know what some folks are like about animals. They treat 'em just like bairns . . .'

'He's a plucky lad, I'll say that for him . . .'

'What's going on?' Walter enquired of a man at the scene.

'That young lad . . . He's gone into t'sea after his dog . . . Hey up! The dog's here. Well, bless my soul! He's got hisself out.'

As the man spoke a shaggy brown dog of indeterminate breed scampered up the steps and shook himself, showering the bystanders with droplets of water. He was apparently none the worse for his adventure, but his master's head could be seen bobbing up and down a few yards from the sea wall, his arms and legs threshing wildly as he strived to swim against the force of the tide towards the safety of the steps. The onlookers, a few more of them by now, were cheering him on.

'Come on, lad. That's it. Another yard and you'll have done it . . .'

'He'll be all right. Seems as though he's a strong swimmer . . .'

But no one, though they were vociferous in their encouragement, was making an attempt to help in any other way. Walter didn't hesitate for more than a few seconds.

'Throw out the life-line, throw out the life-line, Someone is sinking today . . .' The words were echoing in his brain as Walter put his large Bible down by the iron railings and flung off his heavy coat. Then he stepped over the chain into the cold grey sea. He was a strong swimmer and had always enjoyed the sport since he was a lad, but the iciness of the water and the strength of the waves took him unawares. As he struck out towards the floundering boy he could feel the pain in his chest and the heaviness of his limbs hampered by his clothing. The words of the sermon he had preached that morning returned to him. 'I can do all things through Christ who strengthens me,' he whispered to himself as he drew nearer to the drowning boy.

He was there now . . . He had reached him. As he grasped the boy beneath the armpits he was dimly aware of a cheer from the small crowd on the promenade.

'He's done it. He's got him . . .'

'What a brave young fellow . . .'

'Just . . . try to . . . relax . . .' he said to the boy, though he could hardly speak for the restriction in his chest. 'I'll . . . have you out . . . in a minute . . .'

He was nearly there. He swam on his back, pushing out strongly with his legs as he pulled the limp figure towards the sea wall. He felt his shoulder nudge against the hard stone – what a blessed relief it was – then a huge wave crashing against the wall engulfed them both and Walter felt himself being swept out to sea again. He had been so near . . . Walter began to pray, more desperately than he had ever prayed in his life.

Chapter 24

Grace was shocked to see a policeman on her doorstep in the early afternoon, though she was not altogether surprised. She had been sure, by now, that something must have happened to Walter. It wasn't like him to be so late home.

'Mrs Clayton?'

'Yes . . . I'm Mrs Clayton.' She looked at the serious face of the policeman and a dreadful fear seized hold of her. Walter . . . Oh, dear God . . . no!

'I'm afraid I have some rather disturbing news for you, my dear. It's your husband . . .'

'Walter!' Grace put her hand to her mouth in horror and closed her eyes for a moment as she tried to face up to what she felt sure this man had come to tell her. 'Are you trying to tell me that he's . . .?'

She was surprised, afterwards, at the devastation she had felt and the feeling of despair that had gripped her in those few seconds when she had believed her husband to be dead. In the dreadful early days of their marriage she thought she would have welcomed such news, but not now.

'No, love. He's not dead,' said the policeman,

reaching out and holding her arm. 'He's been very brave. Do you mind if I come in for a moment, then I can tell you about it?'

'No, not at all. Come in,' Grace murmured as a feeling of overwhelming relief engulfed her. She led him to the small parlour where little Sarah was playing on the hearthrug with her doll. 'Do sit down. Now, tell me . . .'

She listened in quiet astonishment as the policeman, an avuncular man with kind grey eyes, told her of her husband's rescue attempt.

'He was nearly a goner, though, and the lad an' all, but they think they'll both pull through, thank God. Our lads were on the scene in a few minutes with life belts an' all that, and they managed to get 'em both out. But it were a close thing.'

'And where is Walter now?' asked Grace, feeling bemused.

'In Victoria Hospital. You know, the place they opened a few years back on Whitegate Lane?' Grace nodded. 'They took them both there as a precaution, but I daresay they'll let your husband out in a day or two if all's well. Perhaps you could slip along and see him later on?'

'Yes . . . of course. When I've found someone to look after my little girl.' Grace still couldn't quite believe what she was hearing. 'And . . . you say that Walter jumped into the sea? With all his clothes on?'

'Aye, he did that. It's good to find somebody who practises what they preach, Mrs Clayton. It's not a scrap of good ranting on about good works and then standing aside and doing nowt about it. Your husband's a preacher, I believe?'

'Yes . . . yes, he is. But how . . .?'

'How did we know? His Bible was there on t'promenade, as large as life, with his name inside. Not his address, mind, but one of the nurses on the ward recognised him. She goes to the same chapel apparently, so she was able to tell us where he lived. Seems as though he's very highly thought of at that chapel he belongs to, and he'll be even more so now, of course. He's a brave fellow. You've reason to be proud of him, Mrs Clayton.'

'Yes . . . it seems as though I have.' Grace was still bewildered and she couldn't get over the feeling of thankfulness that she had experienced when she had found out that her husband was not dead, as she had surmised in those first few awful moments. Could it mean that, after all, she . . . loved him?

Grace was even more aware, as she hurried along Whitegate Lane that evening, of the affection that she felt for her husband. At one time she wouldn't have believed it possible that she could look forward so much to seeing him, or could hope so desperately that he would make a complete recovery. She passed, on the other side of the road, the Donnellys' residence, with its carriage drive sweeping round the immaculate lawn, and the flowerbeds, bright with dahlias and Michaelmas daisies, making a brave display of colour before the onset of autumn. Edwin, she knew, no longer lived there. He had moved out several months ago and now had his own smaller house near to the Raikes Hall entrance. She didn't see much of him now since he was installed as manager of his father's new store down at South Shore. Grace, somewhat to her annoyance, was still interested in the doings of Edwin Donnelly, but tonight her concern about Walter was uppermost in her mind.

She pushed intrusive thoughts of Edwin away as she walked through the imposing pillared gateway of Victoria Hospital. The place had been opened some five years previously, in 1894, and was supported mainly by voluntary contributions. Grace and Hetty had attended, only a few months ago, a large bazaar at the Winter Gardens to raise more money for the hospital.

Walter was in a large ward which, Grace thought at a quick glance, held about twelve beds, and she was surprised and relieved to see how well he was looking.

'Grace . . .' His eyes lit up with pleasure as he saw her and he held his arms wide to embrace her. Affectionately she kissed his cheek and she felt herself enveloped in a bear-like hug. 'It's grand to see you, Gracie. Real grand.'

'You're looking well, Walter. I thought you'd be . . . Well, I don't really know what I was expecting, but I certainly didn't think you'd be sitting up and taking notice as soon as this. What does the doctor say?'

'I'm as fit as a flea, don't you worry.' Walter laughed. 'It'll take more than a bit of sea water to finish me off, I'll tell you. The doctor's very pleased. He says I can come home later tomorrow, all being well. Young Arthur over there, he'll be in a little while longer, from all accounts.' Walter gestured across the ward to where a young man

556

was lying on his back with a middle-aged man and woman at his side. 'That's Arthur Jackson, the lad that I . . . the lad that went into the sea after his dog.'

'The lad that you rescued, Walter,' said Grace, her eyes shining with pride as she smiled at him. 'Don't be modest, love. He wouldn't be here if it wasn't for you. I'm very proud of you, Walter.'

Walter shook his head self-deprecatingly. 'It was nowt. It was the policemen who were the real heroes. They had us out in no time at all.' Grace thought what a change there appeared to be in her husband. He was usually so full of bluster and bounce and a sense of his own importance. Now that he really had something to boast about he was making very little of it, giving the credit to someone else, in fact. 'Anyroad, all's well that ends well, and I reckon the Lord still has a few jobs lined up for me down here or else He wouldn't have hung on to me.'

'I'm sure He has, Walter.' Grace smiled at him, then she glanced across the ward towards the bed where the young man was lying. She could see that the woman, the lad's mother she presumed, was smiling in her direction. 'I'll just go across and have a word with . . . Arthur Jackson, did you say he was called? With Arthur's mother; she looks as though she would like to speak to me.' She touched his arm fondly. 'I won't be a minute.'

'Mrs Clayton?' The older woman's eyes filled up with tears as she looked at Grace. 'I can't thank your husband enough for what he did for my Arthur. And my husband, too. We're . . . we're overwhelmed, aren't we, Horace? And Arthur's going to be all right. He's a bit shaken – it took him a while to come round, but he's never been all that strong, you see.' Mrs Jackson smiled at her son and the darkly shadowed eyes in the white face smiled back at her. 'Not like your husband. He looks a robust young fellow. Never had a day's illness in his life, I daresay?' Grace opened her mouth to reply, but didn't get the chance. 'Not that that makes any less of what he did for Arthur. A real Christian act that was, Mrs Clayton. And all because of that dratted dog. When I think of the disaster he might have caused . . . but our Arthur's always thought the world of Barney and I don't suppose I'd have him any different . . . Hark at me going on! My husband always says I'm like a river in full stream when I get going, babbling on and on, don't you, Horace?' Mrs Jackson shook her head and laughed. 'But I'm that relieved, you see, dear. And I just wanted to tell you how grateful we are. You must be real proud of that husband of yours.'

'Indeed I am,' said Grace with feeling. 'Very proud.'

'You're never going back to work, Walter? Not so soon.' Grace stared in disbelief as her husband entered the kitchen in his working clothes and sat down at the table. 'You only came home from hospital yesterday, and you know what the doctor said. You have to take it easy for a while. It was a shock to your system, that dip in the sea.'

'Oh, stop fussing, Grace.' Walter sounded a trifle irritated. Grace knew that he had no patience with malingerers or with people who were said to 'enjoy bad health', but no one could have blamed him if he'd stayed in bed for a day or two at least. He had had a nasty experience and had come very near to drowning in his brave rescue bid.

'I've told you, I'm as fit as a fiddle,' he went on. 'It'll take more than a dip in the sea to finish off Walter Clayton.' Grace smiled to herself wryly as a touch of the old belligerent Walter began to show again. 'Besides, if I don't work I shan't get paid, and I can't afford to lounge around here like one of the landed gentry.'

'It wouldn't matter for a day or two, surely, Walter? We're not that hard up, and the rent's not due for another couple of weeks or so. I don't want you making yourself worse.'

'Shut up, woman,' said Walter, though not unkindly. He grinned at her. 'I'm going back to work and that's the end of it. Nowt that you or anyone else says'll make any difference, so you might as well save your breath.'

Grace knew that there was no point at all in arguing with her husband. He always had the last word. She couldn't recall a time during the three years of their marriage when it had not been so.

The weather was capricious, as it often was on the Fylde coast during early autumn. The sun would blaze from an azure blue sky for a few hours, holding all the promise of an Indian summer, then just as suddenly the sky would darken to a threatening grey and the rain would start. With the rain came the strong winds and the high tide, like the one that had occurred on the day that Walter had

559

rescued Arthur Jackson from the sea. Walter, sitting on the coal waggon behind the two dray horses, was alternately sweating as the sun blazed down, then shivering as the wind howled round him and the torrential rain poured upon him in bucketfuls. Several times he came home soaked to the skin and by the end of a week of such weather even Walter had to admit defeat.

His eyes and nose were running, he had started to cough and he obviously had a high temperature. There was no question now of him going to work. Walter found when he got out of bed that he couldn't even stand, and the only relief he got from his pounding head and aching limbs and the cough which was now shaking his body was when he was lying between the cool sheets. But he stubbornly refused, at first, to allow Grace to call the doctor. He did, however, succumb with a fairly good grace to her wifely ministrations and he obediently took the quinine powders that she purchased from the chemist and sipped the hot lemon drinks she plied him with. But it was all to no avail. By the evening of the third day Walter was delirious and Grace knew that she could afford to waste no more time. A neighbour's young son ran round to the doctor's house a few streets away and he was with her within half an hour.

Dr Hargreaves looked grave. 'You should have called me sooner, Mrs Clayton. Why didn't you?'

'My husband wouldn't hear of it. He's no patience with folks who mollycoddle themselves and . . . well, I never like to go against his wishes. I've not left it too late, have I, Doctor?' The alarm

560

was obvious in Grace's voice and in her eyes as she looked fearfully at Dr Hargreaves.

'I hope not. Indeed, I hope not. But your husband has pneumonia, and the bronchitis has made things worse. He's subject to bronchitis, is he?'

Grace nodded. 'Yes, occasionally. It runs in the family. His mother . . . died after an attack.'

'Mmm . . . He was told to take care, wasn't he, after that episode in the sea?'

Grace nodded again. 'He's stubborn, Doctor.'

'Yes . . . I can see that. And this is the result. It was a much bigger shock to his system than he realised, and he should have taken heed of what he was told. But don't blame yourself, my dear. I know what it's like dealing with a man who's headstrong. You've done your best.'

The doctor was silent for a few moments as he looked in his capacious black bag. He took out a small bottle. 'Give him this in water, every two hours. He must have it regularly, Mrs Clayton. I can't stress that enough. Apart from that there's little we can do except wait for the crisis to pass. It shouldn't be long . . .'

The night seemed endless. Grace alternately bathed her husband's face and body as the fever sweated out of him and he threshed wildly from side to side, then covered him with blankets as the uncontrollable shivering started again. And every two hours she forced the dark-brown liquid past his parched lips, making sure that he drank every drop. He spoke little except occasionally to mutter, 'Grace . . .' as he reached for her hand. Grace found herself praying, in a way she would once have believed impossible, that her husband would recover.

As dawn appeared, a misty grey dawn creeping with a faint feeble light through the thin curtains at the window, Walter seemed to rally. His eyes looked less feverish and his voice, though quiet, sounded clear and resolute as he spoke her name.

'Grace . . .'

She looked up, startled, from the basket chair where she had been resting, but not sleeping. Walter needed her and she hadn't slept properly for three nights.

'Come here, Grace . . . I want to talk to you. Come and sit . . . next to me.'

She sat on the edge of the bed and he reached out and took hold of her hand. 'There's something . . . I have to say to you . . . Grace.' Walter's voice was quiet and husky as though it were an effort to speak, but every word was distinct and audible. 'I want to tell you that . . . I'm . . . I'm sorry.'

'Sorry? What are you sorry about, love?' Grace spoke gently and she put her hand on his forehead which, to her relief, felt cooler. 'There's no need to feel sorry about being ill. I'm here to look after you, aren't I?' She didn't think that it was his illness to which he was referring, but she didn't want him distressing himself unduly. His next words proved her correct.

'No . . . no, it's not that.' Walter frowned slightly, his characteristic impatience showing itself even now. 'I wanted to tell you that . . . I'm sorry . . . about that first night . . . when we were married. I shouldn't have treated you like that. I shouldn't have said those terrible things. It's been on my mind . . . all these years, but I just couldn't . . . I wouldn't say I was sorry. Forgive me, Grace . . . please.'

The look of remorse in his eyes was one that Grace had never seen before, and she felt a lump come into her throat. 'It's all right, Walter. I have forgiven you. A long time ago.' She wasn't sure that that was true, but she knew that his treatment of her on their wedding night had not loomed so large in her mind for quite a while now. They had been perhaps not blissfully happy, but certainly contented recently. And she knew now that she desperately wanted her husband to get well again. 'Don't think about it any more, Walter. Just think about getting better.'

'It was wrong of me, Grace. It was . . . wicked.' Walter tossed his head from side to side on the pillow. Then he stared straight at her, his eyes dark with regret. 'I blamed you because . . . there'd been someone else. It was hypo . . . critical.' His tongue and his mind had difficulty with the long word. ' . . . And deceitful of me, Grace. Because . . . you weren't the first for me either. There had been . . . someone else. A woman . . . in Burnley.'

'I know, Walter.' Grace spoke calmly as she smiled at him. 'I always knew. Don't let it worry you, love. It's all right. And it was all a long time ago.' She patted his hand as she repeated, 'It's all right.'

'But I love you, Grace. I want you to know that. I always loved . . . only you.' Walter's eyes were closing now and she knew that he must sleep.

'And I love you too, Walter,' she whispered, realising as she said the words that it was the first time in their marriage that she had told him so. And she thought that she meant it.

While he slept she made herself a drink and buttered a slice of bread. She didn't feel like eating, but she knew that she must make an effort. At least she didn't have to worry about Sarah; her daughter was next door in the care of a good neighbour who had offered to look after her until . . . until the crisis was over. Until Walter was well again, Grace told herself firmly.

Towards the middle of the morning Walter opened his eyes and lifted his head from the pillow. He tried to raise himself up, but was stopped by a violent bout of coughing. The bed shook with the uncontrollable spasm that seized him. Grace rushed across the room when she saw the blood and phlegm on the sheets. 'Walter . . . Walter, my dear . . .' He lay back exhausted.

'Grace . . .' he said, just once. Then he closed his eyes.

Please God, let him live, said Grace silently as she looked down at him. His breathing became more normal and Grace stood motionless for several minutes, just watching him. Perhaps that's it, she thought. Perhaps the crisis is over. Then she heard the rattle in his chest, a harsh grating sound, and she seized hold of his hand.

'Walter . . .' she cried. 'Oh, Walter, don't leave me!'

But she knew that it was too late. One more horrifying gasp, then his breathing stopped and there was silence.

And as Grace stared down in dry-eyed grief at the lifeless form of her husband she wondered why it was that God, so often, failed to answer prayers. Or to answer them in the way that His children wished.

Chapter 25

It had been over a fortnight after the funeral
when Edwin had first called on Grace. She had
been startled to see him there on the doorstep one
evening in October.

'Edwin . . . Do come in. I've just been putting
Sarah to bed.' She was aware of her somewhat
dishevelled appearance and she hastily patted her
hair and snatched off her apron as she led Edwin
into the small parlour. She saw him glance at the
pile of unfinished sewing on an armchair, for this
was Grace's workplace as well as being the room
where she entertained the few visitors she had.
She lifted up the cut-out pieces of the dress she
was sewing for a neighbour and placed them on
the sideboard along with the other tools of her
trade – scissors, tape measure, reels of cotton,
thimble . . . Gosh, she thought, the place was in a
mess, but it couldn't be helped. She had to work
for a living, especially now.

'Sit down, Edwin.' She gestured towards the
chair. 'I'm . . . pleased to see you.'

'I felt I had to call, Grace, to offer my condolences.' He had written to her at the time of
Walter's death, but it was kind of him to call now

in person and Grace appreciated it. 'I was so sorry about your husband,' he said, 'especially after his brave rescue attempt. It seems . . . unfair, somehow, after he had been so courageous. I'm sure you must have been tremendously proud of him.'

Grace couldn't count the number of times that those words had been said to her, 'You must be very proud of him.' There had been a moving obituary in the local *Gazette* with details of Walter's brave deed and of his prowess as a local preacher and the esteem in which he was held at his chapel.

'Yes . . . I was proud of him,' she said now, looking unflinchingly at Edwin. 'Very proud. He was a brave man. And a good man, too,' she added quietly.

Edwin held her gaze for a few seconds before he nodded. 'I'm sure he was, Grace. And, may I ask you . . .?' He looked down at his bowler hat which he held in his hands, twisting it round a couple of times before he went on. 'You may think it's an infernal cheek, but I'd like to know . . . Were you happy, Grace?'

'Yes, we were happy, Edwin,' Grace answered quietly. She had been going to add 'eventually', but decided against it. It was really no business of Edwin's what had occurred in her marriage to Walter and there was no point in going on about it now. Not that she would have dreamed of divulging the reason for her early unhappiness – she had told no one of the misery of those early days – but there was no need even to mention that she and Walter had once been far from happy.

'Very happy,' she added, a trifle defiantly. 'I was

mistaken about Walter, you know. That time when I thought he was following me . . . frightening me, you remember?'

'Yes, I remember,' said Edwin gravely.

'I think I was letting my imagination run away with me.' Grace knew that what she was saying was not strictly true – there had been occasions when she had felt frightened of Walter – but he had proved himself to be a caring husband in the end and it wouldn't be right to give Edwin the impression that she had been miserable with him. 'He loved me, you see. That was why . . . He didn't want to let me go.'

'And you loved him, Grace?'

'Yes . . . I loved him,' Grace replied simply. That was all that Edwin needed to know. After all, it was really none of his business.

'Good.' The word sounded flat, dropping like a stone into the silence. 'And you're managing all right, are you, Grace? You and the little girl? I don't like to think that you're . . . finding it difficult.'

'We're managing perfectly well, thank you, Edwin.' Grace's reply was a little brusque. 'I've started sewing, as you see.' She pointed towards the pile of half-finished garments. 'I'm working up quite a nice little clientele amongst neighbours and friends. And Walter left me reasonably well provided for. He was always careful with his money. And I shall be helping Mother in the boarding house when the season starts again. She's always glad of an extra pair of hands. So we're all right, Sarah and me. We'll manage.' She nodded decisively, then, aware that she may have

569

been somewhat curt, she smiled at Edwin. 'But it's kind of you to ask.'

They chatted then about Donnelly's and the new store at South Shore which Edwin was managing, and the restaurant business to which, after four years, Martha was still supplying cakes and pastries.

'It's been good to see you again, Grace,' said Edwin as he rose to leave. 'I'll come again, if I may? I would like to feel that we could be friends again.'

'I'm sure we can, Edwin,' said Grace brightly. 'It's been lovely to see you. Do come again. I'd like us to be friends too.'

And now, several months later, in the spring of 1900, that was what Grace and Edwin still were. Good friends . . .

Grace sighed as she put down her sewing on the settee and gazed contemplatively into the glowing fire. Edwin called to see her about once a week now, usually on a Wednesday, when it was half-day closing at the shop. There had grown between the two of them a comradeship, and awareness, certainly, that their mutual feelings for one another were not dead. Grace could tell, or thought that she could, by the softness of Edwin's tone and the affection in his glance. But never, even once, had he made any move towards her, or suggested that their relationship should be more than it was at the moment. Sometimes it was evening when he visited her, but occasionally he called during the daytime when little Sarah was awake. Grace's two-year-old daughter looked forward to the visits of this personable friend of her mother, 'Uncle Edwin'. He was completely at ease with the little girl, which Grace found surprising, but very appealing.

She had listened to Edwin's plans for expanding the business at the new store at South Shore. She had heard of his tentative ideas of, eventually, moving to America. That scheme, however, had been shelved for the moment while he concentrated on the enterprises in Blackpool, but Grace felt that the New World and its wider horizons were beckoning to Edwin and that, one day, he might succumb. She wasn't sure what part she would play in these dreams of Edwin's. None, perhaps. Maybe he just enjoyed her company . . .

She was, of course, still in mourning. Perhaps that was why Edwin was still behaving so reticently. But it was now six months since Walter had died; time, surely, for her to abandon the deepest black she had been wearing and dress in half-mourning colours, grey, lavender or mauve. Queen Victoria certainly had something to answer for, Grace mused, setting a pattern following the death of her beloved Albert that women throughout the country tried to emulate. How long had the Prince Consort been dead now? It must be almost forty years, and yet his grieving widow – the Widow of Windsor as she was sometimes called – still dressed in sombre garments of black and grey, relieved only by her white widow's cap.

But Queen Victoria was a law unto herself and always had been. As far as Grace was concerned she knew that she had no intention of going on grieving for Walter for ever. She had missed him at first, more than she had imagined she could, but the pain and the shock of his death had eased considerably now and life had to go on. And she knew that she was still very, very fond of Edwin Donnelly . . . But the first move had to come from him. There was no doubt in Grace's mind as to that, and if all that Edwin wanted from her was friendship then there was nothing she could do about it. And now, to complicate matters further, there was Amos Armitage . . .

She had been wrong about so many things, Martha thought, as she sat in her parlour one early spring evening in 1900. She had believed at one time that she knew what was best, not only for herself, but for her two daughters as well. Not that she had interfered – not really – but she hadn't been afraid of telling both Grace and Hetty how she felt about things and giving them a shove in what she believed was the right direction. And Martha was forced to admit that she hadn't always been right. She was determined that in future she would keep her mouth firmly shut. It was a funny old life, to be sure, with plenty of knocks along the way. It was a good job you couldn't see ahead or you would never make it. The good Lord in His wisdom withheld the future from His children, and what a blessing that was. Who would have thought that five years after moving to Blackpool both her daughters would have been married and then both widowed? One of them had got wed again, though, praise the Lord . . .

Martha knew that she had been wrong about

Reuben. He had proved to be a good husband to Hetty and he had made the lass so happy. Martha had never seen two young people so much in love as Hetty and Reuben had been . . . for the short time they had shared together. Yes, that had been a marriage made in heaven, as the saying went, and Martha still felt a pang of sadness when she thought of the tragic way in which Reuben had died.

She had been wrong about Walter Clayton, too. He had made Grace so unhappy. The girl had never told her so, but it had been written plainly on her face for all to see in the early days of her marriage. Grace had seemed to be contented enough as time went on, and Walter had redeemed himself in the end, of course, by that brave rescue attempt in the sea. But Martha knew, in her heart of hearts, that it had been a less than perfect union and she felt that she was partially responsible.

Because she had been wrong about Edwin Donnelly, too. Martha was only thankful that Grace and Edwin now had another chance of getting together, and she hoped that they would soon discover that they were right for one another. Edwin Donnelly was a fine young man, and Grace was still head over heels in love with the fellow. Anyone with half an eye could see that by the way she spoke about him.

Martha was thankful that she had, at least, been right about one thing. Albert Gregson was the salt of the earth, and Hetty had now realised so as well. The pair of them had been married a couple of months ago and had moved into their own little home near North Station. Albert hadn't rushed things; he had taken it nice and steadily, as was his way, and gradually Hetty had come to realise that she loved him. Not, perhaps, in the way she had loved Reuben, but it would be a good marriage. Martha was sure of that.

'Hello there. Anyone at home?'

Martha's rambling thoughts were stopped by a knock at the door, then George Makepeace poked his head round. His blue eyes twinkled and his face broke into a smile as he looked at Martha. She smiled back at him. She had been expecting him, waiting for his habitual greeting, 'Anyone at home?'. She knew now that she would always be at home for George.

'Yes, come in George, love,' she welcomed him warmly. 'Make yerself at home – not that you need telling; I know you will – and I'll go and put the kettle on.'

She stood up and he put his hands on her shoulders and bent to kiss her lips, a kiss that told more of friendship, at the moment, than of passion, but Martha was hopeful . . . A glow of happiness surged through her as she busied herself in the kitchen, for this was another thing about which she had been right. George was solid gold – she had always thought so – and very soon, before the season started in earnest, she would be Mrs Martha Makepeace. She had said yes to his proposal of marriage only the night before. The future was full of promise, not only for the young ones like Grace and Hetty, but for the slightly older folk as well.

When Hetty and Albert called later that

574

evening with young Zachary, now three years old, they were delighted to hear Martha and George's news.

'I can't say I'm surprised though, Mam,' said Hetty as she kissed her mother's cheek. 'I could see the way things were shaping up.'

'Aye. Old George there has had a gleam in his eye for quite a while,' said Albert laughing, 'and we all know what that means.'

'Go on with yer bother,' said Martha, pushing at him and feeling a blush staining her cheeks. Albert certainly wasn't the shy lad that he had been when she'd first met him, five years ago now, and his marriage to Hetty had completed his maturity.

'And it'll be grand for young Zachary and his little brother to have two granddads,' Albert went on with a sly grin at Hetty.

'Little brother? You mean . . .?' Martha looked at Albert, then at her daughter.

'Yes, Mam, that's right,' said Hetty happily. 'Zachary's going to have a little brother. Or little sister, of course.' She took hold of her husband's arm and looked up at him fondly. 'We're not fussy either way, are we, Albert?'

'No, we'll all be as pleased as Punch, whatever it is,' said Albert as he smiled at Hetty and ruffled Zachary's black curls.

His love and pride in his wife and his adopted son were plain for all to see, and Martha's heart was filled with thankfulness as she watched them together. They had had their share of sorrows, all of them, since they moved to Blackpool, but now it seemed as though things were on the mend. She,

Martha, had found happiness quite unexpectedly. She would never have thought when George Makepeace first came to lodge here that she would end up marrying him. And Hetty, too, was undeniably happy again. Martha prayed that her elder daughter would also find the happiness that she so richly deserved.

Dusk was falling as Edwin walked briskly along the streets towards Grace's house. He was glad of the semidarkness because the huge bouquet of spring flowers that he was carrying caused him some embarrassment. It would have been much easier, and more usual, to have asked the assistant at the florist's shop to see to their delivery, but Edwin felt that he must present this token of his affection himself. He hoped that when Grace saw it she would realise what was in his heart and in his mind, feelings that, so far, he had felt unable to express in words.

He had chosen the flowers with care. Spring flowers which, to Edwin, held all the promise of new life and new hope. Golden daffodils, orange-eyed narcissi, deep-blue irises and sweetly smelling freesias, all wrapped in shining cellophane and finished off with a pale-blue satin ribbon. He hoped that they might be the means of paving the way for him, making it easier for him to tell Grace that he wanted so much more from her than the friendship they were sharing at the moment. Edwin had known from the first time he had called to see Grace, over six months ago, that he must take things steadily and be careful not to rush her. He had been grateful that she had received him so kindly and been so obviously pleased to see him. He thought at times that something in her glance – a softness and a warmth – revealed that she still retained some of the old affection for him, but he couldn't be entirely sure.

She had loved her husband, Walter Clayton. Edwin was sure of that. He had been surprised – and a little disappointed, if he were honest – at the way Grace had spoken of Walter, saying what a good husband he had been to her and what a doting father to little Sarah. And she had been so very proud of him when he had made his brave rescue attempt, the escapade which had later cost him his life. What right had he, Edwin, to feel churlish about Grace's happiness in her marriage? he thought. He had abandoned her, hadn't he? Cast her on one side like a worn-out coat to take up with Constance Whitehead, or so it must have seemed to Grace. She had had every right to make a life of her own and if it had turned out to be a successful marriage, as Edwin believed it had been, then he should be glad that the girl had found happiness. It was no more than she deserved.

But Grace was a widow now. Whether she had been happy or not was immaterial. Her husband was now dead and she was free to marry again, and Edwin knew that he still wanted Grace to be his wife, as he had wanted her five years ago.

She had been a widow for more than six months now, and her time of deep mourning was drawing to a close. The last time Edwin had seen her she had been wearing a grey dress with a white lace collar, a pleasant change from the sombre black she had been clad in since her husband's death. Edwin was resolute as he approached the house. It was time for him to tell her what was in his heart. She would not be expecting him tonight. Maybe it would prove to be an advantage, taking her unawares. Perhaps he would be able to discern her true feelings in the surprise she showed at seeing him on her doorstep.

She was certainly surprised. 'Edwin!' She smiled brightly at him, as she always did, but confusion and a certain wariness flickered in her eyes. 'I wasn't expecting you. It's . . . it's only Tuesday.'

'I couldn't wait till Wednesday,' said Edwin boldly, smiling at her. 'Aren't you going to ask me in?'

'Yes . . . yes, of course. Come in, Edwin.' Grace nodded uncertainly, and Edwin thought how lovely she looked this evening. Obviously, in Grace's mind as well as his own, her period of deepest mourning was at an end. She was wearing a dress of a soft woollen material in a pale-mauve shade, just the colour of the delicate freesia blossoms in the bouquet that he was holding, somewhat awkwardly, behind his back. He guessed that she had made the dress herself, although it didn't look home-made. Grace was an excellent seamstress, and the gently flowing lines of the dress moulded themselves becomingly round her slim figure. Edwin thought how very much he loved her.

She seemed ill at ease, though. 'Come in,' she said again. 'But there's someone else here . . . I've got a visitor, Edwin. I wasn't expecting you, you see . . .'

Perplexedly he followed her through the door into the small parlour. Edwin surmised at a quick glance that the visitor was possibly in his late thirties; a smallish man, but with powerfully built shoulders, dressed in a brown tweed suit. He looked vaguely familiar.

'This is Amos,' said Grace. 'Amos Armitage. He's . . . he was a friend of Walter's. Amos . . . this is Edwin Donnelly. We've . . . known one another a long time.'

Amos Armitage stood up and held out his hand, Edwin took it, embarrassedly aware of the bouquet he was still holding in his other hand. The fellow's handshake was firm, and his face – by no means handsome, but lively and interesting – creased in a puckish smile as he answered Edwin's 'How do you do?' with 'Pleased to meet you.'

Edwin noticed that Grace's visitor didn't seem at all disconcerted by the new arrival. It was he, Edwin, who was beginning to feel uncomfortable. Neither was Amos Armitage making any move to depart when he saw that Grace had another visitor. But there was no reason why he should do so, Edwin told himself, feeling more sick at heart and confused with every second that passed. The other fellow had been here first, after all, and Grace had every right to entertain whomsoever she wished in her own home.

'I think . . . I'd better go, Grace,' Edwin said as Amos sat down again. 'I can see I've called at an inopportune time.'

Grace didn't contradict him.

'I only called to . . . bring you these flowers.' At last he produced the bouquet from behind his back. 'To thank you for . . . all the suppers you've made for me,' he said lamely. 'And because . . . well, because I like spring flowers. They make me feel that winter's over. I hope you'll like them, Grace.'

'Oh, Edwin, they're beautiful. Thank you very much.' There was no mistaking the delight in Grace's voice as she bent her head towards the heady fragrance of the freesias. 'And what a lovely scent. Yes, I love spring flowers too.'

She smiled at him, but Edwin could see nothing in her glance but friendship and her appreciation of his kind thought. She put the flowers down on the sideboard and stood aside, obviously waiting for him to go.

'Goodbye then,' he said briefly to Amos Armitage, noting how at home he seemed at Grace's fireside, and the fellow nodded in reply. 'Goodbye, Mr Donnelly.'

Numbly he followed Grace along the short hallway to the door. 'I'm sorry if I called at a bad time,' he said again. 'I realise . . . I should have let you know.'

'That's all right, Edwin,' said Grace brightly.

'You say . . . he was a friend of Walter's?' Edwin spoke quietly, nodding in the direction of the parlour door.

'Yes, that's right. Amos Armitage. He works at Henderson's, where Walter used to work, and he goes to the same chapel, too. He's been very good to me since Walter died.'

Edwin remembered now where and when he had seen the man before. That night at Tilda's Tavern, when Grace had been upset by Walter's appearance, this was the chap who had been with him. He recalled, too, a blackened face, and realised that this was also the fellow who delivered his family's coal.

'And . . . you see him quite often, do you?' Edwin was well aware that it was none of his business, and that he was only rubbing salt into his own wound, but he couldn't let it rest. He had to know.

'Yes . . . quite often. He's a good friend. As a matter of fact . . .' Grace lowered her voice. 'He's just asked me to marry him.'

Chapter 26

'Have you seen our Edwin lately?' William Donnelly put down his copy of the local *Gazette* and looked enquiringly at his wife.

'Yes, I've seen him today. He called round this afternoon. Said he had some business in the area, but I think it was just an excuse for a cup of tea and a chat.' Clara Donnelly smiled to herself, then she nodded at her husband. 'Yes, he chats to me much more these days, you know, William. In fact Edwin and I are quite good friends now. Sometimes I can hardly believe it.'

'Hmmm . . .' William grunted. 'You're lucky then. I can scarcely get two words out of the lad. I called round at the new store this morning to see how things are going and I was sorry I bothered, I can tell you. Face as long as a fiddle he had, and just answering me with "yes" and "no". If you ask me it's time that lad got himself a wife and settled down. It's not natural, him pushing thirty now and still single. Of course I know he's had his problems in the past with his love life, but that was ages ago, all that business with Constance Whitehead and . . .' He hesitated, not wishing to mention Grace Turnbull – Grace Clayton, as she was now – remembering what a thorn in the flesh she had been to his wife at one time. Possibly not now though. Clara had changed, but there was no point in stirring up old memories.

Her next words, therefore, came as a shock to him. 'He's been seeing Grace Turnbull again. Grace Clayton, I should say. Didn't you know?'

William looked at his wife in surprise. Of course he had known that Edwin had seen Grace a few times after her husband had died so tragically, but he, William, had forborne to mention it to Clara, not being sure what her reaction would be. 'Yes . . .' he said. 'I know he's been seeing Grace, but I didn't realise there was anything in it. Anyway, she's still in mourning, isn't she? It can't be much more than six months since her husband died.'

'Mmm . . . Mourning or not,' said Clara thoughtfully, 'the lass is thinking of getting wed again, and that's what's ailing our Edwin.'

'Grace Turnbull's getting married again? Who to?' William stared incredulously at his wife. 'And who told you?'

'Edwin, of course. Who do you think? I've told you, William, he confides in me quite a lot these days, and I'm very glad to listen, too. Well, it seems that he called round to see Grace the other night and there was another fellow there. A fellow who's got his feet under the table, according to Edwin, and the lad's got it into his head that Grace is going to marry him.'

'And who is it?' William asked again.

'Amos Armitage he's called. He's the fellow that delivers our coal.'

'A coalman? Grace is going to marry a coalman?'

'So what? She was married to one before, wasn't she? Apparently this fellow was a good mate of her husband's and he's been very kind to Grace since Walter Clayton died. But I don't know . . . I can't believe that she'd want to marry him . . .' Clara paused thoughtfully. She pushed the needle into the cushion cover she was embroidering and placed it on the settee beside her. 'I've been thinking a lot about Grace and our Edwin . . . You know, William, I've a feeling they're right for one another. Always have been . . .'

'Grace Turnbull? You've changed your tune, haven't you?' William continued to stare unbelievingly at his wife. 'I remember a time when . . .'

'I know, William. I know.' Clara held up her hand dismissively. 'Don't say any more. I know now that I was wrong. But I tried to make amends, at least I can say that. I encouraged our Edwin to try to get Grace back after that business with Constance, but it was too late. She was already wed.'

'You never told me that. That you'd changed your mind about the lass.'

'There was a lot I didn't tell you, William.' Clara shook her head ruefully. 'If you remember, it was soon after I'd been ill, and I had a lot on my mind . . . with my father and everything. When it turned out that Grace was already married I knew there was nothing else to be done. Our Edwin would just have to sort his own life out the best he could. Well, she's a widow now, and he wants her back, but he seems to think it's no use.

He's left it too late . . . again.'

'Then . . . why didn't he say something to her before, if he wanted the girl?'

'I'm not sure, William,' said Clara slowly. 'Like you mentioned, Grace is still in mourning, and I suppose he didn't want to rush things. He knew that he had hurt her very badly once, and I suppose he wanted her to be very sure now before she committed herself to him again.'

'And so he's left it too late? Someone's got in before him?'

'I can't really believe that. And I don't think Edwin believes it either, but he's got himself into a right state. His thinking's all cockeyed. He's started talking about going to America again, getting right away from it all. You remember he talked about it once before, but it came to nothing. And he says that perhaps Grace would be happier with someone of her own class. Would you believe it?'

'And what did you say to that?'

'I told him not to be such a damned snob! Class indeed! As if it mattered.'

William laughed out loud. 'That's rich, Clara, coming from you. After all you said before . . .'

'I know, I know,' said Clara again. She grinned wryly at him. 'I've changed, love. I'm not ashamed to admit. Class and religion, they don't matter two hoots, not when two people love each other. And I'm sure that those two do. I don't know why I feel like that about it. Grace went and married Walter Clayton pretty smartish, and now, according to Edwin, she's thinking of getting wed again. But I still feel that Grace and Edwin are right for one another. It's a gut feeling I have.'

'Maybe you're right,' said William. 'I must admit, I always liked the lass, ever since she first came to work at the shop. But it's up to Edwin, you know. If he won't do anything about it, then there's nothing to be done. It's nothing to do with anyone else.'

'No . . . I suppose not,' said Clara. But she was unconvinced.

Grace had never been more surprised in her life than she was when she saw Clara Donnelly on her doorstep one afternoon in April.

'Mrs Donnelly!' She couldn't help but gasp when she saw her. 'Whatever . . .? Is there something wrong? Is it Edwin?' Grace felt a tremor of fear run through her. She remembered an unexpected visitor on her doorstep once before with unwelcome news.

'No, there's nothing wrong with Edwin. At least nothing that can't be put right, I hope.' The older woman grinned at her, to Grace's surprise. 'Do you mind if I come in, Grace? I can call you Grace, can't I?'

'Of course you can,' Grace replied, more surprised than ever. 'And . . . do come in, Mrs Donnelly.'

It was the first time that the two of them had ever spoken together. They knew one another by sight, naturally, and nodded and said, 'Good morning', or 'Good afternoon', on the rare occasions that they met in town, but that was all. Now Grace found herself in a state of confusion and she hastily removed the pile of sewing from one chair and Sarah's toys from another so that they could both sit down. The little girl was upstairs having her afternoon nap, so Grace didn't have to worry about her. But heavens! Whatever would the woman think? The place always seemed to be so untidy since she had started sewing.

She need not have worried, because Clara Donnelly took not the slightest heed of her surroundings. She leaned forward in the chair and looked steadily at Grace in the chair opposite. 'First of all,' she said, 'I owe you an apology, Grace.'

Grace shook her head slowly. 'I don't think so, Mrs Donnelly. Why? What do you mean?'

'When you and Edwin were friendly . . . ages ago. I . . . I interfered, and it all went wrong.'

'But it's ages ago,' said Grace, repeating the older woman's words. 'I don't hold that against you. Anyway, you were ill, weren't you? And then there was . . . Constance, and, like you say, it all went wrong. But I'm sure you weren't to blame. It was . . . a lot of things.'

'That's as maybe. And, yes, I was ill. But I felt responsible, anyroad. I felt it was partly my fault and that's why I've come now. To say I'm sorry, and to stop it from all going wrong again if I can . . .' Clara paused for a moment. 'I suppose you could say I'm interfering again. Maybe I am, and if you tell me to mind my own business then it'll be no more than I deserve. But I want to ask you something, Grace. Two things. First . . . you and this . . . Amos Armitage . . . Are you going to marry him?'

'Of course I'm not!' The words were out before Grace had time to think. Part of her was astounded at the barefaced cheek of the woman, inviting herself in and asking questions like that, but another part of her couldn't help but admire Clara Donnelly. There was something in the woman's manner that reminded Grace of her own mother, a forthrightness and the way she seemed to have of calling a spade a spade. In spite of herself Grace couldn't be offended. 'Whatever gave you that idea?' she added.

'I rather think it was the idea you gave to Edwin,' Clara replied. 'Anyroad, he's got it into his head that you're going to marry the chap. If you'd said to me yes, you were, then I'd have had to leave it, Grace. But as it is . . .'

'Edwin didn't stay long enough to find out,' said Grace. 'Yes, I admit I told him that Amos had asked me to marry him. Then Edwin just gave me a strange look and walked away. He didn't ask me what my answer was going to be.'

'And so you told him no, this Amos Armitage?'

'That's right. Amos is a good friend, but I don't want to marry him. I think he understood.'

'Yes, I see.' Clara Donnelly nodded. 'The other thing I wanted to ask you was this . . . Our Edwin . . . do you love him?'

Grace was silent for a moment before she answered. She stared down at her hands folded in her lap, then she looked unwaveringly at Clara. 'Yes . . . I love him. I've always loved him. Even when I was married to Walter I never stopped loving him. I know that now. But I couldn't let myself think about it. I had to get on with my life. I had my husband and my little girl. It wasn't possible . . .'

'But it is now, Grace.' Clara leaned forward and looked at her earnestly. 'If you love him why don't you tell him so?'

'Surely it's up to him, Mrs Donnelly.' Grace's voice was sharp. 'He's had ample opportunity. He's been calling round here for the last six months or more, but he's never said . . .'

'I think he was going to say something the other night, but he had the wind taken out of his sails.' Clara nodded towards the huge vase of spring flowers that graced the sideboard. 'He brought those, I daresay?'

'Yes . . . he did.'

'A token of affection, I reckon. And then he must have felt that he'd made a fool of himself. That'ud be why he scarpered so fast.'

'But I didn't mean . . .' Grace gave a wry smile. 'To tell you the truth, I only told him about Amos's proposal to make him come to his senses. I'm tired of waiting.'

'Then wait no longer, my dear. Go and tell him how you feel.'

'How can I?' Grace almost shouted the words. 'If Edwin wants me, if he still loves me, then it's up to him to say so.'

'He still loves you, Grace. I know he does,' said Clara Donnelly quietly. 'But he knows that he hurt you once, very badly, and he's not sure that you are still willing to pledge yourself to him after that.'

'He's told you that?' asked Grace, frowning a little.

'No, he hasn't told me, not in so many words. But I know that it is so. And I can't stand by and

590

see the pair of you drifting apart again.'

'But he'll come round again, surely, in a day or two? He can't really think that I mean to marry Amos?'

'That's what he does think, Grace. Or says he does, and I can't tell him any different . . . He mustn't know I've been here, of course,' she added hurriedly. 'One of our Edwin's faults is that he tries to please everybody. Not a bad fault, but it doesn't always do. Sometimes you've got to make up your mind what you want and then go for it, hell for leather. Like I did when I married his father.'

Grace raised her eyebrows questioningly.

'Oh yes.' Clara Donnelly grinned. 'I knew I wanted William and I made jolly sure I got him an' all. It's reckoned to be a man's world, my dear. It's the fellows that make all the decisions and think they're running everything. It's all the same whether it's Parliament or the Church, or even just running a home. They like to think that they're the boss. But they're not you know, Grace, not always. We've had a woman on the throne for more than sixty years now, and I reckon she's done a lot to shape this country of ours the way it's going. A lot more than those ministers of hers give her credit for. We're not called Victorians for nothing.'

'Yes, I'm sure you're right,' said Grace.

'And that's what we've got to do, us women,' said Clara. 'We've got to give the fellows a push in the right direction sometimes or we'd never get anywhere. And that's what Edwin needs, a good shove. A kick up the backside, I've sometimes

591

thought, love.' Clara laughed and Grace found herself laughing too. And to think that she'd once thought this woman was so stiff and starchy.

'And Edwin needs you, Grace,' said Clara Donnelly simply. She looked at Grace steadily and Grace looked back, but she didn't answer for several seconds.

Then, 'You mentioned the Church,' said Grace slowly. 'That was one of the problems, wasn't it? One of the things that you . . . had against me. That I'm a Methodist and Edwin's a Catholic. And I still am; I don't go as much now, of course, since Sarah was born, but it's the way I was brought up . . .'

'Yes, that was one of the things, I admit,' Clara agreed. 'I thought it was a problem, but I've changed my mind now. I don't see that it needs to be at all. Don't ask me what you can do about it; that would be something for you and Edwin to sort out, but there's a way round everything, if you want it badly enough.'

'My mother was just as set against it as you were,' Grace remarked, 'because Edwin was a Catholic, but I think she's seeing things differently now as well.'

'Yes, I reckon there's not much to choose between any of us, Catholics or Protestants, when it comes to being bigoted. We're all so set on our own point of view; we like to think that we're the only ones who are right.' Clara shook her head bemusedly. 'And yet we're all supposed to worship the same God. I'm sure I don't know what He makes of us all.' She glanced towards the ceiling. 'He must think we're a rum lot.'

Grace smiled, thinking again how much this woman reminded her of her own mother, not in looks, of course – Clara Donnelly was much taller than Martha, of almost regal bearing, neither did she look as careworn as Martha did at times; Clara had had a much easier life, Grace mused – but she was so much like her in her manner and turn of phrase. Clara Donnelly was a real Lancashire lass, in spite of the la-di-da manner that Grace knew she could put on at times.

'Neither does it matter that my husband earns a bob or two more than your father did,' Clara said now. 'It doesn't matter a scrap. You know, Grace,' she continued, 'there generally has to be one partner in a marriage who's stronger than the other. Of course the fellow always thinks that it's him, and we let him go on thinking so if we've any sense. A man likes to be top dog. It's 1900 now, though, practically a new century. I reckon women'll have a good deal more to say for themselves in the 1900s than they've ever had before. Pity I won't be here to see much of it, but that's the way it goes.'

'Don't say that, Mrs Donnelly,' said Grace, thinking how much she liked this woman now that she was, at last, getting to know her.

'It's true though, Grace. None of us'll live for ever. But we've got to make the most of it while we're here. Now, think on what I've told you. I'll say no more about it now, but if you're a sensible lass, as I know you are, you'll do summat about it. And . . . mum's the word.' Clara put a finger to her lips. 'This little visit is just between you and me, mind.'

'Of course. I wouldn't dream of letting on that you called. And . . . what you've said makes sense. Thank you, Mrs Donnelly. I'll . . . I'll bear it in mind.'

'Good. Then that's that.' Clara grinned at her. 'Now, are you going to make me a cup of tea, or am I going to sit here for ever with me tongue hanging out?'

Grace laughed out loud. 'Yes, what a good idea. We'll have a cup of tea before Sarah wakes up.' She felt that she and Clara Donnelly were going to be good friends.

Grace dressed with care. She pulled her black coat out of the wardrobe, then frowned and pushed it back again, taking out instead the brown coat with the fur collar which Alice Gregson had given her several years ago. She had worn it, she remembered now, the first time she had gone to the theatre with Edwin. It still fitted her – a shade tighter round the hips and bust, but not noticeably so – and it was appropriate that she should wear it this evening. With it she wore the little round fur hat and, underneath the coat, the mauve dress that she had made recently to replace her black mourning garments. She regarded herself gravely in the mirror, thinking that she looked very little different from the girl who had accompanied Edwin to the theatre five years ago. Her eyes had lost some of their sparkle, but she felt that tonight's meeting might restore to them all their former radiance. All that a woman needed was to know that she was loved . . .

She went downstairs and, on an impulse, plucked a spray of delicate mauve freesia blossoms from the vase of spring flowers that Edwin had brought and tucked it into her buttonhole. Sarah was spending the night with her Aunt Hetty and Uncle Albert – and cousin Zachary, of course; the little girl was always delighted to spend time with her bonny and mischievous cousin – and Hetty, wisely, had asked no questions as to Grace's mission this evening. Grace hoped that she would find Edwin at home. It was very early evening and she presumed that he would be there at such a time. If he wasn't . . . She felt that her courage might fail her if she had to make the errand a second time. She stood in the middle of the parlour, feeling nervous now that the time had come for her to set off. Then there was a knock at the door and she frowned with exasperation. Whoever could that be? Whoever it was, she couldn't afford to waste much time.

She hurried to the front door and cautiously opened it. Then she gave a gasp of astonishment. 'Edwin!' She could do nothing to check the radiant smile that lit up her face at the sight of him. 'How lovely to see you. I was just . . .'

Edwin was smiling too, but as he noticed that Grace was wearing her outdoor clothes his smile changed to a look of puzzlement. He interrupted her words. 'You were going out, Grace?'

She nodded at him, still smiling. 'Yes, I was just going out. You've only just caught me.'

'And . . . may I be so bold as to ask . . . where?'

'Yes . . . you may ask, Edwin,' said Grace pertly. 'I might even tell you, if you ask nicely.'

A tiny frown was creasing Edwin's brow and his eyes were wary, almost fearful now. He sighed. 'I suppose you were going to see . . . Amos Armitage?'

Grace decided that the time for prevaricating was over. She took his arm and drew him inside, closing the door behind him. 'I was coming to see you, Edwin,' she said quietly.

'Me? You . . . were coming to see me, Grace? But . . . why?' Edwin still looked confused.

Grace looked at him gravely for a moment, then she smiled. 'I was coming to tell you that my days of mourning are over, Edwin.' Gently she touched the spray of freesias tucked in her buttonhole. 'Spring is here. A time to start again, I think. I loved the flowers. Thank you so much, Edwin. And . . .' Her voice dropped to the merest whisper. 'I was coming to tell you that . . . I love you.'

'Grace . . . Grace, my darling.' His arms went round her and he held her close to him. 'But what about Amos Armitage?'

Grace grinned up at him and didn't answer for a few seconds. Then, 'What about him?' she asked, raising her eyebrows mischievously.

'You haven't promised to marry him?'

'Of course not. Whatever gave you that idea?'

'I rather think you did.' Edwin frowned at her, then gently touched her nose with the tip of his finger. 'Didn't you?'

'Mmm . . . I might have done,' she admitted before his lips closed upon hers, preventing any further words for several minutes.

Then she took hold of his hand and led him into the parlour. 'Now,' she said, smiling up at him,

'I've told you why I was coming to see you. Now it's your turn. Why have you come, Edwin?'

He folded his arms round her again and drew her close, then he pulled off her little round fur hat and gently stroked her hair. 'Because I can't live without you, Grace,' he said simply. 'I've come to tell you that I love you, that I can't bear to lose you again, to Amos Armitage, or to anyone. I love you, my darling,' he murmured against the softness of her hair and her skin.

And all the longing and the love that she had ever felt for him flooded back, filling her with a quiet happiness. Grace felt that she had come home, that she was safe at last. She knew that she loved this man and to know that he loved her in return was all that she had ever wanted.

'Marry me, Grace?' he whispered, and she smiled up at him, her eyes shining with happiness.

'Yes . . . of course.'

'When, darling?'

'Soon . . .'

'Oh yes, let it be soon, my darling . . .'

And as he kissed her again Grace knew that she was the happiest woman in the world. She felt his strong arms around her, a feeling she had thought at one time that she might never know again, and tears of joy and thankfulness sprang to her eyes. She found herself thinking of the words of a song that Hetty used to sing at the Tavern.

'When a merry maiden marries,
Sorrow goes and pleasure tarries,
Every sound becomes a song,

All is right and nothing's wrong.
From today and ever after
Let our tears be tears of laughter . . .'

Grace knew that her tears of sorrow had come to an end. The winter in her heart had gone and it was springtime once more. A time of new growth, new hope, new love. She and Edwin had found one another again and it was time for them to begin a new life, together.